THE IRON FAÇADE
&
HOUSE OF MEN

Catherine Cookson

CORGI BOOKS

THE IRON FAÇADE & HOUSE OF MEN
A CORGI BOOK : 0 552 14700 1

PRINTING HISTORY
This Corgi collection first published 1999
Copyright © Catherine Cookson 1999
including

THE IRON FAÇADE
Originally published in Great Britain by William Heinemann Ltd.
Copyright © Catherine Cookson 1976

HOUSE OF MEN
Originally published in Great Britain by Macdonald & Jane's
Copyright © Catherine Cookson 1963

Set in 11/13pt Sabon by
Phoenix Typesetting, Ilkley, West Yorkshire

Corgi Books are published by Transworld Publishers Ltd,
61–63 Uxbridge Road, London W5 5SA,
in Australia by Transworld Publishers, c/o Random House Australia
Pty Ltd, 20 Alfred Street, Milsons Point, NSW 2061
and in New Zealand by Transworld Publishers, c/o Random House
New Zealand, 18 Poland Road, Glenfield, Auckland.

Reproduced, printed and bound in Great Britain by
Cox & Wyman Ltd, Reading, Berks.

THE IRON FAÇADE

Catherine Cookson

CORGI BOOKS

Catherine Cookson was born in Tyne Dock, the illegitimate daughter of a poverty-stricken woman, Kate, whom she believed to be her older sister. She began work in service but eventually moved south to Hastings where she met and married Tom Cookson, a local grammar-school master. At the age of forty she began writing about the lives of the working-class people with whom she had grown up, using the place of her birth as the background to many of her novels.

Although originally acclaimed as a regional writer – her novel *The Round Tower* won the Winifred Holtby award for the best regional novel of 1968 – her readership soon began to spread throughout the world. Her novels have been translated into more than a dozen languages and more than 50,000,000 copies of her books have been sold in Corgi alone. Fifteen of her novels have been made into successful television dramas, and more are planned.

Catherine Cookson's many bestselling novels established her as one of the most popular of contemporary women novelists. After receiving an OBE in 1985, Catherine Cookson was created a Dame of the British Empire in 1993. She was appointed an Honorary Fellow of St Hilda's College, Oxford in 1997. For many years she lived near Newcastle-upon-Tyne. She died shortly before her ninety-second birthday in June 1998.

'Catherine Cookson's novels are about hardship, the intractability of life and of individuals, the struggle first to survive and next to make sense of one's survival. Humour, toughness, resolution and generosity are Cookson virtues, in a world which she often depicts as cold and violent. Her novels are weighted and driven by her own early experiences of illegitimacy and poverty. This is what gives them power. In the specialised world of women's popular fiction, Cookson has created her own territory'
Helen Dunmore, *The Times*

BOOKS BY CATHERINE COOKSON

NOVELS

Kate Hannigan
The Fifteen Streets
Colour Blind
Maggie Rowan
Rooney
The Menagerie
Slinky Jane
Fanny McBride
Fenwick Houses
Heritage of Folly
The Garment
The Fen Tiger
The Blind Miller
House of Men
Hannah Massey
The Long Corridor
The Unbaited Trap
Katie Mulholland
The Round Tower
The Nice Bloke
The Glass Virgin
The Invitation
The Dwelling Place
Feathers in the Fire
Pure as the Lily
The Mallen Streak
The Mallen Girl
The Mallen Litter
The Invisible Cord
The Gambling Man
The Tide of Life
The Slow Awakening
The Iron Façade
The Girl
The Cinder Path
Miss Martha Mary Crawford
The Man Who Cried
Tilly Trotter

Tilly Trotter Wed
Tilly Trotter Widowed
The Whip
Hamilton
The Black Velvet Gown
Goodbye Hamilton
A Dinner of Herbs
Harold
The Moth
Bill Bailey
The Parson's Daughter
Bill Bailey's Lot
The Cultured Handmaiden
Bill Bailey's Daughter
The Harrogate Secret
The Black Candle
The Wingless Bird
The Gillyvors
My Beloved Son
The Rag Nymph
The House of Women
The Maltese Angel
The Year of the Virgins
The Golden Straw
Justice is a Woman
The Tinker's Girl
A Ruthless Need
The Obsession
The Upstart
The Branded Man
The Bonny Dawn
The Bondage of Love
The Desert Crop
The Lady on My Left
The Solace of Sin
Riley
The Blind Years
The Thursday Friend

THE MARY ANN STORIES

A Grand Man
The Lord and Mary Ann
The Devil and Mary Ann
Love and Mary Ann

Life and Mary Ann
Marriage and Mary Ann
Mary Ann's Angels
Mary Ann and Bill

FOR CHILDREN

Matty Doolin
Joe and the Gladiator
The Nipper
Rory's Fortune
Our John Willie

Mrs Flannagan's Trumpet
Go Tell It To Mrs Golightly
Lanky Jones
Nancy Nutall and the Mongrel
Bill and the Mary Ann Shaughnessy

AUTOBIOGRAPHY

Our Kate
Catherine Cookson Country

Let Me Make Myself Plain
Plainer Still

1

'I'm going to be sick again.'

'Oh, Aunt Maggie!'

'I – I can't help it. I – don't like it any better than you— Stop the car!'

'I didn't mean it like that. Hang on, I must find a place to park off the road.'

When I saw my aunt put her hand swiftly to her mouth, I didn't wait to find a suitable place on the grass verge but pulled the car abruptly to a stop and, getting out, ran round the bonnet and was only in time to hold her head as she retched for a second time into the ditch.

Straightening up and wiping her mouth, she muttered weakly, 'I'm sorry.'

'Oh, Aunt Maggie, there's nothing to be sorry for. Come on.' I turned her about and led her towards the car again.

'There is to me. I'm supposed to be looking after you.'

'It'll do me good to think of somebody else for a time.'

'It might at that, but I don't want to be sick to

give you that opportunity.' Although she was leaning weakly against a fender, my aunt glanced at me with a shadow of the twinkle that was nearly always present in her eyes. She then said, 'If only I had a drink of soda water I'd be all right. Unless I've lost my bearings altogether, there's a village somewhere near here. We've crossed the River Eden, passed Appleby, Colby and Strickland. Now before we get to Brampton, there's this little place I remember called Borne Coote.'

'You should have let us stop in Appleby and have a meal as I suggested.'

My aunt turned her eyes to mine again, then lowered her head and leaned heavily against the side of the car. I turned and walked a few steps along the grass verge and looked down over rolling green hills, down, down, down to a valley, where the faint froth of water was discernible. Beyond, the hills rose again to fall, I knew, on the other side to more burns and rivulets and cascading water. This was Cumberland, a county new to me, and although beautiful in some of the areas through which I had come, it was wild and desolate in others. But that was how I wanted it – desolate – lonely. That was why I had suggested that we stop for a meal in Appleby. Aunt Maggie, thoughtful as ever, had said she wasn't hungry; all she wanted was to reach our destination.

We had started from Eastbourne shortly after five o'clock that morning. Just before we left, after she had been round the house to give a last check-up to windows and doors, Aunt stopped for a moment in the hall and touching me gently on the cheek had said, 'You'll sleep tonight, Pru, without pills, I promise you.' Then, with her ability to bring laughter out of nothing she exclaimed, 'Pru, pills and promise. You wouldn't like to partake of a little repast before we depart would you?' If laughter had not been dead in me, I would have laughed. I only smiled at her and we had left.

'It's a grand sight, isn't it?'

I hadn't been aware that she had joined me. I turned to her. 'Are you feeling better?'

'Yes, yes,' she nodded. Then she added: 'Until the next time. So much for palliative pills.'

'It's this heat,' I said. 'It's so unexpected.'

Aunt Maggie was gently shaking the neck of her blouse back and forth as she answered. 'It must be ninety – and at the end of August. There's one good thing about it – it won't last. I can't stand the heat, not this kind at any rate. But look, isn't it bonny?'

My aunt moved her hand in a wide half-circle, and my eyes followed its course and saw that the scene was indeed bonny. It should stir me as lovely scenery had always stirred me; my breath should be catching with the effect of all this rolling beauty; my heart should be singing with the knowledge that I was to live in it for three months; but there was no emotional response in me, nothing but an icy numbness which melted only to make room for fear – fear that made me walk with my head down and my eyes fixed on the ground.

'Remember,' Aunt Maggie had chided me, 'when you used to be afraid of getting a double chin? – Come on, lift that head up.'

Could I be the same person who had once had a horror of a double chin, the person who had been careful to sit upright in a chair and never to cross her legs in case her hips spread? It had been said, and not so very long before, that Prudence Dudley, besides being clever, had a lovely figure, and a remarkable face – not beautiful, but remarkable. Yet there was someone who had said that the face went beyond beauty. He had said that there was plainness and prettiness, then beauty, and, after beauty, exquisiteness. That exquisiteness had nothing to do with beauty or prettiness, it was something on its own – yes, that had once been said to me . . .

'Now stop it, you're tired. Come along, stop it.'

My Aunt Maggie's hands were covering mine, pulling them from the lapels of my suit, easing the fingers away one after the other. Her voice, stern now, was saying, 'Pru, you're tired. That's all. Stop contemplating. Remember, you've had bad patches before – they come and they pass. Remember that – they pass.'

I was in the car now sitting at the wheel. My body had stopped trembling, but the perspiration was running down my face, and it was only faintly that

I heard my voice saying, 'I'd better take a couple of pills.'

'But there's no water.'

'I'll swallow them dry.'

'No. No, don't do that, my dear. I seem to remember this road. Go along there and turn off left. I'm almost certain you'll come to Borne Coote. There'll be a café, or some such place in it. Perhaps we'll each get a drink. If not soda water, a cup of tea.'

My hands began to shake again as I started the car but I kept repeating Aunt Maggie's formula, 'It will pass.'

A few minutes later, there was the road Aunt had remembered, and a half mile further along it, we ran into the village and saw immediately, and to my consternation, that there was something on. Most of the villages we had passed through had been sleepy, almost deserted, places. Whether this was natural to them or due to the unexpected heat, I didn't know. But now, at a quarter to two in the afternoon during the hottest part of the day, the village was abuzz. There were at least a dozen cars, none of them very smart, lined up along one side of a low granite block wall which bordered a cemetery as bright with flowers as any park. And sitting among the flowers, on the grass and gravestones, were groups of people, all laughing, joyous people. Similar groups were repeated at intervals all along the main street.

Neither of us spoke. My Aunt Maggie didn't

make the comment that would have been natural, 'It's a wedding.' But, when we had reached the end of the street and had come to a little square with a stone cross in its centre, she said, 'Over there, look, where it says "Ices", we'll get a drink of some sort.'

The shop, I saw at once, sold everything, including paraffin oil, but there was no-one in it. Aunt Maggie knocked on the counter, and when she did so for the third time, she accompanied it with a sharp command: 'Hello, there!' Receiving no answer to her call, she did not, even now, make the obvious statement, 'I bet they've gone to the wedding,' but, taking a basketful of groceries from off an upturned lemonade box, she placed it on the floor, then sat down on the box and, pointing to what looked like a butter cask, said, 'Sit yourself down on that and we'll wait. It's cool in here, anyway.'

I didn't want to sit down; I wanted to stand, or rather walk. At this moment, I wanted to walk quickly away from everything, especially from this village and all its laughing people. I knew the signs, I knew what this feeling would lead to. My heart would begin to jerk, then race. Then my limbs would tremble, and this would be followed by that dreadful feeling that I was about to die. But wasn't that what I wanted – to die? Yes, but not in that fear-ridden way. They – they being the doctors – said I could conquer the feeling. They all said it was up to me now . . .

'Well, Aa never! Aa never knew there was anybody in. It's the weddin' you know. Aa was out back lookin' over the top wall. You can see the side path into the church from there. Well, now.'

The little thin wisp of a woman with the painfully straight hair and bright bead eyes looked from one to the other of us. Then, her gaze settling on me, she said in rapid sympathetic tones, 'It's a drink you'd be wantin'. I should say you do. You look as white as a strip of lint. It's this heat. Did you ever know anythin' like it? And us steppin' into September. Just like the weather, isn't it – contrary? But could you have it better for a weddin'?'

'Do you happen to have any soda water?'

'Soda water?' The little woman confronted Aunt Maggie. 'That's a thing we haven't got. Practically everything on God's earth we've got in this place –' she spread out her short arms '– but no soda water. "Syphons," I said. That's what I said to Talbot. "We want syphons." "Who's going to pay four bob or more for a syphon?" Talbot asked. But, as I said, "That's only at the beginning, you'd get them refilled for next to nothing." But he wouldn't hear of it. No, we haven't got any soda water, but the next best thing's ice-cream soda – look!' She pointed to a row of coloured bottles. 'How about that?'

'Yes, I'll try that – anything.' Aunt Maggie was moving her head slowly in assent.

'And you, miss?' The bead eyes were turned on me now. 'Are you going to share, or would you like one to yourself?'

'Is it possible to have a cup of tea?'

'Oh–h!' As if the eyes were being moved by a

switch, they now did a series of jerks between my aunt and myself. And with this action, the little woman made it evident that tea was going to be a bit of a bother at this moment, so I put in quickly, 'Oh, it's all right; I'll have a bottle of lemonade.'

'Well, now, not that Aa wouldn't make it for you, an', if Talbot had been in, Aa would have done it like a shot. Aa would do it if you'd hang on, but oh, Aa'd like to see the weddin' and Aa daren't leave the shop, you see, not for long like. But, if you like, Aa could put the kettle on and come back in a few minutes.'

'It's all right, I'll just have the lemonade.'

'You sure now?' She bent towards me as if trying to persuade me out of my choice.

At this point, the shop door opened abruptly to the sound of heavy breathing and the sight of a hand thrust in towards where Aunt Maggie was sitting on the lemonade box brought our eyes towards the round, red, slightly indignant face of the newcomer.

'Oh, it's on the floor at t'other side.' The little woman darted forward, picked up the basket and pushed it into the outstretched hand. 'The lady wanted to sit down . . . Is she coming yet?'

There were a couple of wheezy breaths before the woman answered, 'No, not due for five minutes yet. I've run all the way.'

The basket and the round face disappeared, and the little woman, addressing Aunt Maggie, said, 'That's Alice Merely. She used to work up at McVeighs' for years, and her mother and father afore her. The weddin's for McVeighs', but it's not one of the McVeighs. Miss Doris is a Slater. Her and little Janie were old McVeigh's young sister's children, if you see what I mean. They've lived with the McVeighs since their mother died. It's Miss Doris who's being married this day.' The little woman suddenly stopped and patting her lips with a child-like gesture at her forgetfulness exclaimed, 'Oh! You want glasses.'

As she dived into the back room, Aunt Maggie signalled to me with raised eyebrows.

'There you are. Mind, it's fizzy, and it might go all over your frock . . . You're not from hereabouts?' The shopwoman was holding the bottle over the glass as she put the question.

'No. No, I'm not.'

'Aa thought you weren't. But Aa thought you might be.' She was now looking over her shoulder with a cunning expression on her face towards Aunt Maggie. 'Somethin' in your voice, like ours sort of.'

'Well, it should be,' said Aunt Maggie. 'I was born not so far from here – in Evenwood near Bishop Auckland.'

'Well, Aa never! Do you know the McVeighs then? Have you come for the weddin'?'

The froth was spilling onto the shirt of my grey wool suit, and gently I guided the woman's hand aside and took the glass from her.

'No. No, I don't know the McVeighs. Bishop Auckland isn't exactly on the doorstep,' my aunt informed her.

'No, it isn't that, I grant you, an' I'm well aware of it.' The little figure was inclined to bristle now.

15

'But the McVeighs are known far and wide. If you ever lived in the county, you couldn't help but hear of the mad McVeighs. Of course, it was the old man an' his father before him that made the name. The two that are left now aren't very hectic, although Mr Davie is mad enough in his own way. Yet everybody in the county knows the McVeighs.'

'It must be more than thirty years since I was in these parts, you must forgive me.' There was a small note of sarcasm in my aunt's voice. It was a danger signal that brought me from my low seat to my feet. My lovable kind aunt had a tongue like a rapier at times. Although we owed nothing in courtesy to this woman, for she had not put herself out very much on our account, I still did not want her to be hurt. I did not want anybody to be hurt. Some part of me was always wishing for a miracle that would make mankind immune to hurts and the results thereof.

'How much do I owe you?'

'Well, you're not taking the bottles.' The eyes were darting now between the two bottles. 'That'll be elevenpence each. You haven't drunk half of it but that's not my fault, is it? One and tenpence, please.'

We were just going out of the door when the little woman, almost on my heels, addressed me pointedly, practically turning her back on Aunt Maggie as she asked, 'Are you stayin' hereabouts or are you just passin' through?'

As my mouth opened to answer, Aunt Maggie's sharp voice came over her shoulder, 'We're just passing through.'

While I started the car once again, Aunt Maggie, looking straight ahead and speaking under her breath, exclaimed, 'Nosy Parker! These out-of-the-way villages seem to breed them.'

'I should have asked the way.'

'Yes, I suppose you should. She'd have known every step of the road, I bet. Look, there's a car drawing up in front. It looks like some form of taxi. I'll ask him.'

I drew our car once more to a halt, and Aunt Maggie, leaning out of the window and looking along the kerb to where a man was alighting from a dignified pre-war Bentley, called, 'Can you please tell us the way to Lowtherbeck at Roger's Cross?'

The man came to the car and bent down towards my aunt. He was tall, thin, with a grey moustache and a solemn face, the only solemn face I had seen in the whole village. His voice sounded serious as he asked, 'Are you for the weddin'?'

Although I could only see the back of my Aunt Maggie's head, I knew that she had closed her eyes. Her voice told me so.

'We are not going to the wedding,' she answered him. 'We would just like to know the way to Lowtherbeck, if you don't mind.'

'No – I – don't – mind.' The man's voice was slow and held the same note of controlled patience as did Aunt Maggie's. I could remember the time when I would have laughed at the implication in their tones. 'Go round the stone cross there and out of the village that way until you come to the three roads. If you want to get there quickly, take the gully sharp left. It's steep and it's narrow, but it will bring you to the very door and it will save you a couple of miles or more. But if you want to do it in leisurely fashion, take the middle road. There's no shelter from the sun that way, you'll be dead on top of the fells, but it's a good road and five miles long to the very inch – now, is there anything more I can do for you?'

My Aunt Maggie drew her head back inside the car. Her eyes were turned sideways up at him. 'No, thank you,' she said. 'You have been very explicit.'

'The – pleasure – is – mine – madam.'

Oh, if only I hadn't forgotten the way to laugh! I set the car moving slowly forward, and, as we rounded the cross, I glanced to the right. The tall man was standing beside the little woman store-keeper outside the shop watching our departure.

'That,' said Aunt Maggie slowing, 'is Talbot, I bet me bottom dollar.' And then she burst out laughing.

'Oh, Aunt Maggie,' I said.

'Oh, lass,' she said, mimicking my tone. Then she added, 'Oh, well, we know where we're bound for, five miles to the inch or down the narrow gully straight to the front door. Which is it to be? I leave it to you.'

I took the narrow gully.

And you could almost say it *was* a gully. It was a track between two high banks beyond which towered tall trees, a great part of their trunks covered by an undergrowth, the whole making a deep shade over the roadway which was most welcome after the glare of the sun.

'Ah, this is nice.'

As Aunt Maggie spoke, I turned the wheel sharply to follow a bend in the lane, the bend was followed by another and yet another very much on the hairpin style. My foot was already on the brake as the road itself was steep, but, on turning the third bend, I instinctively pressed it down hard, for there, tearing up the incline towards me at a pace that should never have been attempted on such a gradient, was a big black car. My mind registered it as an old Rover.

My hand brake was tight on, and, although I had shut off my engine, I still held my foot on the brake as I stared from my elevated position down through two windscreens into a large face that was screwed up in a sort of amazed perplexity – and something else.

The cars were almost bonnet to bonnet. I did not move from my position at the wheel. Only with my eyes did I follow the other driver's movements. He wrenched his car door open; he took the few steps which brought him to my open window; now his face was thrust through it at me.

His appearance was strange, to say the least. At first I thought I had been looking down at an old man, a white-haired old man – this man could not have been more than thirty-five – his hair was so fair as to look almost bleached. This was emphasised by the colour of his skin which had that ruddy brownness produced by sun, rain and wind. But it was much later in the day before I realised I had taken any note of his appearance, for at this moment he was awakening in me a feeling that had been dormant for many months. It was anger.

'What the hell are you doing on this road?'

My answer was so trite that, again, it was only later when going over the incident in my mind that I censured myself for it; it was the kind of double cliché that I was careful to keep out of my own writing, and criticised when I found it in the writing of others.

'Who do you think you're talking to?' I demanded. 'It's a free country. At least, so I understand.'

Under the chemical reaction of the man's anger, the irises in his dark blue eyes were widening, and he held his breath before bringing out, with a slowness that was in itself a calculated insult, 'Would you care to take a look into that car?' He thrust his arm out. 'You will notice, unless your eyesight is as much affected as your road sense, that there's a bride sitting in it. And, naturally, she's on her way to her wedding – at least, she was . . . What is more, she happens to be late already.'

I did not do as he commanded and look at the bride. I hadn't noticed there was a bride in the car although I had taken in a silvery mass behind the dark blur of the driver. I was about to say, 'Well, you'll just have to go back because I cannot reverse up this steep hill,' when Aunt Maggie spoke my thoughts and in a much cooler manner than I could have achieved. Yet there was a cutting edge in her voice. Bending across me, she peered up at his supercilious face as she said, 'If you're in such a hurry, I shouldn't stand there wasting time. You back down the hill until we can pass you, because we cannot reverse backwards round these bends.'

Again the man held his breath, but not for so long this time, and his tone when he answered was rapid, 'Madam, there are two more cars at this moment setting away from the bottom of the bank, if they are not already halfway up it.'

'Well then!' Aunt Maggie laid particular stress on these two words with which she usually preceded any admonitory sentence. 'Well then! They'll have to back, too, and the quicker you get started the more likelihood you have of getting to the church, if not on time, then sometime today.'

'Davie.'

The man turned his head sharply towards a hand which was waving out of the car window. Evidently the bride was not going to risk damaging her head-dress by getting out. I was looking at her now through the intervening windscreens and an awful feeling of resentment flooded my body. The longer I could keep her waiting, the better I would like it.

'No, no! Don't be like that.' The voice was loud in my head. I looked at the man and said, 'I can't attempt this winding road in reverse; it's too rough. How far before I can pass you downhill?'

I wasn't looking at the man's eyes but at his mouth – it was very thin for such a large face. It was a cruel mouth, I thought. All men were cruel – I hated men, all of them – all of them – all of them! My mind was beginning to race again. 'It's not true.' The voice in

21

my mind was speaking again. 'You only hate one.'

'No – two,' I almost answered the inner voice vocally because, at this moment, I was hating this big face, and these dark blue eyes, and this head covered with odd bleached fair hair.

My gaze, lifting to the man's now, was undoubtedly expressing my feelings and, as his eyes held mine, I shouldn't have been surprised if his hand had come up and struck me. But almost in one leap, he was back at the wheel of his car and talking rapidly to the girl behind him. I could not hear what he was saying for the noise of the engine – doubtless, the substance was vitriolic.

With a driving dexterity that deserved credit, he backed the big car down the incline, and, as I followed, Aunt Maggie's voice came to me, cautiously saying, 'Now, go steady. Don't be silly, go steady.'

Did she know that I had a strong desire to drive my bonnet forward and crash that arrogant bully off the road?

For a moment, the black car disappeared round yet another bend and when it came into view again it had stopped. From my superior position I saw, at two points of the road lower down, two more stationary cars. The man was out of the Rover now and running down towards them. The sound of his voice shouting orders came to me, but now I wasn't paying much attention to it – I was looking once again through the windscreens straight at the bride, who was looking at me. She was leaning forward over the front seat staring at us.

I willed my Aunt Maggie not to say, 'My! she's bonny. Isn't it a pity – all this mix-up?'

I gave another extra tug to the hand brake before I started to get out of the car.

Now Aunt Maggie put her hand on my arm and her voice had an underlying note of anxiety as she said, 'Now, Pru.' Then, again, as I shook off her hold and stepped into the road, she repeated, louder this time, 'Now, Pru!'

I walked the few steps to the window of the Rover, and there was the girl's face staring at me. I have no idea what I first intended to say, nor what impulse brought me to this action, but I surprised myself I know when I did speak.

'I'm sorry for all this,' I said.

'Oh, don't worry.' The happy smile on the girl's face pained me. The kindness in her words pained me. I would have felt much better if, like the man, she had raged. The bride-to-be spoke now as if I knew all about her. 'Jimmy'll wait for years. Don't worry. Anyway, it isn't your fault, no matter how Davie goes on. I've always said there should be a notice at the top of the lane.'

'This way was recommended to us.'

'It was?' There was surprise in the girl's voice. 'Who told you that?'

'A man in the village.'

'Now I wonder who that could have been?'

I found that I was amazed at the girl's attitude. She was going to her wedding and her pleasant pretty face was twisted slightly with enquiry as she wondered who my informant had been. All her concern at this moment seemed to be taken up with this wondering.

From the corner of my eye, I saw the man running back up the bank, and, after saying once again, 'I'm sorry,' I retreated hastily towards my car. But before I was settled in the seat, the face was hanging over me again, the voice snapping out orders.

'About half a mile down the bank there's a grass verge – sort of. It's on a slope. See what you can do about it.'

The Rover was moving backwards again, but more slowly now for the driver had adjusted its speed to that of the cars behind. It seemed a long time before we came to the grass verge. Even then I wouldn't have recognised it as such but for the gesticulating of the man at the wheel in front.

Aunt Maggie objected, 'You can't get on there; that's a bank.'

I stopped the car. Yes, it was a bank – not much of a bank as banks go, but nevertheless a bank. My car was a modern one and had little weight. Likely the old Rover in front of me could have taken this slope and held it, but I could see myself doing a back somersault into the road again.

My head was out of the car and I was shouting, 'It's too steep.'

Now the big face was facing me at an angle. 'You can take it. Look, stay where you are a minute an' I'll show you.'

I watched the Rover mount the bank and hang there at a dangerous angle.

'You'll never be able to do that. Don't you attempt it,' Aunt Maggie protested.

'I'm not going to let that big head get the better of me.' I answered Aunt Maggie without looking at her. Then, as the Rover backed once again onto the road, I went into first gear and slowly, very slowly, mounted the incline.

'Oh, my God, we'll be over! I tell you we'll be over!'

'Be quiet, Aunt Maggie.'

To my surprise, Aunt Maggie was silent. When she grabbed at the handle to balance herself, for she was now leaning heavily against the car, I said tersely, 'Don't move.'

Her answer, a deep intake of breath, was smothered under the noise of the cars as, one after the other with throttles open, they sped past us. The other two cars were packed to capacity and I was aware of a number of bobbing heads and eyes turned in our direction. Then they were gone and we were alone.

For the first time I realised that the road was no longer shaded with trees but was open to the glare of the sun. Gently I reversed and cautiously edged the car back down the bank onto the road once more.

'Thank God!'

Although Aunt Maggie uses the expression 'Thank God!' a number of times a day, it is not in an irreverent way. Not at all. When you hear my aunt use the words 'Thank God', you know they mean just exactly that, and, at this moment, I was endorsing them.

'You did that very well, lass. I would have said nobody could have stuck on that slope without overturning. Well, that was an experience. They say that all experience is grist for the mill, but I can do without that kind, what do you say?'

'I would like to tell that big lout what I think of him!'

I had been thinking along those lines, but with no intention of voicing my thoughts. But that was the way of things. Although I had no conscious wish to hurt anyone either by word or deed, I seemed to have little control in mastering my emotions. That was one of the reasons I wanted to get away from people. I knew as yet I wasn't ready for civilised society, in which you do not say immediately what you think, in which your thoughts, before they leave the channels of your mind, must be sorted out lest they embarrass or hurt the hearer. No, I knew I wasn't ready for an ordered civilised community, for when I spoke I wanted to speak nothing but the truth, plain fact and truth – and life can be very uncomfortable with unadorned fact and truth.

This phase, the doctors had told me, was a natural reaction to having suffered due to lies. All my life I had suffered the one way or another because of lies. I had been brought up on lies. I can still hear my mother saying to me, 'Tell Daddy I've gone over to Kay's.' I was eight before I knew that Kay was a man. I was twelve when I knew that Father did not go to the continent for business alone but for pleasure as well, a special kind of pleasure.

And yet for years they had both lived together, been polite to each other, talked to each other, and acted as if nothing unusual were happening.

I cannot believe now that I was just fourteen when the farce of the three of us living as if we were a normal family ended, for I seemed to have been playing at their game for a great number of years. I say when the 'farce ended', for it ended only to break up into two separate farces, shameful and humiliating farces, at least to me. But not to my mother, or my father either.

My mother said, 'You will love it, darling; Joey is such fun. He's young and gay and has such a lovely boat. Oh, you will love it.'

I didn't love it, and I hated Joey.

When I had attended boarding school afterwards, I had spent half the holidays with each parent and I could never decide which I hated most, Joey's hands searching my waist or my father's bachelor apartment, which could be in France, Spain, or Italy – or wherever the fancy took him. Each apartment was presided over by a different housekeeper who did no work; but all of the housekeepers had one thing in common – they all had big busts – and they all disliked me as much as I did them.

I was seventeen when my mother divorced Joey and said that I must leave school and come and live with her – we 'had only each other'. Those were her words and I believed her. I didn't mind giving up the idea of going to university. I had only been working half-heartedly for it anyway. I knew what

I wanted to be, I wanted to be a writer, and I couldn't see that I was going to be helped very much more by another three to four years of mental slogging.

Mother and I 'had only each other' for six weeks – then Ralph came on the scene. Ralph was four years younger than Mother, which made him thirty-one. Quite suddenly I was packed off to my father.

I was put in the first-class Pullman with chocolates, magazines, a travelling rug – like an old lady, and a last-minute present was thrust into my hand – it was a three-strand pearl necklace. Then Mummy was waving frantically from the platform, with Ralph by her side. Her eyes were full of tears – I swear she had a glycerine phial in her handkerchief. And so she was rid of me once again.

But that was one journey I did not complete. I got off at the next station, put my new yellow hide cases in the 'Left Luggage' office, and went to the coach station. A little over an hour later, I was sitting in the kitchen of my Aunt Maggie's house in Eastbourne. Her arms were around me and her tears, real tears, were mingling with mine as she pressed me to her, murmuring over and over again, 'Don't worry, my love. There now, there now. You'll stay with me. Just let them try to get you – just let them.'

They did try, but not overhard. My mother descended on the little house and accused her elder half-sister of being an interfering, frustrated old maid.

Was I coming back home?

No, I was not.

She would write to my father – something would be done about it.

Nothing was done about it. That was the humiliating thing. The knowledge that they were glad to be rid of me was more devastating than the game of tug-of-war they had played with me for years. And all the love and kindness Aunt Maggie showered on me couldn't make up for the feeling of being rejected, of being thrown aside, put out of the way.

I was eighteen when I first took ill, and neither of them came to see me. My father was in Australia by then. He sent me money to buy an expensive present and said he had been in touch with the doctor and I must get out and enjoy myself. My mother was in France on an extended honeymoon. She, too, had been in touch with the doctor and her advice was similar to my father's. I must get out and enjoy myself. When she returned she would get Ralph to introduce me to some nice boys. With my looks I could pick and choose. But, in the meantime, I must get about and amuse myself. There was no better cure for – *nerves*!

Neither the doctor nor Aunt Maggie had called my illness 'nerves'. The doctor had said it was a form of exhaustion. I was so weak. I couldn't lift hand or foot. I lay in bed day after day looking out the window at the trees across the road through which I could glimpse the chimneys of the big empty house beyond. It was thinking about this house that brought vitality back into my body. I found I was filling the empty rooms with people and making up stories about them.

I made up several stories about the house and, always, the occupants were a close-knit family, a happy family. Then, one day, my dreams turned into reality. A family came to live in the house. It seemed to me at the time that I had conjured them up out of fantasy. It was a happy family; I became connected with it and the connection ruined my life.

It says somewhere in the Bible: 'And their second state was worse than their first.' This was true for me, too . . .

'Well I never!' These words must have escaped Aunt Maggie's guarded lips, for her lips were always guarded on any subject that might bring me added hurt.

The man in the village had said the road would take us to the very door. And that is what it had done. The path had widened out into a kind of drive, and the drive encircled a large round of lawn, and, beyond it, stood the house – a replica of the house I had been thinking about only a moment ago. There were the steps leading to the front door, four in this case, the other house had six. And, on each side of the steps, there were two large bow windows. Above them were six long windows which spanned the front of the house. The windows in the other house had been footed with iron balconies. There were no balconies here, but the side of the house was almost covered along its ground-floor level and halfway up its height with a

conservatory, an exact replica of that other conservatory.

'Well, we're here.' Aunt Maggie's voice was low.
'We'd better make ourselves known. Everything
seems very quiet – no!'

It was at this point we turned and looked at each
other, the same thought speaking from our eyes. We
were at the bottom of a valley. It seemed a dead end
and there was no other house to be seen. The
wedding party must have come from here.

My Aunt Maggie was biting her lip and she
pulled on it hard before saying, 'But this can't be
Lowtherbeck! That woman said the name was
McVeigh – I mean those concerned with the
wedding.'

'No, "Slater", I think. She said the name was
"Slater".'

'Well, Slater or McVeigh, that's got nothing to do
with Cleverly, has it? Miss Flora Cleverly, that's the
name on the letter.' Aunt Maggie rapidly opened
her bag and, producing the last letter of the corre-
spondence that had passed between her and the
owner of the cottage we had taken, she tapped
the signature, saying 'Flora Cleverly!'

'Well, there's bound to be someone about. We'd
better enquire – we can't just keep going on.'

Simultaneously we got out of the car and together
we walked up the steps to the front door. It was
wide open, showing a half-panelled hall with stairs
leading off at the end. On a polished table to the left
side of the door stood two twisted candlesticks with
a bowl of roses between. The hall floor was bare

except for one rug in its centre, and, although the boards showed the dusty marks of many feet, I could see from the surroundings it had been highly polished. I have always had an observant eye, seeming to take in everything at a glance. I suppose it is a natural part of a writer's stock in trade, and, from the first glimpse of the interior of the house, I sensed that there was little money about – at least not enough to keep up with the ordinary wear and tear of such an establishment – for, although I could only see two steps of the stairs, I noted that the stair carpet was worn, so worn it was torn in the middle of the treads.

After I had rung the bell for the third time, Aunt Maggie said, 'Let's walk around.'

So we went down the steps again and along the front of the house, but before we reached the second bow window we had both stopped again, our glances drawn to a length of whiteness stretching from the window to the other side of the room – a table laden with the wedding feast.

My Aunt Maggie's crisp tones brought my gaze from the window. 'Well, I just can't understand this. There's only one thing I know: this can't be the place we're looking for.'

We were now on the side of the house opposite to the conservatory. This side was open to a court-yard – but an unusual type of courtyard, for it was bordered on one side with a hill of stark solid rock. On our journey over the fells, we had passed great outcrops of rock – the fells themselves were composed of such, as were sections of the hills and mountains – but it seemed odd to find the rock so near to the house when all around there was evidence of a green valley which was wooded in parts. The rock looked out of place, as if the house had been there first.

'Hello, there!' Aunt Maggie was calling now, her voice loud. 'Hello, there!' When there was no answer, she turned towards me and lifted her shoulders significantly. 'Surely there must be someone about – they couldn't leave the place to God and good neighbours and all the doors open and everything.'

My aunt was moving now towards the middle of the rock wall in which, oddly enough, there was a door – and the door stood open. I had turned and was looking towards the side of the house, which I realised was the kitchen side.

Aunt Maggie said, 'Here, a minute!'

Her tone was urgent, and when I walked towards the rock I thought how odd it was to see an ordinary doorway in that massive stone. The doorway spoke of a hollowness inside which belied the impression of the rock itself. Then I was standing by Aunt Maggie's side and she was pointing into the dim depths. As I peered I saw what had caused her exclamation.

'They grow mushrooms – look at the boxes. That must be a cave in there. But the smell! Still, it's fascinating.'

'Yes, yes, but let's try to find someone.' I wasn't interested in the mushrooms or the cave. Of a sudden, I was feeling very tired, physically tired; I had been at the wheel of the car for hours. What was more, I hadn't had a solid meal since six o'clock last night.

As we turned away, I almost tripped over a piece of wood at the foot of a small lean-to which covered an old rusty coke stove. I kicked it aside and said to Aunt Maggie, as she was going to some pains to close the door, 'I wouldn't shut it; it was likely left open for a purpose.'

I was to remember these words of mine some time later.

'This is fantastic,' said Aunt Maggie, dusting her hands. 'If this is Lowtherbeck, where are the Cleverlys in all this? Evidently, the bride is from here, and if she is, then so are those McVeighs.'

'Well, if that's the case—'

'Ssh! Look there.'

Stemming my rising indignation, I turned in the direction of Aunt Maggie's gaze. Standing at the corner of the house watching us from underneath lowered lids, I saw a young girl. The sun was full in my eyes and, from that distance, I guessed she could have been any age from fourteen to eighteen.

'Hello!' called Aunt Maggie. She moved forward and I followed her, and now we were standing close to the girl.

As I looked at this being, I felt a tremor pass through me. It wasn't a tremor of revulsion, but a feeling that always prepared me inwardly when I was confronted with something odd in nature. I have experienced it on a bus occasionally, and on board ships when sitting next to someone who looked quite ordinary, but proved to be slightly deranged.

However, it did not require any gift of insight or deep probing to know that standing before us was an unusual person. I was more puzzled than ever now about her age, but what intrigued me more was the beauty of the creature – immediately on looking at this girl, I had termed her in my mind a 'creature', a delicate, rather unearthly, creature. Her head was still inclined forward, but her eyes were wide open now and it was for all the world as if we were looking into the eyes of a young antelope. Her skin was cream-coloured – one could almost imagine that it would feel pleasantly warm to one's touch. Her mouth was full and beautifully shaped. But it was not the face that gave the impression of strangeness so much as the girl's body, for it seemed to droop; rather, it was relaxed like that of a very young child.

'Hello, my dear.' Aunt Maggie's voice was soft and low as if speaking to a child whom she did not want to startle. 'I think we are lost. We are looking for a house called Lowtherbeck at Roger's Cross. Can you help us?'

For answer, the girl turned slowly and pointed towards the house, and, as she did so, there slipped from her hand a book. As it fell to the ground, I saw that it was a Beatrix Potter book. There was nothing strange in that – this was Beatrix Potter's country – yet, was there not something extraordinary in a girl of this age reading such a baby book? Well, why not? I was still reading, at intervals, A. A.

Milne's *Winnie-the-Pooh*. But there was a difference here, for this book seemed to be part of the girl. As if she were reclaiming part of herself, she stooped quickly, grabbed up the book, and held it to her chest with both hands.

'This is Lowtherbeck then?'

The lips parted, the head nodded and she said, 'Yes.' Her voice would indicate her age as six or seven years old.

Speaking for the first time and, also, keeping my voice low I asked, 'Does anyone called Cleverly live here?'

The head bowed again. 'Yes.'

Her answer surprised me. If the Cleverlys lived here, what were the McVeighs and Slaters doing in the same house? – all living together, apparently. If that were the case, that settled that. I was certainly not going to live within sight or speaking distance of the gentleman with the odd-coloured hair – cottage, or no cottage. We would have to find someplace else, even taking into account that already we had paid quite a substantial amount to reserve the place.

'My name is Fuller, and this is my niece Miss Dudley. We have rented a cottage near here, it belongs to—'

'The cottage – yes.'

The girl was smiling quite brightly now and nodding her head. Then, with a darting movement she ran past us onto the drive to the car and, opening the back door, she turned and glanced towards us before getting in.

Neither of us had moved, but Aunt Maggie exclaimed, 'Well, I never!'

With no more words, we went forward and took our places in the front seat.

Because of the luggage stacked on the back seat, the girl was sitting forward on the edge of it, and Aunt Maggie's face was close to the girl's as she asked, 'Will you show us the way?'

'Yes – round the side.'

'Which side, my dear?'

'Side of the house, 'course.' She laughed – the sound was slightly eerie.

'You'd better try it.' Aunt Maggie spoke under her breath.

I set the car in motion and edged it slowly down the path by the side of the house. It was just wide enough for us to pass. Then we came to what should have been the back of the house, but had more the appearance of a front façade because it was bordered by a wide terrace, which was now studded with deckchairs and odd tables. Two French windows leading into the house were wide open.

I spoke over my shoulder, asking, 'Are you sure this is the way?'

'Yes.'

We passed the terrace, then a rose shrubbery and a vegetable garden.

'You're all right. There's been cars along here before.' Aunt Maggie pointed through the window. Then, turning round again, she asked of the girl, 'How far away is it?'

'By the Lil Water.'

The 'Lil' I knew to mean 'Little'.

Aunt Maggie's rejoinder was not, 'That doesn't help much,' as it might have been to anyone else – she only smiled at the girl and nodded her head before she turned towards the front again.

'Oh, look at that! Isn't it beautiful?'

The path had come abruptly into the open – it actually ran on the rim of a hill and the scene below was, indeed, beautiful. There again was the sparkle of water – not a rivulet this time, but a lake.

Aunt Maggie had twisted to the back seat once more. 'Is that the water?' She was pointing behind my back.

'No, that's the Big Water.'

'Oh!' Aunt Maggie, looking ahead, was muttering now. 'Little Water; Big Water, sounds as if we had struck an American Indian reservation.'

I was driving very carefully for there were only a couple of feet between the edge of the road and the steep sloping hillside.

'I wouldn't like to come along here on a dark night,' Aunt Maggie commented.

I endorsed this mentally and was beginning to censure myself for bringing the car along the path. We should have walked to the cottage first, yet it seemed as if it were a goodish way from the house or the girl wouldn't have got into the car. The path now took a deep curve and began to descend steeply. Leaving the sunlight, the trail entered the coolness of a small copse, but only for a few minutes; then we were in the sunlight again and I pulled the car slowly to a halt.

I knew, as I stared at the scene before me, that if nature alone could cure a troubled mind that I would soon be better. There to the right of us lay a small lake, bordered on one side by the continuation of the copse we had just passed through. On the opposite side, rose a hill covered with great patches of heather. Slowly I brought my gaze from the right and looked to the left.

Aunt Maggie was also looking in this direction. She turned her wonder-filled eyes towards me and breathed, 'My, isn't it bonny!'

'Bonny' was not the correct word to describe the cottage. It was two-storied and built of blocks of granite which, in the late afternoon light, had a warm pink hue. Profuse clematis covered one corner and lent an added beauty to the stone. Before the door and the two windows were wide flag-stones intersected with heather. There was nothing between the flagstones and the grass bank that sloped very gently towards the lake. A railing, a garden ornament, even a chair would have marred the whole at this moment. The lake and the cottage were one and I was to live here for three months.

For the moment I had forgotten about the man with the odd-coloured hair.

'Well, well!' Aunt Maggie was slowly moving towards the cottage now with the girl walking slightly in front of her, her face half turned towards my aunt as if she were leading her. And Aunt Maggie might have been speaking to herself, for I was still in the driving seat, but I caught her words as she said: 'She didn't exaggerate – "a haven of peace" she called it.'

And yes, that's what the letter had said, 'a haven of peace'. And the writer had added, 'I'm sure your niece will benefit from her stay, it's worked little miracles with a number of convalescents.' Recalling these words, I felt a quick stab of resentment, resentment that anyone should have lived in this cottage, should have come here before me. I was aware that the feeling was ridiculous and unreasonable.

I got out of the car and watched my aunt and the girl walk out of the sunlight into the dark shadow of the doorway, but I made no haste to follow them for I was experiencing another odd feeling. I was resenting the fact that Aunt Maggie was with me. I had the strangest desire that I should be alone in this place, along with the cottage and the lake. I turned my eyes to the water. A strip of it, near the right bank where the trees were, lay in shadow. The rest of the water was a magnet for the sun, and, as if being caressed with jewelled rain, the surface sparkled and shimmered. So bright was the reflection that I closed my eyes against its brilliance.

'Pru!'

I turned towards the cottage. There was Aunt Maggie beckoning me from the window. I walked slowly towards the door; when I reached the threshold I stopped. Nothing that I saw surprised me; I seemed to know exactly how the place would be furnished. No wheel-back cottagey chairs, no chintz, no gay assortment of coloured cushions. There was no femininity at all about the long low room into which I walked straight from the open door.

I looked first to the left of me where Aunt Maggie now stood near an open fireplace which was just a large inlet in the wall and was made of the same rough stone as the outer walls of the cottage. There was a fire basket flanked by a pair of iron dogs in the aperture. Opposite the fireplace was a long deep brown leather couch holding cushions of the same hue. Behind this, running lengthwise with the room, was a rough refectory table, definitely handmade, and well made at that. Even my cursory glance took in this fact. The wall opposite to me had been boarded halfway along its length, and this was topped by a shelf on which stood, at intervals, three wooden animals: a horse, a fox and a dog. The dog was a perfect replica of a Labrador. Aware that my Aunt Maggie was watching me intensely, as was the girl, I turned and looked towards my right. In the middle of a wall which was entirely stark stone, there was another door which led into, I could see beyond, a kitchen. To each side of me, and flanking the front door, were two windows. They were square and rather high, and the sills were the same thickness as the stone.

'Like it?'

Aunt Maggie's question startled me for a moment and I repeated her words 'Like it?' Then I answered, 'I think it's amazing – out—' I had been about to say 'out of this world' but I checked myself in time. It would have been a trite summing up, an easy summing up. I often became annoyed at myself for lazy expression, for not translating my thoughts into meaningful words, and this cottage – this house – this setting deserved meaningful words.

'Where are the stairs?' My Aunt Maggie was bending down slightly towards the girl now.

With a skipping movement that had about it the jerky abandoned style of a child at play, the girl went towards the other doorway, and we followed.

The kitchen I saw was for use as a kitchen and nothing else. It held a Calor gas stove and a shallow stone sink above which there was a Calor water heater. On one side of the sink was a draining board; on the other, a small table. Beyond this, there was a door which doubtless opened into a pantry. On the wall opposite the stove and the sink was another door, which evidently led outside. And next to this, sprouting almost vertically out of the room, were the stairs.

The sight of their steepness had almost silenced Aunt Maggie. Except for a noise that was a cross between 'Oh!' and a groan she made no verbal comment, and bringing her eyes from the dim tunnel of the staircase she looked at me. Then, being Aunt Maggie, she smiled, although somewhat wryly.

'Shall we try it?' she asked.

My lips at least were smiling as I said, 'I'll go first,' but before I had finished speaking the girl was in front of me and she ascended by the simple method of using both her hands and feet.

I disdained to follow her example, at least for the first four stairs, but before I had reached the twelfth and final stair, I had resorted to her sensible means of going up this particular stairway. There was no landing, and, as I stepped out of the well of the stairs straight into a room, I did not look about me but turned swiftly and, bending forward, held out my hand to assist Aunt Maggie.

But my help was disdainfully thrust aside, not by my aunt's hands, she was using those as I had done, but by her voice, saying, 'Don't fluster me else I'll be over.'

I had never looked upon my Aunt Maggie as old – she was an ageless creature. Some days she appeared thirty or younger, at least in her outlook, and, physically, never over fifty. But, as she pulled herself up into the room and I put out my hand to steady her, I thought – this is going to try her – and I remembered that Aunt Maggie was sixty-five. Yet, when she straightened up, her breathing was even and she seemed undisturbed.

We moved away from the unprotected well of the staircase as if afraid of becoming overbalanced, then we looked around the room. It was the lowness of the ceiling that I noticed first; it was not more than six feet high. A tall person would have had to stoop. I am five feet seven and I felt that my hair was almost scraping it. There was one window in this room, small and square like those downstairs. Under it was a single wooden bed covered with a thick plaid travelling rug. There was a chest of drawers against the wall at the foot of the bed, and on the top of them was a small swing mirror. On the wall opposite was a long oak plain wardrobe like a detached cupboard; and, between the two walls, a door led into another room.

The girl went first. When we followed I found that the same pattern was repeated here; a single bed, a chest of drawers, a mirror and a wardrobe; no facilities for washing. The question did cross my mind at that moment. Not – is there a bathroom? I hadn't expected that. But – was there an indoor lavatory? And where did we wash and bathe? These questions were to be answered when we returned downstairs, but my attention was drawn now to yet another staircase, or, to be more explicit, a ladder placed straight against the wall and leading to a hatch in the low ceiling. When I looked up towards it, then down again, it was to find the girl's eyes fastened on mine. I could see she wanted to speak, so I waited.

What she said was straight to the point. 'That's mine.' She pointed upwards.

'Yours?' I inclined my head towards her. 'You sleep here?'

She shook her head from side to side vigorously. 'Just play – my toys up there – I sleep with Grannie.'

'Oh!' I glanced swiftly at Aunt Maggie. She wasn't looking at me, but at the girl, and, when the girl turned towards her, they smiled at each other.

The girl leading the way again, we descended to the ground floor. I think it was more awkward getting down the stairs than going up. I went face forward but Aunt Maggie, being more sensible, returned the way she had come, using her hands and her feet.

44

In the kitchen once more, dusting her palms against each other, Aunt Maggie remarked, 'There's going to be some washing of hands around here if nothing else. Which reminds me—' She looked from me to the girl and asked on a little laugh, 'is there a bathroom of sorts?'

The girl answered Aunt Maggie's laugh with one of her own which was again of a high squeaking quality exactly like that of an excited child, and, opening the back door, she pointed to the wall. There, hanging on a nail, was a long zinc bathtub.

The girl was already running down a roughly paved path to some bushes, amongst which stood a sentry-like structure.

The twinkle was deep in Aunt Maggie's eyes as she turned to me and said, 'It's been known to freeze up around here in November!'

'We needn't stay that long.' I was thinking with nostalgia, but only for a moment, of the beautiful sanitary arrangements in our house in Eastbourne, but as Aunt Maggie said airily, 'Aw, well, sufficient unto the day . . .' I thought, yes, sufficient unto the day. What did sanitary arrangements matter anyway? So close had I become entwined in my surroundings within a matter of not more than fifteen minutes, that had Aunt Maggie said anything detrimental about the amenities of the cottage I would have resented it as a personal affront.

I turned and went into the kitchen and opened the pantry door. It was dim and very cool. It went quite a way back with shelves all around it; opposite to me was a marble slab on which stood a large brown loaf, two bottles of milk, and a round of butter with an acorn pattern on the top. There was some tinned food on one of the shelves and a number of empty screw-top jars.

Aunt Maggie, coming to the door and looking past me towards the bread and butter, exclaimed, 'Well, that'll give us a start.' She narrowed her eyes as she spoke. Then she exclaimed, 'I've not seen butter done like that for years. Well, now we can get settled in.'

Aunt Maggie turned away and I was about to do the same when the girl almost overbalanced us both as she pushed past us into the larder and, reaching to the far corner of the marble slab, she grabbed up two china mugs. They looked like Coronation mugs, but I couldn't see what was written on them because, like the book, she held them tightly pressed to her chest. Then, looking at me she said, 'Mine 'n' Davie's.'

I had a picture of the bride's hand waving out of the car window calling 'Davie' and the name put my teeth on edge – I had already associated the name Davie with the surname McVeigh. It didn't need much stretching of the imagination to know where the designation 'Mad' came in. But what had this Davie – Davie McVeigh – to do with the cottage? A little tentative quizzing might enlighten me and I was about to proceed with it when the girl, now standing by the kitchen table and still holding the mugs, jerked her head upright and appeared to listen. So definite was her attitude that both Aunt

Maggie and I listened with her. We could hear nothing, but the girl now moved swiftly to the kitchen door and stood on the stone slab outside, her head still cocked to one side. Then we heard what she had heard, the sound which made her turn and run like a deer, past us again, through the kitchen, through the living room and out onto the path that led through the copse. I had just reached the door when I saw the pink flash of her dress among the trees.

'That was a whistle.'

I turned to Aunt Maggie. 'Yes, but from quite a distance away.'

'You don't think it was from the house?'

'No.' I shook my head.

The whistle had been thin and high, like notes from a reed pipe. I turned my gaze from my aunt and looked down the gentle slope to the lake as I said, 'I once saw a shepherd in Spain playing on a pipe that sounded like that.'

I had said I had 'seen' the shepherd; but I had never seen him; he had been miles away in the hills. I went out and walked towards the car, amazement filling me. I had spoken of Spain, I had spoken about the shepherd. I hadn't mentioned the name of the man who had told me that the pipe I was then hearing was being played miles away in the hills, but he had been in my consciousness and he had remained there for some seconds without causing me panic. I stopped and looked back at the stone cottage. Already it seemed to be working, already its calm strength was oozing into me.

I began to unpack the car rapidly, carrying the heaviest cases into the house, making two journeys to each one of Aunt Maggie's, aware all the time that she was covertly watching me. It didn't matter. Aunt Maggie was always watching me. Well, she could watch me now getting better. I couldn't wait to get settled in.

2

It was seven o'clock and Aunt Maggie and I were
sitting in two rather decrepit deckchairs outside the
cottage. We had sat in silence for at least fifteen
minutes before Aunt Maggie commented for the
second time in the past hour, 'You know, I've a
good mind to take a dander over.'

'I wouldn't. They're bound to know we're here;
the girl would have told them. Anyway, as this is the
only place the road leads to, they will know it was
us coming down.'

'Yes, that's the funny thing. As you say, they were
bound to know it was us. Then why hasn't somebody been across? Poor manners, I should say.'

'At a wedding—' There I had said the word, and
I went on boldly, 'there is always so much to do,
everybody getting in everybody else's way. You
know how it is.' I was looking at the darkening
water, but I knew that my Aunt Maggie's eyes were
full on me.

It was some minutes before she spoke and then
she remarked, 'It was odd that bed being used,
wasn't it? You would have thought they would

have stripped it after the last tenant. And, then, it being made up with a sleeping bag – funny.'

Yes, I myself thought it was funny. Underneath the plaid travelling rug, there hadn't been the usual bedclothes but a home-made sleeping bag, comprised simply of an old eiderdown sewn together to form the bag. This was covered inside and out with two sheets which had also been sewn to form bags. Doubtless it was a very easy way to deal with bedding but I couldn't see myself climbing into a sleeping bag each night. In the far room, which was to be Aunt Maggie's, there were three blankets and two pillows under another travelling rug, but no sheets. The lack of sheets she said wouldn't worry her for that night – she was so tired she could sleep on the grass.

We had come prepared with a lot of tinned food as Miss Cleverly's letter had indicated we were off the beaten track, so, together with the bread and butter from the larder and a tin of tongue and some salad stuff we had bought on the way, we made quite a satisfying meal. Later, as we washed up, Aunt Maggie was so funny about the zinc bath, going to the length of giving a demonstration of how she would get in and out of it, which included slipping on the soap, that I laughed outright.

A quaint silence had followed my unusual burst of merriment, then Aunt Maggie put her arm about me and pressing me to her said, 'I'm going to enjoy myself here.'

What she really meant was – she was going to be happy here because she thought that in this charming oasis I would regain health of both mind and body – and, perhaps, enough self-confidence to enable me to live with my fellow creatures.

Because of my parents, I had lived with distrust from my earliest memories, and this did not engender faith in others. Yet I had lived in faith for one glorious year. But the shattering of my faith for the second time was more destructive than anything my parents had done to me, or maybe I had felt it more keenly because of the quicksand foundation they had laid – I didn't know. At this moment, I didn't want to think. Let the past creep back gradually.

I looked over the lake, and saw a swallow darting in and out of the last rays of the sun as it flickered on the water. He was after his evening meal, and, as he darted and bobbed and twisted, I realised I was setting his motions to the distant sound of music.

'They'll likely be having a dance on the lawn,' said Aunt Maggie. 'Well, if they go on till midnight they won't keep me awake. Once I get my head down I'll be gone.'

'It'll soon be dark,' I said. 'I'd better try lighting that lamp.'

'That's not a bad idea.'

Aunt Maggie hoisted herself out of the chair and, folding it up, carried it and laid it against the wall of the cottage. I did the same with mine, and then we went indoors.

The lamp stood on a side table. It was an old-fashioned one with a pink bowl but it had been

converted to take Calor gas. The conversion had
been ingeniously achieved by a tube which ran from
the bowl down to a junction near the floor boards.
There it joined a metal pipe and, so, went to the
main tank in the kitchen which reposed in a
cupboard under the sink and fed both the water
heater and the stove as well. Being so fixed, the
lamp was not movable and I had noted that, unless
one had very good eyesight, it would be difficult to
read sitting comfortably before the fire for the table
was some distance from the couch. I probably could
manage, but I doubted whether Aunt Maggie would
be able to read unless she was sitting directly under
the lamp. But, as she had said, all she wanted to do
tonight was to get her head down on the pillow.

I had the match lit in my hand and was bending
over, my face close to the globe, and was about to
cautiously turn on the tap when I was so startled by
the door being thrust open that I swung round and
almost upset the whole contraption.

'What the blazes!'

Opposite to me stood the man with the odd-
coloured hair. He had appeared a big, bulky
individual on the road, but now his size seemed to
have doubled. He looked enormous, ungainly,
crude; there was about him some quality of the
rugged stone of which the cottage was built. But the
stone of the cottage gave out a warmness; this man
did not. His face was not contorted with anger as I
had seen it earlier, but now was wide with surprise
and what I could only think of as blank amazement
tinged with annoyance.

'You two!'

The words were certainly not complimentary in their implication.

'Yes. We two!' My back was stiff and my chin thrust out. I had said 'We two,' but Aunt Maggie was in the kitchen.

'What are you doing here?'

The man took two slow steps towards me and, as he approached, I was overwhelmed with the fear that we had settled in the wrong cottage.

My voice had a weak note as I asked, 'This place is Lowtherbeck, isn't it?'

'Yes, it's Lowtherbeck.'

'Roger's Cross?'

'Roger's Cross – right again.'

'There isn't another cottage about?'

'No. There isn't another cottage, not hereabouts.'

'Well, we've taken this cottage for three months.'

'You?' He screwed up his face. 'We were expecting a Miss Fuller and – and, I understand, her young niece – but not until Monday.'

'I'm Miss Fuller.' Aunt Maggie came slowly from the kitchen. 'I sent Miss Cleverly a wire saying that we were coming today instead of Monday. She had told me previously that the cottage was ready for us at any time.'

The man had not moved his body, but had turned his head and was looking down at Aunt Maggie.

'We didn't get your wire, unless –' He paused. '– unless it got mixed up with the wedding ones.'

'Well, be that as it may, I sent the wire and here we are.'

'Yes, I can see that, and it's damned awkward. My brother was sleeping here tonight; the house is full.'

'Then you'll just have to let him share your room, won't you?' Aunt Maggie's voice was deceptively civil.

'That, again, is going to be slightly awkward, madam.'

'Miss.'

'Miss.'

He turned his big head gravely towards her. 'You see, I sleep here most of the year. When it isn't let, I could say I live here.'

'Miss Cleverly should have explained this in her letter.'

'There was no need. I'm always out before the tenants arrive.'

I watched Aunt Maggie and the man survey each other, weighing up the form as if before combat. And now Aunt Maggie, dropping into old-fashioned prim courtesy as she was at times wont to do, said, 'I don't know whom I have the honour of addressing.'

As the man laughed, I could have lifted my hand and struck him across the mouth so strong was my anger against him.

'You have the honour, Miss –' he stressed the 'miss' '– of addressing David Bernard Michael McVeigh.'

'Thank you.' Aunt Maggie seemed to be losing ground. She swallowed, then indicating me with a motion of her hand, she said, 'This is my niece, Mrs Lac—'

I closed my eyes for a second as Aunt Maggie, retracting quickly, changed my name to 'Miss Prudence Dudley.'

When I opened my eyes, the man was looking at me full in the face. I did not expect him to say anything so trivial as 'How do you do' or 'Pleased to meet you', and he didn't.

He said instead, 'Why the devil did you come down the lane?'

Here we went again! My chin moved twice before I replied; then, and not too quietly, I said, 'We were directed to come that way.'

Before McVeigh could make any comment on this, Aunt Maggie put in, 'Why are you pretending you are surprised to see us here? You must have known who we were this afternoon. That road leads nowhere else but to the house up yonder.' She thrust a sharp finger towards the large house.

'There, you are mistaken. There's a turning that branches off to the right about a quarter of a mile before you reach our place. It connects with the fell road. If you had taken the fell road, you would have come in by that way.'

'Well, we didn't, and we're here, and that's all about it. And I don't think we're answerable to anyone but Miss Cleverly.'

'Really?' There was question in the word.

'Yes, really! I made arrangements to take the cottage through a Miss Cleverly and I will continue to do business with her – perhaps, you'll enlighten me—' Aunt Maggie was back on the pedantic line again. 'Where do you come in on all this?'

'Me?' He was pointing to his chest where I could see the muscles bulging under a starkly white shirt. 'Oh, me. I only happen to be the owner of the set-up.'

I swallowed dryly. Aunt Maggie swallowed. I clasped and unclasped my hands as my mind repeated again and again: oh, no, no.

It seemed a long time before I heard Aunt Maggie ask in a slightly subdued tone, 'Who, then, is Miss Cleverly?'

'That will take a lot of explaining, Miss Fuller.' There was a trace of sardonic laughter in his voice now. 'Miss Cleverly is a lady who runs my house. She fills the position of housekeeper and adviser, and – performs lots of other functions.'

I felt my face turning scarlet again. Again, I wanted to take my hand and strike out at the mouth from which the deep cool-sounding words had come. There flashed into my mind the picture of my father's last apartment, and his last mistress – the last one, that is, that I had seen. I was glaring at the man's back now for he had turned round.

As he walked towards the kitchen door, he said over his shoulder, 'I'll collect my bed if you don't mind.'

Aunt Maggie moved across the dim room and stood near me. Under her breath she muttered, 'Don't let him get you down. We'll not see much of him – there'll be no need to. Anyway, if you can't stick him, we'll find some other place.'

Yes, we would certainly have to find someplace else, for I couldn't tolerate that individual. I couldn't put up with David Bernard Michael McVeigh for long without bursting asunder. The man did something to me; he made me want to hit out. It was a terrifying feeling for I had only hit out once in my life before, and then I had been driven to it, and was half-mad.

'There is always a fly in the ointment, lass. That's life.' Aunt Maggie's voice was sad now and this broke my thoughts away from myself; I was now filled with concern for her. She had put up with the long hot journey, even car sickness. She had put a good face on everything, and, not only today, but for years past, she had done everything to smooth the granite edges of life that would from time to time dig at me. Now she sounded tired, and not a little sad. Making an effort, I put out my hand and touched hers and whispered a saying to her she had often extolled in my childhood: 'Big balloons make the loudest bang.'

The balloon appeared at the kitchen door.

'Two mugs that were in the pantry?' the balloon asked.

'The girl took them,' I said.

'The girl?' McVeigh was moving into the room now. Under his arm was the rolled-up sleeping bag. 'You mean Frannie?'

'I don't know what her name is, but she took them.'

'Oh, well.'

He was standing with his back to the front door, and through narrowed lids, he looked first at Aunt Maggie and then at me – his gaze taking in, not only my face, but the whole of me.

His voice slightly mocking, he said, 'Well I suppose it'll sort itself out. Sleep well. I put a clean set –' he hitched at the bedding under his arm '– on. You'll find plenty of linen and such in the loft if you require it. Good night.'

Neither of us answered. And, not until I watched through the window the dark bulk of him disappear in the copse, did I turn to Aunt Maggie.

She was seated now and was silent – her silence disturbed me.

'Let's go to bed,' I suggested. I put my hand on her shoulder.

She turned her head, looked up at me, and remarked, 'So Miss Cleverly is the housekeeper. Well! Well! From her letter, I would have said she was around the same age as myself. Funny, the impressions one gets – the wrong impressions.'

'I don't think you could have got a wrong impression about that individual – shall I light the lamp?'

'No, don't bother. If we have a good sleep, we'll see things differently tomorrow, be able to laugh at life again, eh?' My aunt patted my hand where it still rested on her shoulder. Then, with an endearing movement, she lowered her cheek towards it.

These were the moments in my life when I knew that deep feeling was not dead in me. When I could respond to affection. In this moment I knew I loved my Aunt Maggie very deeply.

The bed was placed in such a position that, when you were sitting propped up, you could see the lake out the window and, because of the added height, over the hill bordering the left side of the water as well to a range of higher hills beyond. I could pick out small details quite clearly because there was moonlight, strong white moonlight, that made the scene almost as clear as it had been in the sunlight.

It was nearing eleven o'clock and I had been in bed for almost two hours but I had not yet been able to approach sleep. In fact, I was much wider awake than I had been when driving in the heat of the day. My mind seemed alert and my thinking was devoid of the slightest trace of panic, which was strange to me, especially as my thoughts were delving into the past. It was the moonlight that had done it.

When I had first come to bed, I had been thinking of our visitor. It was odd, but I hated to think of him as the owner of the cottage, yet I found, as I continued to gaze down into the lake where the moon was buried fathoms deep, and watched its light softly dimming now and again as a cloud raced across its surface, that I was forgetting the man. At least, my anger against him had subsided. He was, in this moment, washed of all importance; his rudeness had not the power to anger me any more, and it seemed that it would never again have such influence – he just didn't matter. Yet it was because of the feeling he had aroused in me, the feeling of retaliation, that my mind had slowly sunk back into the past, the not so very distant past, until it reached the point where, for the first time in my life, I had lifted my hands with the intent to hurt another; I had been incensed to the point where I was struggling madly with a man – with my husband.

There was a contraction of the nerves of my stomach now. My mind skirted round the thought of violence and moved quickly away – further back – to the time when I had lain in the bedroom of my Aunt Maggie's house and peopled the empty house opposite with characters. That was until the day when the real characters took over.

A family, as I've said before, came to live in the house. The daughter was at college. When she came home and heard there was a sick girl lying in the room that she could see from her bedroom window, she came to visit me. With that visit began my friendship with Alice Hornbrook.

Alice was twenty-three. She was what could be called an intellectual. She had just received her degree in English and had secured her first teaching post in Eastbourne. When she learned that I wrote stories, she asked to see them, merely I think out of politeness or to give some comfort to a sick person, but her praise of my work, which I knew to be genuine, acted like an injection of elixir on me.

'You must write, write seriously. Go on with this.' Alice's high, clear voice seemed to come across the lake now. A night bird was calling; it was saying, 'You must go on with this; you must go on with this.'

I did go on with it. I wrote a sixty-thousand-word story which, when Alice read it, she criticised.

'I would rewrite this again,' she told me. 'Make it eighty-thousand, and you'd do well to cut out the chunks of homespun philosophy and bitter passages. There's enough acid in your cynicism to make it a winner.'

I did as she advised, and the day I received a letter from a publisher stating that he would take pleasure in publishing my work and asking if I would come up to town to have a talk, my nervous complaint was cured and I got out of bed.

From this distance, I think my early success was on a par with that of Françoise Sagan. The critics hailed me for my youth while praising me for my knowledge of life, for the cynicism of a professional, for the competence with which I had handled the eternal triangle. But, didn't I know a lot about the eternal triangle? Hadn't I been brought up with it, fed on it from my earliest days? The characters in my books were only thinly disguised replicas of my mother and father, together with the second and third husbands on the one hand, and the numerous mistresses on the other.

I wrote three books in just under two years and I was there – I had arrived. I was selling so well, especially in America, that I need not worry about money ever. And I did not worry about money. That was one thing that had never caused me any anxiety. It seems to me strange at times that people should worry so much about money. If I had not a penny tomorrow, I know it wouldn't worry me; truthfully, it wouldn't.

Alice Hornbrook and I were friends for five years. She, too, called Aunt Maggie, 'Aunt Maggie'. And I called her mother and father 'Aunt Ann' and 'Uncle Dick'. Ours was that kind of close relationship. Then Alice's uncle came to stay with them. He was young, as he was her mother's youngest brother. His name was Ian Lacey, and from the moment I first looked at him my life was changed. Not that I fell in love with him straightaway; no, I would say that he gradually charmed me into loving him. But, right from the first moment, I was fascinated by him – for, besides his charm, he was amusing, and he was helpless, so helpless that he needed me – at least part of me.

And we had something in common, a strong bond – we were both writers, the only difference being that I had been published and he hadn't. When I say that Ian was helpless, I mean he was helpless with regard to money. He was helpless as a writer. He wanted someone to lean on, to guide him, and, although he was nine years older than I, I felt the elder. I also thought that I was the only one who understood him – had ever understood him, or could ever understand him. Ian indoctrinated me well.

For the first year of our acquaintance, Ian only stayed for short periods with his sister Mrs Hornbrook. But, on these visits, he spent most of the time with me in Aunt Maggie's house, and during this time my own work suffered – if I may use that word to imply neglect. For I would spend days reading and revising his work, or advising him about some story he was concerned with at the moment.

Before Ian took up his abode permanently with his sister in the house across the way, I was aware that it was impossible for him to follow my advice. Put a pen in his hand and a ream of paper on the table and his words flowed. Showy, flowery, verbose words – words resulting in long sentences with obscure meanings. He would spend hours with a dictionary and *Roget's Thesaurus* looking for a glorious ornamental adjective. But his prolixity did not cause me to withdraw my help, or lessen the love I then had for him.

On the night that Alice came to tell me that she was going to marry a schoolmaster (this came as something of a shock, for I wasn't even aware that she was interested in a man; she didn't seem the mating type, and never discussed the male) – it was on that night that Alice asked me, 'You're not getting serious about Ian, are you?'

For answer, I said, 'Is there any reason why I shouldn't?'

And to this she shook her head as she replied, 'No. Only that he's unstable; he's never been able to hold down a job in his life. Ian was the youngest, and my grandmother spoiled him. When she died, she passed on the task to her four daughters, and now it'll be up to a wife to complete the course. You want to think seriously about it. And, by the way,' Alice had nodded sagely, 'don't waste your good time on his stuff – he'll never be able to write in a month of Sundays. And Ian's kind can become as jealous as hell of another's success.'

I had said somewhat bitterly, 'You seem to love your uncle.'

Alice answered, 'I'm very fond of you and would hate to see you hurt.'

'Is that all you have got against Ian?'

She had considered for a moment, and then had said rather doubtfully, 'Yes. Yes, that's all.'

Many months later, when I recalled this conversation, I knew that Alice had spoken the truth when she said that was all she knew.

But at that time, when Aunt Maggie spoke along lines similar to Alice's, I began to think, and I knew I must get away and sort things out in my own mind. I did not want my marriage to repeat my mother and father's life all over again. I felt that if my marriage went on the rocks it would surely kill me – I had enough experiences of marriages going wrong. So I went away and thought things out, and I came to the conclusion that my parents' marriage had broken up because neither of them needed the other sufficiently. Ian needed me. He might be weak, but was that a great fault? My father wasn't weak, he was strong, and look what he had done to himself and to others. My decision was – if Ian wanted me to, I would marry him . . .

I waited and waited, but Ian didn't mention marriage. Then, one night, the situation, which was becoming emotionally unbearable for me, was brought to a head. It was the night I told Ian that I was going on a tour with Aunt Maggie and might be away for two months or more. At that moment, he seemed to have become hysterical – I wasn't to leave him, he needed me. How was he to exist without me?

I had never felt so happy in my life. I consoled him, saying I would never leave him – we would be married and go touring ourselves. Aunt Maggie would understand.

It was one of the awful blows to my pride when later he reminded me that he had never mentioned marriage to me, it was I who had done the proposing. And, dear God, how true that had been!

Ian and I were married in the autumn and we spent our honeymoon in Spain. It was then that I had heard the thin whistle of the pipe which was like the sound that had made Frannie run to answer the call today. When we returned to England, we stayed, at her request, with Aunt Maggie. She said she would be lonely without us. That I am sure was a lie for my benefit – Aunt Maggie sensed disaster.

And disaster came early in the year, in the form of a letter from Wales. In an old magazine, a woman had seen the picture of a man boarding a plane with the authoress Prudence Dudley. The caption stated that the man was Prudence Dudley's husband. She wanted to know if there was some mistake because the man, she felt sure, was her own husband, and the father of their two children, one aged three and the other seven. He had deserted her three years ago.

My mind had now reached a point where I was

fighting with a man, with Ian, going for him like a savage wild creature as if with intent to kill. And I think that had been my purpose, for when, in his easygoing, charming fashion, he admitted the contents of this woman's letter to be true, I did go mad for a time.

The Hornbrooks were devastated by the turn of events. Our association naturally was broken. I could not bear Alice's sympathy for her eyes seemed to say 'I told you so.' Although she had not known the facts of her uncle's life, from her estimation of his character, she had made a pretty shrewd guess.

When the case was brought to court, the newspapers did not hesitate to make top-line news of it. I had felt very ill during all that time, ill and dazed, and, if it hadn't been for Aunt Maggie, I think I would have ended my life. But it was nearly ended in a natural way by the premature birth of my baby. From the moment I knew that I wasn't Ian's legal wife, there had arisen in me a horrible distaste for the child I was carrying, and when, three months ago, it was prematurely stillborn I knew a measure of relief. But the relief was very short-lived, for in its place came a deep sense of guilt – I felt I had killed the child – I had wished it out of existence.

After the disastrous birth of the baby, I lay in a dark, muddled kind of numbness for weeks. I was back in the state of 'nerves' that had hit me once before. Once more, I was retreating from myself, or, more true to say, I was dragging myself from contact with life – unbearable life.

Again, it was Aunt Maggie, and only she, who

pulled me back to the surface of living. Now, here I was, my head just breaking water. I was looking about me realising that I was a free agent. I could do what I liked, go where I liked – stay put where I liked, and write, write again. The thought of writing again brought back the thought of Ian. Ian's last words to me had been, 'No matter what you think, I love you – above all I need you.'

I didn't know so much about the love, Ian's kind of love was worthless anyway, but I did know quite a lot about the need. Ian had needed me all right, he had needed me to support his ego, for he was a writer who couldn't write, at least, except for his own enjoyment, to satisfy his taste for words, elaborate words. Well, he had plenty of time to ponder over words now. He would have enough food for thought in prison.

Prison! I looked out onto the moonlight-swept scene before me – the wide, wild, free scene, and, for the first time since the sentence of six months' imprisonment had been passed on him, I realised the awfulness of his punishment; after all, his crime had been weakness, breaking the law through weakness. At this moment, he was encased in a cell, perhaps lying there thinking as I was. I was amazed at the voice in my head which said, 'Poor Ian.' Yet I knew at the same time that, if I lived to be a hundred, I did not want to set eyes again on the man who had played husband to me.

I told myself I must stop thinking, I must go to sleep. But I didn't go to sleep; I lay looking out of the window across the water, the Little Water. It was really a charming name for the lakes – the Lil Water and the Big Water, the girl had said. Did the Big Water lie within the grounds too? This thought directed my mind to the house along the hill path. The music and the noise had died down some time ago. Perhaps the guests were indoors now continuing the jollification, as Aunt Maggie would have termed it.

As if in denial of their presence indoors, there came to me now the sound of laughter, the mingled laughter of men and women. It rose and fell as if being carried by the wind, or it may have been the laughter of people running. I sat up straighter in the bed and turned my head round so that my eyes could take in the black blur that was the thicket. The moon was shining on the top of it, but the side of it was casting a deep shadow and, under my widening gaze, there came running out of the shadow a number of people – six or eight – I didn't know how many at first. They were laughing and talking. One figure that had been carrying a basket of some kind ran to the edge of the lake and, after dropping the basket onto the ground, he began leaping madly about.

Someone shouted, 'Look at Alec!'

The leaping figure now stopped and caught hold of a girl and waltzed her madly over the grass. When he stopped, the girl fell over and lay laughing wildly. The man called Alec shouted, 'Give us a jig, Peter.'

A member of the party who stood by the lakeside

swaying gently as if rocked by the breeze brought his hands upwards and began to play what looked like a small concertina. The air became filled with the strains of a Highland reel accompanied by shouts and whoops from the rest of the party.

'Here we go – upsy-daisy!'

'Yipp–ee!'

'Oh! me boys; Oh! me boys of Barrow-in-Furness!'

The laughter was loud now, wild-sounding.

I was kneeling on the bed gazing downwards. I flicked my eyes around as I heard Aunt Maggie shuffling into the room.

'Well, this is too much – it's beyond a joke.'

'Were you asleep?'

'I was dead to the world. The sound frightened the life out of me for a moment. They're all mad drunk.'

'They're certainly not sober.'

'I wish I could see that McVeigh, I'd give him the length of my tongue. Look! look!' Aunt Maggie was kneeling on the bed beside me now. 'It's like a witches' Sabbath. There's two of them dancing in the water. Well, they can dance where they like, but they're not doing it here at this time of night – we've rented this place.'

She had pulled open the window before I could stop her but with the sharp command of 'No! Aunt Maggie,' I prevented her from calling out. 'Let them alone. In their present mood, you don't know what they'd do. They might come in here or—'

My voice trailed off and my eyes turned in the

direction of the copse, for there, coming to a halt on the edge of the moonlight, I saw the tall thin figure of a young man. His hair looked black and his face very white and he was biting on his lip as he smiled. Then, apparently hearing a noise that was not distinguishable to us because of the music, singing, and shouting, he cast a glance over his shoulder. As if the man had been conjured out of the shadow itself, there stood Mr David Bernard Michael McVeigh! I found that, ironically, I was giving him his full title when I thought of him. I saw him grab at the dark man's arm and point; then I watched the young man pull himself away, apparently giving an angry retort.

I kept well back from the window, indicating to Aunt Maggie to do the same. The two men were now standing near the corner of the cottage and some of their words were audible.

I recognised McVeigh's voice saying, 'I told you to keep them clear of here.'

The dark man's immediate answer was lost to me, but I noted that his tone sounded angry; and, then his voice rose and I heard the words: 'You try telling Alec anything when he's on the bottle.'

'That crowd should never have been asked in the first place. I was against it – I told you.'

'You're always against some damn thing – your life is made up of being against things.'

'Look!' McVeigh's voice was deep and low, and I found myself bending forward to catch the words. 'I don't want any trouble with you tonight, Roy. Let the wedding day end in peace.'

'Huh! You're the one to talk about peace!'

'Now, look.' The voice was brittle. 'If you want to take up where we left off, it's all the same to me, but first I'll get this lot away from here.'

McVeigh's head looked as silver as the moonlight as I watched it move towards the man with the concertina. The music stopped abruptly, but the dancers, still laughing and yelling, continued their capers for some seconds before their laughter petered out in spluttering and coughing.

The night returned to its serenity for a second before the ringleader Alec shouted, 'Aw, Davie, man, why d'ya stop it? Come on, come on and fling it! Hoots! Toots! an' a drop o' the hard!'

'Be quiet, Alec.'

'Aw, man, it's a weddin' night. Come on, let your hair down.'

'I've told you—'

The rest of the words were lost, but I knew that McVeigh was telling them that the cottage was occupied for I saw a number of faces turn in our direction.

Then Alec's voice rose again, not so loud this time, but quite recognisable: 'Well, you said yourself they were stinkers, didn't you? "Prudence by name and prudence by nature" – that's what you said – so why worry? I don't give a damn, Davie, man.' The words were slower now. 'It's a weddin' night and nobody should go to bed 'cept those concerned.'

There was a great shout of laughter at this quip. And my hand was moving forward to close the window when the man's next words caught and held my attention.

'Why are you doin' the considerate landlord stunt now, when earlier on you said they were a fossilised pair – the old 'un talkin' like Queen Victoria herself?' he shouted.

'Be quiet, I tell you.'

'Now, Davie, don't tell me what t'do – you know it won't work, not with me it won't.' The voice was menacing one moment, then gay the next. The man now cried: 'Come on, let's have a singsong . . . the one about Pru. How did it go?

Oh Prudence, dear one, take this ring,
And wear it near your heart—'

As the man's voice rang out high over the lake, I saw the silver-headed figure spring forward, only to be stopped by a number of arms. I saw the man retreating towards the water singing tauntingly as he went:

'And give me but one word of hope
Ere I this night depart.'

Aunt Maggie and I exchanged glances, mine indignant, hers surprised. Then we were looking down towards the edge of the lake again. There seemed to be a number of people sprawled about, but McVeigh was standing, and so was the man who had sung the rhyme. I put my hand over my eyes as the fist shot out, yet I seemed to see Alec's feet fly from the ground. I certainly heard the splash as his body hit the water. I kept my eyes covered for two or three minutes, and, when I next raised my head and looked downward, I thought I must have dreamed the whole scene – but for the fact that Aunt Maggie was sitting close to me and was trembling slightly. For the greensward was empty of people; that is, with the exception of two shadows which supported another shadow, and moved into the darkness of the copse. And if I hadn't known that the shadows were two men assisting the drunken brawler whom McVeigh had hit, I might have taken the movement for the swaying of the trees.

'Well, I've seen some things in my time!' Aunt Maggie was shaking her head. 'It didn't seem real, did it?'

When I didn't answer, she patted my arm and said, 'Take no notice of the rhyming; it strikes me the whole lot of them are blind drunk . . . And this –' she spread wide the palms of her hands '– and this is the haven of peace. Wait till I see that Miss Cleverly.'

'When you do see her, you can tell her that we are going.'

'Yes. Yes, I will, indeed. There'll be plenty more places to get. It's the end of the season anyway – people will only be too glad to rent cottages or such. There was never a good but there's a better. Well, now –' she stood up '– do you think we'll get to sleep after this?'

'We'd better,' I said, 'or we'll be dead beat

tomorrow when there'll likely be another long car journey before us.'

'Good night, lass.'

'Good night, Aunt Maggie.'

The strangest thing about that strange day was that almost as soon as I lay down again I found myself dropping into sleep, and, as I lost consciousness, I imagined that the scene that had taken place before the lake was part of a dream, and, as sometimes happens in dreams, I desired to continue dreaming, but I didn't.

I must have slept soundly until the next morning, when I was awakened, not only by the smell of frying bacon, but by Aunt Maggie standing over me shaking me gently, saying, 'There's somebody moving about downstairs – and can you smell that?'

Slowly I pulled myself upwards in the bed and blinked the sleep from my eyes – then I sniffed. Following this, I looked up at Aunt Maggie.

'Peace offering from the lord of the clan, I suppose,' Aunt Maggie was whispering down at me.

'You mean *he* is cooking the breakfast?' I was whispering back.

'Who else? And we hadn't any bacon with us. It's going to be awkward giving someone the length of your tongue when they are handing you a plateful of bacon and eggs, isn't it?' Aunt Maggie's eyebrows were now straining towards her hairline.

I swung my legs out of the bed, slipped my feet

into slippers, and grabbed up a dressing-gown. As I zipped it up to the neck, I said flatly, 'I never eat breakfast.'

Tricky as it was I descended the staircase face forward; I was not going to give Mr McVeigh food for laughter by presenting him with a view of my rear.

When I stepped into the kitchen, the frying pan was on the stove. There was steam from hot water in the sink, and on the side table were two trays set most tastefully for breakfast.

My back stiff again, my chin up, I moved into the sitting-room, and there the wind was completely taken out of my sails, for I was not confronted by McVeigh holding out the velvet glove, but by a stranger. She was a woman well into her sixties – as old, I should say, as Aunt Maggie. She was extremely thin, of medium height, and had abundant brown hair without a streak of grey in it. But the face that I saw in profile, first one side then the other, as she darted about the far end of the room was extremely lined.

I knew that she was aware of my presence for some time before she gave the false start, saying, 'Oh! Oh, my! Well, you're up now.'

She came towards me, her step almost on the point of a run, and, when she was standing opposite me, she looked up into my face and smiled, saying, 'I let you lie, you had had a long journey yesterday. And, oh, I am sorry about the place not being ready. You see, I didn't get your wire – it got among the wedding ones, and half of them weren't read, what with one thing and another, you know?'

The woman had almond-shaped eyes – they had been very beautiful at one time – and these had widened at me as she had asked, 'You know?'

Then she went on, 'And not a flower in the place, and it like a pigsty. Davie – you know Davie? – he sleeps here at times, and you know what men are. You know?' Again the eyes widened with the question. 'And you see I never knew a thing about it – I mean that you were here or anything till they brought Alec Bradley in and then it all came out. They said they hadn't told me because it would fuss me – fuss me, indeed! As if I couldn't cope – oh, good-morning.'

She was now holding her head on one side and looking beyond me to Aunt Maggie. Like a gramophone that was wound up and wouldn't stop until it ran down naturally, she went on, 'You're Miss Fuller? Yes, I can see you're Miss Fuller, and this is your niece. I've been telling her everything. I'm so sorry, but things will be quiet and peaceful after this, dead as a doornail you might say. Nothing much happens here. But it was the wedding. You know?'

I moved aside to let Miss Cleverly get into the kitchen and I was now abreast of Aunt Maggie. As we looked at each other, I knew we were both thinking the same thing: that no matter in what capacity Miss Flora Cleverly served David Bernard Michael McVeigh, it certainly was not that of his mistress.

'Now, your breakfasts are ready. You could have them out on the lawn. It's warm enough and nobody will disturb you.' She turned and wagged her finger at us. 'I promise you that. There's bacon and egg and fried bread and mushrooms. I've brought a couple of bottles of milk over; we have our own milk. We run seven cows, sheep and chickens, and a few pigs, but we go in for mushrooms, you know.'

'It's very kind of you –' my Aunt Maggie had moved forward '– but you shouldn't have done this.'

'No trouble. No trouble at all. All in a day's work.' She was moving quickly here and there as she spoke, mashing the tea, turning the toast. She worked with the sure precision of a robot and seemed to be drawing on a store of energy that would never go dry. That was really the thing that struck me immediately about Flora Cleverly – her outstanding energy.

'We are—' Aunt Maggie hesitated. 'I'm slightly at sea with regards to who's who about here. I understand that Mr McVeigh owns the place.'

'Yes, yes, that's right. The one you met – Davie. He's the eldest – he owns Lowtherbeck and what's left of the land, not fifty acres now. It used to run into thousands – would you believe that? Yes –' she nodded her head at me '– it was a wonderful estate at one time. Still, we're thankful for what we've got – we must be thankful.'

'Are there other McVeighs?' Aunt Maggie's head was inclined to one side with gentle enquiry.

'There's Roy – he's three years younger than Davie. A nice boy, Roy. That's all that's left of the McVeighs. But we have young Janie with us. It was her sister, Doris, who was married yesterday. They're cousins of the McVeighs.'

'Are you a relative too?'

For the first time Flora Cleverly's hands ceased their moving and she looked down at them for a moment before she answered Aunt Maggie.

Then, on a laugh she said, 'No. It's funny I'm not, but I've been connected with them all my life. I brought up the two boys after their mother died, and I've always run the house and seen to every-thing. When Davie was away I ran the whole place, and everything went on just the same. I've run it now on my own – that is, I mean the house – for thirty-two years. But I ran it even before that, because Mrs McVeigh was never very healthy – I mean strong. There, I mustn't talk any more, you must have your breakfast. I've brought you over a piece of lamb and some vegetables for your dinner.' She thumbed in the direction of the pantry. 'And if you will, we'd be pleased to see you at tea – there's so much to be eaten up,' she added. 'And after that you can settle down and only see us when you want to. But, if you're short, you've just got to ask – I'm nearly always sure to have what you want; I've always kept a good larder. There, now.'

With an oven cloth she whisked the hot plates one after the other out of the oven onto the trays and we lifted them up and followed her into the living-room.

'Would you like to have breakfast on the porch?' I asked Aunt Maggie.

'Yes, that would be nice.'

Even as I spoke, Miss Cleverly had lifted the table into position and brought forward a couple of chairs.

'There now, you're all set. Don't forget what I told you – anything you want.'

She was standing on the threshold of the door when I asked, 'Who is the little girl we saw here yesterday?'

'Oh, you mean Frannie? She's from across the hill. She lives with her grannie on the road to Brookfield. But she's always about here, has been from when she was a child. We couldn't get rid of her if we wanted to. The boys have sort of adopted her, you know. Quite daft over the boys she was.'

'How old is she?' asked Aunt Maggie.

'Coming up sixteen. It's a pity, isn't it?'

'Has she always been like that?' I asked softly.

'Oh, no, no. It happened one day on the Big Water. That's the other lake, you know.'

It seemed that whenever Miss Cleverly used the words 'you know' in either the form of a statement or a question she accompanied them by a widening of her almond-shaped eyes. It was an odd co-ordination.

'They were all out in a boat,' she continued, 'her father and mother and her. They were always quarrelling, the pair of them, and he must have hit her – he was a jealous man – and the boat capsized. And that must have been that. Their bodies were never recovered – the Big Water's very deep in the middle – but the child was found lying, late that night, floating face up in the reeds. They thought she was dead at first, but she was just unconscious, must have been like that from the time she hit the water, and that saved her. Anyway, whatever it was, when she pulled round, well, she was like she is now. She's never developed. It's a pity, isn't it?'

Both my Aunt Maggie and I nodded slowly in assent. Yes, indeed, it was a pity.

'Now eat your breakfasts. I'll be seeing you at tea.'

With that, Miss Cleverly left us abruptly.

There had been a matron at my boarding school who used to speak in the same manner. Eat your breakfast, do your nails, tidy your room. I felt like a child again.

Aunt Maggie cut into her bacon, but before she conveyed the piece to her mouth she leaned across to me and said quietly, 'Variety is the spice of life.' Then, with an effort, she smothered her laughter.

3

The day should have passed peaceably enough. The sun was hot again, but not so fierce as the day before, just comfortable enough to lie in, and that's what I was doing. I was lying on the green slope near the lake while Aunt Maggie lay in a deckchair higher up in the shade. Earlier in the day, I had sampled the water but, to my disappointment, I found I could not stay in it very long for the temperature was almost freezing.

Together, Aunt Maggie and I had made lunch, eaten it, and washed up. Now, to all appearances, we were relaxed. Aunt Maggie might be, but I certainly wasn't. I was all keyed up inside waiting for Aunt Maggie to say, 'Well, isn't it time to make a move?' If there had been anyone to send with a message, I would have certainly sent a note with our excuses, for I didn't want to listen to apologies about last night – the rhyme was still running in my head. Thinking along these lines, I found I was wishing that the girl Frannie would make her appearance, but no-one disturbed us.

And then Aunt Maggie's voice came at me saying, 'Psst!'

I rolled over on my face, my hands under my chin, and looked at her. Aunt Maggie was sitting straight up now and pointing towards the copse. She wagged her finger while she mouthed silently: 'Someone coming.' I swung round and sat up, supporting myself with my hands, and waited, my gaze directed towards the hill rising from the far shore of the lake.

'I hope I'm not disturbing you?'

The pleasant voice brought me from my studied pose, and I saw, standing a few yards from Aunt Maggie's chair, the young man whom I had seen last night in the moonlight, the one who argued with McVeigh.

'No, no, not in the least,' said Aunt Maggie.

'I'm – I'm Roy McVeigh and I've come to fetch you over.'

The man was looking across towards me now and, as I rose slowly to my feet, I saw that his eyes, like those of his brother last night, were taking me all in. But there was no covert insolence in his face – interest, perhaps, and, if I had felt inclined to search for compliments, I might have said, some admiration. The fabric of the sun-suit I was wearing had an orange-and-yellow pattern on a white background and was an attractive thing in itself.

'This is my niece, Miss Dudley,' said Aunt Maggie.

'How do you do?'

We each inclined our heads slightly to the

other. Then I said, 'I won't be a moment.'

'That's all right. There's no hurry.' Roy smiled, a wide easy smile. I did not return it, but moved away and went indoors where I changed the sun-suit for a white linen dress that was deceptively simple. I brushed my hair, noting, as I always did when I looked in the mirror now, that there were single grey hairs among the dark brown ones. I applied a lipstick. That was all. I suppose I was fortunate in having a skin that didn't require much make-up.

When I appeared on the lawn, the young man's eyes again moved over me. After a space, during which Aunt Maggie heaved herself up out of the chair with his assistance, Roy looked at me and said, 'It's nice having people in the cottage again.'

'Do you have many here?' Aunt Maggie was straightening her skirt.

'No, not often; not for long leases.' He smiled. 'Perhaps two or three lots a year, for a week or so. It isn't everybody's cup of tea you know, stuck out in the wilds.'

'It suits us,' Aunt Maggie now turned to me and added, 'will I go and change?'

'That looks quite all right,' I said.

'Oh, please, don't dress up for us. Wait until you see our set-up. It's rough and ready, I can assure you.'

'Ah well and good then. That suits me.'

Aunt Maggie moved towards the copse; Roy waited until I was abreast of her, then he walked by my side and I found he did not disturb me one way or another. He made no mention of last night, leaving that to his brother I supposed.

The 'set-up', as Roy McVeigh had called it, was homely and comfortable, yet, over-all, there was a shabbiness that spoke of hard wear. Like the treads in the carpet on the stairs the curtains, chair covers and cushions looked as if they hadn't been renewed for several years. Although the curtains on the windows were thick and lined, their colour, except where the big old-fashioned curtain rings caught them, was drab beige, but the material near the rings indicated that they may at one time have been blue or green. Yet the room we were sitting in was definitely a drawing-room. There were a number of small tables, two of which I noted were Louis Quinze and probably authentic antiques. Then there was a china cabinet holding odd pieces of Wedgwood and Spode; and, lastly, a large deep old-fashioned suite of furniture in faded red moquette.

Flora Cleverly was presiding at the tea table, her hands darting over a two-handled Sheffield silver tray holding an ornamental tea service of the same design, all brightly polished. To her side were two cake stands and a small table laden with eatables. Beside Miss Cleverly, Roy McVeigh and ourselves, the only other person in the room was Janie Slater.

Janie was ten and her face had a similar expression to that of her sister when she had looked at me from the back window of the car the day before. But, as yet, Janie didn't get much chance to talk. *'Hand Miss Dudley the sandwiches, Janie. Pass the sugar to Miss Fuller.'* Do this. Do that. See to this. See to that. I could almost see Miss

Cleverly's brain at work, organising, docketing, thinking, thinking ahead to tomorrow when it would organise, reorganise and docket again. Miss Cleverly also did the talking. Her conversation took the form of questions which were mostly addressed to Aunt Maggie, but, as I sat trying to think of something to say to the shy child beside me, Miss Cleverly addressed me pointedly for the first time.

'And what are you? I mean, in what line of business?'

My head had turned sharply towards her and, whatever answer I might have given, I certainly wouldn't have told her the truth, for I knew what disclosure could mean – even in out-of-the-way places. Dead manuscripts pressed on you to be read. *'When you have a minute, you know.'* But I hadn't a chance to say anything – Aunt Maggie was there before me.

'My niece is the writer Prudence Dudley.'

She didn't say *'a* writer', but *'the* writer'. I knew my face had gone a deep pink; I was also aware that Flora Cleverly had never heard of the writer Prudence Dudley, but that Roy McVeigh had.

So it was he who spoke first, exclaiming, 'Good gracious! Yes, yes, of course, I remember seeing your photograph.' He stopped, embarrassed when it came to him just where he had seen my photograph.

'Davie makes up rhymes. He makes up funny ones.'

Janie, speaking for the first time, was silenced almost immediately. 'Be quiet, Janie! Here, hand

Miss Dudley the cake. Well now, to think you're a writer.'

Miss Cleverly did not look at me, all her attention was directed towards the tea-tray, but she went on talking to me. 'We're honoured. We've never had a writer stay before, a painter, yes – two painters and a singer. We certainly knew we had the singer – he practised morning, noon and night. He even had the piano carted over. Oh, yes, we knew all about having a singer, but we've never had a writer – well, now!'

It was at this moment that the door opened and Davie McVeigh came in. Automatically, I sat up straighter on the couch, thinking, Yes, Davie makes up rhymes all right. He was wearing a white shirt and riding breeches. It was evident he had left his top boots outside for on his feet were a pair of old red slippers. His shirt was buttoned at the neck and wrists. I remember noticing this because Roy's shirt was open at the neck and his sleeves were short. One of the men looked free, and the other encased. Now Roy spoke to his brother as if there had never been any harsh words between them.

'What do you think, Davie? This is Miss Prudence Dudley the writer.'

'Yes, I know.' The voice was calm. The big head was turned in my direction; the man was looking down at me, his eyes smiling quite pleasantly. His face had no aggressiveness in it at this moment.

'You know? How do you know? You couldn't have known.' This was Miss Cleverly, her hands still now as she stared towards Davie McVeigh.

'I know because I happen to read now and again. It may be surprising to you, Flora –' the sarcasm was back in the voice so the man was more recognisable '– but I do read at times. The cottage is made for reading. I think Miss Dudley –' he glanced at me '– will discover that.' After some seconds of silence, he turned and, facing me, said, 'By the way, I never managed to read your second book but I read the first and the third. I liked the third best. Less harsh, more compassionate, if you'll allow me to say so.'

People, I noticed, always added, 'if you'll allow me to say so' after making some cutting criticism. Yet I knew that what he had said was true. I had softened a lot by the time I had written my third book. I also knew that I was pleased, and surprised, that this objectionable man had read my books.

'I don't believe you could have known anything about it.' We were all looking at Flora Cleverly again. 'If you had known she was – *the* Miss Dudley, why didn't you say?'

The atmosphere in the room had changed. The fact that I was a writer of some importance was now of little or no consequence. All that was of consequence was the fact that Davie McVeigh had withheld something from Flora Cleverly.

'And have you turn the place upside down in preparation for a celebrity? I'm sure Miss Dudley would not have wished that. Am I right?'

He was gazing down at me once more, and in my embarrassment at the situation that I had unwittingly brought about I stammered, 'Yes – well, I mean, everything is quite all right as it is. The cottage is lovely—'

'There! Does that satisfy you?' Davie was looking once more towards Miss Cleverly. She had poured him out, I noticed, a cup of tea, but had not handed it to him. He now went behind the couch and took it from the side table; then he filled his plate with sandwiches before taking a seat in a chair to the right of Aunt Maggie near the empty fireplace from which, when he raised his eyes, he could look straight at me.

Roy McVeigh came and sat on the couch beside me. His opening remark did not alter my opinion that he was a nice young man, but it confirmed my suspicion that he was an ordinary one. 'I always wanted to write a book,' he said.

As he spoke, I heard my Aunt Maggie remark to Davie McVeigh in her conversational way, 'I see you go in for mushrooms.'

And the answer she received was, 'Oh, my God!'

But the older brother was not speaking to her. He was looking at his brother, and Roy, his face almost livid, was returning his scathing stare. But the incident was all over in a second.

Davie McVeigh had turned to Aunt Maggie and was saying, 'Yes, we go in for mushrooms, there's money in them; at least, there should be.' He paused before asking, 'Did you by any chance look into the cave yesterday when you came into the yard, Miss Fuller?' His tone was mildly inquisitive and quite civil, yet there was something behind it.

Aunt Maggie cast a quick glance in my direction

before saying, 'Yes, yes, we did. We thought there might be someone inside who could guide us.'

'And you forgot to close the door?' David was smiling now.

It was I who answered him, and stiffly: 'No, we didn't forget to close the door. We purposely left it open because we found it open.'

His eyes were looking straight into mine. Then he said, 'Don't worry, I believe you.'

'Thank you!'

'You and that cave door – you dream about it half the time.' Miss Cleverly poured some water into the silver teapot.

'Oh, no, I don't, Flora. I'm not given to dreaming; there's no time. I only know that before I got into the car yesterday I saw to it that the door was closed, well closed, and, when I came back, it was open. I had let the stove go out.' He turned his head and addressed himself pointedly to Aunt Maggie now, looking sharply into her slightly perplexed countenance. 'If the weather had suddenly changed, say it had rained – if it had, it could have meant a drop in temperature. The matter of a few degrees applied often enough can ruin six months' work – not only that, it could ruin me.'

He gave a laugh – it was a pleasant sound – before adding, 'Never go in for mushrooms, Miss Fuller, unless you are very wealthy and can play at it as a hobby on a losing basis.'

I enquired of Roy McVeigh: 'Have you ever done any writing?' My motives for asking were mixed. I had resented Davie McVeigh's outrageous reaction to his brother's natural statement – natural, because writing a book is the desire of many people, and also I felt I must bring his attention from his brother at whom he was still staring. When I achieved this, he turned on me what could have been a glance of dislike, then drawing his lower lip in between his teeth he shook his head.

'No. No, I haven't,' he said, his voice sounding like that of a youth, a petulant youth.

'Don't you worry, Roy – if you want to write a book, you'll write a book. You can do anything you put your mind to.'

I looked over the back of the couch to Miss Cleverly, who was looking towards Roy McVeigh. Then she shifted her glance to me and added, 'Isn't that so, Miss Dudley?'

'Yes, yes. If you want to do a thing strongly enough, I am sure you can do it.'

I wasn't sure. I was just answering the woman the way she wanted to be answered. There was something here I couldn't understand. The tea party had turned into a battleground, but perhaps the battle had been raging before we had come into the house. I had the feeling that this was so – that it was a battle of long standing. Quite suddenly I found myself thinking, this woman loves one man and hates the other. And, from the little I had seen of the two men, I certainly couldn't blame her.

Even with stretching politeness to its limit, you could hardly say the tea was a pleasant interlude. I found it embarrassing, even unnerving, for the atmosphere from the moment Davie McVeigh had

entered the room had been pervaded with bitterness.

A signal passed between Aunt Maggie and me
which was achieved with our eyebrows, and I was
about to rise to my feet when there came a tap on
the open French window and all the occupants
of the room turned towards it. The girl, Frannie,
was standing there.

With an odd sort of stiff agility, I watched Davie
McVeigh swing his heavy body up out of the low
chair, but, before he was squarely on his feet, Miss
Cleverly was at the window.

'Run along, Frannie, and play. That's a good
girl.'

She was standing in front of the girl to prevent
her entering the room.

'Leave her alone,' McVeigh's voice was quiet.

He did not thrust Flora Cleverly aside, but, in the
position he took up, she was forced to step back
into the room. He was now bending down towards
the girl, talking softly in a different tone than any I
had heard him use.

'Where have you been?' he asked. 'We haven't
seen you for days . . . What's that?'

I could see him now holding up her arm and
examining it. Then he looked at the other arm.

'Who did this?'

He was now touching Frannie's brow.

'Leave her alone. Her grannie's likely had to
chastise her.' Flora Cleverly was seated once more,
sipping at her tea now, and, addressing Aunt
Maggie, she went on in a low tone. 'The girl gets

out of hand – becomes very destructive. Her grannie has got to use the cane; it's the only way she can manage her.'

I prevented myself from saying, 'I don't believe it.' I wanted to rise and go towards the girl; however, I couldn't make myself do it when McVeigh was there. But now, although she was very reluctant to enter, he was drawing her into the room.

'I'll give that old girl a taste of her own medicine one of these days.' He was speaking as he pressed Frannie down on to the wooden seat near the fireplace.

'Not Grannie.'

'What!' He looked down at her bent head. 'Who then?'

The girl shook her head and turned it away until she was staring into the empty fireplace.

'She'll get herself into trouble one of these days.'

So quickly did McVeigh swing round that I started nervously. He was glaring at Flora Cleverly and there was undisguised hate in his eyes but he did not speak.

In a way I admired the man for championing this poor undeveloped girl, but my condemnation of him was much greater than any approval I felt for his kindly attitude. For, no matter what he thought about his housekeeper, he had no right to treat her as he was doing in public. On the other hand, she had certainly goaded him more than a little.

When Frannie suddenly began to cry – and her crying had a heart-rending sound – it had differing effects on us all. It brought a pitying look from Aunt Maggie. It brought Janie to kneel in front of her saying, 'Ah, Frannie, don't cry. Don't cry like that.' It made Flora Cleverly move quickly between the tables, pushing at the plates, arranging and re-arranging their depleted contents. It brought Roy McVeigh's head drooping and his teeth pulling at his lips. The latter gesture I noted seemed to be characteristic of the young man. It drove Davie McVeigh onto the terrace outside the French windows. From there he called sharply, 'Frannie! Frannie, come here!'

The girl rose obediently, her head hanging, the tears dropping off her chin, and when she reached Davie McVeigh he held out his hand and she placed hers in it. I watched them walk over the lawn towards the road that rounded the hill and led to our cottage.

I was about to rise to my feet when Roy McVeigh spoke: 'Will you excuse me?' Getting up, he nodded towards Aunt Maggie before going hastily from the room, not through the French window, but out into the hall.

Flora Cleverly now came and took up her position on the home-made wool rug flanking the wide fireplace. She had her hands clasped loosely in front of her and her jaws moved back and forwards causing the wrinkles of her face to flow into each other before she spoke.

'I'm not going to apologise,' Flora said. 'You can't be expected to live on top of a family and not know all the ins and outs about them. We're no better or no worse than the next.'

'Oh, please don't apologise to us.' Aunt Maggie was standing now, smoothing down the front of her dress.

'I'm not. I said I wasn't, and I'm not. I just made a statement. But you'll be able to pick out the gold from the dross for yourselves. It would be a very unusual family if it had all saints and no sinners, wouldn't it?' Flora was smiling at me as she put this question. But it was Aunt Maggie who answered her, saying, 'Very . . . very.'

'I made a pie this morning. I thought you would like it. If you'll just wait, I'll fetch it.'

If we had made any protest she would not have heard us, for in her lightning fashion she was out of the room so quickly it was impossible to realise she hadn't run or flown. And now we were left looking at each other, and Janie was looking at us, first at Aunt Maggie and then at me.

It was to me that Janie finally spoke, and what she said was, 'Davie's all right.'

Her tone was aggressive; it was as if she felt we were putting the blame for the whole scene on Davie McVeigh.

'He gets the backwash, always has.'

It was an odd, old expression to come from a child of ten, and it brought a twisted smile to Aunt Maggie's lips.

I was too embarrassed to answer and was relieved when Aunt Maggie asked, 'You are very fond of Mr McVeigh?'

'Yes, I am. And so was Doris.'

With this last statement, Janie cast a quick glance towards the hall door, then, with one more direct look shared between Aunt Maggie and myself, she turned and ran out of the French window. A moment later, Flora Cleverly came in with the pie which she handed to Aunt Maggie. I was glad, for I myself had a great desire to refuse her gift . . .

Aunt Maggie and I were walking back along the hill path towards the cottage, but, so that she wouldn't be overheard, it wasn't until we were well past all the shrubbery and in the open that she began to talk.

'It would appear,' she said, 'that the lord of the manor has the loyalty of the young'uns at least.'

'And he would need it,' I said, 'for Flora Cleverly hates him.'

'They hate each other I would say. You know –' Aunt Maggie turned her face towards me '– it's a very queer set-up. If I were in your shoes I'd be saying to myself, here's the nucleus for a very good story.'

I smiled, then looked ahead. Perhaps my aunt was right, I thought. There was everything here for a story, certainly a background, one could even call it a 'romantic' background. I felt no pain at this moment as the world presented itself to me. The people in the house called Lowtherbeck were certainly heading for one big flare-up, and, unless I was very mistaken there was a deep underlying reason for it. But I couldn't compose a story without a love element of some sort, and there was no love element in that house so far as I could gather.

But wasn't I a writer? Couldn't I concoct such an element? If I did, it would be to bring it to an unhappy conclusion. And who would I make the hero, the one who fell in love, to be, in the end, frustrated? David McVeigh? – oh, no, not David McVeigh— And yet, why not? He had all the ingredients needed to make a lover, a strong, passionate, headstrong lover. I stopped dead on the hillside and looked down.

Aunt Maggie asked me, 'What is it?'

I just shook my head slowly before moving on again. In the shaking of my head, I was rejecting, clamping down heavily on the idea of the elder McVeigh as a hero of any story I would write. Roy, yes, perhaps, but David Bernard Michael McVeigh – never!

And no-one had said a word of apology about last night – no-one.

4

When you have done something that surprises you, you search the past to see what elements precipitated your action. What surprised me was that I had now begun my novel and its hero was Davie McVeigh. This change of mind had come about through a series of incidents during the previous three weeks, but I think it really began on the hillside that Sunday afternoon. And it bore fruit one early dawn when I discovered what Davie McVeigh was hiding, but that was later.

On the Monday following that first Sunday at the cottage my aunt and I drove into the village of Borne Coote to replenish our supplies, or rather, stock up with tinned stuff and other necessities. And, as Borne Coote had only one actual shop, we were confronted for the second time with the little woman, Mrs Talbot, and, not only with Mrs Talbot, but Talbot himself. They were both behind the counter and they gave us the full benefit of their combined stares on our entrance. Then, with the embarrassing straightforwardness which seemed to be prevalent in this part of the country, the little woman, pointing at me, spoke.

'I thought you didn't know the McVeighs.'

'Nor did we when we were last here.' My reply was stiff.

'But you were going to the cottage – you were going to stay?'

'I made the arrangements through a Miss Cleverly. Does that explain things?' Aunt Maggie's head was cocked to one side.

'I told you so; I said it would be her that did all the arranging.'

Talbot was looking down at his wife. Then, turning his gaze towards Aunt Maggie, and seeming to pick up the tone of their last conversation, he said slowly, 'The misunderstanding is pardonable, madam. Now, what can I do for you ladies?'

Here was the businessman speaking.

We had written out an order and I handed it to him. The length of it seemed to please him, for he turned, and looking down on his wife, said, 'You leave this to me; get about your business.'

And Mrs Talbot got about her business. Talbot saw to us himself, going as far as to pack the goods in boxes and to place them in the boot of the car, assuring us as he did so that he would be pleased to be of service to us – any kind of service.

He explained, 'The shop's only me sideline, you see, ma'am.' (The 'ma'am' was divided between us now, it had taken the place of madam and miss.) 'I do a bit of taxiing, although there's not much in that line, except for a wedding and a late dance or such over in Penrith. An' I turn me hand to a bit of plumbing and decoratin'. Besides which, I'm the gravedigger for the three villages hereabouts. And in me spare time I go up and help Davie, big Davie. Now, there's a man for you.'

Talbot was pulling down the boot-lid of the car, and he swivelled his long face towards me as he demanded, 'What do you think of big Davie?'

In case I might go so far as to forget myself and say what I did think of – big Davie, Aunt Maggie put in quickly, 'What do you do up there – at the house – Mr McVeigh's?'

'Oh, there's plenty to do up there. He'd have me full time if he could manage it. He thought he would be able to last year, but then he had to buy the horses.' He bent over Aunt Maggie and shook his long face in front of her as he stated: 'You can't grow mushrooms without manure, an' the cheapest way to have manure is to have horses, isn't it? Three he's got now, two old shires. The heavy ones are the best. Like old times to see horses on a farm, an' he uses them all, doesn't keep them just for—' He stopped, coughed, and added the information: 'Well, it's always better from working horses – they eat more, see? It's natural.'

I had got myself into the car. As on Saturday when these two had met, the desire to laugh rose in me. I dared not look at Aunt Maggie as she sat down beside me, but now Talbot's face was close to mine at the open window of the car.

'What do you think of Flora Cleverly?' This was asked in a loud whisper.

'What?'

'I asked, what do you think of her?'

'Well – er.' I glanced at Aunt Maggie, but Aunt Maggie was looking straight ahead. 'I should say she's a very capable housekeeper.'

'A very good featherer of nests if you ask me.' Talbot's nose was almost touching mine, and I couldn't get my head any further away from his long sombre face.

'You know she an' me nearly become related?'

'You did?'

'Aye, she was after me brother. He was gardener up there to the old people in the days when they had land to have gardens, if you know what I mean. But he upped an' skedaddled off to America.'

I shook my head.

'He died just three years gone. An' you know what?' He went on. 'Left her what he made.'

'Really?' I commented.

'Was it much?' This came from Aunt Maggie.

'Two thousand, seven hundred and fifty pounds. I contested it rightly but I lost 'cause we were only half-brothers really, and he had always fended for himself since he was a lad. Aye, Flora got the lot. But do you think she'll spend a penny on the place, or help Davie? No, not a brass farthin'. But she gives young Roy backhanders. Oh, aye, he's her bright boy is Roy, and the biggest cadger from here to—'

Talbot just managed to replace the destination with the name 'Cockermouth'. Then he continued. 'You be on guard, ma'am, if he comes askin' for a sub. You won't be the first one that Davie's had to refund money to afore they left.'

Again, I could only say, 'Really?'

'Aye, really.' The big nose was moving up and down now.

'Do you believe in jinxes?' Talbot asked now.

'Jinxes? – well, I don't know.'

'That means you don't believe in them, but there are such things. Davie's got a jinx on him; it's been put on him.'

Now Talbot withdrew his head a little from the window and his expression changed, even took on a semblance of hauteur. He said, 'I hope you ladies don't think I'm shootin' me mouth, but, as you're goin' to be up there for God knows how long, I thought it best to put you wise to a few things. Ladies are apt to get the wrong impressions at times – bit gullible like.'

And now he leaned forward again and almost across me, and addressed himself pointedly to Aunt Maggie this time. 'I'd like you to understand, ma'am, that I don't talk so glibly to everybody, but I'm concerned with them up at Lowtherbeck.'

'Yes, of course,' said Aunt Maggie.

Now that he thought Aunt Maggie understood the situation and the reason for his verbosity, Talbot withdrew himself, straightened up to his limit and inclined his head slowly downwards. And we took this as a signal that we now had his permission to depart.

We drove off and when we got into a quiet lane, we laughed – I laughed as I hadn't done for many months. Yet, in spite of our making kindly fun of him, I knew we had gathered more than groceries from Talbot's shop, and that we had met a man who could be a very good friend – to those he took to.

We did not return straight to the cottage, but did a round of sight-seeing going as far as Talbot's Cockermouth then on to Maryport, returning around Derwentwater and Keswick, past Ullswater, and on home. I thought of the cottage as home now.

It had been a long drive and, for the most part, a beautiful drive. When we arrived at the cottage about five o'clock, we were both rather tired; consequently, I did not mount the stairs to put our things away until sometime after six. And it was as I opened the doors of the big cupboard that the sound came to me distinctly and brought my eyes upwards towards the ceiling. It was the sound of smothered weeping and I recognised it immediately.

Within a moment, I had mounted the ladder and pushed open the trap-door. There, on the floor, almost on eye level with me, lay Frannie. She lifted her head when I entered and I was quick to note the look of disappointment coming into her eyes. Without getting from my hands and knees, I crawled the short distance to her, asking, 'What is it, my dear?'

On this, the girl turned her head from me and buried it once again in her arms.

'Don't cry like that, you'll make yourself ill. Come, sit up.' I put my hand on her shoulder, but, with the peevish attitude of a child, Frannie tried to shake it off.

'Come along.' I was coaxing her gently. 'Would you like a drink?'

There was no response.

'Come, don't cry like that – don't.'

The sound was hurting me. I wanted to take her in my arms and comfort her, and the next minute that's what happened – she was in my arms – brought there by the suggestion that I should take her over to the house.

'Come along, get up and I'll take you to the house,' I had said. On this, Frannie turned and flung herself on me, pressing her head between my breasts and gripping me with her arms as a frightened child clings to its mother.

'There now, there now. Don't – don't cry any more. What is it? Can't you tell me?'

It was at this point that Aunt Maggie's voice called up the stairs to me and I called back, 'Can you come up a minute?'

When I heard her come into the room down below my voice drew her to the foot of the ladder, and, twisting round on the floor, the girl still in my arms, I leant over the hole and said, 'It's Frannie; she's up here and upset about something. You'd better go and fetch one of them.'

At this, the girl's grip tightened about me and I looked down into Aunt Maggie's perplexed face and said quietly, 'Better try and find – him.'

Whether the girl knew to whom I referred I don't know, but she made no protesting movement.

I heard the creak of the stairs under Aunt Maggie's weight; then there was no sound except the girl's lessening sobs. She was lying now, her full weight on me, her head still pressed into my breasts, her arms gripping me, her legs entwined around mine, her whole attitude that of a child in distress. Stroking her hair, I looked around as I waited.

As McVeigh had said, there was plenty of bedding up here. Half of the small floor space seemed to be taken up with it. The rest of the floor, except where we were sitting, was covered with a conglomeration of books and soft stuffed animals, among them a panda and a teddy bear with long flopping ears. There were no dolls, I noticed. The only light came in through a minute skylight.

How long it was before I heard the quick scraping of footsteps on the stairs I don't know, but I had been aware for some time that one of my legs had gone to sleep and was now becoming very painful.

Davie McVeigh's head did not shoot into the attic, but rose slowly into the room, and he, too, did not rise to his feet but crawled forward.

Davie did not touch Frannie but asked gently, 'What is it?'

I had expected her to turn from me and fling herself on him, but she remained still.

'Frannie – Frannie, look at me.' Davie was bending down close to her now and his face was not more than inches from my own. His eyes were downcast and I noticed that the lids were heavy and fringed with short, thick, dark lashes. I felt embarrassed, slightly disturbed, and very uncomfortable as well. Trying to move my leg, I gave vent to a stifled groan. The lashes lifted and the eyes were looking into mine.

'I – I've got cramp.'

He bent forward to relieve me of Frannie and as his hand cupped her head his fingers touched the flesh of my neck near the breast. Instinctively, I recoiled. In a flash, his eyes were holding mine again.

His voice was low and cutting as he said, 'The action was involuntary.'

I wanted to say, 'I'm sorry.' But how could one explain a thing like that? What I did now was to try to loosen the girl's arms from around me, and, in doing this, I almost lost my balance and had to put my hands behind me to save us both from falling sideways. Then, with a movement that could only be called rough, Davie pulled Frannie from me and, gripping her by the shoulders, brought her round to face him.

Frannie did not protest. She was no longer crying but her head was hanging and she would not look at him.

'What is it? Tell me. Your grannie been at you?'

'No, Davie.'

'Someone said something to you?'

She shook her head.

'Have you been breaking things again?'

'No, Davie.'

He raised his eyes and looked at me. Then turning his gaze once more on Frannie, he smiled. It was a movement of his features I hadn't seen before. There was no sarcasm lifting the lips, no malice in the eye; his whole face looked gentle.

He said now, as he put his finger under the girl's chin, 'Come on, come on, you've got the hump. What do we say when we've got the hump?' He jerked her chin further up. 'Come on, what do we say?' he waited. Then he prompted slowly, 'Buck up and be a rabbit. Come on, say it.'

Frannie was looking at him now, her face unsmiling, but she repeated after him slowly: 'Buck up and be a rabbit.'

'Where's that book?' He was scrambling around the floor like a romping bear now. He pushed me aside slightly as he reached out and pulled towards him a large red-backed book. Then sitting down beside Frannie again, he said, 'Come on, we'll read some poetry – right out loud.' He pointed the words out with his finger and began:

Slowly Frannie repeated, 'Promise to look at a leaf on a tree.'

Then she went on in halting fashion:

'Promise to look at a leaf on a tree,
Promise me, promise me;
Promise to stand and look at the sea—'

Then breaking off, she turned her eyes up to his and tears were in them once more as she whimpered, 'I can't, Davie, I can't.'

Gently Davie laid the book down by his side – which was almost against my knee – and cupping

Frannie's face with his thick square hands he asked in a perplexed fashion, 'What is it, Frannie? You can tell me. Someone has frightened you. Tell me – who?'

I watched her look at him for a moment, then lower her head, and after she lowered it, she shook it from side to side.

'You'd better tell me –' his voice was softly insistent '– because I'll find out anyway. I find out everything, don't I?'

At this, like a slowly overbalancing sack, Frannie drooped forward and lay against him, her head buried in his open coat.

Over the top of her head, he looked at me and asked, 'How long has she been here?'

'I don't know. We've been out all day.'

'Come on. We're going home.'

He made a movement to rise to his feet, but, as he did so, the girl pressed herself tighter to him.

He said sharply, 'Now, Frannie! No more of it. I'm taking you home.'

Then, very much with the reaction of a father who had stood enough from a petulant child, he put his arm around her middle and drew her towards the ladder. Holding her like a bundle of bedding, he descended into the bedroom and placed her on her feet.

He turned and, looking up at me, asked brusquely, 'You coming down?'

'I'll manage, thank you.'

'Good enough.'

I sat on the floor where he had left me, the

red-backed book in my hand. Frannie was an odd creature but so, indeed, was he. 'Promise to look at a leaf on a tree.' I looked down at the book. It was a loose-paged book comprised of thick hand-made paper, and on each page, in spidery italic writing, was a verse of some kind – I would not have called it poetry. The book had a frontispiece which bore the date, January 24th, 1919, which was followed by the strange inscription: 'Came home today with the desire to live.'

Further down the first page, standing alone, were the words: Buck up and be a rabbit. On the opposite page were two verses – the words which Davie McVeigh had tried to get the child to repeat. I read them slowly:

Promise to look at a leaf on a tree,
    Promise me, promise me.
Promise to stand and look out to sea,
    Promise me, promise me.
And at noon on the day look up to the sky,
And make it a habit. Try, Try.

But if you haven't a tree, or the sea, or sight,
    What will you promise me?
To reach inside and find the spark
That started the tree, gave sight, and the sea,
and so say with me:
Buck up and be a rabbit.

The sentiment was simple, but charming. I turned over the pages. The book was full of such pieces, simply rhymed philosophy. I wondered who had written it. There was no name on the book, but the date was 1919. Likely, McVeigh's father – very likely.

Besides the litter of books on the floor, I saw tucked neatly in the corner, a pile of books dealing principally with art, bearing such titles as *Perspective* and *The Art of Etching* by Rex Vicat Cole. There were books on woodwork and large flat books that spoke of art plates. But what drew my attention at once was a piece of paper hung between two stacks of books on which was written simply: 'Don't touch.'

The command I felt was meant for Frannie and not for the tenants of the cottage. It gave me a strange insight into the relationship between these two people. Davie McVeigh had placed that order there knowing that, although the girl would be alone in the attic, she would obey it.

My Aunt Maggie called again from the kitchen, and I descended into the bedroom and then to the ground floor, to be greeted by Aunt Maggie not with: 'What was she upset about?' but with 'I don't like that woman!'

'Miss Cleverly?'

'The same.'

Aunt Maggie turned and marched into the sitting-room, and I followed her. And sitting down there, she looked up at me and said, 'I nearly broke my neck getting there. It was her I saw first; she was in a confab with the younger one, Roy. Those two are as thick as thieves. I must have surprised her when I called through the kitchen window, for she turned on me. You wouldn't believe it but her face was really contorted with fury. The young fellow was sitting at the kitchen table and she had her arm around his shoulders. When I had called, they had both been startled – and she actually yelled at me. "What are you doing there?" she asked. And, when I told her – she was at the door by now and slightly calmer – she said, "Oh that girl is becoming a proper nuisance. I'll have to tell her grannie to keep her home. You'd better go and see what's up with her, Roy."' After a pause: 'You know something, Pru?'

I shook my head negatively.

'There's something between those two. He calls her "Aunt Flora". "I can't do that, Aunt Flora," he said. "I'm due back – I'm taking over for Fenwick. I told you." Did you know that the young one was only a garage hand?'

'No, I didn't know what he was.'

'Well, the way she put it was, he was in the car business and they were very busy at the present moment. But, by the look of his overalls, he had been under a number of cars. It's odd, don't you think, that he hasn't been put to something different from a car mechanic?'

'There's money in cars today, Aunt Maggie.'

'Yes, there might be in the big garages, but I shouldn't imagine there's much in that line in the garages around these quarters.'

'It may be a garage on the main road.'

'Perhaps. Anyway, she told me to go to the shed

– that's what she called that cave – she pointed across to it. She said I would find McVeigh in there and to tell him. And do you know something else?'

Again I shook my head.

'When I walked in, he nearly hit the roof. He was laying pipes or such from that coke stove, and when I pushed the door open I must have moved them out of line. Anyway, he calmed down when he saw it was me and not you.' Aunt Maggie grinned at me. 'And he was off like a shot when I told him about the girl.'

Now Aunt Maggie screwed her eyes up, and nodding her head at me, she ended: 'You know, Pru, I don't like this set-up at all, and, the less we have to do with the folks in that house, the more comfortable will be our stay. At least, that's how I see it. How do you feel?'

'I don't really know,' I said. 'I'm only sure of one thing – and that is that David McVeigh is more objectionable than any of the others.'

Later that night, the weather broke with a really terrifying storm. There was a thunderclap that drove Aunt Maggie and me to cling together. We had been watching the lightning streaking over the hill beyond the lake, and one flash seemed to stab the lake right in its centre. Following that, the thunderclouds burst above us.

We went to bed early, voting it the best place to be as we were cold. I would have lit a fire if there had been anything with which to light one. I guessed that the main fuel used was wood, and, although there was evidence of logs having been stacked against the back wall, at present there were not even any chips there with which to make a flame.

So it was early the next morning, while it was still raining, that I made my way over to the house to see about some form of heating. I made the trip reluctantly, I fear, and would gladly have left it to Aunt Maggie. Surprisingly, she had expressed a preference to stay in bed that morning, as she felt as if she had a slight cold coming on. I knew this was a sensible decision, for the room downstairs, although attractive in the sunlight, was fireless and, lacking any form of heating, it had lost something of its charm. So, as I said, I went to the house.

Thinking I would encounter someone in the courtyard, I went straight there, but there was no-one to be seen. So I crossed over towards the kitchen, but at the sound of Miss Cleverly's voice, I stopped before I reached the door or the kitchen window.

Miss Cleverly was saying, 'How do I know why he's decided to sell the land? You should have been here instead of in your bolt hole.'

There came a pause. Then I actually heard a deep intake of breath before the deep, guttural voice of Davie McVeigh ground out his answer.

'Flora Cleverly,' Davie was saying, 'you'll try me too far one of these days and I'll throw you out on your neck. I warn you, mind, I'll do it, because you've stripped me of all sentiment concerning you or anything you've done in the past.'

'Oh, be quiet! Don't act the big fellow with me.

You'd be finished flat if I left here, and you know it. Who'd work like I have done for years for nothing? And supplied the food for many a mouth at that? You can't do without me, and you know it. Everything you touch dies on you.'

'Yes, because you've willed it. Don't think I don't know who left that shed door open. That's the third time it's happened since I spawned the beds.'

'I've told you I didn't touch the shed door; it was them two up at the cottage nosing about.'

'I'd believe them before I'd believe you, Flora. But that's beside the point. What I want to know is, what made Alec Bradley decide to sell that bit of land and the cottage? The old woman has lived there since she was a child. What's going to happen to her and to Frannie?'

'Don't ask me. I don't know. If you make them your concern, that's up to you – and while I'm on about it, whose concern is it? It's puzzled me a bit why you should trouble yourself so much about the pair of them. It wouldn't have been you who was after her mother, would it? Funny, if I'm hitting the nail on the head.'

There came a long silence, during which I found myself backing cautiously away. It wasn't until I reached the beginning of the courtyard again that I heard McVeigh's voice and the end of his reply as he came bursting out of the door.

He was shouting: 'It's a wonder you weren't hit on the head a long time ago.'

I almost ran round to the front of the house and I was about to mount the steps to ring the bell when

I heard the clink of heavy boots coming in my direction on the stones of the courtyard. So, as if having just made my appearance, I walked back towards the end of the house, and there came up with Davie McVeigh.

I have said earlier that the man's complexion was a ruddy brown, but now I saw that it was grey. His cheeks seemed to have been pulled in and he looked much older at this moment than I had yet seen him. Although he looked straight at me, I am positively sure he did not see me. When I spoke, as I did rapidly out of embarrassment, he jerked his head a little to the side before bringing his eyes back to focus on my face.

'– and my aunt's in bed with a slight cold and we would like a fire – if that is possible,' I finished.

'A fire? Yes. Oh, yes. Of course.'

Again, he shook his head. Then, to my astonishment, he began to apologise. 'I'm sorry about this. Of course, you need a fire. I generally see to a load of wood being dumped before anyone goes in – summer or winter. It's always cool in the evening.' He, too, was talking rapidly now. 'I'll get Talbot to saw some up – he should be along shortly. But in –' he turned from me '– in the meantime, you'd better have an oil heater.'

So unexpectedly civil had he been, so unlike himself, that I answered, 'I'm sorry that I have put you to all this trouble.'

I was following him back across the yard in the direction of the cave wall now, and, as he looked at me over his shoulder, I fully expected some remark, such as, 'And so am I.'

But what Davie said was: 'We've slipped up a lot where you and your aunt are concerned – the place wasn't ready and it should have been. But I suppose you can lay that down to the wedding.' As he pushed open the door and stood aside to allow me to enter, he added, 'They don't happen every day, do they?'

My back was stiffening again. Was he probing? If he had known who I was he had likely got his information from the splash the papers made about the court case and the break-up of my marriage.

We were in the cave now, all the way in, and, for a moment, my mind was diverted from him by what I saw. Stretching away into the far distance was what looked like an allotment, and covering the surface was a network of grey stuff, like solidified mist.

'The – the beginning of the mushrooms?' I pointed.

'Yes. This is the spawn. It's doing fine. It's all ready for the casing now – that is, the soil that goes on top.'

'It's very interesting. Can you make a living out of them – a reasonable living?'

I wasn't really interested in the mushrooms, nor yet in whether McVeigh would be able to make a living from them, not at this moment – for I was almost overcome with the oppressive atmosphere of the place.

'Yes. Yes, I can make a living, if I get the chance.'

On his last words, his head went down and he turned away and walked along the path bordering the beds. I could do nothing but follow him. There had been some light given off by a weak electric bulb, but now, walking away from it, I could barely make out his back in front of me, until he came to a stop in front of the cave wall. There, in the Open-Sesame manner, he pushed at what must have been a door, and we passed into another cave, which was cooler and much lighter. After a moment, I saw that this cave got its light and air from two sources – from an open door in the far distance and from a sort of funnel in the rock that opened up just above my head.

I was looking upwards, trying not to gulp openly at the refreshing air, when Davie said, 'I'm going to do something with that when I get round to it. The wind whistling down there in the winter would cut you in two, and that's no use for mushrooms. That's why one's got to be so careful about doors.'

Our glances crossed for a brief second on this last remark but I did not take it up. Instead, I said, 'It's an amazing size. You'd never dream from outside that there was so much space in here.'

'It's wasted.' Davie flung his hand out with an impatient movement. 'I use it as a storeroom, but one day—' He nodded his head – he seemed to have made a promise to himself.

We were moving towards the far doorway now. Again addressing his back, I asked, 'How does one start a business like this?' For the moment

I had forgotten that I didn't like the man; I suppose it was my writer's instinct at work gathering data.

'You go to school and learn.'

'School?' The word was high in my head.

He had stopped and was looking at me. 'Well, sort of. When you want to get mushrooms beyond a backyard and a seed-box business, you've got to learn many things. There's much more in it than people think. But, whichever way you do it, there's the secret.' He had stepped through the doorway and was pointing across a wide farmyard to an open barn beyond, within which was a great mound of steaming manure. 'Preparation of that,' he said. 'But it becomes so damned scientific, I sometimes wonder how the mushrooms managed before the lads started on them. That's the worst part. You turn that stuff until you hate the sight of it.'

'Have you been growing them long?'

'Three years. But I was nearly finished last year – the crop went dead on me. There can be two a year, you know – if you're lucky. But, when a thing like that happens, it can knock you back somewhat.'

'Yes, yes.'

Our glances had crossed again, and I looked away from him at the farmyard. I saw that it was bordered on one side by stables, on another by byres. In a field beyond the open barn were a number of small black hutches which I knew to be chicken runs.

I turned to him, and, my voice showing my

genuine amazement, I said, 'You would never dream that this lay behind the caves – I mean the hill – not from the other side – the courtyard side.'

'No. It is rather surprising.'

I looked up at the wall of the stone-cased hill. 'It's like a basin,' I said. 'It looks much bigger inside than it does out.'

'It is. This hill gives no indication whatever of the size of the caves inside. They go for miles. I haven't even been in some myself – too big to get through the passages.'

'Really?' I was finding my interest deepening. 'How were they discovered?'

'Discovered? Oh, they've always been there, as far as I understand. My great-grandfather used to hide whisky in the far ones when they used to distil the stuff in the hills around here and were on the run from the Excise. They used to search the caves, but more often than not they got lost themselves and had to be brought out – now, there's material for a story.'

He was actually smiling at me in a kindly fashion. He didn't seem the same person whom I'd heard talking to Flora Cleverly not more than minutes ago. He not only looked agreeable, he sounded agreeable. I had the fanciful thought that passing through the caves had cleansed him of his rough-ness, brusqueness, and boorish manner.

David McVeigh stood now rubbing his hand over the head of a collie dog which was pressed close to his knee. Near a gate at the far end of the yard, with their heads well over it, stood two heavy feathery-footed horses – Talbot's shires.

It had stopped raining. There was no sun, yet this place seemed lit up in a fashion I couldn't describe. I sensed it. And I felt accurately that it was in this part of Lowtherbeck, and only in this part, that this man could feel at ease. I could see him, as it were, cut off from the rest of the household, working here and sleeping at the cottage. He need hardly come in touch with anyone at the house unless he wanted to – I cut off my thinking about him abruptly. I did not want to have to change my opinion of him.

I asked now, 'Do you have help?'

'Only occasionally. Talbot, you know, from the village, when he can give me a few hours. But Janie is a grand help; she's got a marvellous way with the animals. But from today, she's back at school. Her sister Doris – that's the one who was married on Saturday – she was very handy, too. And there's Roy; he helps when he can. We get by.' He squared his shoulders. 'It all gets done in the end.' Again, it seemed as if he was assuring himself instead of making a statement.

I knew absolutely nothing about farming and the work it entailed, yet I would have had to be a very stupid person if I hadn't realised that there was a great deal too much work here for one man with occasional help to get through.

As if reading my thoughts, Davie said, 'There's a bit overmuch for one, yet not enough for two.'

'Your brother works away?'

'Yes, he's in the car business. And that's what he likes – he can't stick this.' He moved his arm to indicate the yard. Then, as if he had been betrayed into saying too much, he added abruptly, 'I'll get you a stove and oil.'

When he came out of a shed carrying a stove and a can of oil, I said, 'I can manage these. I'll make two journeys.'

'No. It won't take me but a few minutes to go there and back. Come this way.'

I could see he would brook no argument and I did not protest, but again followed him. Once more I experienced surprise for, as he said, it was only a matter of minutes before I saw the cottage – but the back of it this time. He had brought me through a narrow overgrown path that I guessed had been used before only by himself. It came out in the thicket behind the sentry-box lavatory. Another minute, and we were in the sitting-room. He did not simply deposit the things, but he filled the stove and lit it.

'There,' he said as he looked at the stove after it had given a final *plop plop*, and settled down to glow. 'That should be all right now. And I'll see you have the wood this afternoon. By the way—'

He had turned from me and was walking towards the kitchen as he spoke. His walk was slow, his head was bent downwards, and his words seemed muffled as he said, 'I wonder if you would mind Frannie coming to the attic occasionally? It's the only place she can feel – well –' I thought he was going to say 'safe', and I'm sure he was, but he changed it to: '– at home. She's played up there since she was a small girl. She gets fits of moodiness and likes to be by herself.'

I hesitated in my reply because my mind had jumped back to the conversation I had heard from the courtyard concerning the child and her grandmother.

Davie turned to me and said, 'I'm sorry. I shouldn't have asked.'

I stammered, 'Oh really, please, it's perfectly all right. Yes, tell her to come when she likes. She won't be in our way.'

'You are sure?'

'Yes, perfectly.'

I wasn't perfectly sure. If I had stopped to think and told myself the truth, I didn't want anyone coming in and out of the cottage, least of all this lost soul of a girl, for I found she disturbed me emotionally, and I myself was staying here to calm my own emotions.

'Thanks.'

David McVeigh was standing outside the back door and, before turning abruptly and striding away, he said – in a tone that was an echo of what I had come to look upon as his natural disgruntled voice – 'If you want anything just tell me.'

As he did not wait for my reply, I did not offer any, but returned to the room, thinking of the words of Flora Cleverly. 'If you make them your concern, that's up to you – and while I'm on about it, whose concern is it? It's puzzled me a bit why you should trouble yourself so much about the pair of them. It wouldn't have been you who was after her mother, would it? Funny, if I'm hitting the nail on the head.'

5

We had been in the cottage, as I have said, for over three weeks now, and I was feeling much better. I had had no bout of nerves, no trembling, no retching, and no fear. That indescribable panicky fear and inability to describe what I was afraid of had not returned.

And during this time, I had, in a way, come to know quite a lot about the occupants of Lowtherbeck. I learned, for instance, that Flora Cleverly had actually been born in the cottage. Her father had been a sort of working manager of the estate. She had been brought up side by side with Davie McVeigh's father, John McVeigh, and she had helped in the big house long before John McVeigh had married.

I further learned, from short conversations I had had with Roy, that, compared to his brother, he was of rather low if not exactly dim intellect, and the rude exclamation that Davie McVeigh had made when Roy had said he had always wanted to write a book was now understandable to me, although I still thought the remark had been unnecessary. As for Janie, I found her a nice child, but I saw little of her. Likely, she spent all her time helping with the animals as McVeigh had said.

Then McVeigh himself. Had he kept up his pleasant manner towards me? Yes – yes – strangely enough, yes. I had been amazed at his change of front, yet I had had further proof that under this thin skin of civility still lay the demanding, dogmatic master of all he surveyed. This was proved one morning when I came upon him and the man Alec Bradley in the farmyard behind the hill. It was almost a week from the time that he had brought me through the caves and shown me the short cut to the cottage. From then on, I had used that way when going for the milk. I was just about to come out of the overgrown pathway one morning when I heard Davie McVeigh's voice raised high in anger.

Davie was saying, 'The hell you will! Not if I can stop you. There's something behind this.'

'There's nothing behind this except that I want to plough my own land.'

I would not have recognised Alec Bradley's voice from my memory of it on the night of the mad dance near the lake, but, from where I stood, I could see his profile with his chin thrust out. It was the same man who had shouted out the rhyme.

'You can't plough within twenty yards of the cottage – it's solid rock underneath. If you want to plough, plough round it and leave a path to the road.'

'I'm pulling it down.'

'By God! I'll see you don't!'

'Try and stop me.'

'Aye, I'll stop you. You take my word for it, Bradley. I'll stop you. I've still got some say around here.'

'Pooh! Don't try to bluff me. Everything you've touched has dropped to pieces under your hand for years. You're nothing but a byword. An' I'm warning you, I'm not drunk this time, so don't try anything with your fists. But you won't, will you, because Cissie's in the car above on the road watching us. You wouldn't like Cissie to see you hit out first, would you? You've never been the same since you lost Cissie to me – and then to go and lose young Doris to Jimmy. It was another bad blow, wasn't it?'

'Get out!'

'I'm goin', but I just stepped in to warn you. Keep your nose out of affairs that don't concern you. Even Meg Amble herself doesn't want you interfering. She's all set to go down to her brother in Dorset, an' the girl with her.'

'You're a liar!'

'Go and ask her!'

'Get out!'

I waited a while until I heard the car on the road beyond start up. Then I still waited – for Davie McVeigh had not moved from the spot on which he had stood while talking to Alec Bradley, and something in the look on his face warned me not to make my presence known, yet for some unexplainable reason I wanted to go to him. I was just about to turn round and go back to the cottage when I saw him stride over to what was presumably a chopping block and there, lifting up the axe high, he swung it down and buried its head in the scarred wood.

The action was so ferocious, so terrifying, that I found my breath checked by my own hand pressed tightly across my mouth. The next thing, I had turned without taking heed to be quiet and I was running along the narrow path to the cottage; and I didn't stop running until I was actually in the sitting-room.

Aunt Maggie, who had been sitting before the fire, turned startled eyes on me. And then, rising quickly, she asked anxiously, 'What is it? What's happened?'

'Nothing. Nothing.' I shook my head. Then going towards the burning logs, I held my hands out to the blaze.

'You're shivering.' Her hand was on my arm. 'What is it? Something's happened.'

'Not to me. Don't worry. It was—' I sat down on the couch, then told her of the scene I had just witnessed, and ended, 'It was the fury with which he wielded that axe, as if he were hitting out at the man, this Alec Bradley. And not only him.' I shook my head and closed my eyes tightly. 'I just don't know; I've never seen anyone so angry before.' For a fleeting moment, I remembered my own anger against the man who had deceived me, but it was not comparable with the anger of Davie McVeigh. His anger seemed to be against the whole world – except, perhaps, the girl Frannie, and young Janie.

Aunt Maggie was looking straight into the fire now. She had her hands joined on top of her knees and her body was rocking gently back and forth. This movement indicated that she was troubled.

I said quickly to her, 'Don't worry; *I'm* not upset. It's odd, but – I was frightened, and yet I wasn't – I can't explain. I had to run away – because if I hadn't, I would have run forward to him, and I felt I mustn't.' My voice trailed off.

Aunt Maggie had turned her head and was looking at me. She said quietly, 'Look, lass, things are not turning out the way I thought. What about us making a move, eh? We can even pay them the full amount. They seem hard up, the lot of them. What about it, eh?'

I considered for a moment. Yes, we could easily pay them the remainder of the three-months rent and pack and leave this moment – we had nothing but clothes with us. But, wherever we stayed this night, I knew that I would be thinking back to this cottage and what was happening to Davie McVeigh and those concerned with him.

It was I who was looking into the fire now, and I spoke slowly as if reading my own thoughts: 'The doctors said I had to fight this thing – didn't they – this thing that has urged me for years to give up and let life walk past me. This thing that won't even let me finish with life. They said that, if I wanted to win the battle, I had to do exactly the opposite. I had to take an interest in things outside myself – pretend an interest, even if I didn't feel it, and, eventually, the shadow life would take on some form of reality.

Well, Aunt Maggie, as you know, I've been trying hard for many months with little result, yet here in this out-of-the-way place I think the shadow is turning into reality because I've become interested in the people in that house in an odd way.' I looked at her now. 'I can't explain it except to say that I suppose it's the writer in me coming alive again. But I want to keep going there and finding out things. I'm not being nosy, you know that.'

Aunt Maggie's hand was patting mine now and she smiled as she said, 'That's good news anyway, and if the place and that lot are having such a heartening effect on you we'll take it on a three-year lease—'

Between that morning and the time I want to describe now, I only met Davie McVeigh three times. I had seen him in the distance, but, even at the distance of a few yards, he took no notice of me, seeming unaware of my presence. But at the other times when he did speak to me, his manner and tone were back to what I thought of as the 'real' David Bernard Michael McVeigh. And then came the morning of the soft dawn, the morning when I knew I had a story, when I knew I had a story of the house, of Lowtherbeck and the people therein.

I had been restless all evening and took my restlessness to bed with me. This was often the case when a story was brewing in my mind. I dropped into fitful sleep and woke as the light was just breaking over the lake, revealing the mist as a grey net that was being dragged gently across the water. I opened the window further and leant out. The air was cool but not cold. It was going to be a lovely day, a rare September day.

Previously, when I had woken up at this time of the morning and had not had this view to look upon, my mind had turned inwardly to my own troubles and coated them further with resentment, but, since I had slept on this narrow bed with my head on a level with this window, my thoughts had been drawn outwards, as my whole being was being drawn outwards at this moment. I wanted to walk near the lake.

I strained my eyes towards the travelling clock. It said half-past five. If I were to get up now, I would likely disturb Aunt Maggie. But the urge to get outside conquered consideration for my aunt. I was wearing a short nightie, but did not take it off; I just pulled a skirt and twin-set sweater over it. Then, donning my slippers, I crept quietly towards and down the stairs. In the kitchen, I changed my footwear, and going from the room, I opened the door.

The daylight was creeping higher into the sky now. It seemed to be drawing night shrouds from the trees, trailing them like stencilled veils over the dewy, weeping grass. Slowly, like one entranced, I walked down to the lake. But here the picture had changed. I couldn't see the edge of the water – I couldn't see my feet either. I was now walking in a swirl of mist. It was a slightly eerie, yet wonderful feeling. The hill beyond the lake was showing a pale mauve tint; it looked high and far away like a mountain and of a sudden I had the desire to climb it. I had walked round the foot of it a number of times. The hill rose from a valley bottom which was a field with a boundary wire running down its middle. I had never been to the top, and now I was going to climb it.

As I walked in the mist-covered grass, I experienced a feeling that was not joy. I knew what joy felt like – this was not joy. Was it contentment? No. No. There was nothing static about it. In fact, one of its ingredients was a desire to run, to skip like a child over the carpeted ground.

At one period I lifted my feet high in a dancing step almost, then admonished myself, 'Don't be silly!' Nerves didn't always show themselves in despondency; they often took the form of high laughter, and silly antics – one must be aware. I found myself shaking my head to throw off my own admonition. I was always too careful, always watching myself. Suddenly, I heard the voice in my head saying, 'Run if you want to; go on,' and I obeyed. I ran through the mist until I reached the foot of the hill, and then I began to climb, and, as I climbed the sun climbed with me. When, panting and laughing to myself, I reached the top, I stood in its light and it warmed me through to my heart.

I had not felt like this for years; truthfully, I had never felt like this in my life before. I knew in this moment I was beginning to live and was experiencing life as I had never done. I knew also that, whatever happened to me in the future, I myself would be in the forefront of its creation. The misfortunes which had happened to me in the past had come through my mother and father – and through Ian. I felt now, and with deep conviction, that not one of the three could touch me again . . .

Why don't such moments last? Perhaps they are just given to us to use as a memory of strength with which to combat our fear when it descends on us again. Perhaps this moment I was experiencing was what is meant by drawing strength from nature. Anyway, I had the urge to throw my arms wide, so forceful was this feeling of new life within me, but warned myself that I was on a high elevation and could be seen. Yet, who would be about at this time of the morning? Who, except myself? I had the world to myself. It was as I gazed over this world that I caught a glimpse of the Big Water.

I had never been near the Big Water and when I blinked the sun from my eyes and shaded my vision, I could see part of it quite clearly. Away across an open stretch of land, which headed the top of the Lil Water – which I could just make out from my bedroom window – was a deep belt of trees. This was the border of the Big Water.

I was going towards the border now. I was going to see the Big Water. I was running down the hill. There was no mist here; that is, until I reached the valley, when once again it swirled round my ankles.

Before I could cross the open land, I had a barrier to surmount. It was a drystone wall; many of them intersected the fields in these parts. But this one was about four feet high and two feet thick and its top was rough and hurt my hands and knees. Although I was now in the valley, the land was still on a slope, and, as I gripped the top of the stonework to heave myself over, I had a momentary impression of men struggling with these great boulders, carrying them up the incline, lifting them into place – all without the help of machinery. These were the men from the stock who had fought to defend this country against the Scots. No wonder they gloried in being tough.

I was not thinking so much of Davie McVeigh at this moment as of Talbot, and was remembering the day he brought the wood to the cottage. He had taken up a great pile of logs in his arms and brought them into the sitting-room; I had remarked about their being too heavy to carry at one go. Talbot had turned on me a look that was almost scornful. Then, over a cup of coffee in the kitchen, he had regaled me with stories of the ghosts of Cumberland and the achievements of her men. It was only when he started to relate the passionate romances of some of the ladies of the county that I withdrew. There were still certain subjects I could not listen to, and one of them was the romantic loves of others.

But this memory fled, wiped away by the floating mist. I was over the wall now. I found I had to tread carefully, because twice I had almost stumbled, for the field was undoubtedly studded with small outcrops of rock.

Then, as if it had been pushed aside by a giant hand, the mist drifted away as I entered the trees. When I emerged on the other side, there was nothing before me but a large stretch of water – at least four times the size of the cottage lake.

I was disappointed in the setting. It did not have the attractiveness of the Lil Water. Although it was bordered for quite some way by trees and had the advantage of what looked, from this distance, like a miniature beach, there was something forbidding about the entire scene. There was a rowboat lying on its side away to the right. It was old and unused and I wondered if it were the same boat that had capsized and drowned Frannie's parents.

Although the morning sun was touching the water, it did not seem to add any warmth to it. I was reluctant to go farther. I said to myself: 'Don't be silly. Walk around it; it's only a lake.' But, instead of doing so, I sat down on a low flat-topped boulder near the fringe of the trees. It was as if the excitement of the morning were seeping out of me. I felt rather tired and I recognised, with a feeling of dread, that a depression was descending upon me. I looked around. I was very susceptible to atmosphere – I had found this out long ago. Perhaps I was experiencing this feeling because two people had died in this water. And not only two – there could have been many victims down the generations who had started to cross this lake and never reached the other side. Yet why should it affect me so adversely? I didn't know.

I was about to make the effort to rise and retrace my steps when there came a movement in the trees away to my right. It brought my head round and then my mouth open as I saw – walking down the miniature beach – Davie McVeigh. I saw him drop something from his hand – it could have been a coat. I realised that he was naked, but what brought my hand up to my face was the fact that my eyes were conveying to my senses a horror because I was not looking at naked flesh, but at limbs that were covered in patches with a sickly looking light pink skin, and in between the patches were patterns formed by scarred flesh – in some places, it was drawn together in a series of weals. The weals moved as his muscles worked; they rippled like dissected snakes with each step he took. I found myself repeating Aunt Maggie's reverent phrase: 'My God!' I said to myself. Then I added, 'Oh, dear God!'

This, then, was why Davie always wore his shirt buttoned up to the neck and the cuffs of his sleeves fastened. But when his body was scarred like this, how had his face escaped? I had noticed a broad scar leading from his collar to the back of his ear and thought it might have been the result of a war wound. A great many men carried these badges of war on them, but he was surely too young to be carrying such a badge. Nevertheless, this man was carrying more than a badge, he was carrying a burnt body around with him. I found myself standing on my feet, my head shaking slowly. I was thinking: what does one know of another? I detested this man – at least, I had detested him. I looked upon him as a sneering, arrogant individual, yet all the time he was carrying, behind the façade of the big he-man, this scarred body.

One thing only was important now – I must get away quietly – he mustn't see me. Knowing I had seen him exposed would be unbearable for him.

Forgetting that I had risen from the stone and it was now behind me, I took a step backwards; then, unable to save myself, I toppled over, twisting as I did so and landing on my side. There was a pain in my elbow and wrist, for my arm had been thrust out to break my fall, but I leaned on it now and I turned my head slowly and looked to where Davie McVeigh was standing facing me. The same distance was between us as before, yet he seemed to be almost breathing down on me. After a brief glance at him, I lowered my head. The front of his body bore the same pattern as the back.

From under my eyelids, I watched his feet moving, not towards me but towards the belt of trees again. His feet weren't hurrying; their pace was steady. I made an effort to rise, but when I put pressure on my hand the pain was agonising, and I found myself stretched on my side again. After a moment, I sat up with the aid of my other hand and rested my back against the boulder, gripping my hurt wrist the while. I made no effort to get up and hurry away. I was waiting – the next move would be his. It was only two or three minutes later that I saw him walking towards me with his coat on. I did not look at him when he approached. When he came to a stop, I still did not raise my eyes to his.

'Well!'

The word had a tight sound yet did not give any indication of anger.

I glanced up and found myself stammering. 'I – I came out to see the dawn. I didn't mean—'

'You needn't apologise. I remember you telling me once before that it's a free country. And take that frightened look off your face.'

'I'm – I'm not frightened.'

'You're frightened all the time. Aren't we all?' He turned his face away from mine now and looked over the water. I was surprised at the momentary feeling of resentment that filled me, swamping my pity for the man – resentment that once again he was, as it were, taking the wind out of my sails. I had expected him to rage at me and, in my compassion for him, I had been willing to submit to his rage without rising against it. But here he was turning the tables.

McVeigh was still looking at the lake as he said, 'You are frightened. Oh –' he shook his head slowly '– not of me. You pride yourself that you can see through me, don't you? No, you're not afraid of me, but you're afraid of everything else – don't get up.' He turned and held the palm of his hand towards me. Then he added, 'I can sit down; I've got at least half an hour before the day starts. Have you hurt your hand?'

McVeigh was sitting not more than a foot from me, his legs stretched out from under his coat, his bare feet pointing upwards. I found I was looking at them. There was no contorted skin on them – the skin was natural and the feet were broad and well-shaped.

I said, 'I think I've sprained my wrist.'

'Let's see.'

I did not extend my hand towards him, and,

when his fingers touched my wrist, the reaction was the immediate stiffening of my muscles, mostly in the region of my stomach.

He felt this tenseness, I knew, for his fingers remained stationary for a moment and his hard gaze brought my eyes to him. There we sat for some seconds looking at each other. Then he asked quietly, 'What's made you like this? You should never let anything get on top of you to this extent. You should fight it.'

To my amazement, I heard myself saying quietly, 'I am fighting it.'

'Was it because of the break-up?' The muscles were more tense now and I was unable to answer, so he went on quietly, as his fingers moved over the bones of my hand.

'These things happen, they happen to us all – in different ways. The world of people and incidents beats you up, kicks you around, and you've only got one life to answer with.'

His fingers released my wrist as he said, 'There's no bones broken. When you get in, put a strap round it.'

And then he turned his body from me, and, leaning once more against the boulder, he pulled one knee upwards and rested his hands on the top of it. He looked across the water, and I looked across the water, and there was a profound silence between us. The silence grew until it seemed to my mind to become almost a solid thing. It filled the air and spread over the ground with a stillness that quietened the spirit. It was all around me, in me.

The essence of that moment will remain with me until I die. Then I remember the atmosphere in the silence changing; it was as if his presence had impregnated it, now forcing an awareness on me. When I became conscious of him, I experienced another strange feeling. I felt that this man and I – this man whom I disliked for most of the qualities he had shown to me – this man and I shared something. It seemed as if we were thinking along the same channels – but what particular channels, I, as yet, didn't put a name to.

I came to myself as a single blade of grass flickered; the movement stood out against the stillness like a water spout in a calm sea. My head turned downwards so I could look at the fluttering blade. It was at this moment that my companion began to talk.

McVeigh was still looking over the water as he said, 'When I got this –' he tapped first his shirt front and then his thigh '– I thought it was the finish; I *hoped* it was the finish. When anything big hits us, that's always the natural reaction – to give way before it.'

He paused, and I asked quietly, 'Was it in the war?'

'Sort of – but nothing romantic.' I saw a twist to his lips. 'No dashing in to save my superior officer. No medals. Just a petrol lorry toppling down a bank and catching fire. They found me with my head stuck out of the window – the door had jammed. My boots saved my feet, but they wouldn't have if I had been there much longer.'

'Where did it happen?'

'In Korea. The big war and all the shouting was over. Things like this don't matter often; and then only to the people to whom they happen.'

'I am truly sorry.'

I was looking down towards the grass as I spoke and I felt his head jerk in my direction.

His voice took on that deep satirical quality that verged on laughter as he replied, 'Now, look here, don't go wasting your sympathy on me. I don't want you or anyone else to be sorry for me.'

His voice, his manner, had sent me back to the steep road and the incident with the cars. Hastily, I got to my feet but, before I was standing straight, he was up, too, and, again, we were looking at each other.

I said, 'I'm not sorry for you. I don't think anybody could be sorry for you.'

My meaning was not what my actual words conveyed literally. I suppose I meant he was too big a man to attract pity; his manner spurned pity; yet this wasn't the reaction my words had on him. To my surprise, I saw a look that was almost pain come into his eyes. His lower lip moved in and out twice and his jaw jerked – it was a spasmodic reaction.

Then, his head bouncing once, McVeigh said, 'That's true, that's true.' There was emphasis as he repeated the words. Then he added, 'Well, I've got to get started. Goodbye.'

'Goodbye.' We turned from each other simultaneously and went our separate ways.

The morning had lost its wonder. Although there was no sign of mist, there was now a chill feeling in the air. I was through the belt of trees and nearing the drystone wall when there came over me an impulse for urgency – I wanted to run. If I had asked, where to? – I would have got the reply, 'Home', and home for me spelt Aunt Maggie. I wanted to be near Aunt Maggie, wrapped round by her common sense, her matter-of-factness. I wanted to touch on her life, a life that had known no unnatural fear.

Yet if I had probed within further and asked why this pressing need, I would have found it was because, deep within me at this moment, although I would not recognise it, was the knowledge of the utter fallibility of impressions, impressions that people gave you of strength. The impression I had first got of Davie McVeigh had been one of strength, perhaps cruel physical strength, but, nevertheless, strength. Now I knew that in that moment of silence when our thoughts had been channelled together, the cores of our beings had recognised, each in the other, the emotion which had dominated our lives – and the emotion was fear. My fear was, and had always been, fear of people and what they might do to me. What they usually did was cast me off in one way or another. My fear had become contorted of late and had acquired strange tangents, but at its root was the fear of particular people and what they could do to me. But what was McVeigh's fear? I did not know – only that it existed.

When I rounded the foot of the hill and saw Aunt Maggie standing at the door in her dressing-gown I ran towards her – actually like a child running to its mother.

And, like a mother, she greeted me harshly. 'Where on earth have you been at this time of the morning? You had me worried.'

'I couldn't sleep, I went out to see the sunrise. But what's the matter with you?' I was speaking casually now. I was within the ring of security; for the moment, I was without fear. 'You are never up at this time.'

'I've got the toothache.'

'Oh, Aunt Maggie, not again!'

She turned on me now an almost comical look on her face as she chided me, 'You said that to me the other day when I was sick. I didn't want to be sick again, and I don't want the toothache again.'

It seemed a most unsympathetic reaction, but I wanted to laugh. Instead, I said, 'Well, you're having that tooth out, and no more shilly-shallying. You've had it filled until there's no original tooth left.'

Instead of replying, Aunt Maggie probed. 'You look whitish and tired, haven't you slept? Are you cold? You're shivering.'

'Yes, I am a bit cold. I could do with some hot tea.'

'It's all ready.'

A few minutes later, after stirring the wood ash into flame, we sat close to the fire drinking our tea, and apropos of nothing that had been said so far, I made a statement.

'I'm starting a book today,' I said. 'I've got the title. It's *The Iron Façade*.'

6

It was strange the effect that my new work had on me. Although, naturally, I camouflaged both the characters and the surroundings of Lowtherbeck, the essence of the atmosphere I felt in this place came through in my writing immediately. But there was one thing which disturbed me; I found that I had put myself into the story. Once again, I was probing inwards. I had been entwined among the characters of my previous three books. My character then had been that of a sensitive, poorly-used individual, but now my character was emerging through these pages as a rather self-centred individual, and I found I didn't like the person I was representing.

I didn't like the character, but I couldn't alter her or remove her from the story, for she seemed an essential part of it. I knew that the action surrounding this particular character would make her forget herself, as I wanted to forget myself, but there was something else I had to bring into her character also. As often, when building a character in a book, it is the character that takes charge of the writer instead of the reverse. I wanted to make this character warm and loving as I knew myself to be deep within. I wanted to make her the kind of person to whom people would naturally turn in times of trouble – a young edition of Aunt Maggie. I wanted to make her someone who could forget herself entirely, even to the extent of giving up her whole life for someone else. This was my early intention, but I could not mould this particular character into the shape I had projected. There was an ingredient missing, and I hoped that, as I went on with the story, it would emerge and I would know how to develop her.

When, in the depth of my bitterness, I had poured myself out to Aunt Maggie, saying I must be a frightful person that all these things should happen to me: my mother and father throwing me off, then my husband turning out to be someone else's husband, and his blaming me for it all. He had said, 'Well, take your mind back. I never asked you to marry me; it was you who did the asking.' It was then that Aunt Maggie had consoled me by saying, 'It's their loss for you're a warm, lovable lass. Those that are deceived by your cool model-like exterior have no depths themselves.' It was a portrait of myself as Aunt Maggie saw me that I wanted to set down, but the portrait wouldn't come alive.

I became so engrossed in my novel that during the next two weeks I saw Davie McVeigh only twice, and then only from a distance. When the weather, which had worsened all of a sudden, became permissible, Aunt Maggie did the daily trek to the house for the milk, and, on returning, she nearly always had some comment to make on Flora Cleverly.

One day, my aunt commented, 'That one's so strung up the spring'll snap one of these days. She cannot stand still a minute. But I must hand it to her, she gets through some work. Do you know she does all their washing? She has about eight lines out in the meadow, full of sheets and things. She must have been up bright and early to get that lot done. And there she was in the kitchen baking when I arrived, and that was half past ten.'

To this particular piece of news, I had replied, 'She's very likely speaking the truth when she says they can't do without her.'

I had told Aunt Maggie about the conversation I had overheard between Flora Cleverly and Davie McVeigh . . .

Then one morning Aunt Maggie came into the room whispering hastily, 'He's brought the wood himself, shall I ask him in for a coffee?'

My first reaction was to say *no, no*. Then I placed the onus on my aunt by asking, 'Would you like to?'

'It doesn't matter to me one way or another.' She was still whispering. Then she added, 'Yes, I think I would, if only to prove I'm not early Victorian!'

She returned to the kitchen laughing. She looked and sounded gay. It was one of her young days.

I was using the refectory table as a desk and I'd hardly risen from it when Davie McVeigh entered the room from the kitchen. I hadn't expected to see him so soon; it was as if he had been standing behind the door. I heard Aunt Maggie's voice and the tail end of her words: 'I'll bring the drink in, in a minute.'

'Am I disturbing you?' McVeigh asked.

'No. Oh, no.' I pushed carelessly at a pile of written work. 'I'm always glad of a break.'

He walked down the centre of the room towards the fire. He did not look at home as he had done on that first evening when he had barged in through the front door, but appeared somewhat ill at ease.

'Are you writing another book?' He was standing on the hearthrug waiting for me to sit down.

'Yes, I'm trying to. It takes some getting into if you've neglected it for a time.'

'That's the same with everything, I think.'

He seated himself now in the high-backed leather chair, and although it was part of the suite, I thought to myself: it's his chair.

He asked abruptly, 'Are you liking it here?'

'Yes. Yes, very much.'

'You're not finding it too lonely?'

'I – we don't mind being alone.'

'Do you mind if I smoke?' He pulled a pipe from his pocket when I answered, 'Of course not.'

When McVeigh had lit the pipe and drawn once or twice on the long stem, he said, 'I was wanting a word with you about Frannie. You'll be wondering why, after I asked you if she could come to the attic, she hasn't been across.'

'Yes, yes. It did make us wonder. I hope she's all right.'

'No, I'm afraid she's not all right. She's hardly

146

been near the house these past weeks. I went across yesterday to see her grannie. The old lady says she's moping. I got her to promise to take her to the doctor's this morning. She's a bitter old stick, is the grannie. I suppose life has made her like that, but it's hard on the child.'

I could find nothing to say to this for Flora Cleverly's suggestion was in my mind again.

Then McVeigh broke the silence by referring to the weather. 'The cold weather has settled in,' he said. 'You won't find it very pleasant in a short while.'

'Oh, I don't mind the cold.'

'I don't think you've experienced our kind of cold.' He was smiling wryly. 'There's been times, even early in December, when we haven't been able to make a path between the cottage and the house – but you'll be gone by then.'

'Yes, yes. I suppose so.'

I felt my eyes widen in surprise when he rose from the chair abruptly and, walking to the window, looked out towards the lake, and after a moment, said quietly, 'I always meant to apologise for the day of the wedding – not for what happened on the road.' His head turned slightly over his shoulder, but he didn't look back at me. 'That was understandable, at least from a driver's point of view. But I mean the evening when that mad lot came across and Alec Bradley—' He stopped now and, turning and facing me, added, 'The truth of it is, I had a drink like the rest and the effect of liquor on me is to turn me into a creator of rhymes, corny rhymes. When I've had a drink I can set anything to rhyme, but, should I try when I'm in my normal state, I find the process difficult and the result laboured. Yet when under – the influence, my verses are fluent and corny.'

I saw that it had taken a great deal for him to speak as he was doing, so I said lightly, 'Oh, I'd forgotten all about it. But tell me, do you write poetry?'

'Poetry – no, it's just this rhyming. My father had a knack too. He filled books with rhymes, sentimental Ella Wheeler Wilcox stuff; yet to look at him, you would never have believed him capable of even that. He was a hard-living, hard-drinking, tough individual but –' He looked downwards now and tapped his pipe against the back of his hand '– endearing for all that.'

'Has he been long dead?'

'He died when I was fourteen; my mother died when I was three.'

And I thought to myself, Flora Cleverly brought you up and you've hated every moment under her dominance.

Aunt Maggie came bustling in now and the visitor moved forward and took the tray from her and laid it on the corner of the table, well away from my writing.

My aunt said to him, 'I've been meaning to ask you, Mr McVeigh, did you carve this table and these?' She pointed to the animals on the long shelf.

'Oh, those!' His voice dismissed them lightly.

'Yes. Yes, I used to try my hand at such things in my youth.'

'They're fine pieces of work. And this table is magnificent. Haven't you kept it up?'

'No, no. There's no time now.' He looked towards the carved horse and the hard lines of his broad face seemed to soften as he said quietly, 'I used to spend day after day chipping away at things like that, wood always appealed to me, but as I said –' he turned abruptly round '– there's no time any more.' He smiled and added, 'Thank you,' as he took a cup from Aunt Maggie's hand.

He had just sat down again in the big chair when he exclaimed: 'Oh! I forgot. I've some mail for you.' Reaching into his pocket, he drew out two letters which he handed me.

As I took them, I saw from the postmark and the printed address on one envelope it was from my publisher; the other letter, I knew from the writing, was from Alice. It had been sent to my agent's address for Aunt Maggie had agreed with me, without making the reason obvious, that it would be better if we left no postal address.

As Aunt Maggie was now talking to Davie McVeigh and making, as I thought, a successful attempt to prove she did not talk like an early Victorian, I offhandedly opened the letter from Alice. I say 'offhandedly'; Alice was a link with my painful past and, although I wanted no more pain, I felt an eagerness to learn what she had to say.

The beginning of the letter was to the effect that she had been to the house to see me and found only

Mrs Bridie there, in the throes of what she called 'doing down a bit'. Alice went on to say that she didn't even know we had left Eastbourne.

It was at the beginning of the next paragraph that my heart began to beat at a quicker rate, for it began alarmingly:

What I'm really writing for, Pru, is to warn you. It may not be necessary, but you never know. You see, Ian is out. He got remission on his sentence and he went straight to Mother's, hoping, of course, to find you across the way. Father, I understand, ordered him out.

Then he came to me, feeling sure that I could tell him where you were. He wouldn't believe that I didn't have your address and stated very firmly that he meant to find you. His idea, Pru, is for his wife to divorce him and then to make up with you. He thinks that once he's divorced he can bring this about. I tried to persuade him otherwise, but it was no use.

I think you had better be on your guard, Pru, wherever you are, because, knowing Ian, I'm sure he'll find ways and means of tracing you. I have no need to emphasise how unscrupulous he can be when he wants anything badly, and of this I'm sure – he wants you very badly at the moment, for, as much as he's capable of loving, he, I think, loves you. But what is vastly more important to him, he needs you if he's going to write, and deep down he knows it.

Two clues he has as to your whereabouts;

these are that you are in the North and that you have rented a cottage somewhere. Apparently, he quizzed Mrs Bridie, and if she had known anything more, I'm sure he would have got it out of her. He has the idea that Aunt Maggie will have taken you to her birthplace or somewhere near. He said she has the Northerner's weakness – the homing instinct. But don't let this disturb you unduly, Pru. Yet I felt I ought to warn you.

'Don't let this disturb you unduly.' My heart was racing now. The old fear was filling me again. My limbs were trembling, and I felt sick. I could hear Aunt Maggie talking, but strangely, I couldn't see her, for the room had become blurred, dark. I said something. What it was, I don't know. Then I felt Aunt Maggie's hand gripping my wrist. So hard did she grip that I winced because the sprain in my left wrist was still painful. Her voice was loud around me now, saying, 'Pru! Pru! stop it. Pull yourself together. Come along now, no more of that! – What is it, Pru?'

Nothing that I had been through before had caused me to faint. I had never fainted in my life. Often I wished I could have, just to blot out all feeling. Now, I felt myself retreating rapidly once more away from all contact with people, and, as I went, I heard a voice shouting, 'I won't see him, I won't! I won't!' And then there was a silence.

I seemed to be dragging myself up through layers of black padding, clawing them aside so that I could breathe. At last I was free and I opened my eyes and looked into the face of Aunt Maggie. She was holding a glass to my lips. When she tipped it upwards a stream of warmth zigzagged down my throat. There was warmth at my side too, and I realised I was lying on the hearthrug near the fire, my head resting against something.

'You're all right. There's nothing to worry about.' Aunt Maggie was speaking softly.

What had I been worrying about? I couldn't recall for a moment until Aunt Maggie's next words brought it racing back into my mind.

'You'll see nobody you don't want to see. Now get that firmly into your head. Nobody can get at you here unless they first get past Mr McVeigh and his house. Isn't that so, Mr McVeigh?'

I started as if I had been poked. I had even forgotten the existence of Davie McVeigh, and, when his hands, which had been on my shoulders all the time, steadied me, I lay still once more realising that he was kneeling on the rug and my head was pillowed on his thigh.

'As your aunt said, you need see no-one you don't want to see. I promise you.'

His voice was low and quiet, it was as if McVeigh was talking to Frannie. I made an effort to rise now but I found I was unable to do so. Then I felt McVeigh withdraw the support of his leg. The next moment his arms were about me, under my shoulders and my knees, and, for a brief moment, he held me against him, as he carried me to the couch.

As he laid me down, I heard Aunt Maggie say hastily, 'I'll get some rugs.'

My eyes felt heavy and I wanted to close them, but I didn't. When I lifted my gaze upwards, his face was not far from mine. His eyes, glinting with dark green-blue light behind the short lashes, were looking deep into mine.

Reaching down, he picked up my hand and held it between his two palms as he said under his breath, 'Don't be afraid, I can't bear to see you afraid – not you.'

As my eyes continued to be held by his, I wanted to ask, 'Why me? Why should I not be afraid?' But I couldn't be bothered. I was tired. Not even the glint in his eyes could hold me any longer. My lids drooped and I shut out his face – and the world. Once again, I was retreating. There was no energy in my body, no purpose in my mind, and I knew that by just allowing myself to drift I could return into complete lethargy – that I would also be hemmed in by the barrier of fear didn't trouble me.

I felt Aunt Maggie's hands tucking the rug around my shoulders, and her voice now had a crisp sound. She was saying, 'You are going to sleep, and, when you wake up, everything will be all right. Do you hear? Pru, do you hear me? Everything will be all right.'

'Yes, Aunt Maggie.'

After a while, I became conscious of soft movements in the room. I was surprised at hearing them, I hadn't gone to sleep. I hadn't retreated. My mind was working again, even calmly. It was, surprisingly, saying to me, 'What can he do? If you were to see him this minute, it would make no difference. He can't force you to live with him. And if we stay here, he'll have to get past Davie McVeigh.'

It was as if Davie McVeigh had heard me thinking, for his voice came to me in a thick whisper from the doorway: 'What is he like, this fellow?'

'Tall, thin—' Aunt Maggie was whispering back. 'About your age, I would say. Very charming manner – as if butter wouldn't melt in his mouth.'

'Yes, that's the sort, the talkers, and they get off with it, don't they?'

'Well, I wouldn't say he got off with it – he was put away for six months. But his sentence must have been reduced.'

There had been no sound for some time, so I thought he had gone, until his whisper came to me again, asking this time: 'Why is it always nice women who are taken in?'

'Search me,' was Aunt Maggie's reply.

When the thought skimmed the haziness of my mind that there wasn't much of the Queen Victoria element about that remark, I realised, with something of surprise, that my attack of nerves had passed. I would not be called upon to spend the next forty-eight hours or even two or three days fighting my trembling limbs and fear-filled mind. Alice's letter had plunged me into the depths, but, like a diver rebounding from the bottom, I had risen to the surface as quickly as I had gone down. This fact left me with a wonderful sense of freedom. I wanted to sit up, even talk . . .

It was well into the afternoon when I awoke. I had slept solidly for four hours.

That evening Janie came to the cottage. She brought with her two extra pints of milk, a dozen eggs, and a jar of cream.

'Oh, this is very kind,' said Aunt Maggie. 'You must thank Miss Cleverly for me.'

'It was Davie who sent them.'

'Oh! Oh, then, you must thank Mr McVeigh.'

Janie turned to me now, where I was sitting near the fire, and asked, 'Are you better?'

'Yes, thank you.'

'Davie says you've got a cold.' She came and stood near me. After scrutinising me for a moment in her old-fashioned way – I had found Janie to be a very old-fashioned child – she asked, 'It isn't a sniffy one, is it? When I get a cold I run all over.'

When I smiled and said, 'No, it isn't a sniffy one, Janie,' it crossed my mind that it was thoughtful of Davie McVeigh to say I was suffering from a cold.

Janie seated herself on the edge of a chair opposite to me and looked round the room before saying, 'It's always funny to me when other people are living here 'cause I always think of this as Davie's house.'

'He'll have it again shortly – in the winter.'

'Yes – I wasn't being rude.'

'Oh, no, of course not, Janie. I understand what you mean.'

'Doris is coming over tomorrow.'

'Oh, she's back from her honeymoon, then?'

'Yes, they've been back nearly a fortnight. But they live right up yon side of Blanchland, near Hexham, and Jimmy's got a farm – not a big 'un, but he's always busy.'

Aunt Maggie, who was sitting on the couch, asked, 'Were you very fond of your sister?'

'Oh, yes. We got on like a house afire.'

This colloquial saying caused Aunt Maggie to put her head back and laugh. Then she asked, 'And do you like her husband?'

'Oh – Jimmy? He's all right, but he's oldish.'

'Oldish?'

This comment came simultaneously from Aunt Maggie and me for we had both imagined the young bride we had seen on that particular Saturday had been on her way to a young groom. Then I remembered the girl saying, 'Jimmy'll wait; he's been waiting for years.'

Janie was continuing, 'Well, not really old, you know, but a bit older than Davie.'

'Really!' Aunt Maggie's head was nodding questioningly towards Janie.

'Yes, and if she was going to marry anybody around that age she could have had Davie, couldn't she? She liked Davie, but Davie went away; he went to Australia. He was only gone a year, but when he came back Jimmy had stepped in – Aunt Flora was all for Jimmy.'

'Mr McVeigh has been in Australia then?'

'Yes.' Janie nodded her head at Aunt Maggie. 'But he couldn't stick it because he hadn't wanted to go in the first place, I think. Aunt Flora had said she could manage, but she couldn't. It was Talbot who wrote and told Davie about things.'

'Talbot?' Aunt Maggie's head was still nodding. Now she asked quietly, 'You're not very fond of Miss Cleverly are you, my dear?'

'Aunt Maggie!' I cried.

My aunt cut off my low censured exclamation with a quick downward movement of her hand as if she were knocking something away from the vicinity of her knee.

'Well—' Janie was looking straight at Aunt Maggie. Now she asked, 'You wouldn't tell her, would you?'

Janie hadn't asked a question; rather she had made a statement: 'You wouldn't tell her, would you?'

'No,' said Aunt Maggie. 'No, I wouldn't tell her anything – nothing about anything.'

I closed my eyes for a second and apologised to Mr Fowler for Aunt Maggie's mangling of the English language.

'Well, then.' Janie picked up the hem of her dress, and, concentrating her attention upon it, she nipped a loose thread between her thumb and fore-finger and gave it a tug. When it snapped, she said, 'I never have been fond of her. She's all for Roy. Nobody else matters. She wants Roy to have the place and not Davie. That's why Davie went away – to give him his chance – Roy, I mean. But it didn't work. She's always putting a spoke in Davie's wheel.'

Janie looked at me now and, with the quick change that is the accepted prerogative of extreme youth, she asked, 'You write stories, don't you?'

'Yes, Janie, I write stories.'

'Davie says you're clever.'

Before I could make any comment on this, Janie went on, 'Wordsworth was born near here, at Cockermouth. He wrote poetry. Do you know Cockermouth?'

'Yes, we went there the other day for a drive.'

'Davie says all the good writers come from Cumberland. Do you know what he says?'

I shook my head.

'If they weren't born here, they come here to die. An' John Peel lived here, in Caldbeck. It's not far.'

'You know your county,' said Aunt Maggie now. Then she added, 'I think you'll write stories yourself when you grow up.'

'If I did, I'd write a story about Aunt Flora.' She gave a little giggle. 'She was crossed in love, Talbot says.'

'Was she indeed? Well, well.'

Aunt Maggie's tone conveyed to Janie that she would like to hear more. I wanted to make a clicking sound of disapproval with my tongue, and I knew that Aunt Maggie was aware of this. Although she did not give me the hand signal again, the movement she made with her body, presumably settling herself in the corner of the couch, told me to be quiet.

'So Talbot says Miss Cleverly was crossed in love, does he? Dear, dear.'

'Yes. She was born here you know, in this cottage.'

Janie perked her head upwards towards the ceiling. 'And two years after, Davie's father was born at the big house. They played together when they were children. Aunt Flora didn't even like my mother playing with them for she was gone on McVeigh, so Talbot says.'

I did not like the child talking this way and was vexed with Aunt Maggie for pumping her, yet this was a bit of surprising news. I did nothing to silence Janie as she went on:

'Talbot said it was all right when they were bairns, but, after Davie's dad came back from college, he wouldn't look at the side she was on, 'cept to be civil to her. Talbot said Aunt Flora never forgave Davie's father for marrying somebody else, but he would never have married her, Talbot said, in a month of Sundays, 'cause McVeigh was so handsome that all the girls were after him.'

She paused, and Aunt Maggie and she exchanged smiles which showed their confidence in each other.

Aunt Maggie said, 'And so you could write a story about all that. And would you give it a happy ending?'

'For Davie, I would. Not for anybody else – oh, except Frannie. But not for her grannie. I don't like her grannie. On market day she was going to take Frannie to the doctor, but they couldn't find her. And her grannie told Talbot to leave a message at Doctor Beaney's, an' he did an' when the doctor called, Frannie wasn't in. That was after her grannie

159

had locked her upstairs. She had got out of the window and down the drainpipe. It isn't very high – she couldn't have hurt herself very much if she had fallen . . . Do you like Davie?'

I was grateful that this pointed question had not been put to me. Janie, her little plain face thrust forward, was addressing Aunt Maggie in a lower tone.

Aunt Maggie, I was slightly amused to note, was in a bit of a quandary. Her eyes flicked towards me for a second, then, as if coming to a sudden decision, she made a deep obeisance with her head and said, 'Yes, Janie; yes, I do like Davie. Mind you –' she lifted her finger and wagged it at the child '– I didn't think I would at first, but I've changed my mind.'

'Nobody does at first, but they all change their minds. Except, that is, Aunt Flora – and perhaps Mr Bradley. Alec Bradley and Davie don't get on. That's because Davie was engaged to Mrs Bradley at one time. It was a long time ago – before he went into the army – but when he came back it was off, so she married Mr Bradley.'

I was relieved that Aunt Maggie had the grace not to press further. We looked at each other and then, hitching herself from the couch, she went towards the dresser and, opening a drawer, she took out a tin.

'Do you like walnut toffee, Janie?' she asked.

'Oh, yes, please.'

Janie's tongue was silent for a time while she chewed on Aunt Maggie's favourite sticky walnut toffee. Then, seeming to remember Davie McVeigh's need for her to do the chores, she bade us farewell, but not before she asked me the embarrassing question of whether I had enjoyed having her, and would I like her to come again? This – from a child whom I had taken to be a shy individual. We live and learn, I thought.

When we were alone, I looked coolly at my aunt and remarked, 'You are an inquisitive old woman.'

Aunt Maggie picked up some knitting from the long wooden shelf, came to the couch and seated herself comfortably before she replied. 'Inquisitive, but not old, Pru – anyway –' she glanced at me, the twinkle deep in her eye now, '– you got a packet of information there, didn't you now? So our Miss Flora Cleverly aimed at being mistress of Lowtherbeck! Well, well! She aimed high, didn't she? But I wonder why she liked one child and not the other? They both have the same father.'

'If you wait long enough, doubtless you'll find out.' I stressed the *you*.

'Doubtless,' said Aunt Maggie with another deep obeisance of her head.

Then we laughed, after which we became silent . . .

I retired early, and, again, it was something concerning the master of Lowtherbeck that erased the harrying thoughts of my own problems from my mind. As sleep overtook me, I was thinking: And when he came back from the war messed up in that awful state, it was to lose his girl to somebody else. He's had it hard, has Davie McVeigh. I was no longer cynical when thinking of him and less and less did I attach to him his string of Christian names . . .

My attitude towards Davie McVeigh tempered still further as the days went on. In a way, I came to look upon him almost as a sort of protector, a protector against Ian. 'He'd have to get past Mr McVeigh,' Aunt Maggie had said, and now I, too, thought along the same lines. Yet even the barricade he presented couldn't prevent me, at times, from being overpowered by the fear of meeting up with Ian again, for foremost in my mind was the memory of the wild reaction his betrayal had aroused in me.

I had always seen myself as a fundamentally gentle creature, yet there was this mental picture of me flinging myself on Ian and clawing at him with my hands. The violence was absolutely out of character for me – at least, as I saw myself – but it held terrifying possibilities as to what might happen should we meet again. Not that I was afraid now of letting myself go as I had done on that particular day, but the knowledge that the sight of him might arouse that strange aggressive emotion in me again was sufficient to give me frequent, although diminished, bouts of nerves.

So my opinion of Davie McVeigh rose steadily – so much so that, by the Fifth of November, when I recognised that he and I were two of a kind – he ceased to be a barricade between Ian and myself.

The revelation was split, you could say, into two parts: an incident in the morning, followed by another in the afternoon. There were some letters

I wanted posted, also an order to be sent in to Talbot, who now obligingly brought in any replenishments we needed on his visits to the farm. It was a very sultry morning, not chilly as you think of November being, but heavy and close. This had been the atmosphere for the past forty-eight hours and I felt that nothing but a storm would lighten it.

I was walking along the hill path that morning, approaching the house by the road down which we had brought the car on that first day we came to Lowtherbeck. As I came up through the kitchen garden out of the shrubbery, I looked towards the house and saw, high up, outlined against the dull sky, the bulky figure of Davie McVeigh. He was doing something to the guttering. Supporting one loose end with one hand, he was hammering in what I took to be a bracket with the other. He was working on the far side of the back of the house where the French windows were, at the corner of the building.

I entered the courtyard from the opposite side, and, when I came to the kitchen door and looked upwards, I could see McVeigh's arm, like a disembodied limb, appearing and disappearing round the edge of the building.

Flora Cleverly was in the kitchen, as was Janie. Janie was sitting at a side table scraping potatoes and she lifted her head quickly and gave me a smile. It had about it a secret quality – we two shared something that Flora Cleverly knew nothing about.

Miss Cleverly greeted me in her usual fashion with, 'Hello. There you are.'

When Flora Cleverly spoke, it did not stop her from working. I had become, over the weeks, fascinated by her seeming tirelessness and her habit of carrying on a conversation while doing two jobs at once. Filling the kettle under the tap with her right hand, she would stack dishes on the draining board with her left, for example. Had I attempted to do this, something definitely would have been broken.

I answered the housekeeper's greeting, then, looking towards Janie I said, 'You're not at school today. Is Guy Fawkes Day a holiday?'

Janie was about to answer when Flora Cleverly put in, 'No. Janie's had a bit of a cold over the weekend. She says she didn't feel like school. But doubtless she'll feel like the Guy Fawkes party tonight. They can always get better for parties.'

Miss Cleverly jerked her head at me as she went on emptying groceries from a large carton that was standing on the table.

'Do you have a Guy Fawkes party?' I was looking at Janie again.

'Not here,' said Janie. 'Over at the Ponsonbys'. Mary and Charlie make a big guy and we all take our own crackers. Do you like bonfire parties?' she asked.

'I can't remember ever having been to one, Janie.'

'You haven't missed much.' Again Flora Cleverly was speaking. 'Although—' She paused for us just a second as she fingered a coloured box she had lifted out of the stores. Looking down at it she said, 'I used to enjoy them when I was a girl. The bigger the bangs the better I liked them.' She pushed the box across the table now, saying, 'There you are, there's your fireworks.'

'Thanks, Aunt Flora.'

It was at this point that the sound of something falling in the yard, a splintering sound, caused us all to look towards the door and upwards, and brought from Flora Cleverly the remark: 'There's another slate down. He'll have them all off shortly. There'll be no roof left.'

On looking back, I am sure it was when the slate dropped into the yard that this enigmatic woman jumped at an opportunity that she thought too good to miss – an opportunity to expose the weakness of a man she hated and to lessen him in my eyes. But it was much later when I worked this out, and, consequently, realised that Flora Cleverly had the power within her to sense forthcoming reactions. Her hate gave her this power. But her power was not omnipotent. On this occasion, the reaction she had foreseen did not occur.

The housekeeper had her hand on the box of fireworks again and there was another almost imperceptible pause in her talking, then she looked at Janie and said, 'Go and try one in the yard.'

'Now?' Janie dropped a potato back into the water.

'Yes. Why not? It will give Miss Dudley and me a bit of a treat; we won't be at the do tonight. Tucked away in bed, I expect.' She turned on me with her tight smile; then, rummaging in the box she pulled out a large, long fire-cracker.

'Ee! not that one.' Janie recoiled a step. 'That's a banger.'

'Well, can't we hear a banger? There are four of them. Talbot must have put them in for good measure.'

'Ee! but I couldn't let off a banger, Aunt Flora. I could a squib.'

'Don't be silly. You just light it and throw it – well, if you won't give us a show, I'll have to do it meself. Where's the matches?'

Janie's face was now shining with excitement; that is, until she reached the yard. Then I watched her eyes lift, as mine did, towards Davie McVeigh. He had evidently moved the ladder around the corner and was now in full view. He was at the top, his head back on his shoulders and his arms reaching up as he screwed a bolt in on a corner bracket. Perhaps it was the stationary figures below him or the flash of the match through the greyness of the morning that brought his eyes towards us. I saw him staring down at Flora Cleverly. For a short time, he was posed like a gnarled fossilised tree, so still was he. I saw his mouth open and his hand lift as if in protest. Then he was startled into movement, but, even before he started his erratic frantic descent down the ladder, Flora Cleverly had lit the fuse and thrown the fire-cracker.

McVeigh must have been about six rungs from the bottom when the fire-cracker, not a yard from the foot of the ladder, exploded with an ear-cracking bang. At the sound, Davie McVeigh's entire body left the ladder, he seemed to fling himself into the air. When he hit the ground, he did not fall but began to stagger like a drunken man.

I knew I had cried out. I was standing with my fingers covering my face up to my eyes. I was aware in this moment that, had the fire-cracker exploded earlier – say, when he had been near the top of the ladder – the explosion would have automatically caused him to loosen his hold, for, at the sound, he had jumped as if he were leaping clear of something – a mortar shell, for instance.

I wanted to run to him, for he was standing alone – swaying and blinking – but Janie had done that.

Janie had raced to him, crying, 'Davie! Davie! Oh, Davie, it was only a big fire-cracker. Oh, Davie!'

I saw him shake his head once again before thrusting her aside and advancing slowly towards Flora Cleverly like some terrible gigantic creature. She backed towards the granite wall of the house, her tongue still for once.

I heard myself shouting protestingly: 'Mr McVeigh! No! Mr McVeigh. No!'

He was about a yard from Flora when he paused only long enough to grind out – and he literally did grind out the words through his closed teeth: 'You! You devil-ridden hell-cat! You!' His arms shot out and he had her pinned by the throat.

At the contact, Flora seemed to come alive, for she kicked and clawed at him; at the same time, I on one side and Janie on the other pulled at him and yelled as we did so, 'Stop it! Stop it!' Even so, I knew that our efforts were as futile as those of two flies attempting to stop a stampeding elephant. Loosening my hold on McVeigh and gazing frantically around the yard for some means of help, I saw, near a big rain barrel that stood underneath a spout, a large wooden bucket full of water. Aunt Maggie had once thrown a glass of water in my face to shock me out of a tantrum. I now heaved up the wooden bucket, which under ordinary circumstances I could hardly have lifted from the ground, and, stumbling forward, I threw the contents upwards and over him, drenching myself in the process.

I jumped away as the bucket clattered to the ground. At the same time I saw Flora Cleverly collapse against the wall, then slowly slide to the ground.

I watched Davie McVeigh shake himself, then slowly push his sodden hair up out of his eyes and over the top of his head. When he looked at me, it was as if he were coming out of a dream, and as if we were all figments of that dream without a trace of reality. Then he moved like a drunken man, aiming, to steady his gait, directly towards the door of the cave. Behind him, tentatively suiting her steps to keep a short distance between them, went Janie.

It wasn't until the door had closed on them both that I turned my trembling attention to Flora Cleverly. She was on her hands and knees now, making an effort to rise. I helped her to her feet, assisted her into the kitchen, and sat her in a chair.

'Can I get you something? Have – have you any brandy?'

Flora Cleverly moved her fingers round her throat, then stretched her neck. Her wrinkled skin was the colour of dirty ivory. She swallowed, then pointing to a cupboard high up on the wall of the kitchen to the right, she muttered, 'My pills.'

I had to stand on a stool before I could open the door of the cupboard. Inside there were a number of small medicine bottles, all holding tablets of different sizes and colours. I took three into my hand and brought them to her. She picked a bottle that held round white tablets, and, after I got her a glass of water, she swallowed two of them.

'Will I make you a cup of tea?'

Flora swallowed again, then said, 'It's made – on the hob.'

After she had sipped at the tea in her pseudo-refined fashion, she looked up at me, straight into my eyes, and said, 'He's mad. I could have him locked up, put away. You witnessed this, didn't you?'

I felt myself suddenly recoil from her. I wanted to step back, but was prevented by the force of her stare.

'This isn't the first time it's happened, but this time I've got a witness and there'll be marks to show –' she touched her neck gently '– besides what I did to his face.' Her lips came together in a tight bitter line. 'I've warned him – I've got him now. I'll ring Doctor Kemp and let him judge Davie's condition.'

As she stroked her neck again, I moved from her, and, speaking very quietly, I said, 'You must remember that it was you who threw the fire-cracker, Miss Cleverly. If he had been further up the ladder, I am sure he would still have jumped. He – he could have broken his neck. What he did was under great stress – emotional reaction.'

'You're for him, aren't you?' There was something frightening in her voice. 'Fascinated like a snake by the great big tough he-man.'

'Miss Cleverly!' My voice was haughty.

'Oh, Miss Dudley, I've seen all this happen before. You'll get your eyes opened before long.'

'I don't need to have my eyes opened, Miss Cleverly. And whatever discord exists between you and Mr McVeigh has nothing to do with me – I'd like you to understand that. And what is more, we won't be here much longer. Our lease is nearly up. Perhaps it's just as well.'

'Yes. Yes, of course. I'm sorry, Miss Dudley. I'm not meself at the moment – that's understandable.' Flora pulled herself upwards and steadied herself against the table. Then, speaking to me over her shoulder, she said, 'You needn't stay; I'll be all right.'

Without another word, I left the kitchen and, taking the short cut, I went back to the cottage, the order for Talbot still in my pocket, as well as the mail.

When I got in, I said to Aunt Maggie, 'Give me something to drink – a brandy and soda or something.'

'A brandy and soda?' Aunt Maggie looked at me through narrowed lids. 'What's happened?'

'Give me a drink first. Then I'll tell you.'

After I had drunk the brandy and soda at a speed that brandy and soda should never be drunk, I gasped and said, 'Davie McVeigh is terrified of noise, and he nearly throttled Miss Cleverly.'

'Dear God!' said Aunt Maggie. 'What next?'

Then putting out her hand, she said, 'You're wet, lass.'

'Yes, I had to throw a bucket of water over him.'

'You – what?' She had just seated herself, and my statement brought her immediately to her feet. With her hand pressed against her cheek, she repeated, 'You – *what*?'

When the brandy had steadied me, I related in detail what had happened. I finished by saying, 'I think I'll be glad when we're gone.'

'Will you?'

I had expected Aunt Maggie to say with me, 'Me, too.' But now, resuming her seat once again and stretching her hand out to the blaze, she leant towards the fire as she said, 'You know, I'm sort of sorry for that fellow.'

'But he would have choked her to death!'

'A man doesn't do that unless he's been driven to the limit. I never liked that woman from the first time I saw her, and I've liked her less every time I've met her since. And, from what you say, she threw the fire-cracker deliberately.'

'Yes –' I nodded my head slowly '– I'm sure she did that.'

'Well, then, she deserved all she got. She must have known what an effect it would have on him.

171

She's a nasty piece of work, I tell you.'

I rose to my feet now and began to walk around the room, and Aunt Maggie, raising her head, glanced towards me, saying, 'Go and change your dress, you don't want to get cold.'

'I'll have to go out,' I said. 'I didn't post the letters or leave the order.'

She looked towards the windows. 'There's going to be a storm and you don't want to be caught out with the car, do you?' She knew that I didn't like driving in a storm, not even through rain.

'I wasn't thinking of taking the car,' I said. 'We can manage with what we have in the larder, but I must get these letters off. I'll go up to the pillar box at the crossroads.'

In my ramblings, I had found that if, instead of taking the back path to the farmyard, I crossed the field beyond the 'kiosk', as we called our unmodern convenience, climbed one of the innumerable dry-stone walls, and went over yet another field and up a very steep incline, I came out just at the top of the steep track down which I had brought the car on that memorable wedding Saturday. And here, affixed to a telegraph pole, was a letter box; I had used it before on a few occasions.

I said now, 'If I hurry, I'll likely make it before the storm breaks.'

'Go and change your dress first.'

'It isn't very wet,' I said. 'It was just splashed – it's nothing. I won't be long.'

'You'll catch—'

'I won't.'

I lifted a light mack off the hook on the back of the kitchen door as I went out and put it on as I walked hastily to the copse, then through it into the open fields. The air was still, the sky was low, so low that there came to my mind a favourite story from my childhood of Henny Penny and Cocky Locky hurrying to tell the King the sky was going to fall. It seemed incongruous that I should think such childish thoughts at this moment, but, looking upwards, I could imagine that the sky was touching the top of the hill.

Long before I reached the summit, I was breathing heavily. Little rivulets of sweat were running down my face, and, as I walked, I heard the first roll of thunder. It was quite near. I'd heard no distant rumbles leading up to it that would have made me think, in Aunt Maggie's idiom, 'Somebody's getting it.' But, by the time I reached the top and the three roads were in sight, I was telling myself I wouldn't make it back home before the rain came.

I had just put the letters in the box when a flash of lightning, streaking across the open fells towards my right, caused me to screw up my eyes and lower my head. Then, right above me, the heavens seemed to split in two. The crash of thunder brought my shoulders hunching and my back bending as if to ward off some gigantic pressure. I turned about now and ran towards the hill.

I could make home, I guessed, in ten minutes. At that moment, I wasn't taking into account any rain. It came with the suddenness of the lightning itself and, strangely, it did not appear to come straight down but struck at me horizontally from the direction of the fells. One minute everything had been so still; now there was turmoil all about me. I could see scarcely a yard ahead, and even this distance was obliterated when my coat whirled upwards like an inverted umbrella. I dizzied round once or twice, thrusting my clothes down, and I suppose it was this that altered my direction. I was running, not away from the road in the direction of the fields and the cottage, but down by the side of it.

I discovered this when I got myself caught up in some brambles. I have described before how this track was overshadowed by trees and heavy with undergrowth and I was now among the low undergrowth. Recognising this, it came to me that it was better than being in the open fields and that lower down, almost at the foot of the incline, there was an inlet.

I had investigated this one day after seeing Floss galloping, as it were, straight out of the hillside. I'd heard a whistle; then the dog had come bounding out of a large hole. It was, I remembered, some way down the path in a space clear of undergrowth. That's why it had seemed so strange seeing the dog apparently leaping out of the hillside.

The weight of the rain was almost bearing me down to the ground, and it was more by blind groping than by any knowledge of its position that I came upon the aperture. I stood about a yard inside it, leaning heavily against the wall, gasping and spluttering. When my breathing steadied, I

straightened up and leant my head back. My eyes
were closed, perhaps that was why when I opened
them my sight was more accustomed to the dimness
and I saw Davie McVeigh.

He was sitting on the ground not two yards from
me with his knees up, his elbows on them, and his
hands hanging between them. His broad face was
turned towards me and it bore the evidence of Flora
Cleverly's handiwork.

The bolt hole!

Flora Cleverly's words seemed to fill the small
space: '*You were likely in your bolt hole.*' Was this
his bolt hole? Yes. And he had bolted to it after the
incident in the courtyard.

At the sight of him, my heart had given a quick
jump, and, when it slowed, I was about to say, 'It's
a dreadful storm,' or some such ordinary remark.
But, when I looked at Davie, at his face – all eyes –
deep and pain-filled with self-condemnation, I
could not utter a word.

I still remained pressed against the wall and he
remained sitting in the same position with his knees
up. There was only the sound of the rain, yet it
seemed distant and far away. As during that
morning by the Big Water, a silence enveloped us.
In that other silence, I had asked a question; and in
this silence, I was getting the answer.

This man was fear-ringed. He wasn't, like me,
afraid of people – his fear went deeper. His were
intangible fears, the kind of fears I only touched on
when I became filled with fear of fear. I recalled a
woman I had met when I was having psychiatric

treatment. This woman was afraid of the moon; she also felt that if she walked one step forward she would topple over the edge of the earth. Hers was an elemental fear, and it was the kind of fear that Davie McVeigh suffered from – part of it was manifested by his fear of noise.

If I wanted proof of my surmise, I received it almost at that instant, for, crashing through the silence, came a terrific burst of thunder. It broke directly overhead and seemed as if it were rending the hill into splinters. One moment I had been looking down into his upturned face, the next I saw his head buried in his arms, and I was crying inside myself, 'Oh, no! no!' It seemed such a humiliating thing for a man, a big man, to be afraid of noise, afraid of bangs, afraid of thunder.

'Don't worry, he won't get past McVeigh.' Aunt Maggie's words came back to me. I remembered that what they had implied had brought me a sense of comfort. Nobody could get past this man if he didn't so wish it – that's what I had thought. That was the impression he gave. As the thunder rolled, his head went deeper down between his knees, and, as I watched it droop, there arose in me a feeling not only of compassion – and this was strong – but of awe and admiration. This man was afraid, innately afraid, yet he showed to the world at large a bold fearless front. Where he thought it was necessary, he struck out and levelled a man to the ground while all the time the mysterious, unfathomable elements of nature were attacking him through his sense of hearing.

I didn't remember moving from the wall, but I had. I was kneeling by his side, and embarrassment overcame me for the merest fraction of a second as I put my arm around his shoulder. His coat was very wet, the result of the wooden bucket of water, and the feeling of proximity was strange, and it must have been so to him, too. My touch must have been like salt in an open wound, for he turned his body half from me. His head was still lowered, and I not only felt, but saw, the shudder that went through him.

As the minutes passed, the thunder gradually rolled away, until silence engulfed us once more. I could not hear even the rain now. I had taken my arm away from him and was sitting on the cold, but dry, earth looking at his bent form when he straightened up. He turned round onto his hips, thrust out his legs and lay back against the wall. I could see his face dimly. He was sweating. He sat looking ahead for quite a while before turning to me. His body was trembling, and, when he spoke, the tremor made his voice shake.

'And – and now you know,' he said.

I shook my head slowly. I found it difficult to answer him. Then I asked, 'What do I know? That you're afraid of noise?'

'Y – yes. I'm a man who's afraid of noise.'

'I'm afraid of many things.'

'It's allowable in a woman.'

I repeated to him what they had said to me when trying to arouse me from my self-pity. 'You're not the only one who suffers like this.'

'I'm – I'm well aware of that.'

'What I meant was –' I was stumbling now '– there's nothing to be ashamed of – nothing.'

It was a moment before he answered. 'Yes, I – I know,' he stammered. 'But I'm such a big fellow phys-physically. "Afraid of noise!" people say. "You – you want to sn-snap out of it, man."'

I now hitched myself back and sat against the wall, near him, but not touching. 'When did it happen?' I asked. 'Before you were hurt?' I could not say burnt.

'All in one go. The l-lorry was caught in cross fire.' He was stammering less now. 'In the ordinary way, the noise would have been n-nothing, but I suppose I had two skins l-less by that time and it nearly drove me mad.'

I had closed my eyes. I could see his head hanging through the cab window while mortar shells exploded all about him. Why did people have to suffer such things? There should be a limit to suffering. When his wounds had healed, it should have been the end of it, but, with him, it appeared that he would go down to his grave fearing noise.

I said, 'My fear is of people – not so much what they do to me but what they don't do for me. They don't—' I couldn't say they don't give me 'love', so I substituted 'security'. 'No-one has ever given me a feeling of security. People generally think that security means having money and the things that money can buy – it doesn't. You know, there's a certain street in Eastbourne that you'd really call slummy, but it used to attract me like a magnet. The children playing on the pavements always looked happy, and the girls, with their cheap clothes and their make-up, looked as if they had the world at their feet – this was simply because most of them belonged to a family. Naturally, there'd be bad hats among them, and I knew that a lot of them drank and fought and that a couple of the men from that street were petty thieves. I knew all about this, yet there was some tie amongst them that I always envied.'

I was surprised to find myself talking to him so easily. I had felt compelled to talk to him, not only to comfort him, but to soothe myself. Yet 'comfort' is not the right word here. It was as if, at last, I was able to explain the complaint that I had always suffered from: simply, the lack of love from my parents – which meant that they had deprived me of security. Added to that deprivation, was the betrayal of my love by the man I took to be my husband. The thought came to me that, in talking freely, perhaps I was picking up the reins of maturity. My next action seemed to endorse this.

If anyone had told me three months ago that I would voluntarily put my arm about a man's shoulders, then reach out and take his hand, I would not have bothered to contradict them. Deep within, I would have known the impossibility of such an action and also the futility of making anyone understand the abhorrence with which even such thoughts would fill me. Up to the previous day, I could not have seen myself reaching out my hands to draw this man to his feet – yet this was what I was doing now. I had stood up and, bending over, I was holding out my hands to Davie. He did not take them, but looked up at me, and the muscles of his face were twitching spasmodically, as if he were trying to say something and the words would not come.

When he did not raise his hands to mine, I bent further and took them from his knees and said softly, 'Come on. Aunt Maggie will have a drink ready.' I had spoken as if Aunt Maggie belonged to him as well as to me.

When he got to his feet we were still holding hands. I felt no embarrassment in this, it was almost an elating experience. I could feel the tremor from his flesh passing along my arm. We stood thus, joined not only by our hands and eyes but by our weakness – we were one with our mutual knowledge of fear.

Slowly I withdrew my hands from his, and, turning, went to the opening. The rain had stopped. The threatening sky had lifted, and I could see the smoke from the cottage chimney moving almost vertically over the shrubbery. I turned and looked at him and tried to smile, but I found I couldn't. I couldn't smile into this big broad face, into what was usually a bold face, but was now so drained as to appear almost bloodless. Hesitantly, I moved forward and he with me, and we walked down the sodden hillside, through the equally sodden fields, until we came to the back door of the cottage. And neither of us had spoken a word.

Aunt Maggie was standing waiting, greatly

agitated, but she did her utmost to cover her surprise when she saw me emerge from behind the 'kiosk' accompanied by Davie McVeigh.

As soon as I reached her, Aunt Maggie put out her hand and patted my chest, saying: 'You're sodden. Get those things off. Where have you been? I was worried sick with you out in this. Wasn't that thunder terrible?'

Her voice trailed off. She must have sensed, from the drawn look of Davie's face, that something further was amiss for she started to cover up in her quick prattling way. 'I've just made the coffee. I think we all want it laced. You go upstairs and get those things off.' She pushed at me. 'Will you take your coat off, Mr McVeigh? Go in the sitting-room and make yourself comfortable.'

As I stepped from the steep stairs into the bedroom, I heard her voice going on and on, releasing Davie from tension. I had just stripped my wet clothes off when there came to me a gentle whisper from the top of the stairway. I saw Aunt Maggie's head rise above the floor level. She beckoned me and I went towards her.

'What's happened?' she asked, alarmed.

'I'll tell you later,' I whispered back.

'He looks like death.'

'Be nice to him.'

I was surprised that I should have put this request to her and I felt the colour rush to my face.

Aunt Maggie raised her eyebrows quizzically as she whispered, 'I'll do my best.' A few seconds later I heard her talking again.

When I entered the sitting-room, Davie McVeigh was sitting near the fire in his shirtsleeves. He rose hastily to his feet at my approach, and his eyes were still on me when he resumed his seat. I had changed into a lime-green dress with a broad scarlet belt; it was a very effective combination and I knew that this particular dress suited me. But I had not worn it for a long time, not, in fact, since before I had become pregnant. Why I had packed it, I don't know, except, perhaps, that it was uncrushable. Certain I was that I didn't pack it with the intention of enhancing my appearance to attract a man.

Aunt Maggie was looking at me, too, and, of a sudden, I had a panicky feeling that she might make some remark about my wearing the dress. And she did, but it was not a disturbing remark.

All my aunt said was: 'That's better. I'm glad to see you are sensible enough to put on something warm. Now, Mr McVeigh –' she turned to him '– let me fill that cup again. As the song says, "Another little drop won't do you any harm".'

The remark was trite, yet it brought normality, an ease, that was badly needed at this moment.

A flicker of a smile crossed Davie McVeigh's face as he replied, 'You're very kind; I won't say no.'

I had asked Aunt Maggie to be nice to him and she was certainly doing her utmost. I cannot recall all she said during the half-hour that we sat by the fire, but it was she who did all the talking, seeming satisfied with monosyllabic replies from Davie and me.

Just before our landlord took his leave, when he was putting on his still damp coat, he asked a direct question, or rather made a statement.

He said, 'Your time is nearly up.' He brought his eyes from Aunt Maggie's and looked at me.

Then his gaze returned to Aunt Maggie as she said, 'Yes – yes, time does fly.'

'Will you be sorry to go?'

Aunt Maggie's mouth opened. She wanted, I know, to look at me, but she kept her eyes directly on his as she answered somewhat hesitantly.

'Yes – yes indeed, we will. Oh, yes, we'll be sorry to go. Won't we, dear?' My aunt turned her round bright eyes in my direction. I had asked her to be nice to Davie, and she was certainly being that – she was lying beautifully. When I turned my glance to him, he seemed to be waiting for it. Was I going to lie, too?

I said, 'I'll be very sorry to leave here.' I made a small gesture with my hand. 'I've been happier here than I've been for a long – long while.'

The room became quiet, a log shifted on the fire and fell inwards; as I turned to look at it, I was surprised to realise that I hadn't lied.

'I must go. It's been nice sitting here like this.' He was speaking to Aunt Maggie.

'But you're used to sitting here – in this cottage.'

'Not like this, not with company, just talking. Usually I'm doing accounts and working out ways and means. And often I'm so tired I drop off and wake up with the fire dead, and it's the middle of the night.'

Aunt Maggie, determined to keep the conversation on the mundane level, said, 'Now isn't that like a man!' and laughing, she rose and moved towards the door.

I rose to my feet too but I did not accompany them. I knew I was afraid that, were I alone with him, the conversation would not retain its ordinariness, but would revolve around personalities. I felt I could not bear that at the moment. I wanted to be quiet to think. I wanted to know no more about him – at that time, at any rate.

At the doorway, McVeigh turned and, looking back across the room, said, 'Thanks.'

The single word dissolved the veneer which during the last half-hour had covered the two startling incidents of the day; it was for my help – at least in the latter of the two episodes – for which he was thanking me.

I could make no reply. He turned away, said a word of goodbye to Aunt Maggie, and then was gone. When Aunt Maggie resumed her seat, I was still standing supporting myself against the mantelpiece and staring down into the fire.

'Well, now, what's all this about?'

I felt her waiting for my answer, for an explanation, but, when I spoke it was not to enlighten her, but to question her. Turning about, I asked, 'Is it really possible for anyone to be absolutely the opposite inside to what they appear outwardly?'

'Well—' Aunt Maggie took up her knitting and her eyebrows were arched as she stared at me.

'You're the writer, you should know that. But aren't we all like Jekyll and Hyde? We've got to be, because if people knew what went on inside some of us, we wouldn't be able to bear it – we'd die of shame. We've got to put up, and live behind, a barricade. And I should say that's what McVeigh's had to do, he's had to build himself a barricade – if he's the one you mean. Well, now, tell me what happened.'

A barricade. Yes, she was right. 'The Iron Façade' so to speak. The title of my new novel was taking on deeper meaning. I looked at Aunt Maggie. She was knitting steadily, her attitude one of waiting. I found I could not pick words to describe what happened between David McVeigh and me during the storm.

'He doesn't like storms,' I said.

Aunt Maggie's eyes came up slowly to meet mine. 'No?'

My aunt waited, and, when I did not supply any further explanation, I watched her eyes narrow – an indication that her mind was working rapidly. I felt the flush rise over my neck and cover my face.

Aunt Maggie had the uncanny knack of previewing my thoughts. She had always seemed, as it were, to hold a key to my subconscious mind, and the knowledgeable look that I saw in her eyes now made me want to protest, not only sharply, but angrily: 'It's nothing like that. How could it possibly be! Don't be silly. I loathe men, all men, and, if I did soften, I could not see myself softening for anyone like Davie McVeigh. Oh, Aunt Maggie, have sense.'

But I said nothing like this. I simply walked to the table, sat down, and in a preoccupied manner, began a new chapter.

7

Aunt Maggie and I were having tea when we heard the knock. We'd heard no footsteps approaching along the stone path. We exchanged questioning glances before I rose from my seat by the fire and opened the door.

Before me, stood Frannie. A different Frannie. She was smiling, not broadly, just with the corners of her mouth. When she spoke, I found that the change was in her voice, too – not so much the tone of voice as in the stringing together of her words.

She asked, 'Can I get some books, please?' Frannie's voice and manner, though still childish, were different. Before, she would have said, 'Want some books.'

'Yes, of course. Come in, Frannie. We're just having tea. Would you like a cup?'

'Yes, please.' When she came to a stop inside the doorway – this was the Frannie I had come to know, still gauche, still childish – I took her hand and led her towards the fire.

'Why – hello, Frannie!' Aunt Maggie's welcome was sincere. 'Come and sit down. Aren't you cold?'

'No, no, I was runnin'.'

'We haven't seen you for a long time; where have you been?'

At this question from Aunt Maggie, Frannie, sitting on the edge of a chair now, hung her head.

'Here, drink this tea. Would you like a sandwich first, or a piece of cake?'

For answer, Frannie looked up at me and said softly, 'The doctor said I was a good girl.' Apart from the surprising context of this last sentence, she had again used the word 'the', she had not said 'doctor said', but had prefixed the noun with the article *the*.

'Did he, Frannie? So you have been to the doctor's. Have you had a cold?'

'No, 'cause I was hurt.'

'Have this piece of cake.'

I passed Frannie the plate holding the piece of iced sponge-cake, and I watched her eyes brighten as she began to eat it.

'It's nice cake – Grannie took me in Penrith and we had cakes.'

'Really?'

I shook my head in perplexity as I gazed at the child. There was some burden gone from her, some weight. What was it?

'Grannie bought me taffy.'

— I had it! The child had lost her fear of her grannie. That's what had been lifted from her – fear. And what miracles can happen when fear is lifted from a human soul – even in a retarded person – such as this child? Already, she was different, more normal. What had brought about the new relationship between the child and her grannie? The visit to the doctor? The child had said, 'The doctor said I'm a good girl.' Why had her grannie been so eager to get her to the doctor? Because she was acting more strangely than usual; or because she feared there was something wrong with the girl; or had she feared that Frannie was – pregnant?

Aunt Maggie's thoughts must have been moving along the same track as my own, for, inclining her head towards Frannie, she said, 'All your nasty bruises have gone. How did they happen? Did you fall down, Frannie?'

I knew where Aunt Maggie's probing was leading, and I did nothing to check her, for I, too, was interested in knowing what had caused those bruises. Frannie's head was again drooping, but she shook it negatively.

'Did someone hit you? Was it your grannie?' asked Aunt Maggie.

The girl's head came up and her tone was alive in defence of her grandmother as she said, 'No, no, not Grannie. I hadn't smashed nothin'. Grannie hits me when I smash things. It was Mr—'

The name had almost slipped out and, consequently, the child was startled into tilting her plate so the remainder of the cake dropped onto the mat.

'Ee Ee!'

'Don't worry, Frannie. It's perfectly all right. I'm always dropping cake.' I was picking up the crumbs. 'Don't worry, have a fresh piece.'

I was kneeling now, and I swivelled round to the low table and picked up a fresh piece of cake and put it on her plate, which I placed on her knee. My face was on a level with hers. I smiled at her and she smiled back at me. As she did so, there sprang into my mind a fragment of the conversation I had over-heard in the yard between Davie McVeigh and Alec Bradley concerning the cottage where this child and her grandmother lived. I had heard Davie McVeigh ask, 'But why do you want to get them out?' Now it came to me in a flash of revelation why Alec Bradley wanted to get rid of the old woman and the girl.

Slowly I took the girl's hand into mine, and asked, 'It was Mr Bradley who hurt you, wasn't it?'

Her thin bony fingers tried to jerk themselves free; her eyes stretched wide, her mouth dropped into a wordless gape.

'Don't be afraid. It's all right, my child.' Aunt Maggie was on the other side of her now.

Frannie turned her startled gaze towards her and brought out rapidly, 'Ee! Davie – Davie'll hit him. Ee! No, no!'

'There now. There.' I patted her hand. 'Don't worry about it. Davie won't know.'

Frannie was looking at me again, and she repeated, 'Davie won't know.'

'No, just us – we three. It'll be all right.'

She nodded quickly now. Then, her head drooping, she muttered slowly, 'Mr – Bradley – was – drunk.'

*   *   *

I'll say he was, I was thinking harshly to myself and wishing earnestly that I had Mr Bradley in the room. I would lash him to shreds with my tongue – if nothing else – for, if he had been here at that moment I may not have been accountable for what I would have done. Aunt Maggie had said that the night of the wedding was like a witches' Sabbath, and, from what I could remember of the scene in front of the cottage, Alec Bradley had decidedly led the witches. In his hunt for strange excitement, he evidently had come across this girl, this child-girl whose mind was held in the fortress of childhood, while her body was in the budding cadences of youth.

In Frannie, that night, Alec had seen pleasures to satisfy his stimulated, unbridled passion. I was certain now, with a feeling of surety, that he had tried to seduce this girl. Perhaps she had run out at night and come across the hills to see the dancing and he had stumbled on her.

I surmised that her grannie had found her missing, then later, observing her physical state, feared the worst. Her grannie's suspicions would be emphasised when Frannie was reluctant to be taken to the doctor's. But her reluctance, her refusing to say how she had come about her bruises, I could see now could be attributed to the fact that she did not want Davie McVeigh to know who her assailant had been. Dimly she must have thought that, by keeping the knowledge to herself, she was protecting Davie. I, myself, was very much aware – from what I had witnessed between the two men

– that had Davie McVeigh known the truth about the matter, murder would have been done. Whatever Davie McVeigh feared – it wasn't any man. This child, in spite of her backwardness, had deep perception stemming from love.

But why did she love McVeigh?

The question again brought back to my mind Flora Cleverly's question: 'It wouldn't be you who was after the mother, would it?' The recollection I found repugnant. My eyes began to search the girl's face for a resemblance, any resemblance to McVeigh, but I could find none. Yet, that was no proof that she had no blood connection with the man she so blindly and instinctively loved.

'Not tell Davie.'

I found myself blinking, Frannie's words had recalled me to the present, and I said hastily, 'No, my dear. No. Don't worry.'

Frannie had spoken again in the clipped way of a child. But now, seemingly reassured, she asked, 'Can I have my books now?'

'Yes, of course, Frannie. You know where to go.'

She got up from her seat, put her plate on the table, then ran down the length of the room, but, before disappearing into the kitchen, she turned her face towards us and said brightly, 'Grannie says I can have my books home.'

We both nodded at her, smiling the while.

'Grannie's had a great change of heart it seems to me.' Aunt Maggie slanted her gaze up towards me.

'It would seem so.'

'What do you make of it?'

'What do you?'

'Well,' said Aunt Maggie, 'I think the grannie thought that the poor child was pregnant. But, by the sound of it, she's found that the child hasn't been touched and her relief is making her more human.'

'I don't think it was Mr Alec Bradley's fault that she isn't in that condition,' I said bitterly. 'And what if he should attempt it again when he returns. He's still on holiday, isn't he? What then? He could get drunk again.' I was looking down at Aunt Maggie.

'We can't tell Davie McVeigh. That's certain.'

'No, we can't.'

'I think somebody should know though. What about the other one, Roy?'

I paused before I answered; then, with a slow negative shake of my head I said, 'No, no. I don't think he'd be able to keep anything like that to himself.'

'Perhaps you're right. I know!' Aunt Maggie sat upright. 'Talbot. If anybody wanted to ease McVeigh's burden, it would be that long-faced individual. He's the one we should tell. He may be able to convey to Mr Bradley on his return that his escapade, if you can call it such, is known, and that, instead of trying to get rid of the woman and child he'd better leave them alone.'

My lips twisted as I looked at my aunt. 'You could arrange blackmail lessons, couldn't you?'

'If need be, yes.' She jerked her head at me and we exchanged smiles. Then looking towards the upstairs room, where I could hear Frannie moving about, I said, 'You know, that child's changed.'

'That's what I was thinking. She seems brighter, different.'

'It could be that her mind's starting to move.'

'Could be – perhaps she got a fright. Perhaps that night Alec Bradley did something after all. Good came out of evil. Who knows? If a fright stopped her development, another fright could start it again. Or could it? These things are tricky.'

'Yes, they are. But it would be wonderful if it were true. Anyway, I'm sure there's a change in her – I can feel it.'

The change in the child was emphasised still further when, five minutes later, coming into the kitchen carrying four books in her arms, she said, 'I've got my *Bambi* books. When I grow up, I'm going to work on the farm, Davie says.'

We both saw her to the door and she turned before entering the trees and waved to us.

Aunt Maggie repeated, 'When she grows up.' She added, 'I've got a feeling she's starting right now. I may be wrong – only time will tell. In any case, we won't be here to see it.'

Aunt Maggie sighed as she turned back into the room, and, as I closed the door, I thought, no, we won't be here to see it.

The following afternoon we set off in the car from Borne Coote. We had talked quite a lot about how we would approach Talbot with the subject of Frannie and Alec Bradley. We planned, after seeing

Talbot, to go on a round tour touching the coast-line, first through Penrith and on to Carlisle, thence on to Silloth, making our way down to Maryport, or, possibly, as far as St Bee's Head. It would all depend on the time – and if the weather held up, which it promised to do as it seemed very settled after yesterday's storm.

As we drove along the hill path, Aunt Maggie, looking down into the valley, remarked, 'You know, I'm going to miss all this, and more than a little. People just think of Ullswater and Derwentwater and the Lakes when you speak of Cumberland, but there's so much more – places like this, off the beaten track. Sometimes you could imagine you were back at the beginning of things – no wireless, television, planes, or motors.'

'You be thankful there are motors; you wouldn't be going to the coast now if it wasn't for them.'

'Yes, you're right.' I could see Aunt Maggie nodding agreement in her reflection on the wind-screen. She went on, 'But there's one place I do wish we weren't going to, or, at least, that we didn't have to pass – and that's the courtyard. I don't think we've ever once been past there that Cleverly hasn't been at a door, or a window, or some place – watching out. That woman gives the lie to the saying that you can't be in two places at once.'

It was true that we had never once passed the house without glimpsing Flora Cleverly. Perhaps the sound of the car drew her attention, or she just wanted to look at us to see how we were dressed.

Whatever her reason, it brought her into evidence when we passed.

But, as I approached the courtyard that morning, I thought: this is one time we're wrong. And I am sure Aunt Maggie was about to make some comment along these lines when, instead, she said under her breath, 'Ah! Ah! Ah! Ah!'

For Flora Cleverly had not only made a quick appearance at the kitchen door, but came running across the courtyard calling to us.

When I pulled the car to a stop, Flora stopped too, but some yards away, and she called, 'Have you a minute?'

'Yes,' I answered, then waited.

'Will you come for a bit?' The housekeeper was backing away as she spoke.

I pulled on the hand brake. Looking at Aunt Maggie, I muttered, 'Are you coming?'

'No, I'll stay here. Go see what she wants.'

When I alighted from the car, Flora Cleverly had almost reached the kitchen door again, and she turned her face towards me, waiting. But she had gone inside before I reached the door and her voice came to me: 'There's someone would like to see you.' I paused on the threshold and my arm went out stiffly towards the stanchion.

'Come in.'

Slowly, I went into the kitchen. My body was rigid, my heart seemed to have stopped beating; there was an icy numbed feeling from my waist upwards. My throat was not only tight, it felt constricted, as if the muscles had solidified. Before

I turned my eyes to the right, I knew whom I would see.

He was standing at the far end of the long table. Tall, thin, attractive, the charm still oozing out of him. He looked no different from when I had last seen him. Prison had not left any mark on him. There was a soft, almost tender, light in his eyes. Flora Cleverly's voice had been going on all the while but I didn't comprehend what she was saying until my body, demanding breath, forced my mouth open and my ribs to swell as I gulped at the air.

Then I heard Flora Cleverly saying, 'Rosie Talbot said there had been a man asking for someone of your name. He was staying overnight at The Bull, she said, so I went along and looked him up. I thought you would like—'

Ian stepped towards me, speaking my name, and, at that instant, I let out a high scream. I was back where I had started. My body was trembling, I was hanging onto the table for support, and I was yelling, 'Aunt Maggie! Aunt Maggie!' I was aware of the startled look on Flora Cleverly's face, and I was well aware that I was making a fool of myself. But I could not stop.

If I had truly improved in the past three months, I should have been able to tackle this situation; I should have been able to face this man calmly and to talk to him as one adult to another. But Ian was not an adult – he was an overgrown boy – and, as for myself – would I ever be adult, completely adult?

My mouth was open again ready to shout 'Aunt

Maggie!' when I snapped it closed. Regret was already filling me for having acted so childishly.

Ian was talking rapidly now, his cultured tone stabbing each word through me. 'Aunt Maggie or no Aunt Maggie, I'm going to talk to you. I've come a long way. I've been looking for you for weeks. I wouldn't have done that if you had meant nothing, would I? Think – think.'

I was thinking. I was thinking fast. I was addressing the trembling muscles in my body, saying, *'Stop it! stop it! get control of yourself. Show him.'*

I heard a movement behind me in the doorway. Aunt Maggie and someone else – because one set of footsteps moved to the right of me and the other to the left.

Aunt Maggie was now standing by my side. She was staring along the table towards Ian. Her voice sounded very detached as she asked, 'Well? What do you want?'

'I want to talk to my wife.'

The word jolted my body.

Aunt Maggie then said, 'She's not your wife – you know that. Your wife is in Wales looking after your children, I would think – and that is where you should be.'

'I have only one wife – that's Pru, and she knows it.' Ian was staring at me now. 'I'm being divorced, anyway. But divorce or no divorce, I want Pru.'

'Of course you do – and it's quite obvious why. You'll never earn a living on your own. You've got a damn cheek, you know, to say the least,' said Aunt Maggie.

'How did you get here?' The question came from my left. Davie McVeigh was standing close to me and addressing Ian. I could almost feel the heat from his body.

Ian was looking past me now, and it was some seconds before he answered. 'This lady brought me.' Ian indicated Flora Cleverly with a movement of his long hand.

'You! I told you, didn't I? You mischief-making—'

'It's all right, Mr McVeigh.' My voice sounded flat, even calm. 'It had to happen sometime, I suppose. The sooner the better.'

'I can't see what all the kerfuffle is about if he's your husband?' the housekeeper interpolated.

'He's not my husband, Miss Cleverly.' I had turned my body round and was looking full at this mean-faced woman. 'He already had a wife and two children when he pretended to marry me.'

'Whatever I did, I've paid for. I've spent four months in prison, don't you realise that, Pru?'

Ian's voice had brought me round to face him again. I did realise that he had spent four months in prison, but it evoked no pity in me.

'I don't think that it is too much to ask that I talk to you alone,' he whined.

'There you are wrong – it *is* too much!' Aunt Maggie was speaking again.

Now Ian was looking at her, his pale face showing his dislike of her. 'You mind your own business,' he said to Aunt Maggie. 'You're as much to blame for this as anyone – cuddling and pampering Pru – that's all you've done for years. If you wanted someone to nurse, why didn't you get married yourself years ago?'

I had to put out my hands and hang on to Davie McVeigh to prevent him rounding the table.

'Get out of here!' Davie's voice was menacing.

Ian turned his angered face now towards McVeigh and asked, 'Who are you?'

'I happen to be the master of this house – that's who I am.'

Ian's glance lifted from McVeigh's face to rest on mine; it switched back to McVeigh again. Ian looked at Davie steadily for a moment before bringing his glance finally back to me. He said, with an effort at control, 'I want to talk to you, Pru.'

I could feel both Aunt Maggie and McVeigh about to speak when I put in, 'Very well, you can talk to me. Come outside.'

'Pru!'

'It's all right, Aunt Maggie, it's all right.'

As I spoke to Aunt Maggie, I turned from her, but, in moving, my eyes were caught and held for a fraction by those of Davie McVeigh, which were saying: *'Let me deal with him.'* And some part of me answered, *'If only you would.'*

But there was a voice in my head, a wise voice which had been trained under Aunt Maggie's coaching, and it said: *Stand on your own feet. If you don't do it now, you never will. This is neither McVeigh's business, nor yet Aunt Maggie's. You have got to prove to the man who played husband to you that he matters no more, your ability to convince him will affect your future success or failure. Failure will mean that you give way to your nerves. He will return again and again until he breaks you down. Success will mean that no matter how you feel inside, you will remain outwardly calm, you will convince him that you are calm, that he can no longer affect you.*

I was out in the courtyard; Ian was by my side. He was looking at me. I kept walking until I reached the car; there I stopped and faced him. We were standing quite close now, and the trembling sensation had started low down in the pit of my stomach.

Ian's eyes were searching my face. He did not speak for some minutes; then he said, 'Oh, Pru!'

He had the power to turn my name into a caress. It fell on me like a stroking hand; but the trembling in my stomach increased.

'It's wonderful to see you. I've searched for you for weeks.'

'You've wasted your time.' The tone of my voice gave me courage and I went on. 'Listen to me, Ian. Nothing you can say, nothing you can do –' I paused here, then repeated '– nothing – do you hear me? – nothing you can do will ever make me take up a life with you again.'

'I could make you alter your decision – give me a chance, Pru,' Ian insisted.

I now leaned my head slightly forward and to the side as I said quietly, 'I want you to believe this, Ian.

I want you to get this into your head – it will save you a lot of trouble in the future. Now, listen. The very thought of you ever again touching me makes me want to retch – can you understand that?'

I felt at this moment that I was being cruel. As I watched his well-moulded lips compress themselves into a line, I knew a moment of triumph. I had struck home, I had shaken his vanity. I had known for a long while now that the main ingredients that made up this man were charm and vanity. The two essentials for a confidence trickster, and that is what he was – a trickster of women.

His lips curled outwards now as he said, 'Aunt Maggie has done a good job on you; she's toughened you up. She must have worked hard to have achieved so much in so short a time.'

'Aunt Maggie has done no "job" on me, as you call it.'

'Well, if she hasn't, somebody has.' His lip curled further. 'Six months ago you would have been throwing a bout of hysteria, shaking like jelly, or getting fighting mad.'

He was remembering the night when, like a wounded tigress, I had wanted, and tried, to tear him to shreds.

He said now, 'I can't think your steady equilibrium is due to the Cumberland air entirely. It would not have anything to do with the burly landsman back there, would it?' He inclined his head towards the house.

Don't panic, said the voice in my head. *Don't deny it too emphatically. Don't lift your chin or stiffen your back, for he'll see his answer in the signs if you do.*

I said, 'The experiences I had recently will last me for some time. I don't wish to repeat them in any form.'

His lips moved in a twisted smile. 'It was only a thought. Yet, he's not your type, I could never see you going for brawn without brain.'

At this, I felt within me a quick reaction. I found I was resenting deeply the implication that Davie McVeigh should be classed as a man without brains. Again the voice said, *Steady, steady.*

I spoke now in a tone that surprised even me with its calmness. 'I want to tell you, Ian, that if you try to see me again, or pester me in any way, I will inform my solicitor and instruct him to take the matter to court.'

I saw Ian wince as if he had been flicked by a whip. Whatever his experience in prison had been, he undoubtedly did not want it repeated. His head began to wag now, his shoulders jerked. I knew the signs – this was the nasty side of him.

I forestalled anything he was going to say with: 'Miss Cleverly brought you, perhaps Miss Cleverly will take you back to the village. Goodbye, Ian.'

As I attempted to move away from him he took a step towards me. His face was livid below his dark hair, and he said through clenched teeth, 'You've gone the way of the rest of them. You used to be different; now you're as bitchy as they come.'

I did not answer. I looked at him coldly, then turned about. But as I walked away from him, my legs began to tremble, for I should not have been surprised if his hand had grasped me and he had held me while he poured forth abuse.

I knew Ian was still standing watching me when I reached the kitchen door. I dared not look back, but I almost heaved a sigh of relief when I stepped over the threshold. Aunt Maggie was standing where I had left her; Davie McVeigh was over by the window – he must have been watching us all the while. Although I did not look at Davie I was aware that he had not turned towards me. Flora Cleverly was not to be seen.

I said quietly to Aunt Maggie, 'We'll go now.'

My aunt said nothing, but walked past and preceded me into the courtyard again. When I reached the yard once more, there was no sign of Ian, but I felt he was still about, standing in some corner watching me. I knew as I walked to the car that Davie McVeigh too was watching me.

Seated behind the wheel, I said to Aunt Maggie, 'I can't drive.'

'You drive that car, lass.'

'I daren't, Aunt Maggie. I'm shaking so.'

'There's no sign of it,' she said.

I was about to turn and look at her when I stopped myself and stared ahead through the windscreen. No, there was no sign of it. I might be trembling inside, but I wasn't showing it. I had won. I pushed in the gears, released the brake, and drove the car past the yard and up the steep bank.

When we reached the three roads, I stopped and said to Aunt Maggie, 'I can't go into Borne

Coote; I couldn't talk to Talbot now.'

'No, lass, I understand. Let's go straight on to Penrith. We'll see him tomorrow.'

When we reached Penrith, I suggested we should have a drink.

Aunt Maggie agreed. 'And a very good idea an' all. And a bit of lunch with it.'

I did not want to eat, but I forced myself to swallow the food. After the meal was finished, I looked across the table at Aunt Maggie and asked, 'Would you mind if we don't go round the coast?'

'Not a bit.' Then her hand came out and gripped my wrist. 'You did well,' she said softly. 'Splendid. You never need worry again.'

My aunt's kindly tone was almost too much for me; I wanted to drop my head on my arms and cry.

She must have sensed this, for she said, 'Now, now, don't. He's not worth a single thought of yours, never mind your tears. Say to yourself – it's ended finally – for, you know, you were bound to have run across him sometime. I think that's what you've been afraid of, what you've been waiting for – a sort of test.'

She was right as always. I had been waiting for it as a kind of examination, and I had passed my test.

'Let's go home -- let's go home,' I said.

'You don't want to look round the town?' she asked.

'No,' I said. 'Some other time. Perhaps tomorrow or the next day – there's nearly a week left.'

'Only four days,' she replied.

'We can do a lot in four days,' I said.

We had reached the top of the gully road and I was braking the car for the descent when Aunt Maggie, pointing towards the road that led from the village, exclaimed, 'Stop a minute. Look along there.'

I stopped and looked in the direction she indicated, and saw, staggering towards us, in the far distance, a figure which I made out to be that of Roy McVeigh.

'He's drunk.'

'He certainly isn't sober,' I commented.

'Good lord!' exclaimed Aunt Maggie. 'He'll be in the ditch in a minute.'

As I backed the car onto the main road again, Aunt Maggie asked, 'What are you doing?'

'Going to pick him up.'

'I wonder if he'll thank you. The other one wouldn't – not if he were in this state.'

No, I guess Davie McVeigh would not have thanked any woman for picking him up if he were drunk, but Roy was not Davie.

When I reached the swaying figure, I stopped the car and, leaning out, called, 'Hello! Mr McVeigh.'

'Ah, hall-o, there.' Roy stumbled towards the window and leant heavily on it. 'Hallo, there.' He was nodding at Aunt Maggie now.

'Would you like a lift?'

'Bet your life – been celeratin'. Been celeratin'.' He chewed on the words; then grinned as he finished. 'Got the sack – oh, high jinks 'n' low jinks!'

I got out, opened the back door, and assisted him

onto the seat, where he sprawled back laughing.

I turned the car once again so we were going down the narrow steep bank towards the house. I could only catch snatches now of Roy's drunken mutterings, but he was talking about us leaving.

'Lucky-you,' Roy was saying, 'leavin' this godforsaken hole. Money to spend – travel. That's it, travel. Lucky-you.'

When I drove in, the courtyard was empty, but, as soon as I shut off the engine, I knew that the kitchen was not empty, for issuing from it came loud angry yelling. And when the shouting penetrated to Roy McVeigh's fuddled brain, he started to laugh. Flopping over sideways into the corner of the car, he spluttered, 'Here we go! Here we go! Up the McVeighs!'

When Roy made no effort to get out, I went around and, opening the car door, extended my hand towards him. Still laughing, he grasped it and eased himself to his feet, but he would have fallen if I had not steadied him. I cast a quick glance towards Aunt Maggie. She got out and took hold of his other arm.

She said briskly, 'Steady up. Come on now. Steady up,' and began to guide him towards the kitchen door.

As I approached nearer, I recognised Davie McVeigh's angry voice so I tried to disengage myself from Roy's hand. But he would have none of it, and, almost swaying with him, I approached the kitchen door apprehensively for the second time that day. As the three of us could not all pass through together, Aunt Maggie released her hold on him, and Roy, stumbling inwards, took me with him. Our precipitous entry brought the eyes of not only Flora Cleverly and Davie McVeigh upon us, but also the terrified gaze of Frannie. She'd had her face buried against McVeigh's waist, and she now turned her tear-blurred eyes in our direction and held her choking breath as she looked at us. In the temporary, yet vibrant, silence that filled the room I led Roy to a chair. After he had dropped into it heavily, he still held on to my hand.

'You good for nothing, lazy—!'

'You leave him alone.'

Flora Cleverly was moving down the long table now and Davie McVeigh shouted back at her: 'You keep out of this. Once and for all, I've warned you, you keep out of this. As for leaving anybody alone, I'm telling you again, you lay a hand on her, just once more, and I'll shoot you up that hill quicker 'n you've gone in your life afore.'

'An' I've told you –' Flora Cleverly was leaning across the table towards him '– if you don't want her mistreated, then keep her away from here.'

'She'll be here as long as I want her to be,' Davie stated flatly.

'Oh, will she indeed? We're getting somewhere now.'

They were talking as if they had the room to themselves. 'I've knocked at the truth before, and now the door's opening, is it?' Flora continued. 'She's got a right here, has she? Because you're the one that fathered her, eh? You're the one that Bill

Tarrent was looking for! He beat the daylights out of Minnie to get her to give your name.'

'Shut up! Shut that dirty mouth of yours.'

'Shut up, will I? Oh, no! You've brought this into the open, and now I'm going to give it plenty of air.'

'Aunt Flo-ra!' Roy McVeigh's hand was stretching across the table, trying to reach the enraged woman, but she did not see it. Again he said, 'Flora! Don't – don't.'

But Flora persisted. 'That's why Cissie Bradley gave you the go-by, eh? She likely knew you were carrying on with Minnie Amble – or Minnie Tarrent as she became just in time – before you joined up. Deny it, if you can – she's yours, isn't she?'

The housekeeper was pointing to Frannie's trembling back. The girl still had her arms around Davie McVeigh's waist, and he had one hand on her shoulder, the other on the top of her head. He was glaring at Flora Cleverly with undisguised hate and was about to speak when Roy, dragging himself to his feet, stumbled towards Flora. When Roy reached her, he pulled her roughly round to him saying, 'No, no. You're wrong. Leave Davie alone.'

'You go and sit down.'

Flora pushed at him offhandedly, for her mind was not on Roy at this moment – it was filled with her loathing of McVeigh. But, in the next second, Roy brought her full attention to him – he turned from her and leaned despondently on the table with both hands. He muttered, 'She's mine.'

'Be quiet! Get out. Don't be such a damn fool.' This was McVeigh speaking.

Roy, lifting his head, but still supporting himself with his hands on the table, looked towards the burly figure of his brother and said, in slow, measured words, 'It's – time – Davie. The truth is rottin' in me. It's time it was out.' Now he lifted one hand up, and half turning his body towards Flora Cleverly, he stated, 'I'm Frannie's father. Now you know, Flora.'

Aunt Maggie was standing beside me, close beside me, gripping my arm. Davie McVeigh was still holding Frannie to him. He had his head bowed and his eyes closed. Roy McVeigh was still managing to support himself drunkenly with one arm on the table. He did this for one second longer, then Flora Cleverly was upon him.

Her hands gripping the collar of his coat, she pulled him upwards as if he were a wooden puppet, and staring into his face, she cried, 'It isn't true! Swear to me – it isn't true, Roy!'

The woman was actually shaking him now. It seemed impossible that such a thin frail woman could have the strength to shake this man. Although he wasn't as big as Davie McVeigh, Roy was of no mean stature.

'Tell me she's his! Tell me!' she cried hysterically.

'She's mine, Flora. She's mine.'

'No, no!' She still had hold of him, but was shaking her head like a golliwog, repeating, 'No, no! It's impossible, you were only a bit of a lad.'

'I was six-teen – sixteen, Flora.'

'Sixteen!' She heaved him once more towards her before flinging him against the table. 'Sixteen!' she cried. 'You couldn't – you wouldn't. I tell you, I won't believe it.'

'What's it got to do with you anyway?'

Davie McVeigh pressed Frannie from him, and, pushing her gently behind him, advanced towards the other side of the table.

Again Davie asked, 'What's it to you? After all it's none of your business. Up to these last three years, you've been paid as a servant – a superior servant in this house, but you've forgotten your place because right from the beginning you've been given too much authority. But Frannie does belong here, she belongs to us both. Roy's her father, and I'm her uncle.'

Flora Cleverly had been leaning across the table looking up into McVeigh's face as he spoke, and she repeated 'Uncle?' And again, 'Uncle?'

Then, straightening herself and putting her hand across her mouth as if struck by some fearful thought, she repeated yet again, 'Uncle?' Her eyes moving slowly towards the dresser where Frannie now stood, she gazed at the girl as if in horror before she whispered, 'And I'm her grandmother!' As if shocked by her own words, she jumped back and gripped at the sink before yelling, 'Do you hear? I'm her grandmother!' Then: 'No! No! It's not true, it can't be. I won't be.'

When Flora stopped yelling, a silence descended on the kitchen and all eyes were on her. Roy McVeigh, standing with his back to the table now, seemed almost sober, and he would have retreated from Flora if the table had not been in his way, for now she was advancing towards him.

When she was about a yard from him, she stopped and, looking up into his face, she cried, 'Don't you understand?'

Roy shook his head in bewilderment. Like someone speaking under the influence of a drug, he shook his head and said, 'No, Flora.'

'Not "Flora" – "mother" – I'm your *mother*!'

'Oh – my – God!'

It did not sound like a man speaking; it was more like the whimper of a woman. Strangely, Roy did not deny her accusation, but accepted it with the exclamation: 'Oh, my God!'

'Don't believe her.' McVeigh's voice, crisp and stimulating, brought Roy's dazed countenance round to face him. Again, he said, 'Don't believe her. She wants a hold on you. She's making it up.'

'Making it up, am I? I've made lots of things up in my time, but not this. Your father taught me to make up stories; when we ran wild around these waters, he taught me all I know.'

'You're lying. It was wishful thinking – it's still wishful thinking.'

'You know nothing about it, Davie McVeigh. He would have married me if it hadn't been for your grandfather. I might have been your mother, too.'

'God forbid!'

I watched Flora's teeth set; they scarcely parted as she went on, '"God forbid!" you say. Well, let me tell you, I'd have made a better mother than the one that bred you, for she hadn't the guts of a louse. When I went down with him –' she now thumbed in the direction of Roy '– when I went down with him, I told her it was your father's doings and she believed me. She knew he was on the prowl in other quarters, and she never questioned a word I said. She was pregnant herself at the time and she whisked me off to Spain with her – to the very house on the coast where she had spent her honeymoon. And she stayed there; she wouldn't let him come near her. He had made me suffer, but by God I got my own back on him. There was only three days between her confinement and mine. Her child died a few days later, and her with it. I passed mine over as hers – him there.' Flora pointed again at Roy. 'It was easy. An old midwife and a drunken doctor with not a dozen words of English between them.'

'You devil!' Davie exclaimed. 'I could kill you. As for my father – he wouldn't have looked at the side you were on, and you know it.'

'What do you know about it?' She glared at the glowering man opposite her. 'You were a baby then, and he left you with your grannie all your young days.'

'No, I didn't know. But there is someone who did – Talbot. He had your measure from the first. He knew what my father thought – thought about you. He might have had his women on the side, but he made damned sure that you weren't one of them. He loathed you, woman. He only tolerated you afterwards because you ran the house and –' he cast his eyes in Roy's direction '– and saw to him. And it's because of him and what you did for him that I've put up with you all these years – but now, thank

God, it's finished.' He pointed. 'Get upstairs, woman, and gather what belongs to you and then leave this house.'

I watched the wrinkles on Flora Cleverly's face move like rippling sand over the bones, and, at that moment, I could have felt sorry for her. That is, until her lip curled back with the action of a snarling cat and she spat at him: 'You're drawing out the last stave that holds this house together. Everything in the past you've touched has gone rotten on you – I've seen to that! And now you'll never pull up. Your land has gone; the house is mortgaged; you've got nothing to raise a penny on. Yes, I'll go, but, unlike you, I'm not without money. An' I'll sit apart and watch you moulder and rot away.'

I saw that Davie McVeigh was trying to control his rage. He was staring, eyes strained wide, towards her when she turned from him and, looking at Roy with a proprietary air, she said, 'Come on.'

Roy was standing away from the table. He shook his head and blinked his eyes; then he turned and looked at the man whom he had always considered his brother. As Davie McVeigh looked back at him, I saw his expression soften. There was a look of sincere pity on his face. It hadn't taken much observation to gather that, in a way, he had despised Roy, but now he was looking at him as if the severance of an apparent blood tie had left him bereft of something. The look on Roy's face was similar.

Roy, although still dazed-looking, appeared to be sober, and, when Flora Cleverly spoke his name, making it a command as she said 'Roy!' he turned his head slowly towards her, and gazing at her a full minute before he spoke, he said quietly, 'I can't come with you.'

'Roy!' The command was high now.

'It's no use.' He dropped his head. 'I tell you, I can't.'

'I am your mother.'

'That's – that's not my fault. I – I haven't been brought up to look upon you as – as my mother.'

'I've always acted to you as a mother.'

'I can't come with you.' His head was sunk on his chest now.

'Where will you go then?' There was scorn in her words. 'You can't stay here. You have no place here.'

'Are you sure of that?' He raised his head slightly.

'Yes. Yes, I'm sure. Why do you think Talbot's brother, Charlie, left me that money, eh? Because he skedaddled off and wouldn't face up to his responsibilities. Charlie Talbot was your father.' She tossed her head in Davie McVeigh's direction as she ended, 'You are no kin to him. As I said, you don't belong here – come on.'

As Roy's head dropped once again, Davie McVeigh's voice came to him across the table. 'You've a home here as long as you want it, Roy. We've been brought up as brothers, and to all intents and purposes that's what we are – differences or no differences.'

In this moment, something within my breast leapt up and out towards Davie McVeigh. Aunt Maggie must have experienced the same emotion, for the pressure of her hand on my arm tightened until it was painful.

Roy had lifted his head, and the two men stared at each other until their gaze was snapped by Flora Cleverly letting out a sound that rose and ended in a scream. Strangely, she was not screaming at Davie McVeigh, but at Roy.

'You! you fool!' Flora cried. 'Can't you see he's just doing it to get his own back on me? He'll treat you like scum. And what have you here? Nothing. Nothing but work – work and hard tack. And my God, let me tell you, when I'm not here to see to the table, it will be hard tack. Don't be a fool.'

'It's no use, Fl—' Roy hesitated on the name, then said decisively, 'Flora. If I don't stay here, then it'll be somewhere else, but – wherever it is, it – it can't be with you. I'm sorry because I know –' he turned his eyes away '– I know you've been good to me, yet – yet, I must say this. I think I'd have been a better man today if – if it hadn't been for you.'

'You – you ungrateful swine.'

'I know. I know.'

'I could kill you. Do you hear? I could kill you. And after all I've gone through – all I've done – and then – and then for you to say that. And on top of everything, for you to deceive me all these years.' Her voice was rising to a high note again. 'And to think that – that –' Flora jerked her head in the direction of Frannie, where the girl was standing tightly pressed against the dresser '– that can claim relationship with me!'

What happened next took only a matter of seconds, but it jerked us all into horrified action. Flora Cleverly had been standing to the side of the sink. She did not turn her head towards it now, but her hand jerked out, groped at the draining board for a split second, found what it was searching for, a broad-bladed, taper-edged old vegetable knife, and with all her enraged strength behind it, she threw it in the direction of the dresser. I don't know if I screamed or not – I was horror-stricken – but Aunt Maggie did. The knife had been aimed at the petrified Frannie, but it wedged itself in the outstretched upper arm of Davie McVeigh.

As I saw the handle quiver and the blood flowing from his wound, I had a frantic desire to turn and fly out of the room – fly away from all this hatred and rage.

'You're mad, woman! You're insane! Get away! Get away!' Aunt Maggie was crying now. She was standing by McVeigh's side, and I was there also, but I couldn't remember moving towards him.

Davie McVeigh had said nothing; after the shock of the impact, he had not even moved. I saw that his face looked ashen white and his left hand trembled slightly as it went to the handle of the knife. With a sharp tug he drew it out of the flesh and his shirt and arm were reddened immediately by the blood gushing from the wound.

It was Aunt Maggie who took charge now. She sat Davie down; she ripped up towels. She turned to Roy who was again shaking so that you could imagine he had fallen back into his drunken stupor, and she brought him to himself by saying sharply, 'Get on the phone! Get the doctor.'

'It's all right; it's nothing, only a flesh wound.'

Aunt Maggie took no notice of Davie McVeigh, but said again, 'Do as I say, and get the doctor. As for you!' She was winding a towel tightly around the upper part of Davie's arm now, and she turned to address Flora Cleverly – but the far side of the kitchen table was astonishingly empty. The door leading to the hall was open and through it came the sound of an upstairs door crashing closed.

'Have you any spirits in the house?' Aunt Maggie was speaking to McVeigh as she busied herself to staunch the flow of blood.

'In the cabinet in the sitting-room.'

Aunt Maggie was about to ask, 'Will you—?' when I hurried out of the kitchen into the drawing-room, and, after a little searching, found a bottle, one-third full of whisky. But as I carried it back into the kitchen I thought – tea would have been better.

I poured out a good measure of the spirits and handed the drink to McVeigh. When he took it from me, he did not look at me nor speak, but, putting the glass to his lips, he threw off the drink in one swoop, gave a slight shudder, and closed his eyes as he returned the glass to me.

'The doctor says he'll be here in about fifteen minutes.' I was surprised to find Roy at my side. He was looking down at Davie, and he added, 'Oh, man! Oh, I'm sorry.'

'We'd all be much sorrier if the knife had found its mark.'

The two men were again looking at each other, and I shuddered slightly as I realised that Flora Cleverly's aim, but for Davie's outstretched arm, would have caught Frannie full in the neck, for the girl had been too petrified to move. Thinking of her now, I turned towards the dresser. She was still standing there, seemingly unable to drag herself away from its support.

I went to her and, putting my arm about her, said quietly, 'It's all right. No-one's going to hurt you. It's all right.'

Frannie gasped and leant against me.

At this point, Davie McVeigh turned his eyes towards us and asked, 'Will you keep her with you – for the time being?'

All I did was to incline my head in agreement. I knew what he meant by 'for the time being'. What Flora Cleverly had been frustrated in accomplishing once, she was quite capable of attempting a second time.

Now, as if oblivious of us all except the man whom he had always looked upon as his brother, Roy pulled a chair close to McVeigh's, and sat down; their knees were almost touching.

Roy said again, 'Oh, I'm sorry, Davie.' Then lowering his head slightly, he asked, 'Did you know all along about – about us?'

'Forget it – it wasn't your fault.'

'But have you known all along?'

'No. No, I knew nothing about it. I always thought that – that we were brothers and – and, to all intents and purposes, we are.'

'Thanks, man.'

There was an embarrassing silence now, broken by Aunt Maggie ripping more cloth for bandaging.

Then Roy said under his breath, 'I've lost me job; I got the sack. But it's likely all to the good. I'll move on and get something. And I'll – I'll support her. She's mine, and I'll support her.'

'It's a bad time for you to be moving on.' McVeigh was watching Aunt Maggie's hands as he spoke. 'This is my right arm; I'm going to be handicapped with the turning for the next few days.'

'Oh, man, I wouldn't walk out on you; I'll stay as long as you want. I only thought – you would want to get rid of me.'

'Frannie needs an anchor. There's the cottage – we'll talk about it later.'

'Aw, thanks, Davie. Thanks, man. I don't know what to say – only thanks.' His head had drooped further.

McVeigh said briskly, 'The best thing you can do is to go and sleep it off.'

'No, Davie, I'm sober. I've never been more sober in me life.' And getting to his feet and looking in our direction, Roy held out his hand, and said, 'Come on, Frannie.'

The girl, moving slowly from me, caught Roy's hand and went with him. Just as they reached the kitchen door, he looked over his shoulder and said, 'I'll take her home and see the grannie. I'll tell her I'm bringing her back here – all right?'

'All right.' McVeigh nodded. 'But be prepared – she won't like it.'

Aunt Maggie said briskly, 'Don't lower that arm, keep it up.' Then she added more softly, 'How are you feeling?'

'All right.'

'Your looks belie you. I wish that doctor would hurry up.'

'He won't thank you for sending for him for this bit of a cut.'

'That remains to be seen.'

McVeigh, turning and looking up at me now, said quietly, with an unsmiling twist to his lips, 'I don't think any more can happen before you leave.'

'I wouldn't be too sure of that.' This came smartly from Aunt Maggie.

McVeigh, turning his head in her direction, said, 'No. No, perhaps I shouldn't.'

There was the sound of a car coming into the courtyard, and the next moment the doctor was in the room. His manner was casual and easygoing.

He began by saying, 'Hello, Davie, what's happened? Had a kick from one of your Shetland ponies?'

McVeigh made no reply. After the doctor had unwound Aunt Maggie's handiwork, he made no comment either except to indicate that Aunt Maggie should open his bag. Then he set to work stitching up the torn flesh.

The procedure was too much for me. The sight of the needle made my stomach heave. I walked to the window and stood looking out.

'There. There now,' the doctor said quietly. 'That's fixed that. Now, perhaps, you'll tell me how you came by it? You know you were lucky, another hair's breadth and it would have been the artery – not saying anything about the main leader.'

'I had a slight accident.'

'That's evident. How did you come by the accident – if it's not asking too much?'

The doctor had gone to the sink now and was washing his hands. When McVeigh did not answer, Aunt Maggie, after taking a deep breath, said, 'It was a knife thrown at him.'

'Yes?' The old man's head came swiftly round to look at her.

'It's got nothing to do with me,' said Aunt Maggie, using the phrase that people adopt when they go all out to make someone else's business their own. 'But, while you're here, I think you should see Miss Cleverly and give her a sedative of some sort.'

'Oh – oh—?' The doctor was shaking his head. 'Flora? Well, well. As to sedatives—' He turned and looked fully at Aunt Maggie. 'She's lived on them for years. Pep pills versus sedatives; this, I suppose, is the result.'

He was walking towards Davie now and asked, 'What are you going to do about it?'

'Nothing.'

'Well it hasn't been unexpected; she's been ready to blow her top for a long time. Eaten up inside for years. Where is she now?'

'Upstairs,' said Aunt Maggie.

'I'd better have a word with her.'

'Leave her alone, Doctor, she's going, and the sooner the better.'

'All the same, I think I'll have a word with her if you don't mind, Davie. I think I'd better put it to her quietly that she'd better not try any more tricks. I can talk to her; I've had to do it before.'

When the doctor had left the kitchen, McVeigh got slowly to his feet and, addressing Aunt Maggie, said, 'Thanks; you've been more than kind.'

'Nonsense!' she said briskly. 'We just happened to be here. Now we'll leave you for a time, but I'll be back shortly.'

I noticed she did not say 'we' would be back. Before I turned to follow her out of the room, I looked at Davie McVeigh who was standing now, supporting himself against the table.

I asked quietly, 'Will you be all right?'

He nodded towards me. 'I'll be all right,' he said. And then, 'I'll see you presently.' It sounded like a promise.

I went out into the yard and followed Aunt Maggie to the car. As we drove to the cottage, we did not exchange any words, but, as soon as we were indoors, she began to bustle about. As she did so she talked.

'Well, I've witnessed some things in me time,' she said, 'but never any like today's do. Flora Cleverly – Roy's mother! She's a devil of a woman that. And Roy – Frannie's father! I wouldn't have believed that! If it had been McVeigh himself – well, yes, I could have swallowed that. But Roy going after Minnie Amble, and him just a lad, and he couldn't have had anything about him really, no real attraction, not like McVeigh. He's a weakling, Roy is. He

223

doesn't take after her; he must have taken after the father who skedaddled off and took the line of least resistance. When you come to think of it, it's very good of McVeigh to take things the way he did, offering to let him stay on.'

I found to my surprise that I was becoming impatient with Aunt Maggie's incessant chatter. I wanted to be quiet to think. I was also surprised in the way I answered her last remark, for I said, 'Well, it's to Davie's advantage to keep him here now, for as he said he can't do much with one hand, turning that mushroom manure takes all of two hands – he's going to need Roy.'

I was not looking at Aunt Maggie as I spoke, but I felt her stop what she was doing and turn her eyes towards me.

'What's the matter?' she asked. 'Are you feeling upset?'

'No, no. Of course not.' Then sitting down with a plop on the chair to the side of the hearth, I followed this up with, 'Yes. Yes. Of course I'm upset.'

She came and stood near me, saying, 'Naturally, you're bound to be with one thing and another. The quicker we get packed up and away the better you'll like it. It's been a day and a half, and no mistake.'

I had turned my face to the fire with my head resting on my hand. 'She could have killed that child,' I said.

'She could also have killed McVeigh. You heard what the doctor said, although I think that it would take more than a knife wound to finish off Davie

McVeigh. Still I'm really sorry for him. Funny things happen in a crisis like this: I think he's made an ally of Roy; and Talbot will certainly see that he gets all the help necessary. It's indoors they are going to be hard put to it. Janie couldn't cope – not a child of ten. Anyway, she's at school. Flora said they'd have to live on hard tack, and it looks as if they will have to. Still, I suppose they'll get some-body down at Borne Coote to help out. Yet, on the other hand, it isn't everybody who likes cooking and cleaning these days. We are very lucky to have Mrs Bridie, but, of course, she sticks to us because she's a widow and looks upon us as her family.' She sighed and, turning away, said, 'Well, it's their problem. I'm going to make the tea.'

What a day! Everything had happened that could have happened. No, not everything. It was possible that Davie McVeigh could have taken that knife directly in the chest. What if he had? What if he had died? How would I have taken it?

'Don't be silly.'

My admonition had been verbal and, actually, I shook my body as if a hand were on my shoulder trying to force some sense into me. My inner voice commented: *'He's got a two-inch wound in the arm. It's stitched. It's only a matter of days before he'll be using it again. So stop it.'*

It was quite easy to say *'Stop it'*, but not so easy to turn my mind from Davie McVeigh, or to avoid the new knowledge that had sprung at me. As I sat, I kept repeating to myself: *'This is awful – awful. What will I do?'* And I gave myself the answer:

'*Pack up and go right now; there's nothing to stop you.*'

But there was – there was Aunt Maggie. I couldn't understand Aunt Maggie's present attitude. I couldn't understand whether she was for or against McVeigh. One minute she was in sympathy with him; the next, she was telling me that the sooner we went the better. If I said to her now, '*Come on, let's get away from this,*' she would more likely than not say, '*What! Don't you think it would look odd under the circumstances? Like rats running away from a sinking ship.*' I could hear her using that exact cliché.

Aunt Maggie came in now carrying the tea-tray, and she said, as if there had been no break in the conversation: 'I hope the next one he gets will do something to the house. It could be made into a lovely place if a little money were spent on it.'

I did not turn my head towards my aunt as I said, 'Well, he's not likely to have any money to spend on the house, is he?'

'Oh, I don't know. He told me once if he makes a go of the mushroom business, it could be quite profitable.'

'Once,' was all I answered.

On this, Aunt Maggie rounded on me sharply, saying, 'Now, don't be another Flora Cleverly for goodness' sake! Have a little faith in the man. Give him a chance.'

I turned my head and looked up.

'All right, all right, Aunt Maggie,' I said. 'Don't shout at me.'

I felt near tears, and, as she turned to the tea-tray, she muttered, 'Oh, I'm sorry, lass, I think I'm worked up without knowing. It's been a day and no mistake. Well, come on. Let's have our tea and forget about the whole business.'

We didn't forget about the whole business.

It was just on dark when there came a knock at the door. I rose hastily from the table where I was attempting to write, and when I opened the door, there stood Janie.

'Hello,' she said.

'Hello, Janie,' I answered. 'Come in.'

'No, I can't stop. I've just brought a message from Davie. He says – he says, will you not come over this night?'

I screwed up my face as I repeated, '*Not* come over?' making sure I had heard aright.

'Yes,' she nodded. 'That's what Davie says. Flora – Aunt Flora's leaving in the mornin'.' Janie dropped her head. 'She's got a van coming. She's going to take the little tables out of the drawing-room and lots of other things. She says they're hers.'

Aunt Maggie was now standing at the door. She asked, 'And are they?'

'I don't know, but Davie says she can take what she likes so long as she goes.'

'He's a fool.'

Janie made no comment on this, but said, 'He looks sick. Talbot says he should be in his bed.'

'Talbot has come?' I asked.

'Yes, he's in the yard. And Roy's there an' all.'

She smiled now. 'Roy's working hard.'

'I'm glad,' I said. And then I asked, 'Where's Frannie?'

'She's at her grannie's, but she's coming to stay with us. Roy said he'll bring her back tomorrow after – after everything is cleared up. I've got to go; I'm helping. Bye-bye.'

'Goodbye, Janie.'

As we turned back into the room, Aunt Maggie said, 'He's mad for letting her stay the night. She could do anything – burn down the place; even do him in.'

'Oh, Aunt Maggie! Talk about me looking at the black side!'

Aunt Maggie patted my arm and laughed. 'Yes, I know. Still, I'm sorry he said we can't go over. I had my mind made up to slip across and make them a meal.'

'You had?'

She looked me full in the face now and repeated, 'I had.'

It was as I said – I really did not know what was going on in Aunt Maggie's mind from minute to minute. Nor was I more enlightened during that evening. When we parted at bedtime, she kissed me on the cheek but she seemed slightly distant.

I lay in bed and looked over the lake. There was a wild moon riding, but its light was fitful, and, at times, it was obscured by great drifts of white cloud. When this happened, it looked as if I were seeing the lake through misted glass. As I lay there, I wondered whether Roy McVeigh, when he took over the cottage, would sit up here and look out on the moonlight. I doubted it. I could see Davie McVeigh quite clearly doing just that, but not Roy. I could even see Frannie looking out into the moonlight; even though unable to comprehend fully its beauty, she would still look at it. There swept over me at this moment a feeling of nostalgia. I was going to miss the place, for here I had felt some sense of security. Over the weeks, I had gathered strength from my surroundings, sufficient to convince Ian that never again would I be affected by him – and that was no small accomplishment.

Following close on this feeling of nostalgia and in direct opposition to it, I began to experience a sense of regret – regret that we had ever come here, for this new emotion that I had now to face up to, and tackle, would colour my future. I was sick of struggling, sick of fighting – I had fought 'nerves' and fear. Was I now going to be called upon to fight – I'd had enough of that particular emotion, more than enough. Why had it hit me again? And why, I questioned harshly, had the emotion to be directed towards – Davie McVeigh of all men?

It was a long time later that I felt sleep coming to me. The moon was full on my face and I remembered thinking: they say you'll go mad if you sleep with the moon shining on your face. *They say; what say they? Let them say.* I repeated the quotation to myself.

My lids were drooping when, through the mist, I saw a figure walking from the lake over the lawn towards the cottage. Standing out against the dark bulk of him was the white sling that held his arm immobilised. I saw him stop and look up to my window. I had tried to keep Davie out of my mind. But now I was going to sleep; I was dreaming – I need no longer be on my guard.

In my dream, I knelt up on the bed, thrust open the window, and called to him – he came and held out his arms. There was no evidence of a sling now and, for in dreams the fantastic takes on the form of the natural, I stepped over the sill and jumped down to Davie. But my descent was not rapid; I hovered over him in the air, in the manner of a Michelangelo figure on the ceiling of the Sistine Chapel, until, reaching up, he caught me and pulled me down to him. As we embraced, I laughed and laughed, and then I heard my Aunt Maggie's voice coming from a distance saying, 'Wake up! Wake up, Pru!'

I opened my eyes and there she was, saying, 'Wake up! You're dreaming. Wake up, Pru!'

My mouth still wide in laughter, I stared at her until, remembering the dream and the context of it, to the consternation of both of us, I burst into tears.

Getting into the narrow bed beside me, Aunt Maggie held me tightly, saying, 'There, there!' She did not ask what my dream was about, nor did I tell her; and, so, we went to sleep.

The next morning when we woke in the early dawn, Aunt Maggie almost screamed aloud from the cramp in her arm. I had been lying on her arm most of the night.

It was now about eleven o'clock. I had been for a brisk walk in the direction away from the house. We had had our coffee and I was settled at the table making a vain effort to get on with my story. But, somehow, it had gone dead on me; all my characters seemed to be marking time. I found I could not use the vibrant material of yesterday, not even if I camouflaged it. Something had come unstuck.

I was staring at a half-written page when Aunt Maggie said, 'I think I'll go for a dander. Better take advantage of the sun. I don't suppose it'll last for long.'

When she returned to the room with her coat on and a scarf round her head, I barely stopped myself from saying, *'Don't go near the house.'* It would have been a silly thing to say. I knew Aunt Maggie would not go near the place now until she received word from Davie McVeigh.

'Won't be long.' She nodded at me, smiled, then went out, and I was left alone with my unfinished story.

Now, I asked myself, what did I want to have happen to these two people – these two main characters? Usually, my characters took hold of me and led me along their own paths, but not these two. I had to mould them, and they would do nothing without me. But how was I to mould them from now on – how? I got to my feet and walked towards the fire.

I knew how I would like to deal with the characters, yet I couldn't do it. But why not? Simply because, in touching on these two lives, I was arrested by a kind of shyness. I had not been confronted with these problems when writing my other books, but this book was different. My writing, the critics would say when they read it, had lost its sting. Some would welcome this; some would regret it, no doubt. I sat at the side of the fire and turned my gaze down the long length of the room.

Would Davie come here at times in the winter evenings and keep Roy company? Would he start on his carving again? No. He'd likely be too busy poring over books and accounts, attending to ways and means. I would never look at a mushroom but I would think of him walking the lines in the caves or preparing 'the gold bed' – as he had once laughingly referred to the enormous heap of manure lying under the Dutch barn.

When the clock on the mantelpiece struck twelve, I turned my face to the window. There was no sun now; the sky was heavy again with rain; and I thought: if Aunt Maggie doesn't get back quickly, she's going to get caught in it.

At half past twelve, my aunt still hadn't returned and the rain had started. I went to the door and stood under the porch roof, looking first to the right and then to the left. I didn't know which road she had taken, or by which she would come back. She might have gone round the hill by the Big Water, or through the back way up to the crossroads. She wouldn't, I assured myself again, have gone in the direction of the house. At this thought, my head turned automatically towards the copse. Then I heard the breaking of brushwood underfoot and thought: she *has* been that way, and I added a mental *tut! tut!*

When the figure emerged from the copse, it was not Aunt Maggie but Davie McVeigh. He hesitated a second when he saw me, then came on, and, as he advanced, I tried to recall the dream I'd had the night before. It had been an odd kind of a dream – he'd been in it, and I'd awakened laughing – then I'd cried. But, like all dreams, it had seeped away when exposed to daylight.

'Hello.' Davie was standing, looking down at me.

'Hello. How are you feeling? How is your arm?'

'Oh, all right. Give it another two or three days and it'll be back to normal.'

'Won't you come in?'

I turned and walked into the room, and he followed me and closed the door. I went straight towards the fireplace and stirred up the logs.

I said, 'Aunt Maggie isn't in, she went for a walk. I'm afraid she'll get caught in the rain. I was looking for her.'

When Davie made no comment, I twisted my head round to see him standing a yard or so behind me. Once more I paid attention to the fire, and, as I replaced the poker, I asked, 'Won't you sit down?'

Again there was no response. When I straightened up and turned about, it was to find him standing squarely before me. He was looking into my face and I into his. Why had I ever thought him big, burly, and roughlooking? His eyes were soft; his lips were kind; his hair, at this moment, held an almost irresistible attraction for my hands – like a magnet, it drew them; I wanted to run my fingers through it. I clasped them tightly and became overheated at the thought.

Could this be me? Wasn't once enough? Hadn't I been through all this before—? But no, I hadn't been through this before. Ian's charm had flattered my intellect while he picked my brains. My present feeling did not touch my intellect, but played heavily on my heart.

'We should talk,' Davie said.

What a strange thing to say.

'Should we?' I asked.

What a silly thing to say.

'I'm not much good at charming platitudes.'

'No?'

'No. I'm going to ask you a question; just answer yes or no.'

My eyes were blurry from staring into his face. The pumping of my heart seemed to be forcing that organ up into my windpipe, making breathing difficult. His features were now becoming slightly indistinct as if a thin veil of mist were floating over them. It was like the mist that covered the grass on the morning that I walked to the Big Water.

'Will you have me?'

What had he said? Would I have him? Not, *'I love you, my beautiful'* as Ian had said. *'I want you; I need you; I can't live without you.'* On, on and on. I, I, I. Nothing like that, just – 'Will you have me?' There was a humility about the question that created a sharp pain, like a jab underneath my breast. Where was the big brash individual who had nearly blasted me off the road on that memorable Sunday? There was no trace of him. The man behind the iron façade was a shy, even humble, being, and a man who knew fear. I had knowledge of the fear, but I had not dreamt of the shyness. Nor had I ever imagined him capable of humility – *'Will you have me?'*

I could not get my answer past my throat. I felt myself swaying gently, then, with an inarticulate cry, I was pressed against him. As his good arm went about me, I seemed to sink right into the warm depth of him. For a full minute we stood pressed close, tightly, tightly close, then, slackening his hold slightly, and with a movement of his cheek against my hair, he brought my face round to his. It was a strange moment, that moment before we kissed, and, then, it was not a long kiss, nor passionate – rather it was tender, tender with the promise of an unusual, compelling love that would control our lives. My head dropped back on his arm.

I was gazing up at him when the trembling started in my stomach. But it was not the signal of fear this time, but of laughter, which I tried to check. This was not the moment to laugh. I was back in the dream – in his arms, and laughing. For a moment, I saw perplexity on his face and a look almost of horror, as if I had been playing a game with him. Then the laughter in me changed and I repeated the performance of last night. A second later, I was sobbing helplessly and we were sitting on the couch, my head buried in his shoulder, and Davie was soothing me as he would have comforted Frannie; only he was using different words.

'Oh, my dear. Darling, darling. Don't, don't. It'll be all right. There's nothing to be afraid of, I'll promise you that. You'll never have need to be afraid of me. I cannot believe that you love me. I don't think you do. I don't expect it – not yet. But it will come. I promise you – don't – don't cry any more.'

'Oh, Davie, Davie, it'll be all right, won't it? Things will work out all right, won't they? I'm – I'm frightened.'

Moving his hand out of the sling, Davie lifted my chin and, looking at me, said quietly, 'I can't speak for you, Pru.'

It was the first time he had used my first name.

'I can only answer for myself,' he continued, 'no matter what has gone bad on me before, this is one thing I know that will work out. There are only a few things we're sure of in life. Death is one. With me, there is another – and this feeling I have for you is it. I know, deep in here.'

Davie brought my hand and laid it so I could feel his hard chest – his seared chest. Again we looked deep into each other's eyes. And, again, his lips dropped to mine.

All I could mutter now was, 'Oh, Davie, Davie.'

Making an effort not to start on another bout of weeping, I tried to return to the commonplace by saying, 'I wonder what Aunt Maggie will say? She should be in at any moment.'

Davie was holding me tightly as he said, 'I don't think she will be.'

'What – what do you mean?'

'Just that she won't be in at any moment. She's busy making the dinner. It'll be ready by now, I should say.'

Davie had turned his head to one side but not before I saw the twinkle in the shaded depth of his eyes.

'Aunt Maggie – making the dinner?'

'Yes.' He was gazing at me again and he began to smile. '*Aunt Maggie* came over about half past eleven. Flora Cleverly and her vanload of what she termed her belongings had just left the yard when your aunt made her appearance. I've an idea she had been watching – and waiting.'

'Aunt Maggie!' My voice was high.

'Yes – Aunt Maggie.' His face was twisted with laughter now. 'She's a remarkable woman – Aunt Maggie. She's already reconstructed the kitchen. She's having a new cooker put in, all the old cupboards pulled down, and units put up. She's got all her own furniture mentally placed in the house, and, you'll be happy to know, we are to have a new water system and bathroom.'

I was holding one hand tightly across my lips. All I could do was to shake my head slowly in wonderment.

'Your – or *our* – Aunt Maggie is, as I've said, a very remarkable woman. She tells me that, if the business of Flora had not arisen yesterday, she still had no intention of leaving here.' He moved his head to indicate the cottage.

'Oh—?' I bowed my head and bit my lip. Then I said slowly, 'Wait till I see her!'

'Then we'd better go now. The dinner will be waiting, and I wouldn't like to hear what she'll say if it's spoiling.'

Davie drew me to my feet, and, as we made for the door, his arm was about me. He said casually, 'And, oh, by the way, we're going to have another addition to the family – a Mrs Bridie who, Aunt Maggie says, works like a Trojan.'

I stopped. 'Oh, Davie!' I shook my head. 'I'm sorry for you.'

With a pull of his arm, I was caught tightly to him again. 'Go on feeling like that. It's not enough that you give me an aunt, a housekeeper, and –' he paused '– a wife. Go on feeling sorry for me, and I will spend my days wallowing in it.'

'But you said you didn't want anyone to feel sorry for you.'

'And I don't – not *any*one – only you, Mrs David Bernard Michael McVeigh. You remember when I saw you for the first time?'

I put my head back and laughed, a free young laugh. Did I remember? David Bernard Michael

McVeigh? *My* David Bernard Michael McVeigh? I put my hands up and ran my fingers through his hair.

'Oh Davie! Davie!' It was the wrong thing to do with Aunt Maggie waiting . . .

THE END

HOUSE OF MEN

Catherine Cookson

CORGI BOOKS

1

As I dressed, my hands shook slightly, as they always did when I was excited, but it was a long while since I had felt excitement over anything – two years, in fact. The excitement then had ended in pain, humiliating pain. I had wanted no more excitement; all I wanted was to live my life out quietly in this cottage high up on the wild fells, with my dear parents for companionship. At twenty-seven years of age that is all I wanted. Sometimes I had to tell myself that I was only twenty-seven and was young enough to forget and to snap out of it. Still young enough to like people and want to be among them as I once had. But all the telling in the world didn't alter the fact that I was now half afraid of people – at least, of the impersonal horde of the town, of even the less impersonal group in the office. Perhaps the latter more so because of their curiosity. 'Why,' they would ask, 'don't you ever go to a dance?' 'Why don't you stay and do a show?' 'Why don't you take up something at night school?' To all this I had one answer. We lived too far out of Alnwick. We were miles even from Shilbottle or Newton. In any case, it took me nearly two hours to get home, for whichever way I went I had a mile and a half to walk over the fells to my home. 'But why,' they would probe, 'did your people want to go and live out in the wilds? It isn't fair to you.' Sometimes I had replied angrily, 'Nor were the pits fair to my father; he didn't deserve silicosis.' I never went on to tell them that the other reason we lived in the outlandish spot was because the cottage, owing to its isolation, had been selling at a gift price, and my mother, who had had a longing all her life to own the four walls that surrounded her and the land they stood on, had taken a plunge and mortgaged three hundred pounds. She would not at the time take the money I had saved, for she said I would be needing it for my wedding. But, as it turned out, I didn't need it. And so I paid off the mortgage on the cottage, and with my wage and my parents' double pension – they were both over sixty-five – we lived a comfortable existence. That is, when I reached home, for the journey over the past few winters had told on me. But if the journey I was about to take this morning proved successful it might mean the end of that long tramp to and from the bus each day.

It was Rodney Stringer, the baker in Rothcorn, who had said to me some weeks ago, 'Bill Arnold is looking for a part-time bookkeeper and typist and such. His building business is growing and he can't see to the books himself, not with his wife being ill and that. Now if you could get another part-time job near at hand it would save you this trek every day.'

Rodney had been giving me a lift in the bread van when he said this, and I had smiled at him and said, 'Yes, if I could get another part-time job, but you know yourself they're as rare around here as gold mines.'

I had always been able to talk to Rodney, even on occasions to laugh with him, but never at him, as some of the villagers did. Too soft to clag holes with. That was their opinion of Rodney. This I knew was because he had allowed himself to be pursued, was even on the point of being bullied into a promise of marriage by Hazel Osborne. Hazel had been born and bred in the village; she had married the village carpenter and odd-job man. Unfortunately, after two years he had died. Some folks put it unkindly and said he had escaped, but, whichever it was, it left Hazel with a young baby and an ardent nature, and with a reputation for hot temper and peevishness. Hazel, at thirty-two, realised that her chances of remarriage were few and far between, so fastened on the most pliable male in the small community, who happened to be Rodney Stringer, the baker. I don't think there was anyone in the village who didn't warn Rodney that Hazel was after his blood.

But Rodney was one of these kind men who couldn't bear to say no or hurt anyone's feelings. And he had almost become Hazel's property when we came to live on the fells above the village of Rothcorn. But after he was seen giving me a lift for the third time in a week, the men in *The Fox and Hounds* began laying bets on Hazel getting her nose put out. Mrs Bailey in the post office gave me this information. I didn't tell her that they would lose their bets, nor, on being given this information, did I shun Rodney, because I had no fear of any overtures from him. I recognised him as a natural, kindly soul, and not so soft and pliable as he allowed the villagers to imagine.

But that he had a deep interest in me and my welfare at heart I had proof of, and only yesterday at the latest, for, meeting me, supposedly by off-chance, at the foot of the fell, he showed me an advert in the *Northumberland Times*, which read: 'Wanted: part-time secretary to writer. Apply Maurice Rossiter, Tor-Fret House, near Long Framlington, Northumberland.'

'But, Rodney,' I had said, 'it's only part-time; I must have a full-time job.'

'Bill Arnold'll take you on. I asked him afore I came up. Only too glad, he said; he's up to the eyes.'

'You are kind, Rodney.'

I had touched his hand, but only for a second, for the colour had risen in his face and he had said quickly, 'It's nowt. It's nowt at all.' And then he added, 'Why don't you phone them and ask for an appointment? I'll take you down to the call-box at Biddys Cross and you can do it from there, eh?'

I became smitten with his enthusiasm and so I let him take me to Biddys Cross, where I phoned the advertiser, Maurice Rossiter, with the result that at ten o'clock on this Saturday morning I was to go to Tor-Fret and see this man.

My mother's voice came from the foot of the stairs at this moment, calling quietly, 'It's ready, lass.'

'I won't be a minute,' I called back. I was washed and dressed, but I decided against putting my make-up on until I had had my breakfast, and so it was actually only a minute or so later when I went down the narrow stairs which led directly into the living-room. A room bright with china and brass, and sunshine; made comfortable with a couple of good rugs and three easy chairs, and made interesting with a piano and one wall completely lined with books.

My father was already seated at the breakfast table, which was set under the window, and, his face turning towards me, he pointed outwards, saying, 'What do you bet I can't see Coquet Island and the lighthouse? The air's as clear as glass. Look. Look there.' He was bending towards the window now.

I sat down opposite to him, and I, too, bent forward and looked out on to the scene that was both majestic and beautiful, for now the sun was softening the fells where they rose one behind the other, mighty shelves of rock, driving forever onwards, touched here and there with grass and heather, and defying anyone at this moment to imagine them blotted out by wet fret or mist so thick that its weight lay on you; or wind-driven snow that blinded your eyes and sealed your lips with ice. And this could happen in a few short weeks from now, for we were at the end of September.

My father was saying, 'Look . . . that speck out there against the blue . . . Down there . . . look.'

'Don't be daft,' put in my mother as she placed the teapot on its stand on the table. 'You'll be thinking next you're seeing Alnwick Castle.'

'That's the Head, or if it isn't it's the Island. I bet you what you like an' I bet I could see Alnwick Castle a morning as clear as this, but I'd have to look t'other way,' he laughed.

'Get your breakfast now and don't be silly.' My mother sat down and began to pour out the tea.

My mother's voice always held a sharp note that would have made a stranger imagine there was no softness in her, and there they would have been gravely mistaken. She was generous-hearted was my mother, and gentle and kind. But she put on a brusque front like the front that lots of women put on when their men are hale and hearty, and working. She kept this front for my father to give him the idea that he was no less a man than he had always been, and it worked well, for my father did not pity himself. Although he couldn't walk far and could never go down into the village unless he was sure of the help of a strong arm to bring him back up the fell, he occupied himself in a thousand and one ways in his 'miner's mansion', as he sometimes referred to our five-roomed cottage.

My father looked at me now and said, 'You're

going to have as far to walk if you get it. Have you thought of that?'

'Oh, I won't have as far,' I said. 'Not half as far. In the summer, or even on good days in the winter, I could go upwards' – I pointed out of the window to the right – 'over Neete Fell. I could get down to the valley that way. I could do it in half an hour, too. And in bad weather I could get a bus from the village to either Long Framlington or Swarland, whichever road is best. I'll have to find out, anyway.'

My mother nodded at me and said, 'Well, when you see him don't let him beat you down. Some of these writers are as mean as muck, I'm told.'

'Oh, Mother.' I laughed at her but said nothing more, for I couldn't see myself haggling with this unknown writer. And, anyway, I was quite prepared to have my wages reduced in order to save myself the wearing journey in the coming months.

A short while later, they both came to the door to see me off, and my mother put out her hands and picked an imaginary thread from the lapel of my suit as she said, 'I'm glad to see you put on your grey. It's a nice cut.'

'Shows off your figure,' said my father. 'An' you've got a grand figure.'

'Be quiet,' said my mother. 'She knows what kind of a figure she's got. Go on now.'

As she pushed me gently forward she bent and kissed me swiftly on the cheek; at the same time my father's hand came on my arm with a gentle pat, and I left them and walked down the rough road between the sloping banks of grass and heather. And when I came to the steep incline that would take me from their sight, I turned and waved to them. They were standing outside the door close together, and they waved as vigorously as if I was leaving them for ever. And I might have been. Little did I know that morning that I might have been doing just that.

There were two paths leading down from our house. The one I was on now brought me just outside the village on the south side, and I always used this one because it was easier to get the bus this way. The other one was slightly longer and met up with the main road on the north side of the village – about a mile, I should say, from the village proper.

Some time later, when I reached Rothcorn, I stood in the little main street among the irregular grey-stoned houses waiting for the bus. And as I waited I was hailed by first one, and then another. Mrs Bailey came to the post office door, which was also her front door, and shouted, 'Grand morning, isn't it?' And I called back across the road, 'Yes. Yes, it's a grand morning.' And Bill Arnold from his yard farther along the street, hearing her voice, put his head around the gate and, seeing me, said, 'Hello there.' And then he added, 'I hope you get it.'

And I called back, 'Yes, yes, so do I.'

And Mrs Bailey, picking up his words, repeated them as she looked towards me again calling, 'Yes, an' I hope you get it an' all.'

This brought Mr Shennel, the butcher, to the front of his window, even though he was in the process of serving a customer, and he raised his hand. As I answered the salute I was well aware that before I returned to the village the whole of Rothcorn would know that I had been for an interview with the younger Rossiter of Tor-Fret.

It was strange, but up till yesterday I had never heard the name of Rossiter, and only once had I seen the name Tor-Fret. That was one Sunday last year when I had gone over the top of Neete Fell and crossed down into the other valley, where, after passing some dense woodland, I came abruptly upon a pair of rusty iron gates hanging from high pillars, on which, at one time, had stood two stone birds. One now lay on its side, its legs dangling over the edge of a pillar, while the other lay some distance away on the grass. At either side the land stretched away flat except for the woodland on the left, and there was no evidence of a road beyond the gates. One could be forgiven for imagining that they were the last remains of an old estate. Bitten into the stone of each pillar was a word – 'Tor' on the one, 'Fret' on the other. I found out, on enquiry, that these gates had at one time been guardian to the main drive to the house, but they hadn't been used for years now.

The voice on the phone last night had said, 'Take the bus towards Long Framlington, and ask to be put down at Peter's Well. The road from there leads straight up to the house.'

Half an hour later I was walking up this road. The sun was shining brightly, I was slightly warm and very nervous. The road wound steeply upwards around the brow of a hill, and from one point I could make out the dark blur of the wood where it covered the fell far away to the left of me. That would be where the iron gates were. And then I was walking between outcrops of rock, hedge-high for quite some distance, but still there was no sign of a house. Then, turning another sharp bend in the road, I almost fell over a pair of legs stretched out across my path. I let out a stifled squeal. It was hard to say who was the most surprised, the man sitting with his back to the rock wall or myself. After regarding each other with different degrees of amazement for some seconds, it was he who spoke first. 'You lost ya way?' he said.

'No, I don't think so. This is the way to Tor-Fret, isn't it?'

'Aye, it is an' all. But what be you doin' on the road to Tor-Fret . . . eh?'

I was inclined to say, 'That's my business,' when he swung himself over on to his two hands and with his corduroy dusty buttocks sticking upwards he slowly straightened himself and confronted me. He was a good head taller than myself – and I was five feet seven – with a thin face covered with a ragged beard, two small bright eyes, and clothes in which he had evidently spent the night.

'Who are ya? Who ya goin' ta see? . . . The Big Fella . . . Logan?'

I was about to answer when again he interrupted, stating, 'You'll get no change out of 'im. You on a begging spree, or somethin' . . . charity like?'

'I'm going on business.'

'Aal reet, aal reet. Divn't get cocky. I was just askin'. I knaw a lot aboot them up there. Could put you reet if you hadn't been near the hoose afore. Aa'll tell ya now for nothin' though: you'd better keep away from the back door or Hollings'll give ya his boot in your backside.'

I bestowed on my informant a look that I hoped would put him in his place and moved briskly on. It didn't, because his rumbling laugh came at my back. I was, although I tried to pretend otherwise, more than a little frightened. He was a queer creature. The fells bred characters, I knew, but he was definitely odd.

It was a good fifteen minutes since I had left the main road; and I was just thinking that I was jumping out of the frying pan into the fire by imagining this new post would shorten my trek, when I saw the house. It was made of local stone and was long and flat-faced. Lying somewhat back from the front façade at each end was a wing that broke the austerity of the whole. The house stood on a natural plateau of rock, smooth and flat enough to have been converted into an enormous terrace. I had come upon the house from the right-hand side, and edging this terrace at the far side was what appeared to be gardens, but from this distance they looked a tangle of shrubs and weeds.

Remembering the warning of the odd man back on the road I made my way towards the front door, but in doing so I had to pass two sets of long windows. It was as I passed the second two nearest the front door that the voices came to me. Two men's voices talking rapidly, apparently trying to talk each other down. When I stood under the pillared porch, the voices were still distinct. Then one voice alone was speaking and it said, 'Julian was an excellent secretary, and he didn't mind the conditions.'

Naturally these words caught my attention and they were followed immediately by the other voice. This voice was deep and cold sounding. It said, 'No, but I did. He was costing much more than we can afford and you know it.'

'I told you I'd square up when this one comes out. Becker says it's nearly bound to go.'

The other voice was even colder now, and deeper, the tone scathing. 'Nearly . . . If I remember rightly, he said that about the last two. I told you before that your work won't have any appeal until you forget yourself and widen your scope. You're not the only one in the world that's handicapped.'

In the blank silence that followed this, I looked about me for a bell. All I saw was a long iron rod going through a ring. The top end of the rod disappeared into the stone roof of the porch. As I pulled on this ancient contraption, what I thought of as the 'nice' voice came again, saying, 'I liked Julian, that's why you made it impossible for him.'

'Different species are housed in different ways.' The cold voice was speaking in an ordinary tone now. 'You put a dog in a kennel, and if you must keep a tiger you get a cage. We have no boudoir in the house – not as yet, anyway – and when we do acquire such a room there will, I hope, be the right specimen in it.'

'I hate you when you're being clever.' There was the sound of rage in the nice voice now.

'And at other times.'

'Yes, by God! And at other times, too!'

I pulled on the bell again, twice now, sharply. I could hear no distant jangle, but what I did hear was a door banging, and then almost instantly the front door was pulled wide and I was confronted by . . . The Big Fellow. The odd man's description sprang to my mind as I looked up into the dark countenance glaring at me.

'Good . . . good morning. I'm . . .' My nervous voice did not finish before the man said, 'Oh yes. Yes. Come in. You're early.' He looked at his watch. Ten o'clock it was . . . 'Come in.' His voice seemed to jerk me through the door and into the hall. 'In here.' He pushed open a door and stood aside to allow me to enter, and when he had closed the door behind me he stood looking at me for a moment very much in the way I had seen farmers look at penned cattle in Alnwick Market. His eyes moved from my feet upwards to the crown of my head. Then they came down again to hold, penetratingly, my wide-eyed stare. For staring I was; I couldn't help but stare at this man. He was tall, say six feet one or two, and broad with it, yet his bigness did not emanate from his size alone. Perhaps the impression of largeness came from his deep voice, or was it from his face? He had an outsize of a nose – my father would have called it a neb. His eyes were dark brown and deep-set. His mouth was thin and long, and I noticed the upper lip had been slit at one time, for from the left corner to about an inch up the cheek was a white seared mark which, strangely enough, gave the lip the illusion of an ever present smile, not a sneer as one would expect. But a sneer, I thought, would have gone better with his voice and manner than a smile.

'What is your name? I didn't quite catch it last night on the phone.'

'Mitchell. Kate Mitchell.'

'Oh . . . Kate.' There was even a wrinkle of distaste to his nose. 'He won't like that. I mean my brother. It is my brother who is the writer.'

I felt my chin moving upwards. For a second my indignation at his rudeness took away my nervousness. I, too, wasn't struck on my name, but it was my mother's name and if for nothing else was worth defending.

I said with a touch of what I hoped was quiet hauteur, 'I have never known anyone else object to my name. And it doesn't interfere with my typing.'

He had lowered his eyes, but they lifted quickly to mine now and he stared at me fixedly for some seconds before he said, and quietly now, 'I'm sorry. But my brother is . . . well, he's a little temperamental. I had better explain. He had polio some years ago and it left him crippled down the left side. Because of his handicap he has been humoured a great deal, you understand?'

No, I didn't, and when I made no answer he went on, 'What wage are you expecting?'

'Well, say four pounds. I could do three hours a morning for five mornings . . . That would cover part of my bus fare, too.'

'I don't suppose he'd want you in the mornings, it would be mostly in the afternoons. He's not too good in the mornings. Well, four pounds, that would be all right.'

Not only because it would be a much better arrangement for me if I could come here in the morning and work for Bill Arnold in the afternoon, but also because I had an unaccountably strong desire to stand up to this man that I spoke now as I did. This alone was surprising, for I was not of an aggressive nature. There was only one man in my life who had made me feel I wanted to hit back, and that was over. But I now said, 'This house is a long way out, and if I came in the afternoons it would mean going home in the dark in the winter. It wouldn't be very pleasant. I don't think I can see my way clear to . . .'

His voice cut me off sharply, when with raised hands he said, 'All right, all right, we'll go into that later. You had better see him first.' Abruptly he turned his back on me only to turn and face me as quickly again, and the side of the lip with the cut in it was uptilted further as he said, 'And don't look so much like a frightened rabbit. That show of defiance was too thin. If you hope to survive with my brother you've got to have a mind of your own and show it to him.'

Again his back was towards me, again he was holding the door open for me, and I stepped into the hall without looking at him and followed him across it.

If I took in the conditions of my surroundings it was unconsciously, for, to put it mildly, I was almost overwhelmed with apprehension, and then The Big Fellow – it was strange, but right from the first I thought of him in my mind by this title – ushered me into a large light room which I saw immediately faced the great expanse of rocked terrace and was the room from which I had earlier heard the argument. And there, his face half turned from me, I saw Maurice Rossiter for the first time.

'Well, there you are.' It was a brusque introduction and farewell at the same time, and before I had time to turn and say a stiff thank you, the man had left the room and I was staring across the wide space towards the most beautiful face I had ever seen in my life. The eyes that looked at me were blue and wide apart. The nose was straight, the mouth thin, but the lips had shape to them. The skin was not pale, like that of an invalid, but cream-tinted, like a delicate shade of sun-tan you see on some women. But it was the shape of the face that gave it its beauty – the bone formation. Years ago, when we had lived in Durham, I went to art classes and I remember being told to copy in detail the light and shade of a skull, and I remember marvelling at what was under our skin. The uncanny thing about this face was that it showed itself to be akin to that of The Big Fellow. The features in both cases were strangely alike, but here they were filed down, melted as it were into softness. The only flaw in the beauty of this man was in his mouth, for it drooped noticeably at the corners.

'Please come over here and sit down.'

I walked towards him and sat down and felt, quite suddenly, at my ease.

'You must excuse me not getting up; I don't move unless I've got to. It's very bad for me. I should keep on the move, they tell me, but I'm naturally lazy.' He smiled at me and I smiled back, a wide friendly smile. Because that is how I felt . . . friendly towards this man.

'What is your name?'

I hesitated, then said quietly, 'Kate Mitchell.'

His blue eyes were looking into mine, and the corners of his mouth came up and he repeated as his brother had done, 'Kate?' but in what a different way could not be imagined. Again he said, 'Kate?' And then he smiled as he said, 'You know, you look like a Kate . . . But please—' He put out his hand which, unlike his face, was not beautiful, being short and thick, even podgy, and he went on, 'But please, I don't mean to be rude. The Kate I mean is . . . well, sensible, shrewd and . . . rather beautiful in a way . . . Am I being really offensive?'

I found myself saying quite glibly, 'No woman is offended when she is told she is beautiful, but in this case I know it is a very kind exaggeration.'

And I did know it was such. I knew I was sensible; I did not think I was shrewd. I would not have been taken in so easily if I had been shrewd. As for being beautiful . . . no, I had what is called a nice face – a kind face you could say. My best feature was my grey eyes, and yet they were my weakness, for I could not control their expression. Whatever I felt I showed in my eyes. And at this moment I was showing that I wasn't offended or displeased, and the man opposite to me let his head rest against the high back of the chair and gave a sigh before saying, 'You know, I'm glad you came. I must be quite truthful and tell you that I wasn't anticipating your visit. Even now you are an unknown quantity. Like the renowned Kate you may have the temper of a shrew, who knows? And I may experience it when I work you too hard. Yet I have the feeling we will work well together . . . that is if . . .' He pulled himself from the back of the chair and bent his head towards me, smiling quizzically as he repeated, 'That is if you can type from my scribble, and take shorthand from my speedy orations.'

'I have a pad in my bag. Would you . . . would you like to give me a test now?'

'Yes, yes. Go ahead.'

I wasn't prepared for the speed at which he spoke, and I was sure he was doing it to test me. Twice I had to stop and ask him to repeat a word. After about three minutes he stopped and said, 'That will do. Read it.' After I had read the letter through he nodded his head slowly twice, saying, 'Very good, very good. Julian couldn't have done that . . . Julian was my last secretary. He lived here for a time . . . Now I'll get you to type one of my usual sheets.' As he made to rise I asked hastily, 'Can I get it for you?' And he paused in a twisted position as he gripped the arm of the chair, and, turning his head towards me, he said, 'If you are to work for me you will have to get used to my shuffling, so I had better give you a demonstration of it now.'

I did not speak but watched him pull himself up and then move towards the desk. With each step the straight right half of him was dragged over sideways to accommodate the shrunken left side of his body. And the effect was weird; it was as if he was doing a step of a grotesque dance, and when the action was repeated again and again it sent a chill through me, and the feeling did not ease until, at the desk, he turned and faced me, saying, 'Come and try this.'

The thin spidery writing not only filled the quartosized sheet of paper but went down the margin on the right-hand side, along the bottom and up the other side. As I looked at it he said, 'I haven't picked you a bad sheet.'

I sat down at the side table where the typewriter was, and I thought as I put the paper into the machine: If this wasn't a bad sheet, then I wouldn't like to see one that was. It took me a long time to do the sheet, nearly fifteen minutes, during which time he did not speak but sat watching me. This brought back the feeling of nervousness. But when at last I handed him the page and a half of clean script he merely glanced at it, but smiled at me and said, 'I don't think we need worry, need we?' Then turning from me, he added, 'I suppose my brother has dealt with the matter of fees?' He did not term it wages.

'Yes. We agreed on four pounds.'

'Four pounds!' His face came round to me, one eyebrow raised. The whole face had a cynical look now which marred its beauty, but I did not blame him for feeling like this towards his brother, for the man had got my back up immediately.

'Ah, well.' The smile was once again on his face, and his head went back as he said, 'You must have a drink of something before you go, you've had a long trek. Coffee or tea? Which is it to be?'

'Thank you. I'd like a cup of coffee.'

He took a hand bell off the table, the handle of which I noticed was made from the hoof of some animal, and, hobbling with his weird gait the full length of the room, he opened a door and rang the bell. I could hear the noise jangling through the house. By the time he had returned and placed the bell on the table there came through the door he had left open a wizened-looking man with white hair. He could have been anything from fifty to eighty years old. Even before Maurice Rossiter said, 'Would you bring two cups of coffee, Hollings?' I knew this was the man whom the queer person on the road had warned me against disturbing. The man was looking at me much in the same way as had Logan Rossiter, in a scrutinising, weighing-up sort of way. And he did not turn on the order he had been given, but continued to look at me until my future employer said, 'I'd better introduce you. This is Hollings. He keeps the house and everybody in order; don't you, Hollings?' The man did not reply, and Maurice Rossiter said with a slight edge to his voice, 'This is Miss Mitchell. She'll be coming here some part of every day to do my work.'

The man moved his eyes and looked at Maurice Rossiter, one long penetrating look, then turned away. He had not spoken, and when the door closed on him, Mr Rossiter smiled and said, 'You'll get used to Hollings. I had better warn you though: he has the idea that Tor-Fret and all it holds is his property. You see . . .' He took a long breath and motioned me to sit down opposite to him again before he continued. 'You see, like all of us he was born in this house. His father served my grandfather, and he and my father ran the moors together as boys. They fished the Coquet, vying with each other for the biggest salmon catch. They rode and shot together. I understand they were more like brothers than if they had been real brothers – for my father had three brothers of his own, but he seemed to prefer Hollings. Well, my father is dead, but his brothers are still with us, and so of course is Hollings. He would, I fancy, like to think he has taken my father's place. In the old days you know this house was known as . . . "The House of Men". I sometimes wonder what my mother felt like when she first came here. But she did not stay long, she died when I was five.' He now abruptly turned his eyes towards the window and changed the conversation by saying, 'Isn't that a beautiful view!'

I followed his gaze and looked across the wide terrace, down the sloping valley. There was nothing finicky about the view. The fields were large. The patches of dying heather covered great expanses of land, and in the far, far distance I could see the gleam of rivulets running down the hillside. And below, far below, away to the right, the ribbon of the river Coquet twisting and turning, tumbling its way towards Amble and the sea. And beyond the river, blurred by distance, the massive hill of Simonside.

'It's beautiful,' I said, 'very beautiful, and much softer than our valley.'

'I have never asked you where you come from?'

'We live above Rothcorn, quite a way above, in a little cottage. I understand it was at one time an inn. Although I don't know why anyone would go that far for a drink or a bed.'

'Above Rothcorn? That's a wild stretch.'

'Yes, it is rather.'

'Why . . . ?' He was about to ask me the usual question, why we lived in such an out-of-the-way place, when the door opened abruptly and in came two old men, for the sole purpose, I knew, of having a look at me, and like Hollings, but in a different way, they stared at me without speaking.

I saw immediately that their appearance had annoyed Mr Rossiter, and he showed it by saying curtly, 'Can't you see I'm busy!' and followed this immediately with, 'These are my uncles: Mr Stanley Rossiter,' he pointed to the taller and more pleasant-looking of the two small men, and then to the shorter, adding, 'and Mr Bernard.'

They both inclined their heads towards me and said quietly, 'How do you do?'

'How do you do?' I said in reply. Except for

their expressions they were so much alike I knew immediately they were twins.

'Well, what is it?' Mr Maurice still sounded annoyed.

'Nothing, nothing.' Mr Stanley smiled widely, and then continued, 'It's a beautiful morning.'

Mr Bernard did not speak, and after one last look at me he turned abruptly about and went out of the room.

Maurice Rossiter, looking now at Mr Stanley, said pointedly, 'Would you mind closing the door as you go out, Uncle?'

This elicited a high laugh from the old man, and before he did as he was ordered he bowed slightly towards me. I had the impression that the two old men would prove rather amusing.

'Well now.' Maurice Rossiter's eyebrows were raised as he looked at me with a half smile and said, 'You have seen five of us, there are only three more. Bennett, who cooks for us, is very old, and so his cooking suffers, and, consequently, so do we. And then there's Patterson, who does outside jobs; and my third uncle, Stephen, who is bedridden.'

At this moment, from a far door Hollings entered carrying a tray, and at the same instant my eyes were distracted from him by the sight of The Big Fellow running past the window and across the plateau towards the pathway by which I had come up to the house. He was running at great speed as if he was chasing someone, but as far as I could see there was no-one in sight.

Maurice Rossiter's attention, too, was caught by

his brother's action. And I watched him pull himself forward in his seat to catch a glimpse of the flying figure. Then he sat back and took the coffee from Hollings. I, too, took a cup from Hollings's hand and said, 'Thank you,' but the man did not speak.

It would seem that the sight of his brother had disturbed Maurice Rossiter, for he gulped at his coffee and did not speak to me as I drank mine; and then quite abruptly he dismissed me by pulling himself once again on to his feet and saying, 'When can you start?'

I, too, was on my feet now. 'I'll have to give a week's notice. I could begin a week come Monday.'

'Very well. You'll come in the afternoons?' Before I could state my preference for the mornings he put in, 'Do so for the first week, anyway. You will help me considerably if you comply in this.' It was as if we had discussed the matter, but we hadn't. He spoke as if he had been present at the conversation I'd had with his brother, moreover his words were now stilted. They had what I call an office politeness about them that took away the friendliness of the interview. 'Very well,' I said. 'Goodbye.'

But he had turned to the window now and was craning his neck forward, and it was a full minute before he brought his face round to me and said, 'Oh, goodbye. Goodbye.'

I went into the hall. There was no-one about so I let myself out of the front door and walked across the terrace; as I passed the first long windows I knew that Maurice Rossiter was still standing there, but I did not look towards him.

I reached the road, and when I was once out of sight of the house I stopped and, as it were, asked myself what I thought. And I got no answer. I did not know whether I was glad or sorry that I had got the job.

I had passed around the second deep bend of the road when I saw Logan Rossiter again. The sight of him brought me to a dead stop, and with my mouth agape. Then I let out a cry and ran on to the heathered slope, shouting, 'No, no, don't! Stop it! Don't!' The Big Fellow was kneeling in the heather, one knee on the chest of the odd man I had met earlier on the road, and his hands were tight around his throat.

I have always been afraid of men fighting, but in this moment I seemed to have lost all sense of fear. The one thought in my mind was to stop him strangling the man beneath him. I clutched the collar of his coat and pulled. I don't think my strength had anything to do with his loosening his hold; it was more surprise that made him relax his grip. As if my action had brought him to his right senses again, he heaved himself backwards on to his hunkers and, his hands falling to his sides, he dropped his head for a moment. I stood looking down at him, my breathing as heavy as if I myself had been in the conflict, and my voice cracked as I said, 'Do you want to kill him? He looks dead.'

As he pulled himself slowly to his feet he growled, 'Yes, I want to kill him, but it's hard to kill trash . . .

Get up!' He raised his foot and kicked at the man's leg.

'Don't . . . don't be so cruel.' There was anger now in both my voice and face and I glared at him for a moment before turning from him. But as I went to bend over the man The Big Fellow's hand on my arm almost jerked me from the ground, and his lips left his teeth bare as he cried, 'Don't touch him!' Then, thrusting me aside, he stood over the prostrate figure again and said, 'Get up.' And to my amazement the man, using the same action as he had done on the road, turned on to his face and with the aid of his hands and thrusting his buttocks once again skywards levered himself upwards. When he stood straight he swayed a little and put his hand to his throat. And then in a whining voice he said, 'Aa was only after some grapes from the 'othouse. That was aall. Aa never went near the hoose an' Aa didn't see nebody. An' Aa never spoke ta nebody.'

'I've warned you what would happen if I caught you about here again. Now this is the last time, you understand? There'll be nobody to save your bacon next time. Get going.'

The man retreated a few steps, went to turn away, then, turning back, said, 'Ya might 've killed me that time, an' then ya would've hung, ya would.'

'The next time there'll be no doubt about it. As to the hanging, your neck will be worth paying that price for.' The tone now was the caustic one I had heard him use to his brother.

I stood dividing my gaze between the swaying gait of the departing figure and this man with the

268

polished, cutting, sarcastic way of speaking, but whom I had just witnessed acting like a savage. He said now, still without taking his eyes from the man, 'If ever you come across that character – his name is Weaver – give him a wide berth.'

'I have already come across him. I spoke to him on my way up.'

Slowly he turned his eyes towards me. 'And I suppose you took him for a gentle eccentric figure. A bit of a dolt, but harmless.'

In answer to this I replied, 'You can't murder a man because you dislike him.'

'No? . . . You have a lot to learn. Well' – he began dusting himself down, still looking at me – 'I suppose you feel very heroic?'

'I feel nothing of the sort.' I was looking him straight in the eye. 'But on the other hand, nor do I feel like a frightened rabbit.'

The white line on his lip moved upwards as his head moved down and he glanced at me from under his eyebrows for a moment, then laughed softly. It wasn't an unpleasant laugh. 'Did you find favour in my brother's eyes?' he said.

'I don't like the way you phrase that, Mr Rossiter. But I have satisfied your brother that I can both type and take down shorthand, and he feels that I would suit him.'

'Doubtless . . . doubtless . . . Where do you live?'

'Above Rothcorn, at the bottom of Neete Fell.'

'That's a long way to come.' His voice had even a considerate tone to it now, but I ignored it and said quickly, 'Goodbye, Mr Rossiter.'

He did not say goodbye, but instead, 'You're going down the road, so am I. We can hardly walk one behind the other, can we?' And with this he took up a position by my side and in the most embarrassed silence I have ever experienced we went down the fell road together.

Not until the main road came in sight did he speak again and then he said, 'I garage my car just beyond Peter's Well, near the cottages there. If you've got a mind to walk along the road with me I will give you a lift to the village.'

'The bus is due now.' I looked at my wristwatch. 'Thank you all the same.'

'Very well.'

Where the path came in to the main road he stopped, and looking at me, a smile squarely on his face now, a smile that softened his big features, he said, 'I don't suppose you and I are likely to meet much in the future; I am away a good part of the week, so I'll say now I hope that you enjoy your work.'

'I'm sure I will.'

'Yes, so am I.' His head moved in small nods and I could see that he was amused, for he repeated, 'So am I.' Then, 'Goodbye, Miss Mitchell.' Even his tone of farewell had a touch of amusement to it.

'Goodbye, Mr Rossiter.'

When he left me I stood waiting for the bus and looking straight ahead across the road to the far fells. I felt indignant, annoyed, 'worked-up' as my mother would say. I didn't like the man, and I, too, hoped that we wouldn't see much of each other.

2

'Do you mean to say the boss of the house was strangling the tramp fellow?'

'Yes, I do,' I answered my father.

'He couldn't have been badly hurt if he got up so quick and walked away,' put in my mother in her matter-of-fact way. 'And he must have been up to something for the man to have done that; there are always two sides to everything. But look, lass, you have never told us a thing about the house. What does it look like? What is it like inside?'

I looked towards the fire in the high grate, and I blinked for a moment trying to recall the inside of the house. It was odd, but I hadn't taken much notice of my surroundings; I had been too shaken up with the inhabitants of the house. Yet now it seemed I was back there, standing in the hall, and I said slowly, 'There is a large hall but it's dull looking. I would say the whole place could do with one of your . . . groundings.' I smiled at her. 'The stairs go up from the far end of the hall, and I remember now, they were quite bare. I think they were oak. The first room I was shown into was small and over-full with books, and old furniture in great need of a polish; but Mr Rossiter's room, the one that looked out on to the terrace with the beautiful view, that wasn't crowded at all. But it wasn't any cleaner than the rest. The place wasn't dirty, if you know what I mean, but it wasn't . . .' I spread my hands wide. 'It wasn't like our kind of cleanness.'

'No spit and polish?' said my father. 'Well, that's to be expected if there isn't a woman about nagging all the time.' He cast a swift smiling glance towards my mother. 'There'll be nobody to stop them puttin' their feet on the chairs if they want to. Although in me time I've known some dirty house-wives, and some men that were more finicky than women about the place . . . How many men did you say there were?'

'Five in the family, I think, and three servants, two in and one out.'

My mother at this point narrowed her eyes and looked at me as she said slowly, 'You won't mind working among them?'

I took my eyes from her face as I replied, 'No . . . no, I won't mind working among them.' My mother, I knew, was thinking back to the time when I had judged all men's actions on those of one man. Of men in general I was still distrustful, but here and there I was finding the odd one I could trust and like. Such a man was Rodney Stringer. Another, I felt, could be my future employer, Maurice Rossiter, but I wasn't quite sure. It was early days yet and I had learned not to judge on short acquaintance.

My mother said now, 'Oh, I'm glad that you're not going to have those long winter treks. You'll be able to get there and back in half the time.' And so I thought.

I worked my notice the following week, and I was surprised and not a little touched at the genuine regret the girls in the office showed at my coming departure. And I laughed when they expressed their envy at my going to work for an author – so romantic, so different from invoices on cattle feed. I myself did not look upon my future employment as bordering on the romantic, but I remember I laughed a lot that week. I felt much lighter, even gay in myself.

And so the Monday morning came when I went down into the village and started work with Bill Arnold. This work was not unlike that which I had just left in the office in Alnwick, the only difference being it was much more casual, less organised and with many, many more tea-breaks. And when I finished at twelve-thirty Bill showed himself to be very pleased with my efforts.

It was impossible for me to get home for lunch if I was to get to Tor-Fret by two o'clock, so I had brought some sandwiches with me. Even then I had not realised until I actually experienced it what a rush it was, getting from one job to another. And later that week I decided to cut my time short at Bill's and make it up on a Saturday morning. This I eventually did. But now, after gulping my sandwiches, I caught the bus and was off to my first session at Tor-Fret.

I arrived at the house at ten minutes to two, hot and not a little nervous. I need not have worried. My first afternoon was as pleasant as anyone could have wished for. Maurice Rossiter was courtesy itself. I was to start typing a book he had done, and he assured me that if I was stumped in any way I was just to come in to him, he would be in the adjoining room.

Around three o'clock the uncles looked in. They stood one at each side of me and watched me type, much to my embarrassment. It was as if they had not seen anyone type before. But I knew it wasn't the typewriter they were looking at – it was me. And through them I began to realise how strange it was for Tor-Fret to have a woman within its walls. These old twins looked to me to be in the late sixties, and I learned that afternoon that it was Mr Stanley who did most of the talking. Mr Bernard sounded rather grumpy. He looked a bit grumpy, too. They both had round faces, small round eyes and thick eyebrows, and they both smelt the same. I was a bit embarrassed by the smell at first, because neither of them appeared to be in any way under the influence of drink, yet they reeked of something approaching the smell of whisky. I was to learn a lot about that smell.

'Do you think you'll stay?' said Mr Stanley.

I stopped my typing. 'I hope so,' I said.

'What about the winter?' This was about the only thing Mr Bernard said that afternoon. I turned and smiled up into his crumpled face.

'I'll manage. Our side . . . I mean where my

home is, is much rougher than here.'

'Tut!' was all the comment he made to this.

And then there was Hollings. About half-past three he entered the room without knocking. He was carrying a very neatly set tray, on which there was a small silver teapot with milk jug to match, a thin cup and saucer, and a plate holding three cakes. The cakes turned out to be very nice indeed and I wondered if the old cook had made them, for Mr Maurice had suggested that his cooking left a great deal to be desired. At five o'clock I took my leave with a sense of achievement, sent on my way by the pleased smile of my employer.

Before the week was up I had a good insight into Mr Maurice's make-up, and this came about through the book I was typing for him. The book was entitled *The Nightmare of the Flesh*, and it began with a man waking up in hospital and realising that he was crippled with polio. The man had been handsome and attractive and, by the sound of it, very virile. There had been women in his life, and, among other things, he lamented the future lack of this pleasure. Part of the story I realised could be fictitious, but before I had worked five days on it I became just a little critical, even a little tired of the whine that ran through it. The 'I' was very prominent in every line, as also was the self-pity. Regretfully, very regretfully, I knew that Logan Rossiter had been right when he had said to his brother, 'You will never write well until you forget yourself.' Yet in spite of this I knew that my employer was a writer, he could tell a story. I had done a lot of reading; I had my father to thank for this, for he was a great reader. I remember the first book he told me to get from the library. It was a book on Northumberland. 'Know your own county, lass, know your own ground and the world will fall into place around it.' He was right, too. He was right in most things, was my father.

That weekend I arranged with Bill about the alterations in my working hours and he only too readily allowed me to make any change I liked so long as I did the work for him. And so it was that on the Monday of the second week I left the village early and came up the long fell, home to have a good dinner before starting out for Tor-Fret, this time by the top road over Neete Fell. It was a beautiful day, like summer. I thought, whimsically, it was as if the weather god had mislaid this day and had pushed it in while there was yet time.

It had been my intention to ask Mr Maurice if there was a way to the house approaching it from over Neete Fell, but it had slipped my mind. So my father and I had pored over a local map on Sunday and came to the conclusion that I had only to skirt the top of the wood that lay beyond the other valley and I would actually be in the grounds of the house. We did not know if the wood belonged to the Rossiter estate or not.

From the top of Neete Fell I could see for miles on every side. The scene was both elating and awe-inspiring. I could see the river Coquet twisting and turning like a silver snake. I could see groups of dots on its flower-strewn banks which I knew to be cattle. I thought I could see the river Alwin where it frothed down the hillside to join the Coquet, but perhaps that was my heightened imagination. As I gazed through the glorious white light of that bright day it wasn't my imagination that the mottled moving patches away up on the steep face of a fell were the massed bodies of sheep, black-faced, long-haired, moorland sheep. And as I looked over and down to my left I knew that the thin column of blue smoke, spiralling upwards, came from the chimneys of Tor-Fret. And I thought: Dad was right. It did not strike me for a moment that I would not be able to get on to the Rossiter land. There were no railings around here. Stone walls yes, but you could climb those. On each side of the Rossiter land lay two large farms and these were bounded by rough stone walls.

I actually ran down the winding path between the banks of heather, and for a moment I heard myself humming a tune. I skirted the wood. I walked along by the side of a low stone wall until I saw an opening in the undergrowth, and then I climbed the wall and found myself on a sort of pathway. It had once been a broad path but was now almost covered with bramble, and I had to stop a number of times and disentangle my coat from the briars. I had not gone very far when I came to a crossroad of paths and with the choice of three before me. As the house lay to the left of me I took the left-hand one, and within a few minutes found myself walking up a steep rise which I knew to be an outcrop of rock – the moors and fells were studded with these obstructions. The path had disappeared now, but I realised that it would be easier to climb this comparatively small rock than push my way through the undergrowth. And I was glad that I had decided to do this, when a few steps further on I reached the top and there saw down below me to my right a surprising scene. A lake, an inland lake. Lakes large and small are not unusual in this county, but I had not known that one was so near at hand, and in the grounds of the Rossiter estate. I could see from where I stood that if I had gone straight on I would have come to the shore of this lake. I looked at my watch, it was just turned half-past one. I looked to my left again. There in the distance lay the house, I could see the entire stretch of roofs. I decided on the spur of the moment to retrace my steps and spend a few minutes by the water.

It is not big issues that decide our destiny but little ones. The pampering of little wishes, little desires. I had the desire to go and stand by the water for a few minutes, and I gave way to this desire and it set the seal on my future life.

Having reached the crossroads again, I walked along the middle path. It was narrow and carpet-soft with pine needles, which I felt had not been disturbed for a long time. The path turned twice, and then I came abruptly upon an obstacle, surprising and yet not so surprising. It was the back of a summer-house, and I saw immediately that I could not make my way around it, for growing tightly up to its sides was a dense mass of under-growth. I was disappointed; I had so wanted to see that little lake. I looked at the black weathered wood and saw just above my eye level, to the right, a knot hole. I raised myself on tiptoe, leaned over the bramble and, placing my hands against the wood, looked through the hole. Then there wasn't a part of my body that wasn't hot and burning with embarrassment. I brought my face quickly from the wood and found that I had put my hand tightly across my mouth. It was at this moment that the girl's voice came to me. It was a refined easy sort of voice and it said, 'Stop it a moment, darling . . . listen. What was that?'

'What was what? Don't be silly . . . nothing. Come here.'

'No, no, listen. I'm sure I heard someone.'

'You couldn't have heard anyone, my sweet darling. Isn't Weaver on the lookout? And nothing or no-one escapes Weaver. He will warn me if anyone comes up – anyone, that is, except our earnest Kate. Our prim, industrious, and delight-fully earnest Kate.'

My hand slipped slowly from my mouth. The voice was the voice of my employer, and it was full of ridicule, hurtful ridicule. Yet he had been so charming, so kind, so thoughtful.

The girl's voice said now, 'But are you sure he's gone?'

'My dearest dear, Patterson drove him to the station en route for London town, then returned the car to the garage. I told you, we had one hell of a row, my dear brother and I, concerning that very journey . . . Oh, come here. I want to forget it for this afternoon, at any rate . . .' There came a pause. I was too afraid to move in case they heard me and when the voice came again it had lost its bantering tone. 'I say I want to forget it but I can't. If he doesn't sell that land I think I'll kill him. Keeping us all on the bread line when he could get a hundred and fifty thousand for that strip. What does it matter if there's a few rows of houses at the bottom of the hill? We won't see them.'

'Listen, darling, listen.' It was the girl's voice. 'I am serious now, really, I'm serious . . . Let's go away. Look . . . I'll get work of some kind.'

Maurice Rossiter's laugh came to me. He was choking with it. And then he said, 'Oh, you darling . . . you darling . . . darling . . . darling.' Each darling was punctuated by the sound of a kiss. 'You'll get work of some kind? Oh, that's funny. The hardest work you've ever done in your life is throw your leg over a horse. You're lazy; beautiful and lazy.' There was another pause.

'But I could try, Maurice. We could take a chance . . .'

'Be quiet, don't be silly.' The tone of my employer's voice had changed with such suddenness that it didn't seem to belong to the same man, and now he said bitterly, 'You know full well I haven't got a farthing. I'm as dependent on him for what I eat as a baby at its mother's breast. Moreover, for years now I've been used to being looked after. I need to be looked after, I must be looked after; I can't manage on my own, you know I can't. I need a man there.' It was like the voice from the novel, the character in *The Nightmare of the Flesh* speaking in person. 'Things are bad enough as they are now, skimping and scraping, everything being cut down. But at least I have my rooms and attention, and I have my work. Could I work if I was in, say, a maisonette or some basement flat?'

'But if he does sell the land would he give you anything?'

There was a long pause before I heard Maurice Rossiter's voice again, and then he said, 'He mightn't give me anything, but he'd give it to you, darling. You've only got to say the word, and you're going to say it, aren't you?'

'But after . . . What about us after, Maurice?'

'Leave that to Maurice. I've told you, just you leave everything to me. I may not be able to use my limbs to the full, but thank God I can use my brain . . . and my good side . . . But now, come on to the water with you, come on. I want to come alive.'

I heard swift movements and a scuffling sound and laughter, and under its protection I lifted one foot slowly after the other and made my retreat.

The day was still bright, but nothing was shining any more. There was one word running through my mind: it was . . . duplicity. It repeated itself again and again . . . duplicity, duplicity. And it wasn't because of what Maurice Rossiter thought of me, but because of the underlying meaning to the conversation I had overheard, that it stayed with me.

Without thinking of where I was going, I had automatically taken the path towards the outcrop of rock again, and had almost reached the top when I stopped. If they were on the shores of the lake they would see me from here. I turned my eyes slowly towards the water. My view was obstructed by a spreading branch of a fir tree, but as I moved my head to the side, there, as in a framed picture, was a section of the lake, and standing poised, quite naked, on its shore was the girl I had seen through the knot hole in the summer-house. Her body was merged into the white light, and from this distance she looked like a young girl in her early teens, but the face I had glimpsed in that hot blushing moment was of someone as old as myself. Perhaps a year or two older or a year or two younger. Then into the picture came the loping contorted figure of Maurice Rossiter. Before he reached the girl she had turned her white body from him and dived into the water. In the next instant he was with her, and then even from this distance it seemed as if I was witnessing a miracle, for I saw, not one arm but both his arms cutting the water like the fins of a fish as he pursued the girl. And not only his arms but both his legs were in action. He had said, 'let me come alive,' and undoubtedly only in the water could he know full life. I had heard how water gave agility to some polio-afflicted people, and now it seemed, as I said, that I was watching a miracle. And I could have been happy for him if it hadn't been for that one word . . . duplicity.

I was hesitating whether to risk crossing the top of the small rock when my whole attention was caught by the flash of moving sunlight, like the sun reflected from glass, and after blinking I looked to my left in the direction of the house. The trees were high here, as also were more outcrops of rock, and I saw lying along the top of a flat shelf, and skilfully hidden, at least from anyone down below on the lake side, a man. He was almost hidden from me but for the top of a bald head and the dark blur of his body. I did not attempt to go forward over the mound of the rock, but stepped backwards, and, kneeling down so as not to be seen myself, I looked upwards. The man was lying flat on his stomach. His clothes were not rough country clothes; he was wearing a black suit. And I noticed that his feet, which were hanging over the end of the sloping shelf of rock, were fitted with shining black boots. The flash that had blinded me was the glass of his binoculars as he brought them to his face, and there he was now looking through these binoculars down on to the lake, on to Maurice Rossiter and the girl, whoever she was. I felt sick. I turned about, and within a few minutes I had crossed over the stone wall again.

It was now a quarter to two and I would be late. But this could not be helped. I would have to walk the length of the wood . . . on its outside, go along the road that led to the stone gates, then cut across the fell until I came out on the path near St Peter's Well, for I must take this path to the house.

283

The man Weaver must see me. If he didn't how would I explain my arrival? Could I say I came in by the path which skirted the lake?

I arrived twenty minutes late, hot, tired and still feeling nauseated inside. At what point on the road Weaver spied me I don't know. I heard no strange bird calls, no signals; the only sound on this hot September day was the persistent cooing of a wood pigeon.

It was quite usual for me not to see my employer for anything up to an hour after my arrival. The last page which I had transcribed would be left on my desk and I would go on from there. If I was unable to make out some word, or the sense of an over-written sentence, I would knock on the third door which led out of this room. This door led into the other large terrace-framed room which was furnished like a drawing-room, but which was actually his bedroom. I'd only had to trouble him three times within the past week, and each time I had found him propped up on a couch busily writing, but today I determined that no matter how bad the script was I would not go near him . . . Prim Kate, earnest Kate . . . Yet I knew it wasn't his private opinion of me that was colouring my thoughts but the two-facedness of the man. Yes, that was an ordinary way of putting it, the way my father or mother would have described him, and it was accurate. I did not like Logan Rossiter, he was rude and overbearing, but I found that equally I did not like the idea of his charming-mannered and handsome-faced brother making a fool of him . . . 'making a monkey' out of him. Again my father's expression was most adequate, because that apparently was what was happening. Maurice Rossiter was 'making a monkey' out of his brother and in a most detestable way. I had no way of telling what the actual relationship was between the dark-haired, white-bodied nymph by the lake and Logan Rossiter, but I hoped, in this moment, that it wasn't deep. I had been hurt, and although, as I said, my disposition towards the man was not kindly, I felt I should hate to see him humiliated . . . 'made a monkey out of'. I had been made a monkey out of . . .

'Here's a day for you.' It was nearly four o'clock when Maurice Rossiter greeted me in this airy fashion. His eyes were bright; his hair, I noticed, was still damp; and although the dragging of his left side was very much in evidence, it appeared to me now like a crippled leech clinging to the side of a giant. For today my employer looked as big as his brother, and I realised that if he had been whole he would have been even larger than Logan Rossiter, and together with his beauty he would, like the character in his book before he was struck with illness, have mown all women down.

'Have you had your tea?'

'Yes, thank you.'

'What is it?' He had stopped opposite my desk. 'Aren't you well?' His head was bent towards me, his expression sympathetic. I would have melted under it last week, but now I looked back at him and lied, 'I have a slight touch of migraine. I'm sometimes subject to headaches.'

'Oh, bad luck.' He spoke now with the indifference of a very healthy person for a sickly creature. It was rather absurd, but perhaps, I reminded myself, he might be feeling very healthy at this moment; certainly he'd had an unusual afternoon. Unusual to me, I reminded myself, perhaps not unusual to him. That was not the first time, by many a score, he had swum that lake, and never, I should imagine, without company.

'Mr Rossiter . . .' He was moving towards the window as I spoke and he lumbered round and looked at me, his face smiling. 'Would it be in order if I took the manuscript home and did it there? I have a typewriter. I could easily, and bring it back when it's . . .'

'No, no. It would not be in order.' His words were spaced and cool. 'I want the manuscript done here. Apart from having only the one copy, anything could happen to it once it left this house. I want to work on the finished script every morning. I find it much easier to correct in type. You understand that?'

'Yes, yes, I do, but I just thought . . .'

'Are you getting tired of it?' Here spoke a vain man, here was the hero of the novel.

'No, no,' I said. 'I'm not getting tired of it. I am very interested in the book. It was merely a suggestion.'

'Well, it won't do. I am sorry. You understand that? I am sorry, but I have to have the work on the spot. I thought you understood that when you came.'

'It wasn't discussed as far as I remember.'

'Kate.' His eyes narrowed and he hobbled towards me again. 'What is it? Don't tell me there's nothing wrong. I can tell by your eyes. I've learnt that much about you already – they give you away . . . Has someone upset you? Or . . . Oh, Kate . . .' He pointed his finger at me, wagging it about an inch from my face as he said with mock severity, 'It's the shrew in you coming out. I told you you'd give me a sample of it. Someone's upset you and you're taking it out on me. Now that's it, isn't it? . . . Have you a boy friend?'

The abrupt and surprising question brought the colour flushing into my cheeks. I felt my face go scarlet. Characteristically now, his head went back and his laugh rang out. 'It's years since I saw a woman blush. Oh, Kate, you're delightful.'

I felt gauche, stupid, and was suddenly on the point of tears. I think it was only the door opening which saved me from this humiliation. It was the twins, and Maurice Rossiter greeted them with, 'Come in, come in. Our industrious Kate has a cross between a headache, a temper and a dose of the blues. What do you suggest for it?'

'Headache?' Bernard Rossiter nodded his white head at me, and said in his terse clipped way, 'Have the very thing to cure headache. Early in the day for it though. Should never be touched before six o'clock, 'cept on special occasions . . . Eh, Maurice?' He turned his head quickly and looked at his nephew. And Maurice Rossiter answered gaily, 'Except on special occasions! You're right there, Uncle, and this is a special occasion. We can't have Kate with a headache, can we?'

Mr Stanley now leant towards me and said quietly, 'Is it bad, my dear?'

'Yes, yes, it is rather.' And it was true, my head was now thumping.

'Go and bring her a glass.' Maurice Rossiter was speaking now to his Uncle Bernard. And then he cried, 'Better still, she's never seen the cellars. That's it, take her down. Come on, come on, leave that toil and sweat.' He put out his hand and gripped my elbow, and I was amazed at the strength and power behind his hold because it brought me to my feet. 'Go on, go on with the old 'uns. I'll give you half an hour. I'm being generous, mind you, very generous. Half an hour from my work.' He moved his head slowly from side to side.

'Come along, my dear.' Mr Stanley had hold of my arm now as if he were escorting an invalid, and Mr Bernard, opening the door, preceded us into the hall.

Again I felt like crying, for now the phrase 'Being made a monkey of' seemed more appropriate still. Maurice Rossiter was enjoying himself. I realised that this man could create situations for his enjoyment. Good or bad, if he created them they would give him enjoyment.

When, after crossing the hall and going down a long passage, Mr Bernard opened a door from which dropped a flight of stairs, Mr Stanley, seeming to sense my feelings, said, 'My nephew's in a merry mood today, you must take advantage of it. It isn't often that he will sacrifice his work for anything, or even anyone. Come along, my dear. You go first, Bernard.'

'Well, isn't that what I'm doing?'

The somewhat querulous reply came up from the dark well of the staircase. And then a light was switched on and a strange, and for me unusual, scene was illuminated.

Following Mr Stanley, I went cautiously down the narrow wooden stairs and gazed over an enormous cellar, which was, I could see, split into sections by low frameworks, frameworks holding bottles, apparently hundreds and hundreds of bottles, and against a side wall I saw the round contours of a row of barrels. Then I reached the floor, which I recognised immediately was rough rock. Mr Stanley, following the direction of my eyes, remarked, 'That surprises you, doesn't it? They built in those days. Tor-Fret is built on rock. The foundations were hewn out of rock.' His voice was full of pride.

'Never mind the foundations.' Bernard's voice was still querulous. 'It's a foundation she wants inside, not under her feet.'

I was now standing in a sort of room, made so by partitions full of bottles on two sides and a long rough oak table on the third side. I sniffed at the air – it was dry, not warm, and yet not cold – and gazed about me. This evidently pleased the old man, and, catching at my interest, Mr Stanley began to point out various things to me, such as one complete frame holding perhaps a hundred bottles all lying on their sides and having red sealing wax on the corks. 'Pretty they look,' he said, patting a bottle affectionately. 'Wax keeps out the rot. Corks rot, you know; a nasty little pest gets in. Won't be drunk for many a day, these. But . . . come now, sit down here.' He pulled a chair forward with the air of a host, then, turning to his brother, he said, 'What shall we give her first?'

As they both looked contemplatingly at each other, I put in quickly, 'Oh, please, I must tell you I'm not used to wines, except for a sherry now and again.'

'Oh, my God!' Mr Bernard raised his hands above his head and cast his eyes ceilingwards. 'Don't mention that word. Bottles'll hear and wine'll ferment.'

I laughed up at the old man. Already I felt better. This then was what caused the peculiar smell that hung around them. They made wine . . . wines, I should say, for there must have been dozens of different kinds in the racks.

'The nineteen thirty-four?'

Mr Bernard looked at his brother, and, inclining his head slowly like a doctor giving a verdict, said, 'Nineteen thirty-four it is.'

As Mr Bernard disappeared around the partition, Mr Stanley drew up a high wooden stool to the table and, sitting down, looked at me, his face straight, and said quietly, almost in a whisper, 'Have you really got a headache, or has my nephew upset you?'

I was startled and must have shown it, for he said quickly, but still softly, 'Don't worry, but you must try not to let him upset you. He is used to having his own way and cannot stand being balked. But you be firm, my dear, you be firm.' He touched my hand quickly. The action was more in the nature of a nervous spasm than a gesture of sympathy, and when the clink of glasses came from somewhere beyond the partition he rose abruptly and went to the opening and said, 'Are you draining the bottle?'

Mr Bernard's answer was merely a grunt, and then he appeared round the framework carrying a pewter tray on which stood three plain wine glasses half-filled with a red wine, a deep rich red, yet clear, you could almost say transparent. And when, with a courtesy that did not belong to this generation, Mr Bernard presented me with a glass of wine, I knew that an honour was being bestowed on me, and that these two dear old men did not take the matter lightly. They were standing one at each side of me now and silently we raised our glasses to each other, and then I sipped the wine.

As I have already said, I know nothing at all about wine, having tasted only sherry and on one special occasion, which I don't want to remember, champagne. But from this glass I recognised that I was drinking something rare. I let the liquid rest on my tongue before gently sliding into my throat. I have no words to describe the taste; I can only say that the sensation of warmth was almost immediate. And I remember thinking quaintly: It's like drinking joy.

'What is it made of?' I asked Mr Stanley.

'Oh, well now . . . Grapes for one thing. Our own grapes, too, mind, and a little brandy added. But it isn't only what goes in, it's how you treat it after . . . Give it rest and it will repay you. Don't you think this tastes beautiful?'

'Beautiful,' I repeated.

'Do you know' – he leant towards me – 'wine has been made in this cellar for over three hundred years. And not only wine' – his bushy brows came low over his eyes – 'whisky . . . In the bad old days, when they wanted to warm the blood before a local fight, they would gather in here.' He embraced the whole cellar with the sweep of one arm. 'I remember my grandfather telling me that as a boy he saw thirty to forty men roaring drunk in this very place. They were celebrating a raid.'

'A raid? On the Scots?'

'On the Scots!' The laughter choked in Mr Stanley's throat. 'Nothing so heroic, my dear. Another farmer's sheep. They'd bring them down here and slaughter them by the dozen. There'd be meat for all through the winter. And in the spring our sheep would go to market and there'd be money for everybody who worked for "The Rossiter". Up till this last generation, you know, every owner of Tor-Fret was referred to as "The Rossiter".' Mr Stanley shook his head. 'Ah, things happened in those days; they lived in those days.'

'Aye, and they died in those days,' put in his brother in a way that sounded to me, for the moment, very like my father. 'And if such things happened today you'd be scared to death, you know you would. So be quiet, be quiet.'

Strangely enough, Mr Stanley obeyed his taciturn brother. I had finished my wine and I rose to my feet now, saying, 'I had better be getting back, but thank you very much. I have never in my life tasted anything so wonderful.'

I held the empty glass towards Mr Bernard, and as he took it from me he said in his sawn-off way of speaking, 'Makin' blackberry next. Come down, watch us . . . at it.'

'Thank you, I'd love to.'

They did not lead me back to the staircase along the way I had come, but without remarking on it they both walked slowly between the different partitions, very much like two ardent gardeners quietly showing off prize blooms. And as they went they made such remarks as, 'That's equal to your Vin de Tete,' and, 'There's race for you' – this latter remark being accompanied by a pat on the neck of a bottle, one of about thirty in a rack separate from others. They now led me round the back of the cellar. It was a place apart, and here evidently was where the wine was made. There was a bench holding boxes of corks, labels, and wooden mallets. There was a long wooden trough with a tap above it, then a contraption of pipes, which were connected to the trough and also to what looked like an old-fashioned boiler. There was also an out-of-date stove in a recess, but it appeared not to have been used for years, and right next to it was a door. This too looked ancient and out of use. Mr Bernard now said with a little grin, 'Make you a Trabhalbodor in the summer.'

I did not know what a Trabhalbodor was, and when I said so Mr Stanley explained, 'He means he'll get you to help tread the grapes.'

'Oh.' I laughed, and Mr Bernard laughed with me, as pleased as a child at his joke.

Mr Bernard did not come out of the cellar with us but bade me farewell from the bottom of the steps, and when I had reached the hall and Mr Stanley had closed the cellar door he stood facing me, and without any preamble he said, 'Our elder brother Stephen's an invalid, bedridden this last six years. Not senile or anything. Quite all right, quite all right. Some time – when you've a minute – after Maurice's work's done, would you look in on him? He'd like that very much – very much.'

'Yes, yes, certainly. Just tell me when it is convenient.'

'All right, I will. Goodbye. And . . . and may I say I've enjoyed your company.'

He turned away from me as he finished speaking, and I looked after him and thought: Oh, they are nice. Unreservedly I liked the old men.

I now went along the corridor and across the hall and into the big room, and thankfully I found it empty. Nor did I see Maurice Rossiter again that afternoon.

The effect of the wine stayed with me for quite a time. At one period of the afternoon I could have put my head down on the desk and fallen asleep. But by the time I had finished for the day my mind was clear and I was once again viewing Maurice Rossiter from the same viewpoint as I had done earlier.

Before I reached home I had made up my mind that I would not tell my parents of the scene I had witnessed that afternoon. But had I decided to tell them I would have been prevented from doing so by the atmosphere that pervaded the house and which I sensed as soon as I entered. It was an atmosphere of apprehension, and I knew immediately I looked at their faces that something was wrong, and I hadn't long to wait to find out what it was.

'Tired, lass?' It was my father's greeting.

'Yes, a little. It was warm walking up the hill.'

'Did you find the way to the house?'

'Yes, yes, I found it all right.' This undescriptive statement seemed to satisfy him. At any other time he would have wanted to know every turn I had taken in the path, but now he just nodded and looked towards my mother. She had her back towards me and was standing at the table arranging and rearranging the crockery. The fact that she hadn't spoken to me was proof in itself that something was amiss. Had she had a row with my father? But no; whatever words she had with father never coloured the atmosphere. I went into the back kitchen and washed my hands, and when I returned to the table she handed me a cup of tea and gave me a smile, a smile having in it traces of nervousness and apprehension and, I thought, pity. And then I knew why. Sitting down at my side, she said, 'You'd better know right away, we've had a visitor.' My eyes did not move from her face until she said, 'Arthur's been here.'

'And he nearly got me toe in his . . .'

'Be quiet!' said my mother. My father's descriptive phrase, like that of the man Weaver, was very expressive and conveyed the kind of reception Arthur Boyne had received. I did not say to my mother, 'What did he want?' I said nothing, for my heart was beginning to race as it hadn't done for a long time. My mother said now, 'I'll give it to you straight, lass . . . condensed. He's parted from her and going to get a divorce.'

I got slowly to my feet and looked down on her and said in a voice that sounded strangely calm, even indifferent, 'That won't make the slightest difference to me. What gave him the idea it would?'

'He's had a hell of a time. He's sorry for himself. He wants sympathy.' My father's tone was caustic.

'Well, I'm afraid he'll have to look elsewhere.'

'I told him that.' It was my father again speaking. 'An' I told him that if he showed his nose in this door again . . .'

'Be quiet, Tom!' my mother put in impatiently, then went on, 'He said, when he left her she took the child and plonked it on his mother.'

I rose and walked towards the stairs as my mother said, 'Have this cup of tea, lass.' But I shook my head.

Upstairs I sat on the end of my bed, my arm leaning on the wooden rail, and I looked with unseeing eyes into the purple light that was spreading over the fells, for in this moment my vision was filled with a picture of a plump face, a plump face above a plump body . . . the plumpness of adolescence. I had seen that face only once. It was on a Sunday afternoon. We had just washed up after having dinner. My mother and father were sitting in deckchairs on the strip of green at the back of the house. I answered the knock at the front door and there she stood. This young self-assured, loud-mouthed girl. And she told me almost immediately that she was carrying Arthur Boyne's child. 'What are you going to do about it?' she asked.

I learnt that she and Arthur had met on a number of Sunday evenings on the train from Alnwick to Durham. Arthur was returning after visiting me. Her people lived in Alnwick, but she stayed with an aunt in Durham, where she worked, and came up to Alnwick for the weekends.

My wedding was set for two months ahead. I had everything ready. The girl was seventeen, I was twenty-five, and seemed old to her, and with the cruelty of extreme youth she did not hesitate to let me feel this. The reason for Arthur's sudden desire to emigrate had been made clear. Also a number of things which had puzzled me during the past months.

Arthur had written to me this particular week-end to say he couldn't get over because his father was not very well and his mother was worried. The reason for the excuse was only too plain now. He was leaving it to the girl to 'spill the beans' as she had threatened. She told me this herself as she stood with a stance that exaggerated the swelling curve of her stomach.

And now it was over for him and he thought that all he had to do was to make his plight known to me and things would link up from where they had broken off. Kind Kate, generous Kate, big-hearted Kate, would understand. 'You know, Kate, one of the reasons why I love you is because you're kind, you've got a big heart. Oh, aye, and you're bonny an' all.' I remember the actual day he had said those words. It was as we lay in the heather just down there below this cottage window. We had taken the bus for a day out and it had deposited us in the village, and from there we had walked right up to this fell. It was that day we had seen the empty cottage and gone home to my parents full of it . . .

I stood up. My heart was racing less wildly now. It was over and done with, dead. It had been dead from the moment that girl had knocked on the front door and we had faced each other. It could never be revived. But, oh, I didn't want to endure any more scenes, any more pleas. My life was settled now; emotionally it was stagnant, and that was how I wanted it to remain.

After a time I went downstairs again and I said to my mother, 'You didn't tell him where I worked.'

'Of course not. What do you take me for? But mind, there's one thing I can tell you – he'll be back.'

For the remainder of that week I was filled with apprehension, but nothing unusual occurred, either concerning my own private life, which included my work for Bill, or my life when I was within the four walls of Tor-Fret, except perhaps one thing, which was, in its own way, very pleasant. It happened on the Friday when Mr Stanley came into the room as I was putting on my coat and said to me, 'Could you spare a minute? He'd like to see you.' He jerked his chin upwards. And I realised he was referring to the brother he had spoken about earlier.

'Yes, yes, of course.'

'You have time?'

'Oh yes. Plenty of time.'

He looked towards the far door, and then he said quietly, 'You . . . you have seen Maurice?'

It was his way of asking if I had told my employer I was going. I shook my head. 'I haven't seen him all afternoon. I think he's out somewhere.'

'Ah, yes, yes. He'll be gone to the pool.' The old man's voice sank lower still. 'He never says when he's going. Lets no-one go with him either.' He nodded his head quickly at this point. 'It's understandable. He won't be helped . . . Doesn't like people viewing him. Understandable, understandable.'

Doesn't like people viewing him! He had made his retreat very safe, had Mr Maurice. The members of the household respected his wishes and left him to himself at the lake. The word duplicity grew larger before my eyes. And I asked myself if I was such a gullible type that I had not seen some evidence of this trait when I first met him. Yet why decry my lack of perception, for wasn't he deceiving, and successfully, other members of his family? But that, I told myself once again as I went out of the room with Mr Stanley, had nothing to do with me, nothing. It wasn't my business.

I went up the broad bare oak stairs on to a wide landing, then from this down a narrow corridor which opened up into a square hallway, the walls of which were covered with pictures, mostly portraits. I guessed I was in the south wing of the house which was to the right of the terraced rooms. It struck me that the invalid's room was a long way from the centre of the house, until I learned that it was almost above the kitchens and easily accessible by a back stairway.

Mr Stanley turned yet another corner, and then he opened a door and across his shoulder I saw Logan Rossiter carrying an old man in his arms towards a bed. They both turned their heads sharply in our direction, and it was the old man who spoke, and with a voice so strong that it denied all connection with his frail, night-shirted body. 'You beardless old goat! Why couldn't you knock, or wait?'

By this time Logan Rossiter had deposited the old man in the bed and covered him up; and as he arranged the pillows and with strange gentleness pressed him back among them, he said, 'Now, old 'un, behave yourself; you have a visitor.'

'That's what I mean, that's what I mean.'

'Now, now. Let me put your two hairs straight,' went on Logan, and I watched him wet the end of his finger in his mouth and take the long wisp of white hair upwards from the brow, before turning to me and saying with studied politeness, 'Good afternoon, Miss Mitchell.'

'Good afternoon.'

'Didn't know you were in, Logan,' said Mr Stanley now. 'When did you arrive?'

'Oh, about half an hour since.'

'You've been up here all the time?'

'Yes. His nibs here' – he gave the old man in the bed a gentle punch with his fist – 'was yelling blue murder for company.'

'Well, not a soul, not a soul near me since dinnertime. You two!' He pointed at Mr Stanley as if his twin was standing by his side. 'You two, never out of the cellar, slopping about . . . A man could die.'

'You don't turn your nose up at the slop.' Mr Stanley nodded towards his brother.

But now the old man did not answer him; he was looking at me as if he was just becoming aware of my presence. And I watched his face soften. He raised his hand and said, 'Come here. Come over here and sit down beside me.' He patted the counterpane.

And when I hesitated to sit on the bed, Logan Rossiter said, 'Go on, sit down. He likes ladies sitting on his bed, the old reprobate.' Again he gently punched the old man, and this elicited a chuckle from him, but he did not take his eyes from me, and when I sat down he took hold of my hand and did not speak for a long time but just stared at me. And then he said a strange thing. 'I felt you. I felt you the first day you came into the house. You were down there.' He pointed over towards the floor at the far end of the room which I thought must be the beginning of the drawing-room. 'Nobody told me you had come, but I felt it. I said to myself, "There's a woman down there, and she's nice."'

'Don't believe a word he's saying,' Logan Rossiter put in.

'It's true, it's true, Logan; I did have that feeling. And it's true that she's nice.' He brought his eyes from his nephew and looked at me full in the face again as he repeated the compliment. 'And you are nice, you are nice, my dear.'

Logan Rossiter seemed to be amused and this brought embarrassment to me. If he hadn't been in the room I am sure I would have felt perfectly at ease with the old man, for, like his two younger brothers, he had a charm that was captivating. My thoughts at this point went off at a tangent. All the Rossiters apparently had charm, except perhaps the eldest . . . and yet . . .

As if he was divining my thoughts and determined to make me see him in a new light, in the light of the Rossiters being a charming family as a whole, he said now to his uncle, 'I think you are right. I think Maurice is very fortunate in his choice of a new secretary.' There was no sarcasm underlying the words, the tone was ordinary; even so, I felt more embarrassed than ever.

I was saved from replying by Hollings entering the room carrying a tray on which there was a meal set. He had come in by the door which led down into the kitchens, and he showed no surprise at seeing me. There was a general movement. I had risen from the bed and was near Hollings as, balancing the tray on one hand, he went to pull a small table towards him. Instinctively my hands went out to assist him, and when he had placed the tray on the table he looked at me and said, 'Thank you, madam.'

It had a strange sound, a nice sound, although by omitting to address me as . . . miss, he had placed me in a category beyond youth. I found I was very pleased by it – 'Thank you, madam.' I had never been called 'madam' before, except in a shop I had once visited in Newcastle, but Hollings's way of saying 'madam' was different altogether; moreover, it was the first time the man had opened his mouth to me.

'Come along, we must all get going and let him have his supper. Say goodbye now.' Logan Rossiter bent towards the old man. 'Say goodbye now, Uncle.'

The old man's interest was riveted on his tray now and he seemed to bring his eyes reluctantly on to me again, but his tone still held the ring of sincerity when he said, 'Goodbye, my dear; goodbye. But promise me, promise me, you'll come up again. Any time, any time . . . But not when I'm out of bed.' He laughed and flapped his hand at Mr Stanley. 'Dolt, that's what you are, dolt.'

After assuring him that I would come and see him again I said goodbye. As I went out of the room with Mr Stanley, we were followed by Logan Rossiter, and when we were crossing the gallery he said, 'My uncle is a character, but he never says what he doesn't mean . . . except' – he put his hand on Mr Stanley's shoulder – 'to his brothers. But that is brotherly licence, isn't it, Uncle?' Without waiting for a reply he turned to me and continued, 'He would, I know, very much like you to visit him now and then.'

'I'll be pleased to.'

'Thank you.'

When we reached the main hall Mr Stanley mumbled a goodbye and left us, and Logan Rossiter, turning to me, said, 'You're leaving now?'

'Yes, I've finished.'

'I'm going down the hill, I'll walk with you.' There was no 'May I?' It was a definite statement. He lifted his hat from the hallstand which was made of upturned antlers, an ugly thing but somehow not out of place in its surroundings, and then we were walking across the terrace and down the fell, and silence surrounded us again. I couldn't speak, and he didn't until we were halfway down the road, and then he said, 'You're finding my brother amenable?'

'Yes. Yes, quite.' I was looking ahead as I spoke.

'You like the work?'

'Yes, it's very interesting.'

'But what do you really think of it?' I knew that he was looking at me, but I kept my eyes on the road ahead as I answered, 'It's . . . it's a little too personal.'

He stopped abruptly and this action brought my

eyes towards him, and I stopped, too. 'You're right; you're absolutely, utterly right. I've been telling him that for years. But please . . . I'd better warn you. If he asks your opinion, don't tell him what you've just told me. For, you know, a writer is as susceptible to hurt with regard to his work as a mother is about her child. You criticise a writer's work, and even if he knows you're right he will hate you. It's strange, but no matter how old a writer is he never grows up in this respect. Other men have to, but not writers. I'm a solicitor, and if I hated all the people who criticise me, then my life would become unbearable.'

As I looked at him I endorsed in my mind what he was saying. Yes, life for him would become unbearable, for he could arouse dislike very easily, whether it was warranted or not. And now, and not for the first time during the last few days, I was wondering if I had misjudged this man as I had, in the opposite way, judged his brother.

We moved forward again and the silence descended on us once more, until, on reaching the main road, a car swept past us to pull up on the grass verge. And I saw Logan Rossiter's face light up as he lifted his hand to hail the driver. The driver was a girl. As Logan Rossiter helped her out of the car she stood just below his shoulder. Her hair was dark, not black, nor yet dark chestnut, but something of the sheen that you see on the dark feathers of a mallard when it is flying against the light. Her eyes were deep brown, the eye sockets long, and the brows curbing them took their hue from the hair.

The mouth was full and wide, the skin of her face a warm peach – not like her body, which I knew to be pure white. Here was the girl I'd seen standing naked before Maurice Rossiter on the shore of the lake, and now Logan Rossiter, taking her hand, brought her the few steps towards me, saying, 'Let me introduce my fianceé, Miss Noreen Badcliff.' Then, turning his head, he said, 'Miss Kate Mitchell. Maurice's secretary, you know.'

The girl and I stared at each other for a long second. She looked straight into my eyes, and I into hers, and I knew that had I not known her real nature I would have found her attractive, fascinatingly attractive. She was small, petite; her figure even in her plain suit was perfect. She was like a miniature Venus – and The Big Fellow was in love with her.

'I'm very pleased to meet you.'

Not the usual greeting of 'How-do-you-do?' but the more sincere 'I'm very pleased to meet you.' I would have been captivated by her had I not known her real nature. Birds of a feather. You could hardly pass a thread between her and my employer. I inclined my head but found that I couldn't speak. To my surprise – for really it was no business of mine – I found myself consumed with anger against her for making a fool of . . . The Big Fellow. It didn't seem right somehow that he should be taken for a ride by his brother and this girl.

What I would have answered her by way of introduction I do not know, for I was saved by the bus coming round the bend of the main road, and I turned my head quickly towards it and then back, saying, 'Excuse me, I must catch the bus. Some of them, they . . . they won't wait.' I darted from them and ran towards the oncoming vehicle. I had been unjust to the drivers of the buses; they would stop anywhere for you on this lonely road.

My anger against the girl persisted all the way home and blotted out the personal matters in my life, and I wondered, among other things, and not for the first time since it had happened, who the man was who had lain on the rock above the lake. The fact that he was spying did not say much for his own character, but I had a feeling of relief engendered by the thought that this unknown man might be the means of exposing the underhand game of Maurice Rossiter and this girl. Unless he meant to use his knowledge to blackmail the pair of them. Of one thing I was certain: the man was not a member of the household. I had by now met them all – Patterson the outside man, and Bennett the old cook – but none of them was as bald as the man I had seen lying on the rock. Nor did any of them wear fine highly polished black boots. Hollings wore a black suit and black shoes, but Hollings had thick white hair.

A little way out of the village I saw Rodney with the van waiting by the roadside near the path that went up behind the village and up to the cottage. It was a path broad and even enough to take the van for quite some way, so I alighted and went back to him. 'I waited for the bus,' he said. 'I thought you'd like a lift up.'

'That's kind of you, Rodney.' I smiled my thanks, and at the same time I was wishing he hadn't, for I was wanting to be alone. Yet I was grateful for the lift up the steep hill. He had hardly started the motor before he said, 'That fellow you used to knock around with when you first came here, he was in *The Fox* last night, and I heard him ask Ossie where you were working now and I tipped him the wink to keep mum – I mean Ossie. I thought perhaps you wouldn't want him to know.'

'Thanks, Rodney. You did right.' I closed my eyes wearily. Villages were rather like enlarged homes, they knew all about you. It was no use trying to hide anything from them. Like the members of a family, they either liked you or disliked you. Yet whatever touched you, touched them. Rodney drove the van straight over a hillock and for a moment we were thrown together, and then he said as he still kept his eyes ahead, 'If you want him dealt with at any time you've just got to say.'

'Thanks, Rodney,' I said. 'I'll remember, but I don't think it will come to that.'

'I'm popping over to Amble,' he said.

'Are you?' I didn't ask why and somehow I thought he was disappointed by my lack of interest. Then when he had stopped the van at the nearest point it could get to the house he suddenly turned to me and said, 'You haven't any time for me as a fellow . . . I mean . . . You know?'

'Oh, Rodney . . .'

'That's OK.' He touched my sleeve. 'Just wanted to make sure . . . It's OK. It's OK. Don't worry.' His voice was high and rushed. 'You and me's good friends. Appreciate it an' all, I do . . . It's OK. Good night, Kate. Good night. Be seeing you.'

'Good night, Rodney.'

My voice sounded sad, and I felt sad. What a pity I couldn't like Rodney. But I did like him, you couldn't help but like him . . . But marry him? Oh! And live a life of platitudes? As this thought came to me I realised with almost a shock how temperamentally alike Rodney and Arthur were, and for the first time since Arthur and I had parted I felt a surging sense of relief at what I had escaped from.

3

It was raining as I crossed the terrace towards the front door on that Monday afternoon, but before I reached the porch there came towards me a strange man carrying a leather bag. And on each side of him were the twins. The man glanced at me casually as I passed, but the two old men nodded quickly at me, and then I heard Mr Stanley's voice saying 'Goodbye, doctor. Goodbye, and thank you for all you've done.'

I hesitated in the hall for a moment, thinking: It's Mr Stephen who must be worse, poor old soul. Yet on Friday he had seemed so alive and well in spite of his fragile look. And then the old men were facing me, both their faces perturbed. It was Mr Stanley who said, 'Oh, my dear, it's been a weekend. What a lot has happened since you were here last.'

'Is it Mr Stephen?' I asked.

They both shook their heads vigorously. 'No, no. Young Logan.' It was Mr Bernard speaking now. 'Fell over the drop . . . Wonder didn't break his neck.'

I found that I was cupping my cheek with one hand as I repeated, 'Mr Logan? Is he badly hurt?'

'His ankle's broken and his shoulder's out,' Mr Stanley said. 'But there's hardly a part of him that's not black and blue. We can't understand it.' He moved his head slowly from side to side, and, looking at his brother, he said, 'Can we?'

Mr Bernard's head jerked quickly and he brought out, 'Knows every rock like back of his hand. Every nook 'n' cranny. Can't make it out.'

'What did he say about it?' My voice was a whisper.

'Not much, not much.' It was Mr Bernard still going on. 'Says he must have slipped. Slipped, be damned, I say. It's funny. It's funny, I tell you, Stanley, it's funny.' He was nodding at his brother now, and Mr Stanley, putting his hand on his twin's shoulder, said, 'All right, all right, don't get worked up.' Then he turned his face towards me, saying, 'We'll be seeing you later.'

When I entered my room I stopped just within the door, because there, sitting at the desk, was Maurice Rossiter, and his eyes seemed to be waiting for me. His face looked white and rather drawn, and he did not give me the usual greeting but said right away, 'I heard the uncles telling you. As they said, we've had a weekend of it.'

I walked towards the desk and looked intently into this man's face. If he was putting on a show of concern, then he was doing it admirably. Even being able to turn pale on command, for pale he was, much paler than I had ever seen him. I felt as

I stared at him that his concern was genuine – at least at the moment.

'When did it happen?' I asked.

'Saturday afternoon. Broad daylight. We . . . we can't understand it.' He looked down at the desk, adding, 'I was just gathering up some papers, although I don't feel a bit like writing. In fact, I feel very much off colour today.'

He looked up at me expecting some word of sympathy, but I couldn't respond; and as I turned from him to go and hang up my coat I felt his eyes on my back. When I returned to the desk he was at the other side but still looking at his papers, his hand fumbling among them, and he said, 'We had such a good time, too, on Friday night. He celebrated his engagement, you know. We were all together at supper. It was like old times. I understand you've met Miss Badcliff.'

I raised my head and looked across the space into his waiting eyes and said in a flat voice, 'Yes, I've met Miss Badcliff.' Perhaps it was the tone of my voice that made his eyes narrow, and as he looked at me I warned myself to be careful, for I was very near to throwing my knowledge at him.

He was staring at me with a puzzled, penetrating look now; then he jerked his chin upwards. I had learned that this characteristic action meant that he was dismissing something from his mind . . . putting it aside. Following this, he left me to my work.

The next hour I worked mechanically because I was thinking . . . thinking of Logan Rossiter falling over a cliff in broad daylight. A man, moreover, who knew the fells like the back of his hand, as had been said. When Hollings brought my tea in I spoke to him. It was the first time I had done this except to thank him for the service. I said, 'How is Mr Logan, Hollings?'

'He's in pretty bad shape, madam. But lucky, very lucky he's alive.'

I ventured further. 'It's odd that he should have slipped in the daylight.'

'Very odd, if he had slipped, madam.' Now the old man looked at me for a moment in silence, penetrating silence. And then he said, 'You use the road to the bottom more than anybody except Mr Logan himself. Have you seen any strangers about lately?'

'No, Hollings.' I shook my head. 'The first day I came I saw a man – I think his name is Weaver. I saw him twice in the one day.'

'And you haven't seen him since?'

I paused. Somehow I felt inclined to tell Hollings that, although I hadn't seen the man again, yet I knew he was about the place watching from some point above the path that led down to the road, but all I said was, 'No, no, I haven't seen him since.'

He leant further across the table towards me now and I could just hear his voice as he said, 'Should you see him at any time would you be good enough to tell me . . . on the quiet, that is, madam. Do you understand?'

I nodded once, then said, 'Yes, Hollings, I understand. I'll tell you if I see him.'

'Thank you, madam.' He straightened up, and with his measured step he walked out of the room

. . . I liked Hollings . . . But then I mustn't forget I had liked Maurice Rossiter. Who in this house was honest, and who wasn't? Could you tell?

'What was Hollings on about?' I was surprised to see my employer standing within the door of his room, his appearance had been so abrupt.

'On about?' I screwed up my face. 'I asked him if Mr Logan was any better and he said not much. He was telling me about . . . about his injuries.' My lie was fumbled, but it apparently satisfied him and I watched him come shuffling across the room with his weird dancing step. He passed my desk and went out of the door, and I looked down at my typewriter and drew in a deep breath.

It was almost at this moment that a wood pigeon flew over the house. At least I heard its call. Coo-oo! Coo. Coo-oo! Coo. You don't usually hear a wood pigeon call in flight but I didn't think of this at the time, though I was to remember it later that day.

I had been sitting typing for about perhaps fifteen minutes when, to my utter amazement, I heard the voice of my employer together with that of another man coming from his room. Startled, I looked towards the door through which he had just recently passed, and then over the wide space towards his room. He could, of course, have re-entered his room by the door at the end of the hall, yet he rarely used this way because of two steps that led down to it. But it wasn't my employer's voice that startled me as much as that of the other man, for I recognised it. It was the whine of the odd man,

Weaver. I would have recognised it from out of a hundred voices. I found myself on my feet compelled to go towards the door. I had a sheet of typescript in my hand. Necessity was making me wily. Should Maurice Rossiter open the door I was on my way to ask a question. But as I stood outside, my head bent forward, I felt my face crinkling with bewilderment. Their voices were behind the door yet seemed distant. I can't explain it; as if the voices were echoes, and too far away for me to make out what they were saying. I did not think about what I was going to do or I wouldn't have had the courage to do it, but as I tapped on the door I opened it, not waiting to be bidden to enter. And there I stood with the door in my hand gaping at the empty room. Empty but for the voices, still like echoes but nearer now and coming from the far corner of the room. Coming – I realised in blank amazement – from a corner cupboard, an old weathered oak cupboard that had not seen polish for years. It was impossible for any one person to be in the cupboard, let alone two. But the sound drew me towards it, and as if I were touching something hot I turned the brass handle. And then the voices were no longer an echo. Although they still appeared to be coming from a distance, what they were saying was clearly intelligible. But for the moment I couldn't take in the words I was hearing because I was looking at the back of the cupboard. The inside did not lead to a point as would be expected from a corner cupboard, but was cut off short by a slat of wood, about – I should imagine –

nine inches wide. And in this panel of wood right on my eye level was a door of about twelve inches high. It was not wide open, but wide enough for me to see from the edge of it that on its inside it was padded with some grey material about twice as thick as the wood itself. And now my attention was jerked from the little door by the sound of Maurice Rossiter's voice, saying, 'You blasted fool!' followed immediately by the voice of Weaver. 'How was Aa t'know, Mr Maurice? There he was goin' down the hill, and when he was near the bottom what did he do but turn his backside 'round an' come back. An' you gone t' the lake, an' when I calls ya don't answer.'

'There was no need, you imbecile. I was alone.'

'But how the hell was Aa to work that oot, I ask ya, when I saw her along the road a while afore, makin' this way?'

'But not to meet me.' The words were a low hiss now.

'But how was Aa to know, I ask ya? An' then he goes in the hoose an' comes oot as if the devil was after him an' makes along by the greenhouses t' the lake. What was Aa to think, I ask ya?'

'I don't expect you to think. I expect you to do as you're told. Do you realise you might have killed him?'

'How was Aa ta know he would topple over? Him as is as steady on his pins as the rocks themsels. An' it wasn't a big stone, an' Aa just toppled it ower as if it was fallin' like.'

'Toppled it over as if it was falling!' The voice

was scathing. 'You might as well have put your name and address on it. Don't you know he's on to you? And may God help you if he gets any proof. He'll send you along the line for life. I'm telling you.'

'He'll send me along no line.' Weaver's voice was suddenly no longer whining but heavy with threat. 'If it's me or him, Aa know who it'll be.'

'Be quiet, listen.' There came a pause, and then Maurice Rossiter's voice hissing, 'Get going. There's someone coming.'

The someone I recognised as Mr Stanley, for his voice came in a high echo of surprise, exclaiming, 'Why, Maurice! What are you doing here? It's a long time since you managed . . .' The voice broke off and I heard the sound of quick footsteps, and then Mr Stanley speaking again in hushed tones, saying, and sternly this time, 'Now, Maurice . . .'

'It's all right, it's all right, Uncle. I only came down for a drink. I fancied it, I'm a bit het up.'

There was another pause before Mr Stanley spoke, and then he said, 'It was agreed that we have wine at meal times only. Now wasn't it? No more high jinks, or low jinks. Anyway, if you wanted a glass why didn't you ask me? I would have got it for you . . . Maurice, you didn't come down here for wine. You . . .'

At this point I almost let out a high scream. Only the action of clapping my hands tightly over my mouth prevented the sound escaping, for there were fingers touching my shoulder. I felt I had been caught in the act of stealing, or something equally dishonest. It was some seconds before I turned my body from the cupboard and looked to see who had found me out. And perhaps the gulp I gave was in relief when I saw Hollings looking at me, and raising his fingers to warn me to silence. Then he, too, was listening. I could not concentrate on what was being said any more and only snatches of the voices came to me. The shock of Hollings finding me had turned my legs to water and I had some difficulty in standing. I turned away from the corner cupboard, and as I did so I heard Mr Stanley's voice, the tone angry, now, saying, 'Don't lie, Maurice. The drain door is unlocked. Look, you can't get over that.'

I sat down on the couch where Maurice Rossiter usually rested in the afternoon and watched Hollings shutting out the voices by closing the little door. He followed this by closing the cupboard door. Then, coming towards me, he said, 'How did you find that out?'

'I . . . I didn't. I just heard the voices from the other room. I recognised the man Weaver speaking. I came in here, and when I opened the cupboard door, well . . .' I spread my hands out to him.

'The trap-door was open?'

'Yes.'

Hollings, putting his hand out towards my elbow, said, 'We'd better go into the other room.'

When I was seated at my desk, Hollings, standing opposite to me, said, 'That ingenious contraption is simply an air vent leading down into the cellar. My late master's grandfather had a number constructed in several rooms in the house all leading down to the cellar. You see, right up to the beginning of the last century this was a very wild stretch of country.' I nodded. I had read quite a bit about the lawlessness that had gone on in the last century, in some parts of the county. 'But my late master had all the vents sealed up. I wasn't aware that the one in Mr Maurice's room had been opened.' He paused now, and, leaning towards me, he said slowly, 'No doubt you are already aware that there are two opposing camps in this house. May I ask which one you are likely to support, madam?'

The question actually made me tremble. I certainly wasn't on Maurice Rossiter's side, although I was working for him, but could I say I was on the side of . . . The Big Fellow? I was sorry that he had been hurt, but I didn't really like the man any better now than when I had first met him. I said, 'I don't wish to take sides. It is really no business of mine, is it?'

'You cannot live in this house, even for a short time each day as you do, and not take sides, madam. You are either for my master or against him.'

'Which master?' I asked, looking him straight in the eye.

'Mr Logan,' he said.

'I would be on the side of right,' I said, still evading a direct answer.

'That's good enough for me.' He nodded his head. 'And now can you tell me what you heard between Weaver and Mr Maurice? And I would ask you to hurry, madam. Mr Maurice might be back at any moment.'

'I understand that Weaver threw a boulder which toppled Mr Logan over the cliff.'

'We know that, madam.' The 'we' referred to himself and Logan Rossiter. 'But did he say why he did it, at that time, and at that particular place?'

I stared across into the thin wrinkled face, and not for the life of me could I say, 'Because he thought that Mr Logan's fiancée would be at the lakeside with Mr Maurice.' And Hollings was prevented from repeating his question by the sound of a shuffling step in the hall coming towards my door. On this, with just a quick nod towards me, he went swiftly towards Mr Maurice's room, and a second after he had closed the door behind him Maurice Rossiter entered by the hall door. He passed me as if I wasn't there. And for this I was thankful.

4

It rained heavily all day on the Sunday, and as I stood peeling the potatoes for the Sunday dinner at the little kitchen window that looked almost directly up towards Neete Fell, my mother, coming behind me, said for at least the fifth time since I had come downstairs this morning, 'Don't worry now; come on, buck up.' She put her hand on my shoulder.

I stopped my work and turned round to her, a potato in one hand, a knife in the other, and, shaking my head, I said, 'I'm not worrying about him; I've told you it was over two years ago. I couldn't alter myself now even if I wanted to.'

She did not move back from me, but she drew her head into her shoulders as if to view me from a different angle. 'If it isn't him, then what is it?' she said. 'For something's worrying you.'

I placed the potato back in the bowl, and resting my hands on the little draining board, looked at the sheets of drifting rain, like waves following one another across the brow of the fell, and I made up my mind to tell her and my father what was worrying me, for I was in a state of uncertainty as to the right thing to do. And so I said to her, 'Come into the room and I'll tell you . . .'

Because of my father's frequent interruptions the telling took some time, for he demanded to know the ins and outs of every incident, asking questions that I could not answer, as I did not know the answers. My mother hadn't spoken at all during the telling, and not until I had quite finished did she say quietly, 'I would leave there, lass.'

'No, no, I wouldn't advise that, Kate.' My father was shaking his head at her sombrely. 'This is really none of her business that I can see. She is just worrying herself about something that doesn't concern her.' He turned to me again. 'You go up there to type that fellow's work. Well, then, type his work and keep yourself to yourself and let them get on with it.'

'It's easier said than done.'

'Yes,' quickly endorsed my mother, 'it's easier said than done. And I say to you again, lass: you leave that place.'

I looked at her for a moment and then turned my eyes away. 'No,' I said quietly. 'No, I won't leave until I've got to.' As I made this decision – and it was a decision, for I had been wavering in my mind since Friday night whether I would give up the job or not – and voiced it, I experienced the most odd sensation. I could only explain it by saying that if Hollings had been standing before me at that moment and had asked, 'Which side are you on?'

I would, without any hesitation, have answered, 'Mr Logan's.'

My father said at this point, 'It seems that this fellow's mind's twisted as well as his body.'

He was right there, I thought, for if Maurice Rossiter had not been stricken by polio he would have led a gay life, even a wild one. His novel gave me glimpses of the kind of life he would have chosen. This being denied him, he was holding a grudge, not against all mankind but against his brother, and the question I was asking myself now was, why? I recalled the conversation I had overheard in the summer-house and I couldn't see him venting such destructive spleen and bitterness on his brother just because he kept a tight hold on the purse-strings. It seemed too small a reason to evoke so much malice.

My father, smiling broadly at me now, patted my knee as he said, 'You go on about your own business and take no heed of anybody. Take all in and say nowt . . . At least you can't grumble about it being a dull job, now can you?'

My mother rose from the chair, repeating my father's words as she looked at him, 'Say nowt . . . except keep you informed of everything that's going on.'

'Aye . . . aye.' He laughed up at her. 'It will be like a story, having a chapter read to me every night. But mind' – he dug his finger towards me – 'you'll have to make it exciting. Aye, aye, I want some thrills. Real or make-believe, I want some thrills.'

Now his hand came and clasped my arm firmly as he continued quickly in a soft serious tone, 'I'm only funnin', don't lass; don't look so glum. Everything will turn out all right, you'll see.'

In the kitchen again and behind the closed door, my mother said once more to me, 'I would leave there, lass. You take my advice and leave there.'

Real or fancy, I could report no thrills the following week. Tor-Fret was quiet. I did my work; Maurice Rossiter's manner towards me was ordinary, business-like and ordinary. I enquired every day how Mr Logan was and was told he was improving. The twins asked me to go up and see Mr Stephen but warned me that, should he refer to Mr Logan's illness, I was to speak of it as 'flu. No, there was no exciting episode to relate to my father. And in my private life only one thing happened out of the ordinary. I was in the bus coming back to Rothcorn. It was almost full and I had to take the last empty seat and sit next to Hazel Osborne, who, after keeping a steady silence the whole of the journey, turned towards me just before I was about to alight, and with primmed lips said, 'You thought you were putting me nose out, didn't you? Well, yours is out now. Mr Rodney's after somebody in Amble . . . How d'you like it?'

As I stood up I smiled at her and whispered back, 'I like it very much,' and left her with that to chew on.

In the kitchen that night we laughed over this. It was the first real laugh I'd had for some time . . .

But the following week at Tor-Fret was not so

324

quiet. The change started almost before I had settled down to my work on the Monday afternoon. After a very cursory greeting Maurice Rossiter said, 'You'll have to do all Friday's work over again, the script is a mess.'

'How do you make that out?' I said after staring at him blankly for a moment.

'How do I make that out? . . . How do you spell incredulous?'

'i . . n . . c . . r . . e . . d . . u . . l . . o . . u . . s.'

'Oh, you do? Well, look at that.'

I took the sheet from his hand and there under-scored in red ink was the word incredible.

My father, and many of those with whom I had been brought up in the mining village, would often make the statement, 'It's hardly credible.' In conse-quence I had always found myself using incredible rather than incredulous. And last Friday I had been so disturbed with one thing and another I hadn't paid attention, with the result that I had used the familiar term.

'I'm sorry,' I said. 'It's my mistake.'

'And there's hardly a page where you haven't forgotten your spacing. Look at that . . . and that.' He pointed pages out to me where joined words were scored heavily through with the red pencil.

Again I said I was sorry. I told him I had been in a hurry and hadn't checked the work.

'But you're supposed to. That's what I engage you for.' He stared at me fixedly for a moment, then, dragging himself round, said, 'All right, all right, get on with it.'

On this, something flared up in me and I only stopped myself from crying at his back, 'No, you get on with it,' and walking out.

At three o'clock, when Hollings brought my tea, I was still fuming. He also brought me a message from Logan Rossiter. It was to the effect that he would like to see me after I had finished my work. I had as yet no inkling that this message was the reason for Maurice Rossiter's bad mood. I paid particular attention to my work all afternoon and checked it thoroughly before leaving it in a neat pile at the side of my desk. I hadn't seen anything more of my employer and didn't want to. I picked up my hat and coat and went out into the hall in search of Hollings, and almost immediately he appeared from the far passage-way. He beckoned me and we mounted the stairs, and neither of us spoke. He crossed the broad landing and knocked on a door, and when a voice from within the room bade him enter he opened a door and stood aside, allowing me to pass him, then closed the door again. And I was in the room looking towards the window, where sat Logan Rossiter. Discounting the plastered foot and the arm in a sling, I was startled at the change in him. Sitting there he no longer appeared to me like . . . The Big Fellow. He seemed to have shrunk. Perhaps this illusion was helped by the outsize winged leather chair in which he was sitting.

His eyes were on me as I went towards him and I spoke first. 'Are you feeling better, Mr Rossiter?' I asked quietly.

'Yes. Yes, I'm much better. Please sit down.' He pointed, and then added, 'You will be thinking by now that Tor-Fret is full of doddering invalids.'

'No. No, I don't think that.' I could find nothing original to say but kept looking at his face where one side was mottled with bruise marks from the chin to the brow. One eye looked swollen still, and was yellow tinged. And as I stared at him, pity rose in me. Yet I wasn't thinking so much of him at this moment as of the man Weaver. I could see him as I had done that first morning on the road, and there sprang into being a hatred for that rascally individual.

Logan Rossiter was saying now, 'I wonder if you will do me a favour?'

'Certainly, I will if I can.' My voice was low, and, as Maurice Rossiter would say, earnest sounding.

'It's a busy time. I have a lot of work piling up. My clerk was here at the weekend and he suggested sending one of the girls out to take down my letters. But it's such a long way from Alnwick and I wondered . . . I wondered if it wouldn't be too much for you – that is, whether you could give me an hour after you have finished with Maurice? I would get Patterson to run you home later.'

I did not stop to think, or even hesitate, but said, 'Yes, yes, of course. It won't be any trouble. And as long as I can get away before dark I can easily get the bus.'

'Thank you. It will be only for a week or so – a fortnight I should say at the most.' He now turned his head and looked out of the window. The view,

I noticed, took in a number of greenhouses, some of them in a sad state of repair. Beyond these I knew lay the lake, but it was shut from view by the trees and the outcrops of rock. Quite abruptly he said, 'How are you going to manage in the winter? We're often cut off up here. A few years ago I wasn't able to get up to the house for a week; I had to stay down in the town.' Then before I could make any answer he turned to me and added, 'You could quite easily do Maurice's typing at home, couldn't you? Have you a typewriter?'

I dropped my eyes away from his and said, 'Yes. Yes, I have a typewriter. And I have put that to Mr Maurice, but . . . but he wants his work done on the spot.'

'Oh, we'll see about that.' For the first time since coming into the room he sounded like the Logan Rossiter I had come to know. The tone sharp, the words clipped. And then, his tone changing abruptly again, he said, 'But should you not come up here Uncle Stephen would miss you . . . he's quite taken to you.' His eyes were hard on me, yet the whole expression on his face had softened. He looked different altogether when he was speaking kindly and I felt a warmth spreading over me. 'I like Mr Stephen,' I said.

We were looking at each other, and strangely now it was not my eyes that dropped away but his, and, changing the subject yet again, he said, 'Do you like your other work? You do work down in the village, don't you?'

'Yes. And I like it in a way,' I said, 'but it's

routine. There's nothing exciting about it, although you do a bit of everything, costing and wages, all things connected with a builder's business.'

'Have you any brothers or sisters?'

'No, I'm the only one.'

'What is your father?'

'He was a miner. But he got silicosis.'

'Oh dear, dear.' His brows drew together and I felt the stretching of his skin to be painful.

'Is he bedridden?'

'Oh no, not at all.'

'What does he do with himself to pass the time?'

As I looked at this man whom I had thoroughly disliked – let there be no mistake about that – I got the strange idea he was merely asking questions to keep me with him because he was lonely. Disregard this feeling as I would, it persisted, and so, after a little hesitation, I found myself relating my father's activities. I told him that he was very handy about the house, that he read a great deal. I told him the names of some of his books and how he had introduced me to selective reading. I told him also that he played the piano, being quite an accomplished pianist, although self-taught, mostly through Star Folio albums. And all the while he sat looking at me, his eyes on my face, his big-framed body relaxed in the leather chair, until a voice broke in. The voice came from outside the door and it said, 'All right, darling?' It was a question, and Logan Rossiter, turning his eyes sharply from my face, looked across the room and called, 'Yes, yes. All right, my dear,' and in came the girl.

I was on my feet before she reached the chair, and as their hands joined I turned away, saying, 'I'll come up tomorrow night, Mr Rossiter.'

'Oh, stay, don't go.'

'No, please don't go.' It was the girl speaking now. She was looking straight at me, a smile on her face. 'Please don't go because of me.'

'I'll miss my bus if I don't hurry.' I looked at my watch, and as I did so I thought that this was becoming a lame excuse. This was the second time that I had almost dived out of this girl's presence under the excuse of catching a bus. I glanced towards Logan Rossiter and asked, 'It will be all right for tomorrow night?'

'Yes, thank you . . . Thank you, Kate . . . Good night.'

'Good night, sir.'

'Good night.' I looked towards the girl, then went out, and as I crossed the landing I wasn't thinking of her but that Logan Rossiter had called me by my name . . . the name he had turned his nose up at on our first meeting. And I liked the way he had said it . . . Kate.

When I reached home I gave my father another episode, but I didn't stress the fact that I had found Logan Rossiter vastly changed . . . at least, in his manner towards me.

The following morning Rodney Stringer put his head round the door of the cubby-hole of my office in the yard, and after saying, 'Hello there,' added, 'I'm going to Shirston this afternoon; I could give you a lift as far as the well . . . OK?'

'OK, Rodney,' I said. 'Thanks.'

As he went to withdraw, one of the workmen, stacking slates just outside the main door, shouted, 'You be careful of him, miss. Proper Casanova he's turnin' out to be.'

Rodney looked back at me rather sheepishly as he said, 'You can't move in this village. I've sworn afore I'll get meself into the town . . . See you later then.'

'All right, Rodney.' I smiled on hearing him doing verbal battle with the man outside . . .

Later that morning, when I came down the hill after having my dinner, there he was, and I had hardly got into the cab beside him before he said, 'Well, I'd better tell you right away before that lot' – he jerked his head back towards the village – 'get one in. I've taken up seriously with a girl in Amble.'

'Oh, I am glad, Rodney.'

'Yes, I thought you'd be.' He swung round the bend before going on, 'Well, as there was no look-in with you – oh, I realised that almost from the beginning – I had to do something.'

'But I like you very much, Rodney, you know that.'

'Yes, but likin' and the other thing are poles apart, you know that too.'

'Yes . . . yes.' I looked straight before me. And now he took his eyes for a second from the road and, glancing at me, with a twinkle commented dryly, 'I had to do something or Hazel would have had me pinned for life . . . Oh, I couldn't have stood that. No.' Then, looking ahead again, he added, 'You'll like her.'

'I'm sure I shall, Rodney.'

He sighed and, after a short silence, asked, 'How you getting on up there?'

'Oh, all right.'

'What they like?'

'Like men. There's eight of them.'

'No women?'

'No. No women.' I did not add, 'Not yet.'

'My hat!' We laughed again.

'I heard something funny the other day,' he said. 'But you can't believe anything they say, it's so stretched. But I heard they had big drinking bouts, went as mad as hatters.'

'They might have done years ago, last century, but not now,' I said.

'Oh, but this was only recently. Or at least that's what was inferred.'

'I think they're mistaken.'

'Aye; as I said, everything's stretched. It always is in a village. Oh, aye, more so in a village . . . don't I know.' He laughed again. He was still laughing when he dropped me at the end of the road . . .

Fifteen minutes later I entered Tor-Fret. I crossed the hall, opened the door of the room and came to a dead stop. There, with his back to me, stood a strange man. He was dressed in black, he had a completely bald head and was wearing black shiny boots, and when he turned from Maurice Rossiter towards me I saw, to my gaping amazement, that the stranger was a minister. He was well into his sixties, perhaps older than he looked, for his portly figure and round red face gave the impression of vibrant health. I had been wrong in summing up character before, and this warned me against the instant recoil I had from this man. This recoil was not only caused by my sure knowledge that here was the person I had seen spying from the top of the rock, but by something behind the geniality in the pale-blue eyes.

'Ah . . . Kate.' Maurice Rossiter seemed in one of his happy moods today, and he introduced the minister on a light note, saying, 'This is the Reverend Fallenbor . . . Retired. And this, Reverend, is Miss Kate Mitchell, my . . . my very efficient secretary.' What a different diagnosis of my capabilities from yesterday.

'How do you do, Miss Mitchell?' The minister was shaking my hand, holding it firmly – I could almost say gripping it hard, as some men do when they try to impress you with their hand-shake by bruising your bones. 'Very pleased to make your acquaintance, Miss Mitchell. . . . My, my, you don't know what a phenomenon you are. For to my knowledge you're the first female to be on the staff of Tor-Fret for many, many years. In fact, Maurice' – he turned his head towards my employer – 'I can't remember one, can you?'

'Yes, oh yes.' Maurice Rossiter's voice was sober. Then he added, 'But Kate is only the forerunner. There are new times coming to the house. There'll be a permanent lady shortly, and some of us will have to pull our socks up then, I'm afraid.'

'Yes, indeed, indeed. Pull your socks up. Definitely you'll have to pull your socks up.' The minister was laughing now, his stomach thrust out, his hand squarely placed across it as if to stop its shaking. And it seemed as if his hand had accomplished this, for quite suddenly his laughter ceased and I could see no reason for its abrupt ending except that my employer, who was standing somewhere to the side of me, had made some gesture which had cautioned the minister to check his gaiety. And this could have been so, because on looking at my employer I was surprised at the complete change in him also, for his face at the moment was stiff. But he quickly assumed his expression of charm and gaiety of manner as my eyes rested on him, and he heckled the minister playfully now, saying, 'Come on, I'm going to throw you out. I want some work out of Kate, because one of these days she's going to tell me politely – Kate is always polite, Vicar . . .' He cast his eyes sideways at me before going on, 'She's going to tell me that I must take a week's notice, for she is going into Alnwick to work for Logan.'

'Never, never, not after she's worked for you.' The minister was holding his hand palm upwards towards Maurice, and for the moment I felt my stomach heave a little at the smarminess of this individual. Evidently this man was someone whom my employer knew and trusted, someone who was in the know. Yet I had seen him spying on them, watching their every move through binoculars. My stomach heaved again. And I felt my lip

334

curling. There was something in my make-up, some quality bred of my parents, that jibbed at this kind of nastiness. I turned from the two men and sat down at my desk and lowered my eyes to the typewriter.

'Goodbye, Miss Mitchell.'

I inclined my head without raising my eyes and said, 'Goodbye, sir.'

They went out and the door closed after them, and I had a strong desire to open all the windows wide.

I did not start typing but sat with my hands clasped tightly on my lap, staring towards the broad terrace, and asking myself if I should tell Hollings what I knew about this minister. I couldn't tell Logan Rossiter, but Hollings was different. Hollings, I felt, would sift and sort out information and pass on only that which would help his master. Yet as I sat there I knew that I was afraid to divulge my knowledge of this man's actions to anyone, even my parents, and in the episode I would give my father tonight there would be no mention of the man who had been lying on the top of the rock . . .

At five minutes past five I went up the stairs and across the landing to Logan Rossiter's door, and when I knocked I was bidden immediately to enter. He looked a little brighter tonight, more impatient, more himself, but his voice held no impatience when he spoke to me. It was unusually quiet, but his first words surprised me. 'You're late. I thought for a moment you weren't coming. It's just on twenty past.'

'Is it? I'm sorry. I thought it was only turned five past.'

He turned a little travelling clock round on the table at his side. 'It says twenty past, I must be fast.' He smiled, and as I looked at his stretching skin I felt again rising in me an unusual surge of pity. His face looked so sore, so stiff and sore. I said to him, 'How are you feeling today?'

'Oh . . . oh, much better. I'm better if I can work . . . Look' – he held out some sheets to me – 'I've been writing with my left hand. Can you make it out?'

I took the papers and began to read, then said, 'Yes, yes, I can.'

'They're just notes but they'll give me a lead. Oh, but before we start I must tell you, I've started on Borrow's *Lavengro*. Your telling me last night of some of the books that your father had read rather whetted my appetite. Look, I've got almost a third of the way through.'

He had leant towards the window where some books were placed on a low table and his hand was on one of them when he stopped speaking, and, pulling himself up sharply with the aid of his one good arm and his stick, he almost overbalanced in his effort to look further out of the window. In fact, for a moment, I saw his cheek pressed against the glass as he strained his eyes downwards. This room, as I have said, looked towards the greenhouses and the lake. There was also a path which led round the side to the back of the house and the stables, and it seemed to be towards this that his straining eyes were directed. When with an exhausted sigh he flopped back in the chair he drew in a number of sharp breaths before saying to me, and in a tone that belonged definitely to The Big Fellow, 'Are there any visitors downstairs?'

'There was earlier on this afternoon, a minister, the Reverend Fallenbor.'

The reaction that my answer to his question evoked was startling. It was as if I was seeing him on the hillside again, trying to choke the life out of Weaver. His one good hand gripped the arm of his chair until the knuckles strained white through the flesh, and his painfully stretched skin moved across the bones of his face as he ground his teeth together.

I was standing up now, quite close to his chair, and I bent towards him and said, 'Don't agitate yourself. You'll only make yourself ill . . . please.'

He looked up at me, right into my eyes, and I watched the tenseness fall from his face, to be replaced by an expression of weariness. I could almost say disillusionment. And as he stared at me I had the odd feeling that he was in need of help. And there came back to my mind a fairy story that my father used to read to me. It was about a giant, so big that no-one could go near him, and so he was left lonely in his castle on a hilltop, until one day a little girl came to the gates and talked to him through the bars. And when he opened the gates she did not run away like the rest of them but went in because she knew he was lonely. And then a miracle happened, for the giant decreased in size until he became a boy, just a little older than herself. And of course they married and lived happily ever after . . . Here was the giant then, and he was lonely, but the girl at the gate was not me, it was Noreen Badcliff. Didn't she know that her giant was lonely? My thoughts were pulled from such fey thinking as he said, 'Fallenbor's a reprobate, a real reprobate.'

'But he's a minister.' My voice was soft.

'Minister? Psst! . . . Minister who's lucky not to be defrocked. The valley got too hot for him years ago and he was moved, but after he retired he came back. I . . . I've forbidden him this house.'

'I'm sorry. I'm sorry, I shouldn't have told you.'

'You shouldn't have told me? . . . You should have joined the conspiracy of lies and deceit? . . . Oh!' He moved his head from side to side. 'You don't want to hear all that. But you know—' He stopped abruptly, and, looking up at me again with the same intent look, he moved his big head slowly before going on: 'But you know, Kate, if there was anyone I could talk to I think it could be you.' His head was still moving when, after another pause, he added, 'This might seem strange, for I'm not deluding myself that you like me; in fact I would, at a rough guess, say you disliked me . . . At least . . .'

'No! Oh no!' My eyes were blinking and my face scarlet as I gave him this denial, and then, turning my glance away, I said, 'Not now. I did at first, but not now. Your manner . . .'

'Yes, my manner, to say the least, is unfortunate. Overbearing, arrogant. Oh, I know. Oh, I know . . . Sit down, Kate.'

I sat down and watched him lean towards me,

putting his weight on the arm of the chair as he said, 'Can I talk to you?'

'Yes, if it will help.' I was breathing rather quickly as if I had been running.

'The person I should talk to, I know, should be Noreen, but I can't; she's too closely linked with Maurice.'

My eyes, giving me away again, brought from him now the explanation. 'You see,' he said, 'we were all brought up together, more or less, and at one time she was very fond of Maurice, so much so that . . . well, I thought . . . I thought it was Maurice she loved, not me. Even after his illness I still imagined things hadn't changed . . . but they had, unfortunately for him. Added to this, my brother and I don't see eye to eye on a number of things. I could never countenance his type of friends, for one thing. He was rather cosmopolitan in his tastes. We had numbers of queer people staying here at one time, among them the Reverend Fallenbor. He . . . Maurice even palled up with men like Weaver. You see, he was of an irresponsible romantic turn of mind and tried, in his way, to push Tor-Fret back a century . . . I cannot go into all those happenings, but I had to put my foot down and this caused bad feeling between us. And then he was struck with polio and somehow things never righted themselves. Anyway, because Noreen is still in sympathy with him I cannot talk with her, at least about what is troubling me most at present.' He paused here for a long moment before he said, 'Three times in the last year someone has tried to polish me off.' He pointed to the white line of the slit running down his lip. 'That was a knife. It was aimed at my temple, but the point just grazed my lip.'

Just grazed, I thought. Just grazed was definitely an understatement.

'Then one night last winter I was knocked senseless on the terrace there, below. It was snowing and I could have frozen to death, or at least been finished off by loss of blood from a scalp wound.' He put his hand to the crown of his head where the hair was combed sideways away from the natural parting, then went on, 'Now this . . . and I'm quite well aware who the culprit is.'

'The man Weaver.' My voice was a whisper.

'Yes, the man Weaver, Kate. Yes, I know who wants to finish me. But what I don't actually know is why. There could be any one of a number of reasons. I couldn't, for instance, think he wants to kill me just because I cut him off from free drinks. Of course, men have been killed for less, yet I can't think that's the reason for these attacks, or any of the other things that come to mind; he would have attempted them earlier, and not waited until this last year. And the odd thing is that they've always happened after I've left the house and have returned unexpectedly.'

I could not meet his eyes now, and I said, 'But why don't you call in the police?'

'No. Not yet, at any rate. I feel there's something behind all this, something personal, something connected . . .'

He stopped, and now it was his turn to shift his gaze, and he was silent for a moment before looking at me. And then he smiled and said, 'Anyway, it's done me good to talk. I feel better, lighter somehow. You know, Kate' – his head drooped forward – 'I think you would make a very good friend.'

My face was hot again, but I could look at him and say, 'I hope so.' I could look at him because my eyes had nothing to betray as yet . . . as yet I did not know what was to happen to me. His hand came towards me and I put mine in it. It was a quiet grasp, and then he said, 'Well, now shall we get down to work?'

'Yes,' I said with a laugh to cover the confusion that was creeping over me, 'or else it will pay you to get someone out from Alnwick.'

And so we worked in a harmony that is imposs-ible to describe; and later, when I went down the hill, part of me was worried about Logan Rossiter, but the greater part was happy because of him.

I had almost reached the main road when I saw Noreen Badcliff coming towards me, and as we came abreast she stopped and said, 'Hello.'

'Hello,' I answered, and self-consciously made to move on when her hand touched my arm, and after compelling my gaze for some moments she said quickly, 'Why do you dislike me?'

The forthright question, so much the reverse of her nature as I saw it, nonplussed me, to say the least, and it was natural in such circumstances that I should deny my feeling towards her, saying, 'What makes you think I dislike you?'

She put her head on one side and smiled, a quiet smile that heightened her beauty still further, as she answered, 'Your manner, the look in your eyes the first time we met. I can't remember anyone looking at me like that before, at least not without some good reason.' She moved her head slowly.

It was on the tip of my tongue to say I had a very good reason, but I told myself yet once again it wasn't my business, and so rather inanely I reverted to the old excuse, 'If I don't hurry,' I said, 'I'll miss my . . .'

She cut off my words by closing her eyes and exclaiming, 'Oh, don't tell me you're going to miss your bus again – that will be the third time. This only proves you've something against me, and for the life of me I can't think what it can be.'

'No?' The question was out before I could stop it, and the inflection I gave to the word proved to her conclusively that she was right in her surmise. I had made a mistake and I regretted it immediately, but it was done now and I would have to give her some explanation, and I could think of none other than the truth, at least part of it. I paid no attention to the warning that told me to keep my mouth shut, but said quietly, 'I know you are not playing straight with Mr Logan, that's why.'

I had never given any thought to how this girl would react to exposure; if I had, doubtless I would have imagined her taking a high hand, a very high hand, so I was amazed at the effect of my words on her. I watched the colour drain from her face, and then she clapped her hand tightly across the lower half of it. The fingers digging into her cheek distorted her face momentarily into a caricature of herself, and the eyes that looked at me over the rim of her hand held fear. It was this expression more than anything else that amazed me, puzzled and amazed me. Her hand slowly slipping down from her face, she stood staring at me, her small compact breasts rising and falling rapidly. 'How did you find out?' she now asked.

'At the lake. I came into the grounds over Neete Fell . . .'

'No!' It was her fist that was on her mouth now, as if she was blowing through it.

'When?' The question was muffled.

'Shortly after I started to work here.'

'I know, I know.' Again she closed her eyes. 'I remember the day. I thought . . . Oh . . . my . . . God.' After a moment she opened her eyes wide and said, 'I must talk to you.'

'I really must be getting . . .'

'Oh no, please. Give me a few minutes. Come down to the car, we can't stand here. Come down to the car. I must talk to you, please.'

A few minutes ago I had actually hated this girl, but now I found myself being sorry for her. Again she had hold of my arm, but now as if she was afraid I would run away.

We didn't speak until we were seated in the front of the car, and then to my embarrassment she gripped my hand and her beautiful eyes looked appealingly into mine as she said, 'I wonder if I can make you understand?'

'You can but try,' I said.

'Well, you see, it all started so long ago, twelve years, or even before then. When I came home from school for the holidays, there were always the Rossiters, big Logan and handsome Maurice. Heavenly Maurice I used to call him in those days because his beauty was something not quite real. He was gay then and not a little mad, and all the girls were after him, but he always said that as soon as we both left school we would be married. He was only a year older than me. We used to play at getting married. The last time we played that game was on his eighteenth birthday. We had high jinks in the cellar. Logan was away and we all went mad, even the uncles. Logan wouldn't countenance parties, especially in the cellar, and he was right. Oh, he was right, because they always led to trouble. It was the day after this party that Maurice took ill and there was no further talk of us getting married. I offered to marry him, I wanted to marry him, but he just laughed at me. He seemed different after his illness, queer at times. Then I went away. My mother, who was a widow, married again, a Frenchman. In a way I was glad to escape. We stayed abroad three years, but my mother's second marriage was even more disastrous than her first. We had kept on the house across the valley' – she motioned now with her head – 'but that had to be sold. My mother and my step-father separated and we came back and lived in the lodge, where we still are. And for the last four years I have been in love with two men. It is odd, but it's true.'

I released my hands from her grip and, returning her stare, I said, 'I think it's impossible to be in love with two men at the same time.'

'It isn't, it isn't. I can't explain it. I want to marry Logan. He is good and steady and in him lies security, and oh, I do need security. But apart from that I . . . I do love him. I am greatly attracted to him, and yet Maurice has just to look at me, just to touch me and my blood turns to water. Maurice has a power that can't be explained, you can only feel it. And . . . and a year ago Maurice and I . . . well . . . we . . .'

I cut in on her here, saying sharply, 'So you are quite prepared to marry Mr Logan and keep up an affair with Mr Maurice? I think it's . . .'

'No, no. Once I marry Logan . . .'

'Listen . . . I think you had better know that I was behind that summer-house for some time and heard quite a lot of your conversation with Mr Maurice, and from what I remember you were marrying Mr Logan because Mr Maurice wanted you to.'

'No! No! Oh no!' She was shaking her head vigorously. 'And you can't judge me from what you heard. You don't know what it is like to come under Maurice's charm. When you're with him you never want to leave him, you'll promise him anything, and when you are away from him you want to remain away but feel yourself drawn back. And another thing . . .' Her eyes opened wide now. 'Whatever you do . . . listen to me carefully.' She was gripping my hand hard again. 'Whatever you do you must not let Maurice know that you are aware of what is between us. Even if you make up your mind to expose me to Logan, you must do it in some way other than letting it come directly from you. You don't know Maurice. You see . . .'

'Are you suggesting that he'd do me an injury? Say . . . have me pushed over the big rock like Mr Logan was.'

'No no. Maurice wouldn't do anything physical, but there are worse ways of hurting than by physical pain. And he didn't push Logan over the rock. Even if he could, he wouldn't have done that.'

'No, but he knew who did it.'

Her eyes narrowed at me now and she said, 'You do, too?'

'Yes, I know.'

'There's very little you don't know, is there? You have learned a lot in the short time you have been up at Tor-Fret.'

'It wasn't my seeking; the knowledge has been thrust on me.'

'All through your walking over Neete Fell and coming in the back way.' She shook her head slowly. 'It's funny the little things that change destiny. And you know about Weaver?'

I merely inclined my head and she turned her gaze from me, and, looking out of the car window into the slow twilight, she said, 'I could pity Weaver.'

'After he has tried to kill Mr Logan three times?'

'He's as much under Maurice's spell as the rest of us.'

'Is that why he tries to murder someone?'

'No, that really has nothing to do with it. It's

346

something else that prompts him to go too far. You see, he feels that he's a Rossiter and Tor-Fret is rightly his home.'

My eyes widened and my mouth opened slightly as she turned to me and said, 'He was born at Tor-Fret. His mother worked in the kitchen. Weaver was born over the stables and his mother claimed no man as the father of her child, for it was an understood thing that it was "The Rossiter", as Logan's grandfather was called. Weaver grew up here and was accepted by everyone, at least in his boyhood, as a side-shoot of the family by everyone, that is, except Logan, who could never stand him. When Logan's father died the death duties were such that it was thought they would have to sell the place. But Logan cut down and dismissed the hangers-on – there were a number of these – and one of the first to go was Weaver. But he never really went; he has haunted the place ever since and takes Mr Maurice as his master . . . There you have the reason for Weaver's animosity towards Logan.'

I was thinking back to Logan Rossiter questioning the reason for Weaver's determination to kill him. It was understandable he would not tell me of the blood relationship. Yet why look for a stronger reason?

'But what do you intend to do about . . . about me?' The question was urgent. We were looking at each other; the girl's eyes were wide, seeming to stretch across the entire surface of her face, and I was not proof against the pleading I saw in them. If I had intended taking steps to inform Logan

Rossiter of how he was being duped, I could not now have gone on with it. I said to her simply, 'Nothing.'

Again I watched her close her eyes, but this time in evident relief. Once more she had hold of my hand, and as I saw the glint of tears on her lashes I had the impulsive urge to put my arms about her and hold her, but I was prevented by a little voice which said, 'She could be playing you up. She's just as charming a double-dealer in her way as Maurice Rossiter, and she could be laughing at you behind your back.' And she forced me to bring this sore matter into the open within the next few seconds, for she said, 'You are kind. Logan told me you were a kind person. He said it was in your face. I was a bit jealous of you before I saw you. He thinks you're sweet.'

For no reason that was evident at this moment I found myself not only confused by her words but my heart beginning to thump, and when she added, 'You know, Maurice too thinks very highly of you,' I could not help but snap back, 'Yes, I know. Our prim, industrious and delightfully earnest Kate. I know what Mr Maurice thinks about me.'

She had the grace to lower her head, but it came up instantly again as she said, 'But he talks like that about everyone. He laughs at people, makes fun of them, but that doesn't say he doesn't like them. Take no notice of that. I'll say this in Maurice's defence – I must in fairness to him. He's suffering under a great handicap. You see, he cannot get over the unfairness of fate, he's still fighting it. I think . . .

I think at times that part of his mind is affected also.'

She waited, and when I made no further comment she remained quiet until I said, 'I must really get the next bus. I have quite a walk up from our village.'

'I'll run you there.'

'No, no. I'd rather you didn't.'

She looked hurt and I said quickly, 'You don't want Mr Maurice to know that you took me home. Who knows but we are being watched.' In trying to explain my reason for refusing her offer I saw that I had hurt her and it was my hand that went out and touched hers now as I said, 'I'm sorry. I did not mean to be nasty.'

She put her other hand on top of mine and through the dim light she looked at me and asked, 'Are we going to be kind, Kate?'

It was such an unusual phrase for a girl of this type to be using. The term 'Are we going to be kind?' was one used by children. I had used it myself for years as I had played or fought with my companions: 'Aa you kind with me?' I would ask, or, 'Aa'm not goin' to be kind with you.' Only a short time ago, when I happened to be passing down a street in South Shields, I was interested and amused by a group of children having a squabble and one of the leaders shouting to the others, 'We're not goin' to be kind with you any more, so there!' It was an idiom of the South Tyne and yet here was this educated girl asking me to be kind with her. Engendered by the distrust my employer had bred

349

in me, my thoughts for a moment were: Is she being condescending and thinking she is coming down to my level in speaking this way? But no, there was nothing condescending about her manner; and, what was more, I no longer spoke in the idiom. At this moment the light of the oncoming bus sent a glow through the back window of the car and I made no answer to her request but said hastily, 'I really must get this bus, my mother will be worrying.'

'Yes, yes, I understand. And it's all right . . . Kate?'

I was half out of the car, but I turned my head and looked at her steadily. 'Yes,' I said, 'it's all right.'

I had to put the torch on going up the hill, and when I was still some way from the cottage my mother's voice came to me, saying, 'That you, Kate?'

'Yes, yes, it's me.'

When I reached the door she said, 'What's kept you? You're late.'

'I . . . I met someone,' I said.

Her hand was on my shoulder helping me off with my coat. 'Arthur?'

'No, not Arthur.'

'I had the feeling that's what was keeping you. He was in the village just about tea-time. I was coming out of the post office and I saw him getting off the bus near *The Fox and Hounds*. He didn't notice me and I kept out of his way . . . You haven't seen him then?'

'No. But,' I added, 'I think the sooner I do, the better.'

'Well . . . there's something in that. By the way, I didn't tell your father. He hasn't been too good the day.' She was whispering now.

'Is it his breathing?' I couldn't see her face because we were standing in the passage and the room doors were closed, but her voice told me that she was troubled. 'Yes, that, and he's off colour. In some way he's not himself. See if you can cheer him up.' She patted my shoulder and I preceded her into the sitting-room.

'Hello . . . there.' The words were spaced by a sharp pull on his breath.

'Hello,' I said, standing at his side. 'Not feeling too good?'

'Oh, I'm all right. It's your mother, she keeps fussing. Oh, I'm all right,' he repeated. 'It's the weather. We're in for a hard winter, I can always tell. Bet your life there'll be snow afore the end of the month.'

'I wouldn't be surprised,' I said. 'It was nippy coming up the fell.'

'Anything happened the day?'

'Yes,' I said, 'quite a lot. I'll tell you after tea.'

And so when I had finished my meal and the table had been cleared I told them what had transpired between Noreen Badcliff and myself, and for once my father did not see two sides to the situation, but said immediately, 'She's lying, I bet you a bob she's lying. No woman can love two men at the same time . . . impossible.' He heaved a number of short breaths and was about to speak again when my mother cut in sharply on him, 'And why not? I don't agree with you. Of course a woman can love two men at once.'

I was more than a little surprised at my mother's championship of the girl she knew to be playing a double game, and more surprised still when she went on and emphatically now, 'I suppose you would say it was all right for a man to love two women at once and that he could do it.'

'Well, aye . . . yes, I would 'cos it's different for a man, his temperament's different and everything. Women are more single-minded, they're not capable of it; it's not in their make-up, if you know what I mean.'

'One set of emotions for the man and one for the woman.'

My mother, to my consternation, got up and went out into the scullery, and my father smiled towards the door and nodded to me and in a conspiratorial whisper said, 'I know all her tactics. She's taken that line to get me to argue . . . thinks . . . it'll take me mind off meself.' He shook his head and his smile broadened. 'I'm not worrying about meself; it's her that worries; she never stops.' He now held his finger up for silence, and when my mother came into the room again there was no more talk. My father and I read while she knitted. The evening was changed.

Later, when my father had gone up to bed, I said to her, 'You really don't believe a woman can be in love with two men at the same time, do you, Mother?'

I put the question because I was slightly puzzled. She had been so quiet all evening, and when she was worried about my father she usually chatted and talked and went for him a bit to distract him from himself, as he had said. And now her answer to my question came, I might say, as the biggest surprise of the day. 'Yes,' she said, 'I do believe it, for when it happens to you personally you know it must be true.'

We were looking at each other, standing on the rug within the circle of light from the cream-shaded oil lamp, and I said with some wonderment, 'Mother!'

'I was in love with two men for over three years. I picked your father. I didn't make a mistake, I haven't regretted it, but that doesn't stop me from even now waking up in the middle of the night and thinking of the other man . . . and knowing that some part of me, after thirty years, is still in love with him. It makes me furious when men, your father or anyone else, allows emotional licence for the male breed but not for the female . . . All men are narrow.'

I was twenty-seven and I had never been separated from my parents for more than a fortnight in a year. I would have said I knew my mother inside and out, and yet here she was appearing to me as a different woman. I could not associate what she was saying with the woman I knew to be my mother. It was like something coming out of the mouth of a fictitious character, like one of the women in Maurice Rossiter's book.

'Don't look so worried now.' She touched my cheek. 'I've been happier than most women, and as long as I have your father I will go on feeling like that. But life's a funny thing. Come on.' She took my elbow. 'Let's go up.'

As I lay in bed peering through the darkness I was not thinking at this moment so much about the people at Tor-Fret, but about my mother who had loved two men. But as I went to sleep a thought wove itself along the fringe of unconsciousness and there, as if standing outside myself, I read it. It said, 'I'm glad you were kind to Noreen Badcliff.'

5

Things went very smoothly during the following week. Maurice Rossiter could have been the man whom I remembered during the interview, so charming and considerate was he. Even on the Tuesday, when I was an hour late, owing to my father, who was now in bed, having a rather bad turn, he did not greet me with coolness, as I expected, but was all concern and solicitude when I explained the reason for my lateness. Nor did his manner alter when twice during the week we ran into each other in the hall following my session with his brother.

Logan Rossiter was improving rapidly. His robust constitution coming to his aid, he could now hobble around. It was on the Friday of the following week that he said to me, 'Dare I ask you if you can come over tomorrow morning and help me to get through this?' He pointed to a stack of work.

As I have said, because I cut my hours with Bill during the week I did Saturday morning to make up my time. I glanced up from my table towards him.

He was standing with his back to the long narrow window; the pale sun was outlining him and he looked The Big Fellow again. I said, 'Oh, I'm sorry; I'm due at Mr Arnold's on Saturday morning.' And then without hesitation I added, 'I could come over in the afternoon, if that would do.'

'Oh no, you want your Saturday afternoon . . . your weekend, to yourself.'

'No, I don't; it doesn't matter, I have nothing else to do. I'll come over.' I was finding now that I could talk to Logan Rossiter in a way I could never talk to Maurice, and I was surprised each time I thought about it. In fact I could almost believe that the cynical overbearing individual did not exist, but not quite, for my common sense told me that he was still active below the surface and would break through when the occasion demanded. Because I was obliging him I was being treated to the Rossiter charm; whereas the charm was painted thick on Maurice, there was only a thin veneer on Logan; nevertheless it was definitely evident now and had successfully broken down any feeling of animosity I had towards him . . .

So I came up to Tor-Fret on the Saturday afternoon. I came up through a gale of wind that nearly swept me off my feet. When I reached the Hall I stood inside the doorway panting to regain my breath.

Because it was my custom to do so, I went towards what I called my room to take off my outdoor clothes. There was no need for me to go near Maurice Rossiter's apartments, but I did it without thinking – force of habit you could say. It wasn't until I opened the door that I thought to myself, Oh dear, he could have been in here resting. But the room was empty, yet seemed full of noise, for the long windows in their wooden warped sashes were rattling like castanets, and from the wide chimney-piece a copper draught sheet fixed to the lower part of the chimney joined in with a running rattle of sound like a badly timed tambourine. It was likely the wind and the noise it was creating that covered the sound of my opening the door, and I was about to close it behind me, when from the next room I heard Noreen Badcliff's voice saying, 'You were eager enough for me to go on with it a short while ago.'

'I'm only trying to do the decent thing.' This was Maurice Rossiter's voice. Yet I hardly recognised it, there was no laughter or cynical amusement in it, nor yet bitterness. If I could have associated humility with him, I would have said his tone was humble.

'And it's your idea of doing the decent thing to stop me marrying him? Had you made up your mind to blackmail me when I married him and now you've got cold feet?'

'Oh, Noreen . . . don't say that.'

'Well, what am I to think? You've been breaking your neck to get money out of him, and when he doesn't respond you think it will be a good idea if I marry him and act as liaison officer between you and his pocket. Well, Maurice, it may surprise you to know that I had thought of marrying Logan long before you suggested it.'

'Don't say that.' The voice had changed completely. The tone was so bitter, so sharp, that the words seemed to cut through the sound of the wind, and they came to me so clearly that I started and pulled the door further open, ready to make my retreat, which I did the next moment as another burst of bitterness came from the inner room, the tone lower now, the words thick sounding. 'If you married him in every church in the county, you'd still be mine. Nothing or no-one can alter that now.' What impression these words made on Noreen Badcliff I don't know, but they sent a chill through me.

I stood in the hall, my eyes darting about me. Where was everyone? Were they all in their different niches listening? Did they all know what was going on between those two in there? Were they all in the know except the one person who was particularly involved? As I gripped the handle and noiselessly turned it to close the door, I heard snatches of Noreen Badcliff's voice: the word 'marry' and then 'why?' and then on a high note two words repeated twice, 'I must, I must, I must.'

Still with my hat and coat on I went across the hall and mounted the stairs and tapped on the library door, the room where we now worked. There was no answer, and when I opened the door I found the room was empty and I did not enter. As I looked towards Logan Rossiter's bedroom door there came the sound of footsteps from the far passage, and Hollings appeared on the landing. As I was about to speak I heard the sound now of distant laughter, men's laughter. It was a nice sound, comforting, I thought, so different from the sound in the room downstairs.

'They're all with Mr Stephen, madam; he was in need of company. Would you care to go along?'

'Thank you, Hollings.'

Hollings preceded me along the passage, knocked on Mr Stephen's door, and as he opened it announced, 'Miss Mitchell to see you.'

'Oh, come in, come in.'

This welcome was not only from Mr Stephen, but from the twins, and also Logan Rossiter, who added, 'Oh, you're early. But come in and sit down.'

'Come and sit near me.' Mr Stephen patted the bedspread and Mr Bernard made way for me, while Mr Stanley took my hand as if to assist me on to a throne. And there I sat on the foot of the bed, feeling all of a sudden very shy in the midst of these four men.

'We're just talking of weddings. Do you like weddings?' Mr Stephen was poking his sharp nose towards me as he spoke and I made a great effort to breathe naturally and to ignore the constricted feeling in my chest as I answered briefly, 'Some.'

'All weddings are risks. We never had the guts to take the risk, had we?' Mr Stephen looked towards Mr Bernard and Mr Stanley, and Mr Bernard muttered, 'Wise . . . wise.'

Mr Stephen, ignoring him, glanced at his nephew, and, as if he hadn't been interrupted, went on, 'But Logan's going to brave it. Stout heart, Logan.'

On this, Logan Rossiter laughed as he replied, 'You may not have been married, Uncle, but it didn't stop you being a gay dog, did it? So don't talk as if you've led a lonely bachelor existence. Being saintly in your old age doesn't suit you; you're still a wicked old man.'

This caused Mr Stephen to chuckle so much that I felt his thin body shaking under the bedclothes. Then, heaving himself up, he bent towards me and, taking my hand, said, 'Know what I said to those two last night?' He nodded to his two brothers. 'I said if I was only twenty years younger I would've tossed me cap at you.'

My face was warm and I could not but smile and reply with equal gallantry, 'And if you had been twenty years younger I would have caught it.'

We all laughed, and the laughter was hearty; even Mr Bernard had joined in. But it was his laugh that ceased first and his face was straight as he mumbled, 'Wouldn't mind you 'bout the house . . . sensible.'

I lowered my head and shook it somewhat sadly, but I was still smiling as I answered, 'Some women think, Mr Bernard, that it's the worst thing that could be said of them . . . being sensible.'

'Nonsense. Nonsense.'

Mr Bernard was going from the room now, and Mr Stanley, following him, pulled faces at his brother's back. And now I rose from the bed and said my goodbyes to Mr Stephen, promising once again to look in on him, and when I left the room Logan Rossiter came behind me. He was hobbling slowly, and I suited my steps to his as we crossed the gallery. We didn't speak until we reached the library and he was seated, and then he said, 'Do you believe that?'

'What?' I did not know to what he was referring.

'About women not wanting to be thought sensible.'

I looked down towards the floor. 'Well, it's really hardly a compliment. When a woman is plain and has nothing else about her the best thing they can say of her is she's sensible.'

'But you're not plain, Kate.' His tone was emphatic. 'You're . . .' I was looking at him and he at me, and we stayed like this for some moments. His mouth was partly open as if he was going to continue speaking, and then he shook his head from side to side and looked away as if he was embarrassed, yet I couldn't imagine this man ever feeling embarrassed, or at a loss for words. Nor was he, for quickly I watched him sweep away the personal platform on which he had for a brief moment stood, by saying, 'Well, let us both be sensible and get down to work, eh?'

We got down to work. But as the afternoon wore on I became enveloped in a heavy feeling of sadness. It weighed on me until I had the desire to put my head down on to the table and cry, and when I asked myself what had caused this I got no reply, except that it was late autumn and the dying year had always affected me.

Nor was my sadness lessened by a visit from Noreen Badcliff herself. Logan Rossiter had left me after giving me directions with regard to the work he wanted doing. And I saw no-one for the rest of the afternoon, except Hollings, who as usual brought me my tea but spoke of nothing but the weather, which was worsening considerably, until Noreen Badcliff came into the room. She tapped on the door and entered, and said, 'Hello there.'

'Hello.'

'What is it?' she now asked. 'Aren't you well?'

I could have put the same question to her, for apart from her face, which was paler than usual, there were dark rings encircling her eyes. In fact, her lovely face had a strange, drawn look; perhaps, I thought, it was the result of her doing battle with Maurice. Yet I was to remember this particular afternoon when I knew the reason for her pallor. I said now, 'I might have caught a little cold; the wind was piercing coming up.'

'Yes, and it's worse now. I just said to Logan I would run you back, but he's already made arrangements for Patterson to do that.'

'Oh, he shouldn't. I could easily get the . . .' I checked myself.

'The bus.' She was smiling, a whimsical little smile, which I couldn't resist returning, but I said, 'Yes, I could just as easily get the bus.'

'Well, you're not going to, not today. It was very good of you to come up, and in your leisure time too . . . You know' – she came round and took a seat right opposite the desk – 'I should hate to be tied to so many hours a day. Even if I was capable of doing anything, which I'm not.' She spread her hands appealingly towards me. 'I'm useless, utterly useless. Mother wanted me to go in for teaching because I was good at English. I should have loved to teach. But how can you teach when there's nothing in you? I have nothing in me . . . Oh, I know I haven't.'

How could you hate a girl who talked like this? A girl who had two men in love with her, and others perhaps, and who admitted there was nothing in her. Even with all I knew about her I could still find her endearing at this moment.

'The trouble with me,' she went on, 'is that I'm bone lazy. I hate getting out of bed in the mornings; the only thing that gets me up early is the thought of a horse.' She smiled, and then she sighed and ended, 'But I'll have to alter my ways from now on.' I waited as we looked at each other. 'We're going to be married on the thirtieth of November.'

I knew now that she had come in precisely to tell me this piece of news. She had led up to it in a roundabout way. She had put herself over as lazy, naïve, almost unintelligent. Lazy she might be, but the latter two characteristics were a mere pretence, a mere façade to hide . . . what? I found myself once again filled with suspicion, then this in turn was swept away on my remembering what she had said to Maurice Rossiter earlier this afternoon.

Like my mother, this girl might be in love with two men. I did not know on which side the scale dipped, for dip it must one way or the other, but I was aware she was fighting in her own way as if for her very existence, and who was I to kill happiness for another. I who knew so much what the death of it meant. I looked at her and smiled as I said, 'I hope you'll be very happy . . . That you both will be very happy.'

On this she stood up, came round the table and put her hand on mine for a moment, then went out without another word.

Slowly I placed my elbows on the table and pressed the cushions of my thumbs over my eyes. I was crying, but inwardly.

During the next few days the weather worsened considerably, although winter had not officially begun. The storm on Saturday had heralded winter to the fells. The morning air began to hack at your throat as if it was laden with minute icicles, and some mornings the far Cheviots were obscured by mist, and the valley where ran the Coquet was lost so completely that you doubted if it had ever existed, so levelled and impregnable was the mist that filled it. On these mornings I shrank further inside my clothes. On these mornings I longed to stay in close to the high red fire, wrapped about with the smell of my mother's cooking and the feeling of security I always experienced when with my parents.

It was such a morning as this that began the day on which I was faced with another heartbreak, a heartbreak that made my experience of two years ago seem a pale anaemic thing. And it was brought about by the very man who had caused that heartbreak.

Because of the condition of the weather I had definitely made up my mind to tell Maurice Rossiter that if he still required my services, now that the long screed was nearly finished, I would have to come up to Tor-Fret in the mornings because the nights were cutting in sharply, and even if I left the house promptly at five-thirty it still meant me walking up our fell in the near dark, which I didn't relish. When I asked Bill Arnold that morning if it would be all right my coming in the afternoons, his answer was, 'You come any time you like, Kate. Make your own time, any time in the twenty-four hours. The only thing is . . . come . . . 'cos I've never had it so easy for a long time. Those books and accounts nearly drove me round the bend.'

I didn't think, in fact I knew, that any similar proposal to Maurice Rossiter would get such a kind reception, and yet again I was to be mistaken as I had been so often of late.

'Yes, of course, Kate,' he said. 'I understand you don't want to go home in the dark, not when it's like this. It's vile. Yet you know,' he added, 'I would rather be here, even with the weather as it is, than anywhere else on earth. But why . . . why have we been allotted such chilling cold? It's a different kind of cold from that in any other county. Don't you think so?'

'I haven't been in many other counties, but I know I don't like it.' I found I was smiling at him, as much in relief at escaping the bout of high-flown temper that I had steeled myself to receive as at the pleasant, considerate acceptance of my proposal.

There was a quietness about his manner today, and an ordinariness that was disarming, but I warned myself not to be deceived by it. Yet later in the afternoon, when he called me into the other room to take some pages of the script he had been re-checking, and I saw him wince and his eyes flicker as if he had been jabbed by something sharp, I forgot for a moment his duplicity and found myself feeling compassion for him as I had done when I first met him. And he, sensing this, smiled at me and said, 'You know, I don't know what I'd do without you; I don't know what I did before you came.'

'You had Mr Julian,' I said.

'Yes, I had.' He nodded at me. 'And I thought he was good, but he didn't get through half the amount of work that you do, and took twice the time over it.' He now pulled his chin into his neck and looked at me from under his lids. 'I went for you like a tiger the other day, didn't I? Complaining and criticising.' He shook his head slowly. 'You'll get to know me, Kate, by and by, and take those days in your stride. But remember, should I subject you to another one, don't believe a word I say. Some days I've got to let off steam or burst, and it's just unfortunate if you're the one that's in front of the steam-roller.' He laughed, and I smiled as I said, 'I'll remember . . .'

The clouds were low in the sky when I left Tor-Fret. Hollings, who had been in the hall, came to the door with me and, looking out across the expanse of the terrace, said, 'I'm afraid you'll get wet before you reach home, madam.'

'I don't mind that very much, Hollings,' I said, 'as long as I get home before it's quite dark.'

'Well, I should hurry,' he said solicitously, 'because that cloud isn't going to lift. It'll be dark soon tonight . . . Good night, madam.'

'Good night, Hollings.'

I wondered about Hollings as I hurried down the fell road. He had never spoken of either his master or Maurice Rossiter since the day I had heard the voices coming up the air vent from the cellar. Yet he still appeared watchful, unobtrusively on the alert. I couldn't imagine him allowing himself to be swayed by Mr Maurice's charm as, I told myself rather ruefully, I was. Yet in my own defence I knew that were Maurice Rossiter to talk to me seriously I would not believe a word he said. Nor would I ever be able to understand how, when loving Noreen Badcliff as he surely did, he could press her to marry his brother. I thrust aside the thought of his disability and the obstacle of money, the lack of which he gave as his reason that memorable day by the lake. No, I knew I would never be able to understand this man or his motives.

I was thinking along these lines, my body bent forward, my head down against the wind as I rounded the bend halfway down the bank, the very bend where I'd stumbled over Weaver's legs the first time I had used this road, when I only just managed to shut down on a scream as a man's figure and outstretched arm blocked my way. I actually jumped backwards to avoid contact, and then I was staring at Arthur Boyle, seeing him face to face for the first time in two years.

'I'm sorry, Kate. I'm sorry I gave you a start.'

I tried to swallow and moved my chin back and forward with the effort. He was standing squarely in front of me now, his arms hanging by his side, looking like some big helpless schoolboy. He had changed in the two years since we parted, much more than I had, and some part of me even in this moment of fright was human enough to be glad about this. He said, 'I had to see you; there seemed a conspiracy down there.' He motioned over the fell in the direction of the village. 'Nobody seemed to know where you worked in the afternoons. They all told me where you worked in the mornings, when I wasn't able to get over.' He was smiling faintly now as if trying to turn it into a joke, and then his face became straight and he said quietly, 'It's good to see you again, Kate . . . My God, I've missed you. I must have been stark, staring barmy.'

'What do you want?' I asked.

'Isn't that obvious? I want to see you. I must see you again, Kate.'

As his hand lifted towards me I took another step back. 'The person you should be seeing at this moment is your wife . . . and your child.' I said the last words slowly, and with emphasis. 'There is nothing more to be said between you and me, and nothing can come of you trying to see me, understand that.'

As I stared at him I watched the boyish look fade from his face. His large full-lipped mouth, which at one time I had kindly termed generous, forced itself into a straight line as he pulled his lower lip inwards and bit on it before saying, 'I made a mistake. I did you a wrong, there's no getting over that, but by God I've paid for it. Hell's nothing to the life I've led this past two years. If you ever wanted your revenge, then I can say you've had it . . . Look, Kate.' He took a tentative step towards me. 'I'll do anything, anything if you'll put the clock back. Some men sow their wild oats early and some late. Well, you would have no reason to worry about me scattering any more wild oats. Kate . . . I'm yours for life if you'll only forgive me.'

'I have forgiven you, Arthur.' My voice was quiet now. 'But I don't want to see you or have anything to do with you again, you must understand that.'

He spread his hands out before me now, saying, 'But you couldn't have changed as completely as that, not after the way you loved me. You loved me, you know you did.'

'I'm afraid I have changed as completely as that, Arthur.' I could say his name without any pang. 'And the love that I had for you is so dead that nothing on this earth could ever resurrect it.'

'Give me a chance to try again, that's all I ask . . . I'll take it that you don't feel the same, not anything like the same, but give me . . . just give me the chance to make things up to you. Do that, Kate.'

'. . . And your wife?'

He closed his eyes and swung his head from shoulder to shoulder. 'She's never been my wife, not really. A few words yammered over you doesn't make you man and wife . . .'

'I understood it did.'

'You know what I mean, Kate; we've never been anything to each other. I just stayed with her because of the child. I married her to give the child a name . . .'

'Well, you married her, and she's your wife. But let me tell you that if she wasn't and you were free tomorrow it would make no difference.'

'It's got to, Kate, it's got to.' I watched his pale complexion deepen into pink and then into red. Slowly he was being consumed by a fury of temper, the temper that I had twice before seen take control of him. And as I stared at him through the darkening light on this empty road I was quite suddenly filled with fear, and not without cause, for within the next second I was struggling within the frantic grip of his arms.

'Le . . . let me go. Let me go, Arthur . . . Don't! Don't!' I am no weakling, but my efforts to release myself were as futile as those of a child. Arthur in this moment was mad.

His lips were trying to pin down my mouth, and as I moved and jerked my head I was vaguely conscious that somewhere on the road ahead was a moving blur, dark against the fading light. But it was only a fleeting impression, for I was swung round, my back bent over, and then my breath was almost stopped by the roughness of Arthur's mouth on mine.

For a second I thought dazedly that it was the kick I had given him on the ankle that had made him release me – that was before I took in the large lop-sided form of Logan Rossiter as he stood balancing himself on his good foot, his stick raised high over his head. To me it seemed to hover there for a long time as the two men glared at each other, but that must have been an illusion, for the yell Arthur let out came almost immediately after I was released from his grip.

'Oh no!' The cry escaped me as the stick was raised once again. Arthur was bending over gripping his shoulder. He was evidently hurt and looked dazed, and knowing him I realised that his bout of temper had subsided as quickly as it had risen. But even with the fury gone Arthur was no whelp and he advanced towards Logan Rossiter, yelling now, 'You try that on again. Go on, try it on again and see what'll happen to you, as big as you are. Who the hell do you think you are, anyway? What's it got to do with you? I wasn't molesting her – she knows me.'

'Do you know this man, Kate?' Logan Rossiter did not turn his head towards me as he spoke.

'Yes.'

'There, you see.' Arthur was now nodding vigorously. 'You want to mind your own bloody business.'

'Was this man being objectionable to you? Or was I imagining the whole thing, Kate?' Again he was speaking without looking at me, not taking his eyes from Arthur.

I did not know how to answer this in case that stick was wielded again, and this Arthur I knew would not stand for. There would be a fight, an unfair fight with Logan Rossiter's handicap of one damaged arm and foot. So in a garbled explanation I said, 'We used to know each other but that's over. I don't want to see him again.' And now I addressed Arthur, trying to keep my voice steady as I said, 'As I told you, nothing can be altered. You've got to believe that. Don't go on hoping because I'll never change.'

There was silence between the three of us for quite a while. My words seemed to have at last got through to Arthur, with the result that he looked utterly deflated. He was no fighter at heart, and could only whip himself to extremes when he resorted to the weapon of his temper.

'You heard what she said. Go on.'

Arthur, stung once more into some retaliation, barked, 'I'm going, but not on account of you. Get that clear. Likely you and I'll meet up again . . . when you haven't got your stick with you.'

'If I had the use of my arm I would have no need for a stick . . . Now, go on!'

Arthur turned towards me, but I could not look at him. My head was hanging now because I felt sick, and I had the dread on me that I was about to vomit. But I saw his feet turn away, and then he was lost in the thickening dark.

I stood with my hand tightly pressed across my mouth. Nothing seemed to matter now except that I shouldn't be sick. Then Logan Rossiter was standing in front of me, his voice low and questioning, 'Are you all right, Kate?'

I didn't answer, for besides the feeling of sickness

I was shivering all over, and there was a weakness in my legs such as one experiences following shock. Then to my own surprise I found that I was crying, and not just crying with the tears dropping down my face, but with them gushing from my eyes, blocking my nose and choking me. It was then, in this moment when I couldn't fully appreciate it, that I felt the strength and tenderness of Logan Rossiter's hold, for his arm was about me. At first I experienced no amazement that my head was lying on the broad expanse of his chest, and my wet mouth was pressed on to his shirt in the vee above his waistcoat, for, like a distraught child, I was spilling words out, telling him who Arthur was, or had been. In broken, choking snatches I even told him about the girl. When the break-up between Arthur and myself had come two years ago I couldn't remember crying like this, nor talking like this. It was as if it had all been bottled up inside me and now the stopper had been cork-screwed out and I was experiencing a sense of relief that I hadn't known before. I had no encouragement from his voice, for he had not spoken, only from the pressure of his arm, the pressure that seemed to be changing my life, for I was now aware that standing within this circle I was a different being.

At last I stopped talking and, sniffing and gasping, I raised my face from his chest and looked up at him. I looked into eyes that seemed to be waiting for mine. I stared into their depths until I became lost and could see nothing but them. They covered the face of the fells, they covered the dominion of my entire world. I was aware of my heart racing, racing towards something terrifying, something beautifully terrifying. But I was not racing towards this thing alone, I was aware that what was happening to me was also happening to him. We had both left our surroundings, our responsibilities, our world, and were in some dimension where emotion alone mattered. Although I was still standing within the circle of his arm, we weren't close. Then, like two people coming together following long and lonely separation, we were joined. His grip had tightened about me and was forcing me into him. My arms were about his neck, our mouths met, and we were lost.

How long the kiss lasted I have no recollection; I only know that I was brought back to this planet with a bang, for I felt myself actually being thrown off him. It was as if an electric shock had wrenched us apart. I stood for a moment at arm's length from him, swaying and dazed. He was glaring at me as if he hated me, and I became overwhelmed with a feeling of utter, utter dejection. I knew what it was to be rejected, but this feeling was comparable with nothing I had experienced before. I had been rejected by Arthur Boyle and that had hurt, but in comparison this was like having the skin ripped off your flesh while remaining conscious of it.

Logan Rossiter was now no longer looking at me, for his big body was turned from me as if in shame. Once again I knew I was going to cry, cry tears that would wrench my being in two, but I could let no-one witness this crying, least of all this man. I swung blindly away, and my feet were lifting to run, when his hand caught me, and so swift had been his effort to reach me that he almost overbalanced, and me with him. And again we were clinging to each other, and now he spoke my name in a way that no man had used it before. It was like a loving caress, but it was also, I knew, a farewell. His voice was thick and almost lost in his throat as he muttered, 'Kate. My God, Kate.' Then, 'Forget this. You must . . . Oh, Kate.'

I could not look at him, and I made no answer. He put a little distance between us and his hand was only lightly on my arm when he spoke now. 'Come on up to the house; I'll get Patterson to take you home. Come, Kate.'

I shook my head. 'No. I'm . . . I'm all right . . .' I nearly added, 'I'll miss the bus.' If I had, I am sure I would have subsided in a bout of hysterical laughter.

'He'll be waiting at the bottom of the hill. You don't want that, do you?' His voice was soft.

No, I didn't want that. I didn't want any more conflicts tonight; all I wanted was to get home and think, and sort this out. But did it need sorting out? There was nothing to sort out. Just a plain state-ment of fact. I was in love, in love I think for the first time in my life, because this was a different feeling from anything I'd had for Arthur. This lacerating, choking, even shameful feeling was quite different. Why it should be I was at this moment incapable of explaining to myself.

His hand now came to move me forward, but I

remained stubbornly still. Like some young bewildered girl I tossed my head, muttering, 'I can't go back; they'll want to know why . . . Asking questions . . . I can't.'

'No-one will ask you any questions, Kate. There'll be no-one about at this time. The uncles will be in the cellar and Maurice resting. You can stay quietly in the breakfast room until I get Patterson . . . come on. I can't let you go down there alone. Come, Kate . . . come.'

Like a child who didn't know what she wanted to do I allowed him to lead me back up the hill. It was dark now, but we needed no light, nor did we walk together. I said he led me back, but there was no contact between us.

Far from the uncles being busy in the cellar they were walking across the hall when Logan opened the front door, and they turned their surprised glances on me, and in a moment they were at my side exclaiming, and asking questions. Above their heads Logan Rossiter's eyes were saying to me, 'I'm sorry.' Then quite abruptly he thrust them aside. 'Come into the drawing-room and sit down, Kate,' he said.

'Did you fall?' exclaimed Mr Stanley at my back.

'Fright . . . had a fright?' put in Mr Bernard. 'Get you a drink? Settle you.'

They were in the drawing-room now, and it was Mr Stanley who pressed me into the deep low comfort of the settee in front of the fire, saying, 'There you are now, settle yourself.' Then, looking up at his nephew, he asked, 'Well, what happened?'

I could not see Logan Rossiter, for he was behind me, but his voice sounded tired when it came to me, saying, 'She was attacked.'

I wanted to turn and protest. I hadn't been attacked, not in the way he implied, but I remained staring towards the fire while the old men exclaimed, their voices high with indignation, 'Attacked! Did you see him?'

'Yes, yes, I saw him.'

'What you do?' It was Mr Bernard asking the question.

'I couldn't do much, I was rather handicapped. What I did was with my stick.'

'Did you know the fellow?' asked Mr Stanley. There followed a small silence, a waiting silence, then Logan Rossiter spoke again, saying, 'No, I didn't know him, but Kate did. And if you don't mind, don't bother her any more tonight with your questions. I'm going to see Patterson. What about that drink you were going to get, Uncle?'

'Yes, yes.' Mr Bernard bustled away behind the couch and Mr Stanley with him. And I laid my head back, drew in a deep breath and made an effort to relax my tensed nerves and to quieten my racing mind.

I had not been in this room before. What I could see of it showed a surprising amount of comfort. Deep armchairs, faded chintz, old furniture. Looking at it from my mother's standpoint the whole place was in need of a good clean, but this didn't detract from the character of the room and I realised that at one time this had been an elegant place. My gaze was fixed on the portrait of a horse and rider that dominated the whole length of the broad mantelpiece. A part of my mind was wondering vaguely which Rossiter this was when I was startled by the voices of the present-day Rossiters coming from the hall, both Logan's and Maurice's together, and it was not difficult to gauge that they were once again having a battle of words. And I was brought upright in my seat as Logan Rossiter's voice came to me, muted, yet clear, crying, 'There's no need to have her here at all, she could take the work home.'

And now Maurice's voice high and excited, shouting, 'Where I have my work done is my business. You were quite willing that she should do yours here, weren't you? Why didn't you send it down to the office?'

'The circumstances were quite different . . .'

'Oh yes, of course, my dear brother, I forgot. When you want things your own way the circumstances are always different.'

I swivelled round on the couch and looked towards the old men. They had been gazing towards the closed door and now they turned as one to me and shook their heads, and it was Mr Bernard who muttered jerkily, 'Like tigers those two, not brothers. Hopeless . . . hopeless. Always the same. Never change.'

The voices from the hall were now becoming indistinct as if they were moving away, but Maurice's voice, even higher now, came to us crying in answer to something Logan had said, 'Or else?

. . . I do what you order or else? What does that imply? That if Mr God Almighty isn't obeyed he'll cut off my allowance?'

It was as if Logan Rossiter had suddenly sprung out of a room and into the hall again, because his voice was clearer than ever now as he cried, 'Don't be such a blasted fool. All I'm asking . . .'

'You're not asking, you're telling me. As usual you're telling me.'

It looked as if the battle was going to rage afresh, when Mr Stanley, squaring his bent shoulders, marched to the door and into the hall and joined his voice to that of his nephew, and nothing was distinct any more.

By the time Mr Bernard came round to the front of the couch and handed me a glass of wine the house was quiet. Abruptly he said, 'Drink it up', and, literally obeying him, I drank it up. In two gulps the wine was gone. At another time it would have appeared as a sacrilege to the old man, but not tonight. He took the glass from my hand and nodded his white head and then disappeared behind the couch again.

I sat wondering now why Maurice Rossiter had not told Logan that we had already discussed altering my time, and that he was agreeable to it. Very naturally he had been nettled by his brother's approach. He was not to know that Logan was disturbed, not so much because I had been attacked, as he put it, but because for the few brief seconds – or, like me, had he felt it an eternity? – he had been wafted out of his ordered world. He had allowed something to happen that he would have definitely condemned in others. There was a tinge of bitterness in my thoughts now and I encouraged it, for as long as I could feel bitter I would not cry.

There came a knock on the door and there stood Patterson. He looked across at me and said, 'When you're ready, miss.'

I was ready now. I rose from the couch, said goodbye to Mr Bernard, who patted my hand in a fatherly fashion, and then went into the hall.

Did I expect to see Logan Rossiter waiting at the door to say goodbye? I don't know. But I do know that when I found the hall empty I was overcome by a strange feeling, and as I stepped on to the terrace my mind presented me with a still stranger thought, for of all people it was of Weaver's mother, the woman who had given birth to Weaver in the room above the stables, that I was thinking. She had been used by 'a Rossiter'. What her life had been I don't know, but I had a good idea that happiness hadn't played much part in it. I hadn't been used by 'a Rossiter', but I had been as it were thrown off by one. I could still feel the impact of that electric current that sprang between Logan Rossiter and me a short while ago, and he had undoubtedly created the current. Weaver's mother had remained here all her life. Perhaps once touched by 'a Rossiter' she was unable to get away. The bitterness coming to my aid again, I said to myself, 'It won't happen to me. I'll get away from the Rossiters, all of them, and Tor-Fret and all it stands for.' For what did it stand for?

Unhappiness. For who was happy in this house?

My mind was lifted from myself for a moment by the voice of Patterson, saying, 'Careful how you go, miss.'

Patterson was a quiet man, much younger than Hollings or Bennett, and I couldn't remember having spoken to him until this night, and then it was only to thank him for his escort. He went before me down the road swinging a lantern, letting the light shine at my feet. When we reached the main road he looked about him sending the rays of light here and there. He was, as he had doubtlessly been ordered, looking for the man. Then we walked along the road to where stood three workmen's cottages clustered together in a little dip. At the side of these was a barn-like structure which Logan Rossiter used as a garage. Within a matter of minutes I was in the car and on my way home.

When we reached the point in the road where the lane led off up the fell towards the cottage, I thanked him and said, 'I'll be all right now.' And to this he answered, 'I'm to see you to the door, miss. Mr Logan's orders.'

I did not argue, and now it was I took the lead up the steep fell path. As we neared the house my mother's voice hailed me, and when she came within the rays of the lantern I saw the quick widening of her eyes as she peered at my companion. 'This is Mr Patterson, Mother. He . . . he has seen me home from the house.'

'Good evening.' My mother inclined her head towards the dark figure.

'Good evening, ma'am.' Now Patterson turned to me and said, 'Good night, miss.'

'Good night and . . . and thank you, Patterson, it was very kind of you.'

'Not at all, miss. Good night.'

'Good night, Patterson.'

I went past my mother and into the house, but she did not follow me for some seconds, and when she came into the light of the sitting-room there was a half-smile on her face as she began, 'That was short and sweet.' Then looking at me fully she exclaimed, 'What is it? You've been crying. What is it, lass?' I sat down in the armchair near the fire and dropped my head wearily back into its worn comfort as I said, 'Arthur met me as I was coming down the road from the house. It was getting dark and I think he went mad for a time.' Then I lowered my eyes. 'Mr Logan came on the scene and . . . and there was a fight of sorts.'

'Oh, my God, lass. Did he do anything to him, I mean Arthur?'

'No. Mr Logan hit him with a stick. His arm was still in a sling, but Arthur was in a rage and . . .' I shook my head quickly and finished, 'It's over, it's over.'

'You're upset, lass. I knew you would be when you came across him.' She came over to me and, putting her hand on my head, stroked the hair back from my brow, and the gentleness was too much for me, and once again I was crying, helplessly now, and she was kneeling by me talking softly, 'There, there, now. Cry it out and let it finish. As you say, it's over. There, there. But, it has upset you. Don't let your father see you like this. I've got a nice tea for you. Come along, wash your face and have something to eat. Oh, lass, don't cry like that . . . I've never seen you so upset, not even when it happened.'

I couldn't tell her that I wasn't crying over the loss of Arthur Boyle, but over the irrevocable loss of something not fully realised, something just glimpsed, some world where reigned love. Not just an everyday love that helped you to suffer your existence, but a love that coloured life with almost unbearable intensity, a love that was part-wonder, part-pain not unmixed with fear, fear of the wonder fading, fear of the day when the pain would no longer hurt. It was a love like that, and all I had seen of it was a glimpse, and now it was gone, gone for ever.

6

The Kate that presented herself at Tor-Fret the following afternoon was not the earnest, prim, industrious Kate; it was a washed-out Kate, yet a new Kate, in which bitterness at the moment was uppermost. Why should this have hit me? I didn't want any more emotional tangles, I had had enough. I had been quite content to go on living outside of love, except the love of my parents. This was to have been enough for me, yet here I was in an emotional state I'd never dreamed possible. In the dark hours of the night I had asked myself angrily how, when I had heartily disliked the man, when his presence had filled me with unease and trepidation, when the very sight of him made me steel myself against his sharp sarcastic utterances, how, knowing all this, I could have fallen in love with him. Because it was as simple as that – I was in love with Logan Rossiter. And yet I could not apply the word simple to this feeling. It was anything but simple; it was something larger than myself, something that I was being caught up in . . . And what of him? Did he feel the same? When I asked myself this question I had been standing at the window looking into the black night that coated the fells and the valley and the river that separated Tor-Fret from this house and me. Is he awake? I had asked myself. And the answer came bluntly, No.

My father had said men felt differently. Their emotions were keyed to a different pitch. Yet in that moment on the hillside Logan Rossiter had, like me, been lifted on to another planet. Yet, when he realised the significance of what was happening, he had thrust me off. Make no mistake about that, I had told myself. He had been shocked at what had hit him and would have none of it. There would be no intrigue between this Rossiter and myself. He was no Maurice . . . But a man can love two women at the same time my father had said, and my mother had said the same thing about a woman. I doubted, even allowing for the wildest conjecture, whether Logan Rossiter would love two women at once; and if he should, strangely I knew that I would not want to be one of them. This feeling that had broken loose in me would, if given licence, demand something equal, or even greater than itself, in return. Either that or it would remain alone. I had nodded out into the lonely night and had whispered aloud, 'It will remain alone all right, there is no doubt about that.' I had sense enough to know that I, with my homely attractions, could in no way supplant a girl like Noreen Badcliff. I was also straight enough with myself to realise that if I left Tor-Fret it wouldn't be because I had given in my notice. I knew I couldn't do this, it was as if I were tied to the place by unseen shackles.

This morning my mother had tried to dissuade me from going to work, but I assured her and my father that I was perfectly all right. I also assured them that I had seen the last of Arthur; yet I doubted this.

Bill Arnold had said, 'You look under the weather. You'd think you'd been up all the night.' To this I replied that I had. I'd had a nagging toothache. It was the first excuse that came to my mind, and I was in a bit of a dilemma when he suggested that he'd run me into Alnwick and the dentist, for he said, 'There's nothing that will wear you down more than toothache.'

I lied further by telling him that it was a tooth I'd just had stopped, a matter of an exposed nerve; nothing could be done about it. It came and went. How glibly one could go on when the necessity arose . . .

As I went up the hill towards Tor-Fret the sun was shining. It was a brittle shine, yet the light was soft on the heather and turned the dying patches into cloaks of velvet. Yesterday I would have stopped and drunk in the changing scene, and would undoubtedly have thought that there was no place in the world to compare with this, this particular corner of Northumberland. But today as I looked over the hills I wished myself miles away. Any place in the world but here.

Remembering the exchange in the hall between the brothers last night, I steeled myself for what Maurice Rossiter would say on the matter. And as so often had been the case with me I received the reverse from what I expected.

As I crossed the terrace I saw the contorted figure of my employer standing with his back to the long window, and when I opened the door from the hall into the room I braced myself against the onslaught.

Evidently Maurice Rossiter was waiting for me, and his approach took the wind completely out of my sails. To say the least, it was kind. 'How are you feeling, Kate?' he began as he hobbled towards me, even before I had taken off my hat and coat.

'Oh, I'm all right, thank you.'

'Well, you don't look all right. You still look shaken up. I'm very, very sorry you were upset in that way.'

I went towards my desk and he followed me, saying, 'Tell me how it came about?'

I looked up at him. I did not know how much Logan Rossiter had told him of what I had spilled out in my distress. And then again I could not imagine Logan telling him anything after their clash in the hall. But he might have told the uncles and the uncles could have passed it on to Maurice, I didn't know. So the best thing to do, I saw, was simply to tell the truth. And this I did.

'It was a man I was engaged to two years ago,' I said. 'We disagreed and he married someone else, and now he finds it was a mistake. He was trying to convince me that I could rectify it. I couldn't see eye to eye with him.'

I had related this coolly, dispassionately, like someone else, not like myself at all, and this was proved in the next moment when Maurice Rossiter, after looking at me with a critical expression for some moments, threw his head back and laughed. And he was still laughing as he said, 'You know . . . you know who you sounded like? You sounded just like Logan. You could in fact have been the solicitor himself making a statement to the Bench. Oh, Kate, you're delicious . . . Oh, now, don't look like that. I don't mean anything derogatory. Please get it out of your head that I hold you in anything but the highest esteem. You know what I think?' He leant on the desk now towards me, his manner one of high good humour. 'I think if I had the proper use of my limbs you'd consider me a real bad lot, capable of any kind of roguery. I have seen this in your eyes, Kate. You have very telling eyes, you know.'

I had expected my employer to be on his high horse, and here he was laughing and joking with me, talking as if we were life-long friends. Talking as if every word he had shouted in the hall last night hadn't been a blow hitting out at Logan. Perhaps he had some cause to hit out . . . I wouldn't know. Yet this constant change of manner made him suspect to me. Ignoring what he had said, I came back with, 'Referring to what you said yesterday, Mr Maurice, it will be all right if I come in the mornings?'

'Certainly, certainly. I said make your own time.' His words were clipped now.

I was looking up into his face. 'I could be here by nine and leave at twelve. Would that suit you?' I said.

'Yes, yes, definitely. Of course, of course. That's settled, then.'

On this he turned abruptly away from the desk and hobbled into the bedroom, and I was left with a stronger feeling still that what had transpired in the last few minutes had come from the façade of the man, and that underneath he resented the fact that I, and not he, had suggested the alteration in my time. And in this moment I glimpsed a truth about him that was later to be proved: Maurice Rossiter resented any change being brought about in his daily life that hadn't been suggested by himself.

Later the uncles came in and enquired how I was, and I could smile at them and say I was quite all right now. One patted my shoulder and the other my head, and then they changed positions and one patted my arm and the other my hand. At another time I would have laughed and thought, They're treating me like a Great Dane. But I was soothed inside by their presence and their thoughtfulness . . . I liked the uncles.

At three o'clock as usual Hollings came in with the tray. And after unnecessarily rearranging the tea-things he spoke to me, but with his attention still centred on the tray. 'I'm sorry to hear about the incident last night, madam,' he said.

'It's over, Hollings, and I'm all right.'

'It wasn't Weaver, by any chance?'

'No, no, it wasn't Weaver. I happened to know the man.'

'Oh. Oh, I'm sorry, madam.'

'It's all right, Hollings.'

When he had left the room I thought, at least his master doesn't tell him everything, for then he'd have known it wasn't Weaver I had been struggling with on the road . . .

Five minutes before I was due to finish my work Patterson, after knocking on the door, entered the room. He did not say anything but looked towards me.

Maurice Rossiter had been on the point of going into his room, taking with him part of a new story I had started on some days earlier, and he turned about and looked towards Patterson but did not speak. Then he went into his room and the door banged behind him.

The noise had made me start, and when I looked back at Patterson his eyes were directed towards the floor. I wanted to say to him, 'There's no need for you to come, thank you,' but I felt the uselessness of argument. He was carrying out Logan Rossiter's orders and, like Hollings, I gauged that Patterson was Mr Logan's man. The banging of the door had somehow confirmed this.

On our journey down the hill Patterson was more talkative than he had been last night. He spoke first of all about the weather, and then about fishing. He was a fisherman and I gathered before he had said very much that salmon fishing was the one joy of his life. He was still talking of fishing when we got into the car, and by the time I got out at the bottom of the fell road I knew also that his master was a fisherman, and that they fished together.

It was still daylight when we neared the cottage and because of this he did not come to the door, but, raising his hat, said, 'Good evening, miss,' and then added, 'It isn't many people who like to talk about fishing – I mean ladies.' And when he had gone I smiled rather whimsically to myself. There had only been one person talking about fishing that I knew of and it hadn't been me. Another man was deluding himself. But in Patterson's case it was a harmless delusion.

My father was downstairs when I arrived home and his smile was warm on me as he said, 'Hello, there, lass.'

'Hello, dear, how are you feeling?'

'Oh, grand, me own self again. I've told the winter where to go because I'm having no truck with it.'

I smiled at him and he pulled some papers from the head of the couch, saying, 'I've got somethin' to show you.'

'Now let her get her tea, Tom,' chided my mother. 'You can go into that after. Come on, lass, sit down. I've been baking all afternoon and I don't want to see it go stale.'

I looked towards the laden table, but it didn't whet my appetite. Yet I knew I would have to eat to stop them both from worrying over me.

After the meal my mother exclaimed, 'Well, you won't get fat on that.' And then she added, 'I'll make a panhackelty for the supper.'

Panhackelty, a mixture of potatoes, onions and meat or left-overs done slowly over the fire, was a winter evening favourite of mine. My grandmother had first introduced it to me when I used to visit her on the Tyne. But the thought of it on this particular night only made me think, Oh dear, oh dear. And then my father, catching hold of my hand, drew me to him and, pulling me down into a chair near his, he said, 'Have a look at these.' And he thrust on to my knee a number of catalogues showing on their covers types of shining machines – motor-cycles. I gazed at him in amazement until, selecting one quickly, he said, 'Oh, them others are what they sent along, this is what I want you to look at.' And, opening the folder, he pointed to the picture of a scooter, saying, 'Now wouldn't you like one like that?'

'What!' I looked from him to my mother, who was standing at the kitchen door, a tea-towel in her hand, smiling. 'What,' I asked them, 'do I want with a scooter on these hills?'

'You won't be riding it on the hills, daftie.' My father pushed me. Then, becoming serious, he added, 'It's like this. We thought that if you had a mind to get a job in Alnwick, or even Morpeth, and you were independent of the buses, you could do the journey in no time. And it would be a sort of pleasure to have a thing like that.' He dug his finger at the catalogue while still looking into my face.

'What about the winter?' I said.

'Oh, they soon clear the roads if there's a heavy fall in the winter. You won't be out in it half so much as you will be if you stick at that job on the fell top. Look, lass. We've been worrying for some time about you having to go up there. And now that that fellow's having to bring you home . . .'

'He's a nice man.'

'We've nothing against him, it isn't him; but somehow we're not happy about you being there at all, are we, Kate?' He looked towards my mother, and she, coming across the room, stood before me and said quietly, 'I would leave that place if I were you, lass. I've got a feeling about it, I'm uneasy. Have been for a long time. This was my idea.' She pointed towards the catalogue. 'And I thought it would give you a bit of an interest and take you out a bit. It isn't always winter and you know you're too cooped up with us. We're not young any more.'

'You speak for yourself.' My father nodded at her, then, turning to me quickly, he said, 'But your mother's right. We appreciate all you do for us, don't think otherwise, lass, and God knows it'll be a sorry day if you were to leave us, but you want younger company. You haven't been across the doors but to go to work for over two years now, it isn't right. You're young and' – his hand came out and stroked my cheek – 'and you're bonny. You're me own, and I suppose I shouldn't say it, but you're bonny. You're far bonnier than your mother was at your age and she had looks. Isn't that a fact, Kate?' He looked up at my mother, but she did not answer him, she was looking down at me and I could not meet the tenderness in her eyes. I dropped my head and tried to get rid of the lump that was rising in my throat, and before it reduced me once more to tears, as I knew it would, I muttered, 'I can't leave there, not yet.'

'But why, lass?'

'He . . . he depends on me.'

'The crippled one?' This was my father.

I nodded. Here was another lie, but how could I speak of the thing that tied me there, this new-born emotion. Even its effect of humiliation had not the power to arouse my pride and make me leave Tor-Fret. Not yet at any rate, I now told myself. I would wait until the thirtieth of November. Something might happen before then, something that would come between Noreen Badcliff and him . . . Not through me. No, not for a moment did the thought enter my mind of giving this girl away, for, oddly enough, I liked her. I liked her for herself, yet at the same time I hated the very thought of her need of Logan Rossiter. For it was this need – and from whatever source it sprang I did not know – that would make her marry him.

My father's voice came to me as if out of a thick mist, saying, 'You're not for it, lass?'

I shook my head slowly, and my mother's hand came on to my shoulder, gripping it firmly now, and her voice was bracing as she said, 'Well, don't worry, it was only an idea. Now, come on, no more crying. There's nothing gets you down so much as crying. A little is all right, it's a relief, but enough is as good as a feast.'

The lump in my throat was forced to subside. My father gathered the catalogues from my lap now and my mother, thrusting the tea-towel at me, said,

'Come on, give me a hand, I've got a stack out here.'

As I went towards the kitchen my father said quietly, 'I think I'll play a bit.' And a few minutes later as I stood silently drying the dishes the little house was filled with strains of Beethoven's *Für Elise*. As I listened I was soothed and once again thought, This is all I want. This peace. This close unity. Yet my parents were aiming to thrust me out like a chick from the nest. Their very love for me told them I must fly and so they had thought up a scooter. Some part of me smiled at this. Me on a scooter. I had never had the nerve even to ride a bicycle.

So from the following morning I began my new time at Tor-Fret. It was different coming up the steep road at this time of day. Some mornings everything within a few yards of my feet would be obliterated by patches of mist. Then I would step out of it and into a wonderland of pearl sunshine. Other mornings, through the clear white light the contours of the fells and the distant mountains would take on different shapes. This was caused by laggard patches of mist and isolated tufts of low cloud which from the distance had the appearance of being caught for the moment in clefts on the peaks.

And the house, too, seemed altered. I would encounter Patterson in the hall, mopping and dusting in his own fashion. I had not known previously that he worked inside. He always gave me a pleasant greeting. Apparently, too, he cleaned Mr Maurice's apartments, for on the first morning I was there he came into the room and said, 'I'll see to this later.'

There was much more bustle about the house in the mornings. I could hear Hollings talking from some distant place. Perhaps the butler's pantry, a small room between the kitchen and the dining-room. I judged he was chatting to Patterson. Then, too, the uncles showed me another side of them-selves and their activities. I had imagined they spent the best part of their lives down in the cellar seeing to the wine. But no; apparently they, too, fished, for I saw them going across the terrace the first morning laden with paraphernalia as if they were off on a long, long trek.

In changing my time I had not expected to encounter Logan Rossiter, and during the first week we did not come face to face, yet on the third morning when I came up the hill, a morning when the sun was shining brightly, I saw in the distance a man on horseback. The animal was picking its way among some heavy scree on the hillside, then was brought to a halt near a high boulder, and I was reminded of the picture that hung above the mantel-piece in the drawing-room.

October was drawing to its close and November would soon be upon me. I thought of it in this way: it was like a month of doom. And yet the sensible streak in me told me that if anything should put off the marriage between Noreen Badcliff and Logan Rossiter it would make no difference to me, except that I might be deluded into hoping. And when I got this far my thoughts invariably turned towards

Weaver's mother. What had she hoped for? I had seen nothing more of the man Weaver, and this feeling of sympathy towards his mother didn't alter my feelings towards him.

It was at the beginning of the second week of my changed time that I heard Logan Rossiter talking, but again we didn't meet.

Maurice Rossiter did not get up – at least he did not make his appearance in my room – until about half-past ten or eleven in the morning, but this particular morning I heard the brothers talking as soon as I entered. The voices were indistinct across the long length of the room, but when I was seated at my typewriter I could hear snatches of the conversation which I admit I did not close my ears to. For once, the voices were not angry. Logan Rossiter's in particular had a reasonable sound, although his voice became much louder as he said, 'Nothing on God's earth will make me sell any more land, Maurice. Now don't let us fight over this, and I want to remind you that I won't be persuaded to do so by Noreen . . . Now, now. Don't get het up. Let's talk quietly for once and put our cards on the table. You don't want to see the house sitting like a giant in a backyard, do you? And that's what she'll look like if any more land goes. And there's not enough to run sheep on as you suggest. It's out of the question, for it would mean engaging a man and providing him with a house. It can't be done. Anyway, we gave up all ideas along those lines when we sold the farms, you know we did.'

And now Maurice's voice; it, too, quiet, reasonable. 'That would be quite a narrow strip to let go. Quite unnoticed at the bottom of the hill. Nobody wants to buy land on the heights.'

'I've told you, Maurice. I couldn't bear to go down to that road each day and see bulldozers hacking the land to shreds, and then rows and rows of little houses springing up like a fresh batch of mushrooms every morning. If they would erect one or two decent ones, then I might have consented; but no, when these fellows buy land these days they've got to pay for it, and they get their money back by crowding as many houses on it as possible.'

'You were quite willing to let it go for the hospital site.'

'That was different. I didn't like the idea, not really. There would still be bulldozers, yet the end was more in keeping with the surroundings.'

'You know, Logan, you amuse me at times. Your logic is very odd. You won't have a few rows of houses holding three or four people in each because you imagine there'll be too much coming and going. Yet you will suffer a hospital, or, as it would be, a sanatorium, and cars lining the roads on visiting days, and people walking up to this our very door out of curiosity, visitors and patients alike. Had you thought about that?'

'Yes.' There came a sigh. 'Yes, I'd thought about it all, and I still feel that the end justified my views. But, anyway, don't let's talk about this again, Maurice. It only creates bitterness. Both the houses and the hospital are out of the question. As I tell you, I'd rather sell the lot than have any more bits chopped off.'

'And you'd never do that?' This was a question.

'There's no saying what I might do.' There was a different note in Logan Rossiter's voice now. 'I could do just that, why not? The whole place is like a millstone round my neck; in fact, my neck is breaking with it . . . Believe me, I could do just that.'

'You don't mean it.' Maurice's voice had changed, too. 'You can't even think about it. What would happen to the uncles? Don't forget you have your responsibilities.'

'You, Maurice, reminding me of my responsibilities! That is really amusing. The uncles could be taken care of. They are getting old, and things don't matter so much to them. There are very nice guesthouses along the river where they would survive . . . fishing all day; they would survive, oh yes.'

'You must be mad.' Now Maurice's tone was full of anger. 'They were bred here, they can't stay away from the place for a week. And what about the others? Hollings, Bennett and Patterson? Especially Hollings and Bennett, they would never survive anywhere else.'

'They could be taken care of.' Logan's tone was more moderate than ever. 'They could all be taken care of for less than half that it costs to keep them here. But there, don't upset yourself, it won't happen. I'll do nothing of the sort as long as I'm not driven too far. I'm just keeping my head above water now; I shouldn't even dream of having the top floor redecorated, but it will have to be done.

One last word, Maurice; when you're feeling unduly bitter about my meanness remember this place was never meant to be run on a solicitor's practice.'

There was silence now and I heard the click of a door, and then another sound, one that I hadn't heard before, a dull thump, thump, thump, thump. It was some minutes before I realised that Maurice Rossiter was banging his fist, either into his pillow or the bed itself.

The conversation I had overheard had repercussions. Although later that morning, when we met, Maurice Rossiter was civil to me, I could see it was with an effort. He made no such effort, I noticed, when speaking to the uncles, or Hollings, or Patterson.

From time to time during that week when I looked at Maurice I knew that he was thinking, thinking deeply, pondering on something, and I got an inkling into what this was some time later. It happened on a Wednesday and the first of November. The month I dreaded had come upon me.

The house was a bustle now because the decorators were up on the first floor. The whole atmosphere of the place had changed. Everything seemed to be hurrying towards an end and I too began to imbibe this feeling of hurry. I realised now that the sooner it was over and done with the sooner I would pull myself together.

I found on my desk this particular morning a small pile of quarto sheets. These were two articles that Maurice Rossiter had discussed with me the day before. He seemed to be working at a feverish pace now. He had stopped me going on with his second book – which, by the way, in my opinion, was much better than the first – and had taken to writing articles, and these I found were far superior in writing and interest to either of the novels. One was dealing with the nature of the fells from Durham to the Cheviots, the other was on wine-making. The pages were higgledy-piggledy and I blocked them together to get them straight. But one piece wouldn't go into place, it insisted on sticking out from the side. Its texture and colour, too, were different from the quarto paper, and when I pulled it from among the sheets I saw it was only half the length of the quarto, also that it was a letter. It was open and my eyes took in the heading straight away . . . Darling Maurice. Perhaps I shouldn't have read it. Perhaps I would have blamed anyone else in my place for reading it. But the fact is that I did read it, and if I had been harbouring any hope of something preventing Noreen Badcliff's coming marriage, the words I read quickly dispersed it.

'Darling Maurice' – my eyes flew across the lines of writing – 'What you suggest is impossible. Why, at this late hour, have you changed your mind so completely? I have been begging you to marry me for months and always you have been adamant in your refusal. Even up to a few weeks ago. I have given my word to Logan now and I must keep it. You say you want to do the decent thing . . . well, I'm trying to do it, too. Although God knows it would be better for him if I were to break it off. But I must go through with it, Maurice, and you must believe that nothing you can say now can alter my decision, because, Maurice – I don't say this with the intent of hurting or in any form of retaliation – I want to go through with it. Not that any one on this earth can take your place, but, darling, I am tired and not a little frightened. And I have reason to be.

'If you were to examine your motives, darling, you would recognise, I am sure, that your frantic offer of marriage at this stage is made, not to placate me so much as to hurt him. Although you have gone so far as to deny this emphatically in your letter, knowing you, I can see no other reason for it. Darling, you will always be dear to me and not for a moment do I regret the wonderful times we've spent together. One last thing I would beg of you, Maurice: don't draw me into argument when we meet. Don't try to press me, or change my mind; it won't be any use and it will only upset me. Please . . . please be kind to me because you have a part of me that can belong to no other. Noreen.'

Please, please be kind to me . . . Are you kind with me? . . . Please, please be kind to me. That phrase alone stood out from all the letter. This girl begging Maurice Rossiter to be kind to her, as she had begged me. There was a need in her for love and comfort as great as the one that filled the huge void within me. I was sorry for myself and my own plight, but I was equally sorry for her. And oddly, in this moment, for Maurice Rossiter. Yet how hopeless was the suggestion he had made to her, for if she had consented they could never have stayed in this house. As I remembered him saying, he needed this house, he needed its space, its kind of comfort. He needed the kind of attention commanded here as his due. Yet he was willing to throw it up if she would marry him. But how and where had he imagined they would live? For he depended on his brother for everything he had. I couldn't puzzle it out and I didn't try. What I was concerned with at the moment was putting the letter back between the sheets of paper, and when I had done this I asked myself: What now? If I went on typing the articles I would eventually come to the letter again. The sheet was about halfway down, there was about an hour's work before I would have come to it in the ordinary way. What if he didn't discover its loss before then? I moved it rapidly nearer to the end. But I need not have worried. Before ten minutes had passed the door burst open and he came into the room in his pyjamas and dressing-gown, his dancing step so pronounced as to be almost pitiful. He did not give me any greeting but started to speak right away as he moved towards my desk, saying, 'Those articles, have you started on them? I have mislaid some papers. Have you come across . . . ?'

I looked towards him and, making my voice ordinary, even a little apologetic, said, 'I haven't got very far yet, I've just done the first page.'

Even before I had finished speaking he had whipped the script from the table, and, supporting it against his withered arm, he flicked through the pages. Then stopping, he placed his hand flat on the top page and pressed the papers around his arm until they formed a cuff, and, smiling at me in a sickly fashion, he said, 'I've just thought of something I want to alter, it won't take me long. In the meantime, I wonder if I could trouble you, Kate, to go and tell Hollings that I need him for a minute . . . Would you mind?'

'No, not at all.' I got up immediately and went out of the room in search of Hollings. I knew that if I had only crossed the hall and then gone back into the room he would have had time to remove the letter and the articles would have been on my desk again. But I didn't hurry. I found Hollings in the pantry and I gave him the message. He was cleaning a lot of very dirty-looking silver which I guessed hadn't seen the light of day for many years. This was in preparation for the thirtieth of November, no doubt. He put down the ornate sugar bowl and said hastily, 'Has he had a turn, madam?'

I shook my head. 'No, he didn't seem ill. He just asked me to fetch you.' As he loosened the apron round his waist he said, 'It wouldn't surprise me if he did have a turn; he's been walking the floor every night this week.' On this he hurried towards the bedroom door and I went more slowly towards my own room.

Evidently Maurice Rossiter was deeply troubled. Because of his affliction he liked rest, yet he had been walking the floor. My pity for him mounted, yet at the same time I was still suspicious of his motives. Why at this late stage did he want to break up the marriage between his brother and Noreen Badcliff, when only a few weeks ago he had been all for it, even commanding her to marry Logan? Was it because he realised now that he would be no better off financially with Noreen as Logan's wife? That in some way, once she became his sister-in-law, he would lose his power over her? As she had once accused him of doing, had he hoped in a subtle way to blackmail her and now could see the futility of it? I didn't know.

It was just on twelve o'clock when I finished the two articles and I took them to his room. I knocked and opened the door, expecting to find him, as I usually did at this time, propped up on the couch writing, but today he was sitting near the window, his elbow on a small table, his hand covering his face. He did not seem aware of my presence until I spoke, and then, turning his head towards me, he said, as if coming out of sleep, 'Oh, it's you, Kate.'

'I have finished them, Mr Maurice,' I said.

'Oh, all right. Thanks, Kate . . . thanks.' He still continued to stare at me, then he said something that surprised me more than anything that happened at Tor-Fret. Even the discovery that I was in love with Logan Rossiter had not the element of surprise that Maurice Rossiter's words had as he said, with a kind of unbearable sadness in his tone, 'Kate, I wish I was dead.'

My mouth dropped slightly open, my eyes widened, and with my head leaning sideways I walked towards him, and, standing at the opposite side of the little table, I exclaimed, 'Oh, don't say that, Mr Maurice.'

Looking back at me, the sadness hanging like a cloak from him, he said, 'I'm ten different kinds of a devil, Kate. I'm not a nice person. I demand a great deal of sympathy because of my affliction, but I don't deserve it. I really don't need it. I'm sufficient unto myself, but I must demand, I must have . . .' He broke off and I moved my head slowly. In this moment I was being overwhelmed with pity, genuine pity, for I felt that this was not an occasion when the man before me was playing on my sympathy, striving to arouse it. He was in some kind of mental anguish. I said softly, making excuses now for him to himself, 'Of course you're not bad, Mr Maurice, you're no worse than the next. We are all weak in one way or another.' And now I smiled, trying to lift him out of this depth, adding, 'And you know what they say of the devil? He isn't half bad when you get to know him.'

He answered my smile now by a stretching of his lips, and he nodded, then sighed, and, lying back in the chair, asked me, 'Why do people tell you things, Kate? Do you find that everyone you come in contact with talks to you?'

'No, not particularly,' I said.

'The twins talk to you. Uncle Stephen talks to you. Even dour Hollings talks to you, and that's something from Hollings, I can tell you . . . And my brother, the astute lawyer, he's talked to you, hasn't he?'

We were moving away now from the plane of pity on to dangerous ground, and I said, still looking him straight in the face, 'I took Mr Logan's letters down, that's all, so of course he had to talk.'

He smiled now more widely. 'One of my devils is at work . . . I'm probing, Kate, and not without reason, but you're very diplomatic. But as I said, everybody talks to you, even Noreen.' Our eyes were holding now and I was on my guard. Definitely one of his devils was at work and it surprised me when, speaking through him, it said, 'You had a long talk in the car the other night. What did you talk about?'

I stepped back from the table. I felt my face closing as I answered, 'We hadn't a long talk, Mr Maurice. I sat in the car for a time with Miss Badcliff and we talked about . . . Well, we talked about the things that women do talk about.'

'Kate . . .' His voice was low and urgent, and he stretched his hand across the table towards me. 'Believe me when I say to you that it's important for me to know what she said. There's a reason why I want to know, it concerns us all . . . Logan, too. Him most of all. I feel you know much more than you say, Kate. I see it in your eyes. Tell me . . . tell me what she said, what she thinks. I used to know, but now . . .'

At this point his eyes suddenly lifted from me and looked upwards. There was nothing to attract them but the sound of a wood pigeon cooing. When he lowered his eyes again to mine he seemed, for the moment, to have forgotten the gist of what he had been saying, and then, recalling it, he exclaimed, as he pulled himself to his feet, 'It was unfair of me to ask. Anyway, I might have known you'd keep mum. You'd make a very good friend, Kate.'

Those were the very words that Logan Rossiter had said to me some time ago. But I couldn't see any woman being friends with this man. His mistress, yes, but not a friend. He was a man who couldn't have a woman friend. She would either love him or hate him. Perhaps both, but she could never be friends with him. I said, 'Goodbye, Mr Maurice.'

'Goodbye, Kate,' he answered. 'And forget about the last few minutes. I'm a neurotic individual . . . let's face it.'

'Goodbye,' I said again. And again he answered, 'Goodbye, Kate.'

Thoughtfully I put on my hat and coat, and thoughtfully I went down the hill. There had been a heavy shower of rain, but now the sun was shining, and hollows here and there were glistening like patches of silver, and my eyes were taken into the distance by the gleam of these patches. I was looking towards my left to where the land flattened out into a wide stretch before dropping steeply downwards again. And then I saw an odd thing happen, an amazing thing – a thing that made me imagine I was suffering from an hallucination. I saw the figure of a man standing at a point on the flat piece of land. One minute I saw him standing in the sunlight and the next minute he had disappeared. It was as if he had fallen down a crevasse. It wasn't an impossibility for anyone to fall between a cleft in the rocks on these fells, but that particular stretch of land appeared like pasture-land, and yet I told myself there could be a crevasse there which I couldn't see from this distance. Lower down, where the hill flattened out into the valley, I could see sheep grazing. Was the man a shepherd and had he fallen? No, no. I rejected the idea. It was as if he had dissolved into the air. I hurried farther down the road now to get a different view of the field, but this view only confirmed what I had already imagined. The field was pasture-land, giving way to bracken as it rose to the next fell. I looked back towards Tor-Fret, I looked around me. Behind any of the mounds dotting the hillside a man could be lying watching me, and my movements would be reported to Mr Maurice. This knowledge prevented me from cutting across the fells to investigate, but as I reached the road I determined that tomorrow morning I would get off the bus a stop earlier and make my way towards Tor-Fret from the direction of that field. The incident struck me as odd. It had not left me with the impression that the man could be lying hurt . . .

That evening, while sitting round the fire, my father said to me, 'Would you like to go and stay with your Aunt Peggy in Durham for Christmas?'

I turned on him wide-eyed. 'And leave you two here?' I said, bringing my mother into my glance. 'Don't be silly.'

'You like your Aunt Peggy, and there'll be a houseful and it'll be jolly.'

I drew in a breath and then said, 'I couldn't

imagine anything more tedious or more wearing than being jolly with Aunt Peggy and the rest at Christmas. No,' I nodded my head at them. 'As dull as you two are I'll stay here and put up with you.'

My father, laughing now, gave me a playful dig, and as I resumed my reading I thought here was another effort to throw me out of the nest.

Since the night I had returned home so distraught my father hadn't asked me for an episode on Tor-Fret. And I seemed to surprise even myself when quite suddenly I lifted my head from the book and said, 'A funny thing happened on my way home today.'

On this my father let out a bellow, saying, 'You sounded just like a comic on the wireless, lass.'

'Well, it wasn't anything comic.' And then I told them of the man I had seen disappearing into the ground. And when I had finished, my father said, 'That seems funny. I'd take a dander across there tomorrow morning on your way up. Perhaps you'll find out where he went. You didn't think he was hurt?'

'No.'

'I would do nothing of the sort.' My mother had risen from her chair, her face full of concern. 'I don't like the things that go on up there, and I'm telling you straight, lass, I won't be happy until you leave there.'

As I looked back at her trying to frame an answer I knew that in spite of the secret burden of misery I was carrying I would not want to be deprived of one minute of my time at Tor-Fret. I knew that the lost feeling I was experiencing now would be nothing compared to the overall misery were I to cut myself off from that house. Apart from the feeling I had for its master, the house itself had claimed me also. So I could give my mother no answer. I merely shook my head and returned to my book.

The following morning I got off the bus at the stop before Peter's Well and I walked straight from the road up the steep heather bank. There was no path at this point. The morning was dry and cold, with no sun. It was the kind of morning when one would take a sharp walk, so if I was spied approaching the path directly across the fells I had the excuse that I needed to stretch my legs.

Distances are deceptive. I had to do quite a hand-over-hand scramble to reach the actual field where the strange occurrence had happened yesterday. And when I stood on its edge looking downwards I saw, tracing itself in a zigzag way to the road below, a path which started from a point of the field further along from where I was standing.

Yesterday, from where I viewed it, this stretch of land had looked level, but now I saw that it was uneven in patches, and I felt a little silly when I realised that the man could have dropped flat and been hidden by one of the heather-covered mounds, for the fields were not all grass. Yet, nevertheless, I walked in the direction of what I imagined was the spot where I had seen him disappear, but when I reached it the ground showed no crevasse, only small mounds and clumps of dying bracken. And it was as I looked towards the bracken that a slight sound came to me, a gentle pleasant sound, which I recognised as a trickle of water over stones. I walked towards the sound and, bending over the bracken, I saw a ditch with a rivulet of water running away towards my right. This was nothing strange, for the fells were streaked with rivulets running to the rivers. But what was strange was where the water came from. I had moved slightly upwards towards my left now and there I discovered how the earth had swallowed up the man. Sticking out from the bracken and the slope of the ground was a drainpipe, a large culvert; it must have been four feet deep, large enough for anyone to walk into if they bent down. This then was the explanation of the man vanishing. But why should he go into the culvert? I stood still and lifted my head and looked upwards in the direction of Tor-Fret. I couldn't see the house, not any part of it, but I knew instinctively that this drain led to it, and there came back to my mind the voices in the cellar, and Mr Stanley talking of the drain door.

As if I'd been discovered looking at something very private, I swung round and hurried away. And before I reached the path that led to the house I knew for a certainty that the man I had seen dropping into the earth yesterday was Weaver, and that he had been on his way to Maurice Rossiter. Going back to the time when I was standing opposite to my employer, and going over what happened during that time, I could again see the point where his manner changed, where he put an end to the conversation. It was when he had raised his eyes to the ceiling at the sound of the wood pigeon, and it came to me that I had heard that wood pigeon on different occasions.

By the time I reached the house I was shivering with apprehension and I expected someone to say to me immediately, 'Poor Mr Logan!' But my imagination had run away with me. I was greeted almost cheerily by Hollings. There was the clatter of ladders being moved and the jangling of pails from the upper floors. And on my desk I found a note from Maurice Rossiter which read, 'Take half an hour off and go and have a word with Uncle Stephen, he's been asking for you.'

With my new time-table it had been almost impossible for me to visit the old man. So, shortly after ten o'clock, I went up to Mr Stephen's room and I found him very depressed and very grumpy.

At first he did not show any pleasure at my arrival, and not until after I had made the usual enquiries about his health and showed signs of cutting my visit short did he seem to come alive. And almost at once he gave me the reason for his grumpiness. 'Have you heard the latest?' he said.

'The latest?' I repeated. 'What about?'

'The wedding.'

I remained silent, and he, hitching himself up on to his pillows, leant towards me and went on, 'Hole in the corner, that's what it's going to be. Marrying early morning, ten o'clock, then going straight off, and not coming back here for a drink or anything. Can you imagine it? And they call that a wedding.'

Still I said nothing, and he continued, 'It isn't him, it's her. He was quite prepared to make a bit of a splash, even talked about it a week or so ago, but now first thing in the morning, and straight off. Huh! I did think I was going to see a little jollification in this house before my time was up. But jollification, they don't know the meaning of it these days; not the young ones . . . Why does she want everything quiet like that, eh? They could have come back here and had a drink and then have gone off, couldn't they? But no, straight from Alnwick they go . . . Now what do you think of it, eh? I know what his friends'll think. Mean, they'll say, mean.'

It was impossible to tell the old man what I thought of it, truthfully thought of it, so I said, 'She doesn't like fuss.'

'Noreen not like fuss? Funny, huh! Wildest piece for miles she used to be, skittish as a mountain goat, and now no fuss . . . Huh!'

He was slumping down on his pillows now, and his old wrinkled face losing the temporary firmness his temper had given to it, he smiled at me, and, reaching out for my hand, held on to it like a child clutching at an elder, and his voice matched his age and pathetic appearance as he said, 'Funny thing about weddings. Do you know, there's never been a wedding from this house. Funny thing, but I've always wanted to see a wedding from this house. Right back in the family men have married women away from the house. My great-grandfather met a woman in Spain and married her; my grandmother was a woman from the wilds of Cornwall; fey she was, I remember her well. She was married down there, it was all done before she had seen this house. My own mother was French and it was in France that my father married her; she was another fey one. They are all a bit fey in this family, have you noticed that, Kate?' He was grinning widely now, and I shook my head at him as he went on, 'And Logan's mother. Ah, she was a bonny woman, was Logan's mother. My brother came across her in Dublin. I can see her now the first time she came in through the hall door. She was big and stately. Bigger by inches than her man. Logan is the spit of her. She didn't like it here. Her nature was happy and gay and she longed for the life of Dublin . . . But she didn't stay long, anyway. She died she did.' He laughed gently here. 'She talked like that. That's what she would have said . . . She died she did. Oh, I can remember her well, and at the last it seemed as if she was glad to go . . . You know something?' He was gripping my hand with a renewed strength now and he craned his skinny neck forward as he whispered, 'This house doesn't take to women – not foreign women, anyway. You know what I mean? I've a funny idea it wants someone belonging to the soil on which it stands, to the rocks and the crags and the screes, to the high fells . . .'

Now he thrust himself back on the pillow and raised his hand at me as he said, 'And that is why I had such hopes of Noreen. She was born in the county, she belongs. And yet' – his voice sank – 'she won't be married from the house.'

Aiming to soften his disappointment, I said, 'But it's usual, you know, for the bride to go from her own home to the church.'

'Fiddlesticks. Nonsense. They should do as they do in America: be married in the house, that's the place for marriages. Have your priests, and your parsons, but let 'em do it in the house. They've got to live in the house. They've both got to carry out the "I will" in the house, so why don't they start where they mean to carry on – in the house? But, anyway, they could have come back, couldn't they? After they had done it they could have come back.' His voice was pathetic now.

Yes, I thought, they could have come back. If there hadn't been Maurice Rossiter to look at the bride with eyes that made her remember what she was desirous of forgetting, then she would have come back. But as it was, I thought, she was doing the wise thing not to face Maurice until she was settled in her new life. With such thinking I turned a knife between my ribs, but there it was, it was something I had no power to alter. I could only hope that they would both find a certain amount of happiness. Yes, I could hope that, especially for him. This love that had been sprung on me was already great enough to desire this.

The old man now brought the conversation on to a personal level by exclaiming, 'I want my coffee. Hollings never brings it before eleven. An' I want it black. I'm as dry as a stick.'

This gave me an excuse to rise to my feet. 'I'll go and tell him,' I said. 'Goodbye now, Mr Stephen.'

He blinked at me and smiled his toothless smile, saying, 'I like seeing you. Will you come up every morning?'

'I can't promise every morning, but I'll try to slip up as often as I can.'

'Yes, yes, do . . . I like seeing you . . .'

In the kitchen I found Hollings and delivered Mr Stephen's message, to which he replied, 'He's not getting it black, madam. 'Tisn't good for him.' He gave me what was, for him, a smile. And I returned it, then went to my room.

I did not see Maurice Rossiter until about fifteen minutes before I was ready to leave. His manner was cheerful, too cheerful to be natural. There was no reference to our conversation of yesterday. He talked only of his work. He expressed great satisfaction with the articles, and told me he had done another.

More for something to say than anything else, I remarked, 'You must work all night.' And to this he answered, 'I do very often.' And I was left with a picture of him sitting propped up in bed during the small hours of the night writing, writing one of his devils out of his system.

7

When I look back I can remember very little of what transpired from the beginning of November until the day of the wedding. Only one thing stands out, the rest were mundane happenings, such as my mother insisting I have a fry before I went to work. This was because she said I was getting scraggy. It was true I had lost weight, but I could never see myself as thin, let alone scraggy. And then there was the Sunday that Rodney brought his girl from Amble up to see us, and my mother asked them to stay to tea. And when they had gone my father had looked at me with his head on one side and said, 'You're not regretting anything in that quarter, are you?' To this I replied, 'Oh, Father, don't be silly.' And he answered, 'Well, you didn't sound very bright at tea and I thought you might be regretting something.' Again I had said, 'Don't be silly.'

And then there was the morning of the first really hard frost, a black frost. There was a patch of ice outside the door some yards long and impulsively I slid along it, much to my parents' amusement. As usual they had come to the door to see me off, and my father had cried laughingly after me, 'Enough of that now. You wore enough shoes out when you were a bairn; don't start that all over again.' I waved to them from the bend on the hill. Braced by the steely air, I became almost joyful, intoxicated you could almost say. But it did not last for long. Before I reached Tor-Fret I was sober once more.

But the one thing that remains clear in my mind took place one morning as I was once again going to visit Mr Stephen. It was about a week before the actual wedding day. The decorators had finished their work in the rooms on the left side of the landing, and the door of one room was ajar, and in spite of myself I had to stop and look in. It was furnished as a sitting-room, and from where I stood I could see a moss-green-coloured couch set at right angles to the fireplace. It was standing on a red Turkish carpet, not the ordinary hard red that inclines to purple, but a scarlet red with a yellow and green pattern, and the walls appeared a creamy grey. The glimpse afforded me drew me to the threshold of the doorway and then into the room. I had just noticed that the curtains were the same soft green as the couch, when a voice from somewhere behind me, said, 'Do you like it, Kate?' As I started round I put my fingers to my lips and muttered apologetically, 'Oh, I'm sorry.'

'Why be sorry? What is there to be sorry for?' Logan Rossiter stepped from where he had been standing at a bookcase in the corner of the room and came towards me, but not too close. When he stopped and looked at my flushed face he said quietly, 'Don't be disturbed like that, please. I'm so glad it was attractive enough to draw you in . . . Do you like it?' he asked again.

'Yes, yes I do, very much.' I took my eyes from his face and looked around the room now, taking it in as a whole, and as I did so I knew a feeling of deep envy. 'I think it's very beautiful.'

'I hope . . . I hope Noreen thinks so too. She hasn't seen it yet.'

My eyes were on him again, and his were tight on my face as I replied, 'No?'

Now with a quick movement he stepped behind me and closed the door, then, coming and facing me again, nearer this time, he said quietly, 'I wanted to see you, Kate, to have a word with you. To tell you how sor—'

'Please. Please don't. Don't talk about it.' My hand was out as if warding him off. I couldn't bear to hear him apologise for what had taken place.

'But it was my fault—'

'It was nobody's fault. It's over and forgotten, please . . .' I looked at him appealingly.

'All right, Kate, as you wish. But there's still something I'd like to tell you. I feel I must tell you, if only I can find the right words.'

Now I experienced a terrifying feeling, a racing through my system that made me want to cry out. I didn't want to be confronted by another Arthur Boyle. The thought was unbearable. Arthur had met a girl in a train and because of her I was thrown aside, rejected. Although I would not forgo one minute of the time Logan Rossiter and I had clung together on the hillside, I did not want to be another 'girl in the train' and that 'The Big Fellow' should lose my respect by becoming a mere Arthur. Although if he walked out on Noreen Badcliff an hour before the wedding it would be nothing less than she deserved, yet he was not to know this. If he retracted now he would, in his own mind, be letting down a lovely girl, a girl he had known all his life, and admired all his life . . . had loved all his life.

He now put up his hand and patted the air, and so meaningful was the gesture that I almost felt it on my flesh. Then, as if he had been travelling alongside my whirling thoughts, he now said, 'I understand you, Kate. All that you'd like to say, all that you want left unsaid . . . I understand. The only thing, the final thing I will say to you is, if I caused you any distress, please forgive me.'

My throat was tightening but before it gave me away and choked my voice I managed to say, 'There's nothing to forgive, nothing. Goodbye.' And I paused before adding, 'I hope you'll both be very happy.'

He made no answer whatever to this, and after a second, during which we again looked at each other, I turned and opened the door and went out. I remember that I did not go on my way to visit Mr Stephen but returned to my room.

That's all I can recall of that month, until the wedding day.

Have you noticed that the weather seems to match itself to certain happenings? This is not always so, but I think the weather was in keeping with the events that followed Logan Rossiter's marriage to Noreen Badcliff.

For days now my father, looking across the vast expanse of land that formed the fells, had watched the weather signs. The startling squalls. The clouds dropping on distant peaks as if bent on sweeping them away. Then intervals when everything stood out against the stark white light peculiar to this part of the country. And he would say to me when I returned home at night, 'We're in for it; it's going to be a winter and a half, you mark my words.'

Then on the eve of the wedding the world became still. The cold was intense; and when I returned home that night with my heart as chilled as my face, my father said, 'This'll break in a storm, you'll see. There's hardly a blade of grass moved all the day; there'll be snow 'afore the morning.' And my mother said, 'I saw a grey wagtail the day; it's a long time since I've seen a grey wagtail. It was lovely and yellow underneath; oh, it was bonny. I put out some bread, but it didn't come near, but a missel-thrush did. By, he golloped it up. Oh, I'm sorry for the birds days like this.' And my father put in now, 'I'm sorry for anybody outside days like this.' Then turning to me, he added, 'You won't be going in the morrow, anyway, I suppose?'

I turned from his keen glance, and, settling myself in a chair before the roaring fire, I replied evenly, 'Yes, I'm going in.'

'But he won't be working surely . . . not on his brother's wedding day?' This was from my mother, and I cast a glance at her, saying, 'Well, he's told me to come in and that things are to go on as usual.'

I turned from their probing stares and looked into the heart of the fire, and there I could see Maurice Rossiter when he told me that things would go on as usual. It had never dawned on me that he would want to work on this particular day, and certainly I had not thought that he would expect me to come up to the house, even if there was to be no reception. It was as I was leaving the room that I turned to him and said, 'You won't want me tomorrow then?' I took it as an accepted fact that he wouldn't require my services on this day, but he had turned a completely blank countenance towards me as if I had said something utterly idiotic, and then he had asked in a voice that was too calm, 'Why not?'

'Well, the . . . the . . .' I found I was stammering in confusion. 'Well . . . the wedding.'

'I'm not getting married.'

I was completely nonplussed and showed it.

'It is my brother who is getting married and there is to be no reception, so why shouldn't we go on as usual, Kate?'

I had looked at him blankly for some moments before I was able to say, 'Very well, I'll come in.'

I thought now that cruelty was such an integral part of Maurice Rossiter's nature that he couldn't help but inflict it on himself. I could not blame him for inflicting it on me, not on this occasion, for he was ignorant, at least I prayed he was ignorant, of my feeling towards his brother. I told myself I would die of shame if what had transpired between Logan and me was ever made known to him.

My father now put his book down and took off his reading glasses as he said, 'Listen to that. There it comes, the wind.' And my mother, seating herself on the other side of the hearth, a stocking in her hand, clicked her needles together and smiled at me, but, speaking to my father as if he were a frightened child, said, 'There's no need to worry. The house has stood many a gale and not a stone moved. I think it will ride out another.' She pulled a face at me, then concentrated on her knitting, and I lay back in my chair and opened a book and looked at its pages without seeing the print . . . This time tomorrow it would be all over.

My father, as if he had discovered himself to be a prophet, shouted from the landing the next morning, 'What did I tell you, Kate? Snow, heavy. Have you seen it?'

Yes, I had seen it, and I called back to him, 'You were right.'

Later, down in the kitchen, my mother said, 'You're not going out in this, lass, surely? You'll get down this hill but what about getting up to the house?'

'It isn't thick,' I said, 'and it won't lie. It's much too early for it to lie. It's just a shower.'

'Oh. Don't you bluff yourself. The sky's laden with it. Your mother's right. You stay put.'

'I must go,' I said. And I knew I must go. I was glad now that Maurice Rossiter had insisted that I go. I could not have borne to stay penned up in the house all day thinking. I had to do something, and struggling against the elements was as good a way to forget myself as any other.

As yet the snow was nowhere thick enough to stop traffic on the road, but the people in the bus, like my father, prophesied more to come. But my father had been right. It was one thing getting down the hill into the village but quite another getting up to Tor-Fret. And when I arrived, chilled to the bone and quite out of breath, I was greeted in the hall by the twins, who quite openly were amazed to see me. 'Why, Kate!' said Mr Stanley. 'What brought you up here in this? We're in for a good thick blanket, didn't you know?'

Mr Bernard, now peering into my frozen face, said, 'Maurice? Maurice tell you to come today?'

'It's all right,' I said. 'I . . . I wanted to come. I'm not in the way, I hope.'

'In the way?' Mr Stanley replied while Mr Bernard shook his head. 'No, of course not, Kate.' And then he patted my arm and said, 'It's nice to have you here at any time, but I think we're more glad of you today. It's a funny day today.'

The two old men now looked at each other and nodded in agreement; then, turning to me, they waited for me to say something. They looked very old at this moment, and pathetic, sort of lost. What was it about the men in this house that brought to me a sense of not only loneliness, but aloneness, as if each in his own way was encased in a private world from which he was groping, groping in vain for a hand to anchor to?

I made myself smile and say, 'I'm glad I've come then.'

And now Mr Stanley, brightening, said, 'We'll have a glass of wine, eh, instead of coffee. You'll join us in a glass of wine, Kate, won't you?'

'Yes, I'll be glad to, thank you. Tell me when you're ready.' I turned from them and went into my room. It struck cold; the fire had just been lit and was still sullen, so I sat with my coat on for some time – in fact, until the big old wall-clock in the hall boomed ten. Then I stopped my typing and let out a long breath . . . It was done. It was over. Now it was up to me to pull myself together. It was no use repining or thinking any more about it. I wasn't the first woman in the world, I told myself, that this had happened to, and I could do one of two things. I could become maudlin under it, full of self-pity, asking why? why? why? Or I could use it as an incentive to drive me to do something with my life. As my parents were aiming to throw me out of the nest, then I must also tear myself from the magnetism of this house and one of its occupants. I was a good secretary, I knew my own worth, I could go away and get a decent post, say, in Edinburgh, or London even. And who knew what might happen to me there? Yes who knew?

It was as I was injecting myself with this brave philosophy that I heard the thumping, the same kind of thumping I had heard before, the thump of a fist being beaten into the bed or pillow. And, turning my eyes towards my employer's door, my resolutions fled and for a moment I cried inwardly for us both. And then the uncles came in.

'How 'bout this glass of wine?' Mr Bernard cried. Then added, 'Where's Maurice? Not up yet? Dear, dear.' As he made his way towards the intersecting door it opened and there stood Maurice Rossiter fully dressed.

I had known this man for a number of weeks now. I had seen him in varying moods, which altered his face accordingly. But never had I seen him as he looked at this moment. His skin was so white as to appear powdered. His eyes seemed to have fallen back into their large sockets and were merely dark pools, yet bright with a strange light. I had once, many years ago, shone a torch down a deep well and I was reminded of this incident now. Candidly I was appalled at the change in this man, and pity for him once more flooded over me. The old men, too, were vitally aware of their nephew's mood, and their manner was tender. Mr Stanley spoke first to him, saying, 'Ah, there you are, Maurice. Come on, come on, we'll have a quiet glass together. What do you say?'

And now Mr Bernard, going forward, began in his staccato manner, 'No restrictions, no rationing, not today. Sample some of the bottles, eh? Eh, Maurice? Sample some old bottles, that's the stuff.'

Maurice Rossiter now shambled forward and passed the old men, making for the chair before the fire without speaking. I felt that he could not speak. If his face was anything to go by his feelings were so ravished at this moment that he was incapable of any utterance. And now Mr Bernard, hovering over him, pointed towards the fire and spluttered, 'Look at that, dead as a doornail. Morning like this. Where's Patterson?' He turned from his nephew and was making his bustling way towards the door when he was stopped by Mr Stanley saying quietly, 'Leave Patterson alone, Bernard, he's got his hands full. There's a grand fire in the drawing-room, come on. Let's all go there. And you, Bernard, go and bring the bottles up . . . Go on.'

'Yes, yes, that's it, that's it.' Mr Bernard scurried out, and Mr Stanley, looking at me, said, 'Come along, my dear. We'll go to the drawing-room. Maurice will follow; won't you, Maurice?'

Not for the life of me, even knowing all I did about Maurice Rossiter, could I have left him sitting there in his lonely pain, and so I bent towards him and said, 'Won't you come? Come now.'

He brought his eyes from the struggling embers of the fire and looked at me and blinked once. I was sure he had not been aware of my presence until this actual second, and now he inclined his head forward and, pulling himself up on to his feet, went out of the room. Mr Stanley and I, keeping well behind him to give him, as he always needed, room to swing his body.

As Mr Stanley had said, there was a grand fire in the drawing-room, and the room itself looked inviting, for it was filled with snow-light from outside and fire-light from within, and their mingling lent to it a charm, a comfort and a charm.

We had hardly seated ourselves round the fire

when Mr Bernard bustled in with three bottles in his arms. 'Brought a bottle nineteen-fifty-two up . . . Remember? Christened it Tor-Freto.'

'Good. Good.' Mr Stanley was now acting like an excited boy, an act no doubt put on to bring Maurice out of his depression. He clapped his hands together and shook them as he exclaimed, 'Wait till you sample this. It's as good as your Austrian Petite Tokay. Two years in the barrel it was, smooth as a liqueur. And what else, Bernard?'

Before Mr Bernard had time to reply Maurice Rossiter said flatly and quietly, 'I'd like a drop of hard stuff.'

Following this request there settled a silence on us. It only lasted for a matter of seconds, but during it the two old men exchanged quick glances, and then Mr Stanley said soothingly, 'Now you know there's none left, Maurice.'

'I'll have a drop of the fresh.'

'You won't! You won't! Deadly.' Mr Bernard was now spluttering in agitation. 'Another year at least. Two better. Remember last time. Don't want . . .'

'All right, all right.' Mr Stanley now silenced his brother, but not before he had cast in my direction a very uneasy glance. I knew that 'hard stuff' referred to whisky . . . Did the uncles make whisky? But it was illegal. I recalled the workmanlike corner of the cellar. Was that where they made it? I wouldn't know.

'This one is very good, Maurice, warming.' Mr

Stanley picked up the bottle his brother had referred to as 'Tor-Freto' and proceeded to pour out the wine. He did it with a slow dignity as if he was performing a ceremony – I think he always looked on the serving of wine in a ceremonious light – and then we all had a glass in our hands, and for a moment there was another awkward silence. I say for a moment, but this one seemed to me to go on for an unbearable length of time, and then thankfully it was broken by Mr Stanley raising his glass to eye level and saying, 'Well, let us drink to them.'

It is usual to repeat a toast but no-one replied, 'To them.' Mr Bernard inclined his head, that was all, then raised the glass to his lips, as did Mr Stanley, and the wine was on my tongue when it almost spluttered from my mouth as the stem of Maurice Rossiter's glass snapped in two. As the wine soaked into the carpet we all looked down, and the strangest part of it was there was no exclamation of any kind either from the old men, myself, or Maurice Rossiter. No 'Oh dear!' or 'How did you manage that?' or 'It's all right, I'll get you another.' There was not a single word spoken. The atmosphere had an eerie feeling. If I can explain it, it seemed pregnant with a force that pressed against all of us, even its creator. And there he sat, staring before him, not into the fire, not at the picture of the rider above the mantelpiece, just before him, looking, I thought, into his own mind and watching the torture manufacturing itself. What would have happened next I don't know, but the old men and myself were diverted by the sound of the front-door bell ringing. We all looked towards the drawing-room door as if it was a means of escape, and then Mr Stanley exclaimed in a high tone, 'Who can it be on a morning like this? Hollings wouldn't ring. Anyway, it's too soon for him to be back.'

I hadn't up to now known that Hollings was out, but I knew that there would be only one place he would go this morning. I knew that for this occasion Logan Rossiter would have preferred Hollings to do him this service rather than anyone else.

Now there was a tap on the drawing-room door and Patterson opened it, and in came the minister. The man was blowing on his hands, his face a ruddy beam. He seemed in high fettle, which is more than I could say for anyone else in the room. For the twins' greeting had, I thought, a coolness about it. As for myself, I felt that odd tremor of fear as when I had first come face to face with this man. Evil in any shape is a force to be reckoned with, but when it is hiding under an authorised cloak of goodness its power becomes terrifying. Yet the presence of this man – I couldn't think of him as a minister – seemed to lift the dark depression that was weighing Maurice Rossiter down. For although he didn't smile at the visitor, he greeted Fallenbor in a tone that was almost normal. 'You're just in time,' he said; 'you must have smelled it.' He looked towards his uncle, and Mr Stanley went to the side table and poured out two more glasses of wine. In the meantime the minister had taken his stand with his back to the fire, and he rubbed his buttocks vigorously as he beamed around him, saying, 'What a day! Do you know, I had almost to claw my way up the hill. It's early this year . . . Well, well.' He extended his hand towards Mr Stanley and, taking the glass, went on, 'Isn't this nice! Thank you, Stanley, thank you.' Then, raising his glass and bowing slightly to one after the other, he sipped at the wine and his round eyes widened, and, looking towards Mr Stanley again, he exclaimed in a loud voice, 'Ah! Ah! This is special, isn't it? Of course, of course, what am I thinking about? It's for a special occasion. Well, I will drink to it, but not alone – come along.' He chuckled now as he held up his glass.

I did not sip the wine again but watched Maurice Rossiter closely, and couldn't but be surprised when I saw him put the glass to his lips and drink in quite an ordinary fashion. It was evident that the minister was having a soothing effect upon my employer, and this became more evident still when in the next moment, placing the glass on a low stool at the side, he looked towards the man and said, 'I'm glad to see you, Fallenbor. I was in the doldrums; I want cheering up. Tell me something to make me laugh.'

I couldn't bear to hear this man playing the raconteur. Doubtless he could tell an excellent tale, but I didn't want to hear it, or listen to him. So, rising to my feet, I said, 'If you'll excuse me, I'll get back to my work.'

'There's no need, Kate, there's no need.' It was

the first time that Maurice Rossiter had addressed me since I came in, and, looking at him, I said quietly, 'I would rather if you wouldn't mind, Mr Maurice.'

He was looking straight up into my face now as he said, 'As you will.'

I handed my glass to Mr Bernard and smiled at the old men, then, inclining my head towards the minister, I went out of the room.

When I opened the door of my room it was to find Patterson peering out through the snow-smeared window. He turned quickly on my entry and, looking towards the fire, said, 'It's going all right now, miss. Couldn't get it to brighten at all today.' And then he added, 'I was on the look-out for Hollings. If he doesn't come in a little while I'll go down the hill. He'll have a job to make his way, it's getting worse.'

I looked past him towards the window. I could see nothing now but the snow-flakes falling gently on to the drift on the low sill. 'I'm going to find it a job to get home, too,' I said.

'Well, if I go down I'll see if the road is clear enough and I'll take you in the car.'

'Mr Logan didn't take the car then?'

'No, no. They were going south by train. And Mr Rankin, his partner, picked them up at the bottom of the hill.'

So he had had someone with him besides Hollings. As I turned to my desk, Patterson, looking towards the window again, said, 'Awful day for them really,' and then he added with a little smile,

'Well, I don't suppose they'll mind, do you?'

I turned my head towards him. As I said, I liked Patterson. He was a kindly man, uncomplicated. 'No, Patterson,' I said, 'I don't suppose they'll mind.'

'I wouldn't in his place, at any rate.' His smile was broader now and I dared to say, 'Nor I in hers.' We both laughed now as if it were a joke, a private joke, and then he went out, leaving me alone.

Nor I in hers. As I repeated the phrase the common-sense Kate asserted herself, saying, 'Stop it. Get some work done. Get down to it.' And my weaker self obeying her, I got down to it.

It was just on twelve when Mr Stanley entered the room, saying anxiously, 'I'm afraid, Kate, you'll have to wait awhile before venturing out. Patterson isn't back yet. He went down to see if Hollings had arrived on the eleven-thirty bus, for he would have come straight back. Hollings isn't the one to stay out. Never moves really. So he must have got held up somewhere.'

'Oh,' I said, 'I'll be able to manage. I've had two winters on the fells, I'm quite used to snow.'

'Have you been to the front door?'

'No.'

'Well, go and have a look out; it's no use looking out of the window.'

I went past him through the hall and opened the front door on to a massed white world. I knew it had been snowing steadily, but I hadn't realised how heavily and how thick it was lying. Under the portico lay about three feet of drift, and I gauged that it must be anything up to a foot in depth beyond. That wouldn't be too difficult for walking on the level, but on the steep fell road it was another matter. I turned to where Mr Stanley stood behind me and said, 'I see what you mean. I'll wait until Patterson comes back. Yet it's hard lines on him having to go down again.'

'Oh, Patterson's tough, he's fell-bred. Come in, dear, and shut the door; the blood in my veins is very, very thin.' He smiled at me, then added, 'Leave what you are doing; come along, come and join us. There's only Bernard and I. We're upstairs with Stephen; the minister is entertaining Maurice.'

And so, not a little worried, I went upstairs to find Mr Stephen in a very querulous mood. Unlike his brothers, he was not hiding his disappointment over the wedding. And he greeted me immediately with, 'Serves them right; serves them right, doesn't it? Don't deserve any better weather.'

'Now, now . . .' Mr Stanley began, only to be shut up abruptly with, 'Never mind "now, now". You won't stop me saying what I think . . . not until I'm dead.'

'Not then.' This staccato quip came from Mr Bernard, and the twins laughed together. Then Mr Stephen, turning to his one remaining pleasure, asked, 'What's for lunch? Not the usual, I hope, today.'

'Grouse, man, grouse.' Mr Stanley was leaning towards the bed.

'Grouse. Ah, who brought them in? Logan?'

'No, Patterson. He was out with Burrows on the lower farm.'

'Well, that's something . . . grouse.' The old man smacked his lips, then added, 'Pie or roast?'

The twins now looked at each other in enquiry, then Mr Stanley said, 'Roast. Roast, I suppose, if nobody's told Bennett otherwise. Bennett can't stand pie himself.' Again the twins laughed.

It was half an hour later that I went downstairs with Mr Stanley to ascertain whether Patterson had returned with Hollings, and before we reached the kitchen we knew that they were back, for we heard Patterson's voice saying, 'There now, there now, take it easy, let me get them off you,' and when we entered the kitchen it was to see Patterson kneeling on the floor pulling off Hollings's snow-encrusted boots. The old man was leaning back in a deep cane chair. His face was rimmed with snow, and there was a ridge of hair on his neck sticking out like miniature icicles, where the snow had caught him between the collar of his coat and the bottom of his cap. He turned his weary eyes towards me, and I gave an exclamation of concern as Mr Stanley, hurrying to his side, exclaimed, 'My God! Hollings, you look all in. As bad as that, is it?'

It was Patterson who answered, 'It's as bad as anything I've seen for many a long day, sir. Bus got stuck a mile away, he had to walk. No traffic moving at all. I don't know how we got up the hill . . . I really don't.'

'I'll get you something . . . warm you inside.' Mr

Stanley scurried from the room, and Patterson, getting to his feet, inclined his head to me and said, 'You're not going to get down there yet a while, miss.'

'But I'll have to, Patterson; my people will be worried.'

'They'll be more worried if you get stuck out in that. It was as much as I could do to get up the hill. I'm telling you, I wouldn't risk it, miss. In fact it would be madness; it's blowing a blizzard. If it stops, well, that's another thing, I'll get you down. But it's not only getting you down, it's getting you there.'

Yes, it was getting me there . . . home. I said now, 'I'll have to get word to my people somehow. The wires aren't down, are they?'

'No, not that I know of, not yet. But they won't last long in this, the wind is enough to crack a steel plate in two.'

I was about to turn away when Hollings's hand came wavering towards me, and his voice was weak in his throat as he said, 'Don't risk it, madam. Don't risk it.'

I nodded at him and turned towards the kitchen door, but before I could reach it it was pushed open and there entered Maurice Rossiter. He rolled a few steps, then supported himself against the long white scrubbed kitchen table, and, looking first at Patterson and then at Hollings, he said, 'Pretty bad out then?'

'Yes, sir.' It was Patterson who answered for Hollings.

But now Maurice Rossiter, his eyes still on Hollings, asked the old man pointedly, 'And how did it go?'

Hollings, easing himself straighter in the chair, and turning his head fully towards Maurice, replied, his voice seeming to gain strength, 'Very well, sir; it went very well.'

The old man and the young man surveyed each other for a full minute, and then Maurice Rossiter made a deep obeisance with his head before turning away. I was holding the door open and he passed me without a word, and I followed him. And when we were opposite my door I said, 'Would it be all right for me to use the phone, Mr Maurice? I'll have to tell my people I won't be home for a while.'

'Yes, Kate; yes, certainly.' He spoke over his shoulder and added, 'You must stay for lunch.' I looked at him and saw that he was smiling, and I realised that already he was carrying quite an amount of wine.

I crossed the hall and went into the room that I had entered on the first morning on coming into this house, the room where Logan Rossiter had scathingly repeated my name.

It was with a feeling of thankfulness that I contacted the exchange, and in a few minutes Rodney's voice came to me muffled and unfamiliar, but when he knew who it was speaking he exclaimed, 'Oh, it's you, Kate. Where are you stuck?'

'Up at the house,' I said.

'Well then, you stay there. Don't attempt to come

down here for a while. The roads are blocked and it's blowing a blizzard.'

'But my mother and father, Rodney. They'll be worrying themselves sick.'

'They'll guess that you'll stay put. Anyway, look, don't you worry. I'll have a shot at getting up to them.'

'Oh, will you, Rodney? That's good of you.'

'Don't you worry, Kate. And if I manage it, I'll give you a ring back. That all right?'

'That's fine, Rodney. I'm sorry to trouble you.'

'No trouble at all, you know that, Kate. By the way, I hear the big one, the eldest's, getting married the day?'

'Yes, yes. It was this morning.'

'How did they get down?'

'Oh, they went early. They didn't intend to come back, anyway.'

'Lucky for them. But what a day for it. Ah, well. Are they having any jollification?'

'No, Rodney, no jollification.'

'Well, that's a pity; it would have passed the time away. You'll get something to eat though, surely?'

'Yes, I'm staying to lunch.'

'Good. Now don't worry, I'll have a shot at getting up to the house . . . take some bread with me and things and then if I can I'll ring you back. How's that?'

'Thanks, Rodney. You are so kind. Goodbye.'

'Goodbye, Kate.'

I put down the phone and my mind was easier . . . That was until I sat down to lunch.

Maurice Rossiter sat at the head of the long dining-table, which was only half covered by a cloth. The table would, I am sure, have seated two dozen people comfortably, and doubtless in the not so distant past it had served that number often. But now we sat at one corner of it, I on Maurice Rossiter's right and the minister opposite me on his left, the twins one on each side of us. My employer's manner had undergone a complete change. I myself could hardly believe that this was the same morose creature of a few hours ago, and of the two facets I knew which I would have preferred, for his wine-inspired gaiety was getting on my nerves. But apparently it did not upset the uncles in this way. I think they preferred to have him cheerful and had slackened their restrictions on the wine to keep him so. The minister too, I noticed, had also drunk deeply, if his flushed face was anything to go by. He refused nothing, either of wine or food. And it was hard to see how he could talk so much while eating, and drinking so rapidly, but talk he did, and in a very amusing fashion, even I had to admit this.

Maurice Rossiter was for pressing me to empty my glass, saying, 'Come on, Kate; come on, stop dithering. You've been playing with that for the last half-hour.'

I'd had two glasses of wine with the meal and with the one I'd had earlier this was more than enough for me. Its effect I termed as feeling nice. And I did feel nice. The past was pushed just a little way behind me now; I could look at it without straining. I was enjoying sitting in this dining-room that smelt of leather and smoke, and whose walls had once been red but were now a delicate pink where the paper showed between the huge pictures of men and women . . . all Rossiters. I liked the look of the old-fashioned silver and the way the meal was served. Patterson was serving today; poor Hollings wasn't yet up to it, I supposed. Yes, I was feeling nice . . . mellow, and all due to the uncles' home-made wine. I knew lots of people who made home-made wine, but I knew that they didn't make wine like this. I can remember my father saying of my grandmother's efforts: 'She calls it parsnip and says it tastes like whisky . . . Whisky, huh! Boiled turnip water would be a better name for it.' Yet as much as I had enjoyed the wine, I knew that I mustn't have any more. And I was placing my hand over the top of my glass to prevent Maurice Rossiter refilling it when I and the rest at the table were distracted by the sound of Patterson's raised voice coming from just beyond the door. He was saying, 'How did you get in here?'

I recognised the voice that answered him and was quick to pick up the glance that passed between my employer and the minister. The voice was that of Weaver, and it was not low or even of ordinary tone as befits a servant in his master's house, but came loud and defiant as he cried, 'The way Aa've come in many another time. An' let me tell you Aa've more right than you in here . . . Go on, house-boy, tell Mr Maurice.'

'By God! If Mr Logan was here he'd kick your backside over the topmost fell and I'd help him.'

'Aye, ya would, Aa know. An' . . . well, he isn't here, is he? An' not likely to be, so go on.'

'Go on yourself, don't give me orders.'

I was amazed at the change in Patterson's voice. Then the next moment the door was thrust open and there stood Weaver. He was wearing a ragged snow-covered top coat, the collar turned up, and he still had a cap on his head.

Mr Bernard had risen, his face red with anger as he cried, 'Get out, away, do you hear? This minute. Away you go.'

'Not so fast, Uncle, not so fast.' It was Maurice Rossiter speaking, and he put his arm across in front of me and pulled at Mr Bernard's sleeve, adding, 'Sit down, sit down.' Then, because Mr Bernard showed no sign of obeying him, his voice changed to a deep growl as he said, 'Logan is no longer here remember. I'm head of the house at present, Uncle, the next in line. Maurice Alastair Rossiter, the next in line . . . sit down . . . And you, Weaver.' He now waved his hand, beckoning Weaver further into the room, and his tone became lighter, even jocular. 'Come in, come in. Is it a drink you're after? Well you've come on the right day.'

Mr Stanley had now risen from the other side of the table, and, looking towards his nephew and ignoring the fact that his brother had been told to reseat himself, he said with quiet dignity, 'We'll leave you then, Maurice. Come, Kate.' He motioned me to my feet, but as I made to rise Maurice Rossiter's hand became a grip on my arm as he said, 'Stay where you are, Kate. We're all friends together, for this day at least.'

'I . . . I would rather, if you don't mind, Mr Maurice. I . . . I'd rather get on with some work.'

'Let the young lady go.' It was the minister speaking. It was the first time he had looked at me directly, or addressed any remark to me during the meal, and again he repeated, his voice soft but insistent, 'Let the young lady go, Maurice. It's better so.'

Maurice Rossiter's hand came from my arm and I rose to my feet and went down the long table, past Weaver without looking at him but knowing all the time that his eyes were hard on me. Mr Bernard had walked by my side, and at the bottom of the table we met up with Mr Stanley, and together we went out of the room, across the hall and into the drawing-room without exchanging a word.

I could see that the old men were deeply troubled, and, thinking that they might want to talk, I made an excuse to leave them to themselves and returned to my room. Not, I'm afraid, to work – I wasn't feeling like work. Nor was I feeling nice any longer. I was feeling frightened . . .

By three o'clock in the afternoon the storm had increased if anything, and the sky was so low and dark that it was like late evening. Intermittently there came to me sounds of rumbling laughter. Maurice Rossiter and his two companions were still in the dining-room and the sound made me ask myself, What if I have to stay the night? This thought drove me in search of Patterson, and I found him in the kitchen talking with Hollings and the old cook.

'Is there any chance of me getting down to the road, Patterson?' I said. 'I feel I must get home.'

It was not Patterson who answered me now but Hollings, saying, 'We've just been talking about it, madam. It would be asking for serious trouble to let you go in this; even if you got down to the road there would be nothing running. There's nothing for it, I'm afraid, but that you must stay the night. It's almost dark now . . . look.' He pointed to the window.

Now Patterson turned to me. 'We were thinking, miss, that the best place would be Mr Logan's office. It's a small room and I'll put a fire on. The couch is comfortable. You'd do fine in there, I'm sure, miss.'

I looked from one to the other rather helplessly, and said, 'Thank you . . . Very well.' Then, turning from their concerned gaze, I went back to my room, the feeling of fear more pronounced now.

At four o'clock the phone rang and I went to answer it. It was Rodney. He had managed to get to the cottage and my mother's message to me was definitely to stay put, not to risk coming down while it was like this, and not to worry. I thanked him warmly and was reluctant to ring off.

Although I told myself that there was Patterson and Hollings and the uncles in the house, the feeling of fear grew. The only one that could make any impression on Maurice Rossiter, or rather on his two companions, would be Patterson. There were two camps under this roof – one, with the exception of Patterson, being made up of old men. This I knew was the main cause of my fear, and was not unreasonable, knowing Weaver and judging the minister . . .

Looking back, I don't know exactly at what time I left my room and went into the study. I think it was some time after eight o'clock. I'd had tea with the twins in Mr Stephen's room. It had been a quiet affair, devoid of laughter. I had come downstairs about five o'clock. When I refused an evening meal Patterson had brought me some hot milk and biscuits . . . that was about half-past seven as far as I can remember.

It was about this time, too, that I first heard the sound of distant laughter coming as if through the floor, as indeed it was. Maurice Rossiter, the minister and Weaver were now in the cellar. There had been heated words between the uncles and Maurice in the hall about this move, which had ended with Mr Stanley saying in a voice pathetic with pleading, 'Have what you like, but don't touch the brew, Maurice . . . please.'

What was the brew? Was it the hard stuff that Maurice had wanted this morning, the raw whisky? If so, the effect this would have on top of all the wine he had drunk was something I didn't want to think about.

As Patterson was about to leave the room he had said, 'I'd stick a chair under the knob, miss. It mightn't be necessary, but you never know – men in drink are queer creatures. There's no key. Never been any need for keys in locks in this house, not having any—' he paused, 'well, ladies about – not for years, anyway.'

My foreboding fear drove me to ask him, 'Will you be in the house all evening, Patterson?'

'Yes, I'll be about. I sleep over the stables, as you know, but I'll see things are all quiet before I go over the night. Don't worry.'

And so assured, up to a point anyway, I had gone into the study. It was a cluttered room, but comfortable, and it was warm. And about it hung the presence of its owner. I sat down on the couch that was to be my bed, but did not even take my shoes off. Looking back, I realise I had been ready to run from the minute I had seen Weaver enter the diningroom. Even with the wind howling like a battalion of demons round the house, I think I would have risked throwing myself on its mercy rather than have been confronted by either Weaver or the minister in drink. Strangely, I did not include my employer in my fear.

At times the house, but for the noise of the wind, would become free of all sound, and I thought . . . I hoped, that sleep had overtaken the three men in the cellar. Then hope would be whipped away by the smothered echo of their laughter breaking through once more.

I put my feet up on the couch but made no attempt to read. I could only sit taut, thinking. I thought quite a bit of the sitting-room at home, and of my mother and father, and I hoped they weren't worrying. I thought of many things, but I tried not to let my mind touch on Logan Rossiter . . . or his wife. This title, when I'd thought of it earlier, had pricked me like a sting.

At what point I dozed I don't know, but it was the sound of a door opening that brought me stiffly awake. This door had a particular sound of its own, being the front door. It was built of massive oak and had a chain on the back which jangled when the door was moved either one way or the other. I turned my head in the direction of the hall. Had Patterson come in by the front door? No, I rejected this idea; the stables were across the courtyard right opposite the back door . . . I hadn't stuck a chair under the door handle . . . I was swinging my legs from the couch when the study door burst open and I actually screamed at the sight of the figure standing there . . . The Big Fellow himself. Rimed with snow from head to foot, he looked like something inhuman. In fact, had I not associated the opening of the front door with his appearance I must have thought he was some fearsome apparition. He showed no surprise whatever at seeing me, but with slow lifting feet, as if he were still treading the snow, he moved towards the couch. Putting out his arms and groping like a half-blind man at its back, he stepped round it, then, flopping down, he dropped his body sidewards and lay there panting for some minutes. With one great intake of breath he turned his frozen face towards me and with a weary lift of his hand indicated that I close the door. Up to now I had been too stupefied to move; I had just stood, my hand to my throat, gaping at him, but at his signal I sprang forward, and when I had shut the door I was back like a flash to his side. And now words poured out of me. Words of compassion, of enquiry, of amazement. 'Oh, Mr Logan! Oh, Mr Logan! What's happened? How did you get back? Where is . . . ? Let me take your coat off.' My hands were fumbling at the button of his great-coat when wearily he thrust me off, which simple action, I knew later, went towards saving his life. And now pointing to a cupboard that stood next to the window, he spoke for the first time. 'Get me a drink.'

Again I was flying to his bidding. There was half a bottle of whisky, a syphon of soda, and a glass in the cupboard. Within a minute I had filled the glass to the rim and was holding it to his lips. He swallowed it in one draught, then closed his snow-laden lids for a fraction before handing me the glass and saying, 'Another.'

When he had finished the second glass he lay back against the couch again, and his breathing gradually became steadier. All the while I stood in front of him, until at last, realising the condition of his clothes, I said, 'Let me take your shoes off, you must get changed.' Then I added, 'Where is Mrs Rossiter? Has anything happened?'

For the first time he brought his gaze to bear fully upon me, then, drawing his hands down over his now running wet face, he shut me out for a moment, before saying, 'Where are they?'

'Who?' I asked as if I didn't know what he meant.

'There's no lights in the front. Is he in the dining-room?'

'You mean Mr Maurice?'

He nodded his head slowly at me, and as he did so there seeped into the room again the echo of laughter.

Definitely it wasn't the first time that he had heard that echo, for immediately his eyes were drawn towards the floor. And as he stared at it I felt my throat tighten and constrict my breathing, and then the fear was flooding over me, so much so that for a moment I seemed to lose my head. I was kneeling on the floor gripping his hands as I beseeched him, 'Please . . . please wait till tomorrow. Whatever it is can wait till tomorrow. There'll only be trouble. Please, Logan.' The name came naturally.

His eyes were on mine again and his hand came out towards me and pushed me gently aside, but even so I overbalanced and fell on to my hips. And from there I watched him, still with slow snow-weighed step, move towards the door. He had opened it and was in the hall before I had pulled myself to my feet. And he was halfway down the passage towards the cellar door when I came up with him. And I clutched at his arm with both hands, which did not hinder his walking at all, but now he spoke quite quietly and evenly, saying, 'Go away, Kate.'

The laughter came louder here but still distant, and then it lashed harshly at my ears like a lusty wave, for Logan Rossiter had pulled open the cellar door.

As I watched him descend the first few steps the laughter was still high, which indicated that as yet they were not aware of him. I was at the top of the stairs now and could see over the rack dividing compartments of the cellar. In the little room where the uncles had wined me were a number of men. I could just see their heads and there were more than three. And then one of them happened to look up, and it was me he saw, not Logan, for he gave a yell of drunken glee. Following on this there seemed to me to be a crowd of men spilling themselves through the partitions into the main space that fronted the stairs. But when they had once gathered there, their faces all turned upwards, the cellar became quiet as if it were night and the whole place was about its own business, the business of fomenting the wine that gave the uncles so much pleasure, in making and sampling. And the quiet was not broken by any of the gaping men below but by a whisper coming from behind me, saying in awe-stricken tones, 'Oh, my God, what is this?' I had no need to turn, I knew it was Hollings, and now his hand was gripping my shoulder and his mouth near my ear was hissing, 'Go to the stables; quick, get Patterson.'

If Logan Rossiter's life had depended on my obeying this order he would have lost it, for I found it impossible to move, to tear myself away from this scene. There on the bottom step stood the master of the house, and about ten feet away was his brother supporting himself with the aid of his stick and a stout rack against which he leaned his back. I could see that although Maurice Rossiter was mad drunk he was still capable of feeling amazement, for his eyes held a glazed sort of wonder as he gazed towards Logan. Just to the side of Maurice stood the minister, again I should say leaned, for he and another man, whom I had never seen before, were supporting each other, swaying gently together as they, too, gaped. Standing to their side was yet another strange man, a small man, the build of a pit man, short and wiry. But away from them all, standing alone, was Weaver. If anything he was more drunk than any one of the other four, yet more steady on his feet. He seemed to be braced by the sight of the man who had thrashed him more than once.

And it was to Weaver that Logan Rossiter spoke first, yet he embraced the rest of the company with a sweep of his great arm as he thundered, 'Get out! Get out, you scum!'

'Put us oot?' It was Weaver who had spoken. No whine in his tone now; he was fearless with drink.

It was at the instant when Logan was on the very point of springing on this man that Maurice interrupted with a high cry of, 'Ho . . . hold your ha . . . hand, my de . . . dear brother. These are my friends, all my fri . . . ends . . . Always have been. Don't you recognise them?'

Logan, taking one step nearer to Maurice, brought to me the awful conviction that he was going to pounce, not on Weaver now, but on his

451

brother. And I almost cried out in protest. Logan Rossiter wasn't drunk, but at this moment he was in a worse state. He was mad. But Maurice seemed undaunted by this; perhaps he was too drunk to recognise the danger. Still bracing himself against the support of the partition, he stuttered, 'C . . . come on, t . . . tell us, what's brought you home so early? the s . . . snow blocked the line? . . . Where's y . . . your dear wife?'

On this there came a loud hiccoughing laugh from the minister, to which Weaver added a thin whining sound like the neighing of a horse.

Logan Rossiter was standing stock still now staring at Maurice. The laughter frittered itself out and there was silence again, and they waited for him to answer the question. Which he did, slowly bringing each word up from the agonised depth of him. 'It's all been one great howling laugh, hasn't it? And your friends undoubtedly enjoy your confidence . . . Well, let them laugh, let them laugh as much as they like, it's going to be their last laugh . . . You ask where my wife is, Maurice?'

Now his voice became level, even calm, and he finished with a staggering statement . . . 'She's in Newcastle, in the hospital having a miscarriage.' The voice changing now came like the crack of a steel whip. 'As if you didn't know, you . . . you devilish swine!' He was standing over Maurice, towering over his crouching figure, his two fists quivering above his head. But he did not bring them down. It was doubtful whether he would have had time to strike Maurice before the others were upon him, for they were all waiting at the ready. And now motionless, I watched Logan's arms drop to his side as he moved swiftly back, putting a safe distance between them. My eyes were drawn to Maurice again, for I sensed that Logan's news had come to him, as to me, with a breath-checking shock of surprise. Then a strange thing happened. Maurice, pulling himself from the partition and with the aid of his stick only, stood erect. He seemed to grow straight before my eyes, as he said, almost as if he were sober, 'Really!'

'Y'uve got one ower on him this time, be God I'll say ye hev, Mr Maurice.' Weaver's head was lolling on his shoulders with his laughter.

'Be quiet, Weaver.' Maurice lifted his stick and waved it towards the man; and now, addressing himself to Logan with a hint of the old sarcasm in his voice, he said, 'So Noreen is having a miscarriage. You couldn't, of course, stay with her. Oh no, because you had to tear back here to wreak vengeance on her se . . . seducer. Is that it? Well, now I've news for you, my de . . . ar brother, for you mean business, don't you? So we'll all put our c . . . cards on the table. This is the end, so why not? Why not indeed? . . . Well.' He paused here and with a swift stroke of his hand wiped the sweat from his face. 'Well, I have great pleasure in informing you, The Rossiter . . . The Big Fellow, that Noreen is not your wife and never could be, for she happens to be mine and has been for years . . . There now . . . how do you like that?'

I had moved slowly down the stairs, Hollings

behind me. And I knew that the uncles were behind him. I saw Logan Rossiter move his head and look round the cellar, taking us all in, even those on the stairs. His glance, for a moment, was like that of someone whose senses had been knocked out of his body by a terrific blow. And now looking at Maurice again, he said in a voice that did not carry any conviction to me, 'You're mad, stark staring mad.'

'Oh no I'm not. Ask our dear friend, the Reverend. He married us; didn't you, Fallenbor? It was the night before this happened to me.' Maurice patted his side. And you, my sanctimonious spoil-sport, were away from home, so we decided to have a party and we called in all our friends. And after the party Noreen and I thought it would be a good idea if we were to get married. And Weaver here and the Reverend accompanied us, dancing across the fells. Isn't that so?' As the confirmation to this came, he went on, 'There was one other. You remember Lawson? My dear friend of college days, Lawson. He acted as best man, and about a week later the devil took him in a road accident, you remember? But that's how it happened. Noreen and I were married. She, I must admit, thought it was a game. I have never disillusioned her. But she's my wife, Logan . . . my wife. But I was quite willing to loan her to you, for it was all to my benefit to do so. Yet my conscience tried to force itself through at one point and I did my best to persuade her not to have you, but to marry me, yet once again. But she would have none of it, and now I can see why.

Yes, I see why. She didn't want to make me a father, for I'd be rather a handicap as a father. Dear, dear, considerate Noreen.'

Logan Rossiter was still standing before his brother, but his body looked no longer taut – it looked limp. I was crying for him; with every pore in my body I was crying for him. It was as I made a step towards him that Mr Bernard's voice came yelling from the stairs, spluttering in its anger. 'Don't believe him, Logan; don't believe him. That old reprobate Fallenbor, he couldn't marry them. Illegal. Illegal. Only be married in church. He had no church, not at that time. And what about banns? You know the law.'

'He's right, Logan. He's right.' This was Mr Stanley shouting now. 'I'm ashamed of you, Maurice, ashamed to own you. Get the scum out of this cellar, and this minute. Get you out, Fallenbor . . . And you, Weaver . . . Out!'

On this Weaver stepped forward, shouting, 'Neebody's goin' a order me oot; Aa'm a Rossiter, same's you. Weaver ain't me name, Aa'm a Rossiter, an' don't forget it.' He was now flaying his fist up towards the staircase and the old men. Perhaps it was this that broke the spell that was on Logan Rossiter, this claiming of kinship with his house and forebears, for, like a panther springing from a tree, his body hurled itself on to the man, and as their locked bodies struck the floor the sound made me retch.

I was in the cellar proper now, my back against the rough whitewashed rock, my hands gripped in front of my breast. The other men had moved away from the contorted struggling bodies on the floor. I saw Logan Rossiter's fist pounding Weaver's face, and Weaver using both feet and fists in retaliation. I had no doubt in my mind that Logan would overpower this man. But I also had no doubt that when he had finished with him the other two crouching men would then set about him. This thought made me turn and yell up the staircase: 'Get Patterson! Get Patterson!' I don't know if anyone even heard me. I only know that in the next moment my hands were clasped tightly across my mouth as I saw what was about to happen. Logan and Weaver had rolled near a rack of bottles and Weaver, freeing one hand, was groping blindly and madly at the rack. I saw him grip one of the bottles by the neck. I saw his knee wedge itself in Logan's stomach and his teeth clamp on Logan's ear like a ferret on a rabbit. This was enough to give him leeway. Logan released his grip for a second and that was all this crafty vermin wanted. His arm swung sideways and the bottle crashed down on the side of Logan's skull. But it did not break, nor did Weaver let it escape from his hold. As Logan fell back and my scream rent the cellar I closed my eyes tightly, but I could not close my ears to the sound of the sickening crunch as the bottle descended once again on Logan's head.

A great moan filled the cellar. It seemed to rise above the cries and yells from the staircase. When I opened my eyes again it was to see a bloody crumpled mass that had once been 'The Big Fellow'. I could hear myself screaming as I ran towards him, and when I knelt by his side I moaned between crying, 'Oh, my God. Oh, my God.' I could see no feature of his face for blood, and I had nothing to staunch it with except a woollen coat I was wearing, and I tore this off and tried to wipe his face clear. I ascertained enough with my frantic efforts to know that the blood was coming from a slit which started above his left eye and went up into his hair. As I worked I cried and talked and moaned, and was only dimly aware of the bustle around me. I didn't realise for some time that the staircase was clear and the cellar door closed, but when I did I also took in the fact that Mr Maurice was going for Weaver and that the minister was trying to calm him down. I was holding my blood-soaked coat tightly against Logan's head and was about to appeal to them, any one of them, for help, when Mr Maurice, shaking his stick at Weaver, yelled, 'You bloody fool! You won't get away with this so easily. Haven't I enough to contend with? He'll put you along the line. I've told you.' And now I found myself straining up from the inert body at my side and yelling, 'And I'll see he goes there. If it's the last thing I do I'll see he gets his desserts for this,' I think I must have been quite frantic myself. My hands were covered with blood, my clothes too. My eyes were blinded with tears. I was bawling and jabbering like someone demented. You hear of women being cool and calm in an emergency . . . I'm not one of them. It was in this state that I was pulled to my feet by the taller of the two strange men. I struggled to free myself from his grasp, but he held me firm and pushed me towards a bench, and, forcing me to sit down, he stood over me, with his hands pressed tight on my shoulders. Weaver was just a few yards away and he was yelling at Mr Maurice. 'An' Aa've told ya, him nor neebody else'll put me along the line. Aa'm goin' to see this through finally, once an' for all. Anyway, ye hate his guts as much as me, but if ye've got cauld feet get up above and leave it to me.'

'Get out! Go on, get out.' Maurice was swaying towards Weaver now, his step wildly erratic, but Weaver did not move. And when they came abreast Weaver's hand shot out and, gripping Maurice by the front of his coat, he said, 'Ye can't frighten me, Mr Maurice, ye never have been able to. Aa've let ye play ya game of master, it's suited us both, but now it's ended. There'll be no more high jinks in this cellar, for ye or neebody else. So . . . are ye in with me or oot?'

'You're not going to touch him any more.' Maurice looked at the bruised and swelling face of this man in whose veins ran the Rossiter blood, who, as he was forever claiming, was a Rossiter, and his tone now had a despairing note when he went on, 'He's had enough. It could be serious as it is.' I saw him glance towards the prostrate figure of his brother. And then he ended, his voice dropping, 'He'll need a doctor in any case, and how are we going to get one up here?' It appeared to me that Maurice Rossiter was now stark sober.

'Good enough,' Weaver cut in quickly. 'We know where we stand. Smithy?' He now jerked his head to the smaller of the two men. 'Bottle them both up.'

'Mr Maurice an' aall?' There was amazement in the man's voice.

'Aye . . . Mr Maurice, an' aall.'

The minister had been standing aside during this, casting his furtive eye every now and again to where Logan Rossiter lay. He was now evidently nervous and apprehensive, and Weaver's question startled him when it came at him, 'An' what about you, parson, eh?'

'Well' – there was even a little laugh from this obnoxious individual – 'you know me, Weaver, I'm just passing through. Still, I advise you to go carefully. This could be a very nasty business for . . . for us all.'

'Aa understand, parson, divn't worry. Yer hands won't get mucky. Leave that to Weaver as ye've aalwiz done, ye and Mr Maurice here.' And now Weaver actually pushed Maurice backwards on to the bench on which I was sitting. The backwards jolt must have been painful, for I heard Maurice stifle a groan.

But I wasn't worried about him, only about Logan, and, pointing to the spreading pool of blood, I cried, 'You've got to do something. Let me go and get some bandages. He could die. Do you hear? He could die!'

Now followed something that I want to try to forget, yet even in my dreams it keeps recurring and I wake up choking, and spluttering and spitting out wine . . . No, not wine . . . whisky.

'Ye'd better drink it,' said the short man, handing me a glass. 'It'll be easier that way for us aall.' As the man forced the glass into my hand Maurice Rossiter cried, 'Look, leave her out of it. She has nothing to do with this.'

'No?' said Weaver. 'Only help to push us along the line.'

'There are others besides her who could be used as witnesses, don't you realise that? Don't be such a damn fool, let her go.'

'The old boys think too much of this here cellar an' their whisky-still to split. Anyway, they'd nivver hev the guts.'

'But what's the object in bottling her?' Mr Maurice now demanded.

'Ye leave that ta me. Aa was aalwiz full of good plots. Remember, Mr Maurice? Aa could give ye yarns for yer writin'.' Weaver was laughing.

I looked up into the repulsive and battered face of Weaver now and said in a quiet voice, trying to appeal to the better part of him, 'I don't care what you do to me, only do something to stop the bleeding. Mr Logan could bleed to death.'

'Worried, are ye? Aa thought ye might be. Aa knew ye're all in up to ya neck the first time Aa clapped eyes on you. But ye leave The Big Fellow to us. Whichever way he'll peg oot he won't bleed ta death, that ain't my idea. There's plaster in me sack. Smithy . . . stick some on.'

'You're forgetting Hollings and Patterson in your calculations.' Maurice's voice sounded tired now.

'Hollings won't squeak. He's got a couple of nieces this side of Amble. He likes them. He won't squeak. As for Patterson, there's a woman livin' in

Gateshead who'd very much like to know where he is. She's been lookin' for him noo for a long while. Aye . . . there's reasons why they'll aall keep their mooths shut . . . But this one's different.'

He was pointing his thumb towards me, and Mr Maurice put in harshly, 'Don't be such a damn fool, man, you're mad. You think trifling things like that will stop Patterson or Hollings getting you what you're asking for? And you, Smithy, and you, Connor, use your heads. If anything happens to my brother you'd be as guilty as he is.'

'An' what about yersel, Mr Maurice?' Weaver's voice was quiet.

'I know all that's going to happen to me, Weaver. My number's up as well as yours. I know quite well what's coming to me, so look . . . let's call it a day. You go on out your usual way and take these two with you and leave him to me.' He nodded towards Logan.

'Oh no. No no.' Weaver shook his head slowly. 'Either way Aa know what Aa'm in for. Aa've got nowt to lose, Mr Maurice. In for a penny, in for a pound, that's me. When he comes round he'll hev me hounded like a fox. After the night there'll be nee chance for me around here. This is the finish. So Aa'm goin' to de things me own way as Aa aalwiz intended te . . . Keep goin' with the stuff, Smithy, and you an' all, Connor.' He pointed towards a barrel over in the corner. And Smith and Connor kept going.

The stuff was raw whisky, the hard stuff that Mr Stanley had warned Maurice about touching. At first it merely burned and ripped at my throat while I spluttered and coughed. But by the time they had forced the third glass between my lips my whole body seemed on fire, and my resistance was noticeably less. So expert were they in making me drink that I knew that this was not the first time by many a count that this trick, if you could call it such a thing, had been worked. The voices were now becoming very indistinct. I could not take in what was happening around me. There was bustle of a sort, and once, when I raised my head from the table, I imagined I saw Logan Rossiter standing on his feet. I did hear Maurice's thick trailing tone saying now, 'Don't force me, I can take it.' My whole body was now like a flaming furnace and I was drunk. This, I thought, is what it feels like to be drunk. It wasn't a bad feeling except for the burning. I didn't care what happened any more. At one period I imagined that someone was kissing me; who it was I didn't know. But I knew when they were pulled away from me. Nothing mattered now. Nothing, nothing.

I was sitting upright again, and then I was on my feet, and a voice from somewhere far off said, 'They were on the spree together, it's a clever idea.' And another voice said, 'She'd hev to hev a coat, aye, she'd hev to hev a coat on. What about this?'

I felt like a baby being dressed. Then with my feet dragging I was walked through a door and along a passage, and now I was pushed on to my knees, and I was crawling. I seemed to be moving towards a swaying lantern, but I never reached it, it was always just that much ahead. Then a hand gripped my shoulder and pulled me on to my feet again. It was all very confusing. At one period I had a great desire to rock with laughter. It was then I walked on ice and slipped and fell on my back. When I was dragged to my feet my head struck the roof and I had to walk bent forward. I remember thinking I was like Alice in Wonderland and wanted to laugh again. Then I was on my knees once more and the lantern, swinging in front of me, showed a round hole and, beyond, an expanse of whiteness. Now I was pulled to a halt and there was a confused mingling of bodies about me, and curses and directions. But nothing mattered, nothing mattered any more. I was quite happy inside and quite warm. I was lying against someone, close, pressed tight to a body. It felt nice. The voices faded away from around me. A great silence settled on me, and I slept, deeply, deeply . . .

'Wake up! Wake up!' The hissing sound had been probing my befuddled mind for a long time. It was like a faint echo from across the fells. 'Wake up! Wake up, will you? Sh! . . . sh! . . . don't make a noise. Come on, wake up . . . wake up, miss.' My head began to wag violently as if it was being rocked off my shoulders, and I gasped and spluttered, 'Wh . . . what is it? Leave over . . . leave over.'

'Listen, miss, it's Patterson. Listen, wake up.'

I didn't care who it was, I was too far douched in sleep. And then I almost yelled out, and would have done if a hand hadn't been clapped across my mouth. The snow that had hit my warm flesh running down between my breasts had the effect that Patterson intended it should. My eyes sprang open and I sat gasping as I pulled my clothes away from my body.

'Are you awake?'

'Ye . . . yes.' I was awake and that was all. My head was not on my shoulders but dizzying in a space some distance from my body.

'Listen. Sit up . . . careful or you'll bump your head against the pipe.'

I pulled myself on to my knees, groping at Patterson in the dark. I had not the vaguest idea where I was until Patterson said, 'Don't move now or you'll tumble into the snow, you're on the end of the drainpipe.'

On the end of the drainpipe! If I had been told I was sitting on the edge of a volcano I couldn't have felt more surprised. I tried to make my befuddled brain grasp at the significance of this, but I couldn't get anything clear. And then my head was brought down from its height and somewhat nearer to my shoulders, when I heard Patterson saying. 'Sir. Can you hear me, sir? Look, wake up, sir . . . come on, drink this.'

With a flop that actually shook my body my head fell into place, and now I remembered but still dazedly, but nevertheless I remembered the sight of Logan Rossiter lying on the cellar floor in a pool of blood. I put out my hands and wildly groped about me until Patterson caught hold of my arm and his calming voice said, 'Steady, steady. And quiet, miss. Make no noise.'

'Is he . . . ? Is he . . . ?'

'He's coming round . . . Come on, sir, finish this up. Try now.' There was a long groan, and then I heard Logan's voice muttering thickly, 'Oh, my God. Oh, my God.'

'It's all right, sir. Look, I've tied up your head. Do you think you could get on to your knees?'

'No. No, leave me.' His voice was very tired. 'Leave me alone.'

'No, sir. Come along. Get on to your knees.'

'I can't, Patterson, I can't.'

'M . . . make an effort, p . . . please. Please try.' It was my own voice that was imploring him now and it was stuttering, not only with the effects of the drink still very much upon me but with my shivering, for now my whole body was shaking as if with ague.

'Come on, sir, give it a try. If you can once get up out of the drain you'll be all right. I've brought the sled. You remember the old sled?' His voice was now as soft as a woman's, and as persuasive, as if he were humouring a child.

'Leave me be. Leave me be.' The voice faded away.

I felt Patterson's breath on my face now as he said, 'Lower your feet into the snow and see if you can stand up. Here, sit on the edge of the pipe.'

With Patterson directing me, I sat on the edge of the drain and lowered my feet down into the snow, and when I stood up the bottom of the pipe came to my waist.

'Now,' said Patterson, 'if I get him out do you think you can hold his weight against the edge of the pipe until I pull him up out of the ditch?'

'Yes, yes,' I said, not knowing whether I could or not.

I couldn't see anything that Patterson was doing, and my mind didn't imagine anything, for I, in this moment, became wholly concerned with myself. I was shivering from head to foot, and in my fuddled, bemused, unnatural state I was only barely aware that my feet were in running water, that the storm was over and the thaw had set in. All I wanted was to drop my head forward on to the icy rim of the drain and sleep. I was not concerned with self-preservation, yet it was the preservation of the man lying in the thawing ice that got through to me and warned me that if Logan Rossiter sank into the snow, Patterson would never get him out until it was too late. When I felt the bulk of him against me I pressed my body to his and, putting my hands under his armpits, I gripped as far up the icy circle of the drain as it was possible for me to reach. In this way I kept him upright until Patterson's hands were groping over us both. I felt the clothes on Logan's body lift upwards, and automatically I heaved too. As he was dragged up over the edge of the ditch his body made a tunnel in the soft snow, and a few seconds later it was through this that Patterson dragged me also.

I can't remember if I helped to get Logan on to

the sledge. I can only remember wondering why there was no light, no torch being used. I faintly recollect Patterson's voice hissing, almost angrily at me, 'You'll have to pull back harder than that or I won't be able to hold it.' How he ever did hold that laden sledge from running amok in that white sloping wilderness is still a mystery to me. My job, I understand now, was to pull on the back of the sledge and so act as a brake. I can remember twice lying quite flat in the snow and Patterson pulling me to my feet. He's told me since he did this five times. I do remember, and with a sense of shame, that when we finally reached the road I was blubbing out loud, crying unrestrainedly like any child. I remember also saying to Patterson, 'Are we going to the cottages?' and I can still feel my sense of amazement when he said abruptly, 'No.' And I can hear him adding fervently, 'Thank God the plough has been along.' I now started to jabber, crying, 'I can't go on, I can't go on, I feel sick. I want to be sick. Want to sit down.'

'Well, sit down.' His voice was hissing at me, really angry now. 'Sit by him until I get back, and don't make a sound, I'm telling you, don't make a sound.'

I was only too thankful to sit down. I could just make out the huddled form of Logan as he lay with his knees up on the short sledge. And I remember I sat close to him and took hold of his hand. Then I must have lain my head on his body and slept again, for I actually yelled out when Patterson dragged me to my feet. And there, as if it had been conjured out of the air, was the dark bulk of the car. I did say to him, but not as plainly as I'm stating it now, 'But you'll never get the car along the road – it's madness trying.' Yet I longed to get inside the car, into its warm shelter. But again he had to force me to get up and to help him get Logan on to the back seat, for I was reluctant to do anything but follow my own need, which was to drop where I stood and sleep, just sleep.

'Keep him upright against the back; don't let him fall over.' It was just as I was admonished harshly to do this that Logan stirred and spoke.

'Patterson,' he said.

'Yes, sir.'

'Where . . . where am I?'

'You're in the car, sir. Don't worry.'

'What time is it?'

'Oh, I should imagine . . . somewhere around one, sir. Now don't worry, we'll get you to a doctor.'

A light suddenly sweeping over the car from somewhere along the road made Patterson bang the door and get into the driving seat, and after two quick attempts on the starter the car moved forward. I was still supporting Logan, but now I felt his body move of its own accord into a more comfortable position. As he did so I mumbled a question to Patterson that was going round in my mind. 'Why didn't we wait?' I said. 'There was someone coming with a light.'

He did not answer for what seemed a long time,

and then he said, 'Someone was coming all right. Connor lives in one of those cottages.'

I became quiet. I was shivering less. The slight rocking of the car lulled me. And then I was woken yet once again from sleep by Patterson saying, 'This is as far as we can go.'

I shook my head and drew in a deep breath, making an effort to regain my senses. 'Where are we?' I asked.

'As far as I can make out quite a step from the village. The snow plough is just ahead, this is as far as it's got. Now look, I'll have to get to the village somehow and get help and phone a doctor. You lock yourself in and don't open up for anyone but me. You understand?'

'Patterson.' The voice was just a whisper.

'Yes, sir.'

'I'm . . . all . . . right now . . . I . . . I can walk it.'

'No, sir, out of the question. Just you rest. Stay with miss here, I'll be back.'

He pushed up the handle which locked the door, then banged it, and I settled back into the deep comfort of the car. My shivering had almost stopped, but I had a weird feeling, a sick weird feeling, and the desire for sleep was heavier on me than ever, so without effort I allowed myself to sink into it . . .

I don't know how long it was after this that I heard Patterson's voice again, and not only his but a number of other voices, two of them so familiar that I imagined that the car had been got through somehow into the village. The voices I recognised were those of Bill Arnold and Rodney. It was Bill's voice that came to me as if from the end of a tunnel, saying, 'Well, as we've got to go back to the village, anyway, I'm for taking him there.' Then Rodney's. 'It's him we've got to think of; the quicker he's between sheets, I should imagine, the better. We can, with a big push and two of you going ahead, get him up to Kate's place in under half an hour. But it'll take every bit of a couple of hours to get through these road drifts back to the village. And I bet you what you like, a lot of this fell will be clear of snow. The wind'll have whipped it off the slopes and down into the valley. You know how it does.'

'But will the doctor get up to him?' said a voice.

And another answered, 'But aye, there's the track leading up from yon side of the village, almost straight as a die. Rodney said he went up there yesterday to tell Kate's folk. Didn't you?'

It was many hours later when I thought of the man's description of our road being as straight as a die, and wondered what kind of a road would qualify in his mind for a winding one. But now there were hands on me easing me out from the car, and Rodney's arms were about me, his voice tender and soothing as he said, 'Aw, Kate. Aw, Kate. Now don't worry, you're going to be all right.'

I opened my eyes with an effort, and just glimpsed the swinging lanterns and the bustle of men before I was overcome with the dreadful feeling of nausea again. It was a frightful feeling like nothing I had experienced before, and to my own disgust I was crying again, and whimpering now, 'I want to go home. I want to go home.'

'You're going home, Kate. You're going home.'

It seems dreadful to think now, but I had forgotten completely about Logan, for my whole body and mind was consumed with sickness. I felt myself being half carried through the snow. Then this gave way quite abruptly to the feel of hard rock under my feet. Whoever was on my other side now turned and shouted, 'It's as he said, it's clear.' A voice ahead was calling, 'This way. This way, to your right there. That's it.'

I lifted my weary lids and glimpsed the fairy-like scene created by the swinging lanterns. Then, with a suddenness that was startling, my whole stomach turned a somersault and I was sick. And Rodney and the other man held me up, and Rodney soothed me as my mother would have done, saying, 'That's it, get it up. The more you get up the better. There you are, there you are.' And the other man said, 'Phuh! Whisky!' And somehow this filled me with deep shame.

I began to shiver again and I can't remember anything more of the journey except that I looked upwards and saw a blaze of lights, and deep within me my soul cried out: You're home, you're home. And then my mother's voice swept over me, repeating two words, just two words, 'My God! My God!' And this went on for a long time.

There followed confusion and bustle and voices, then quiet, quiet that I likened to the peace of Heaven. I was in my own room and my mother was undressing me, still at intervals repeating the two words, 'My God! My God!' She said other words, but these were the only two that seemed to get through my bemused, whisky-fogged brain. And then I was in bed and nothing mattered – nothing, nothing at all.

8

'I'm sick. Oh, Mother, I'm sick.'

'You'll be all right, lass. Lie still.'

'I want to be sick.'

'No, you don't. No, you don't. There's nothing more to come up, you just feel like that. The doctor has given you something. You'll be all right in a little while, just sleep.'

'Oh, I am sick. And my eyes are funny, Mother. I can hardly see.'

'That'll pass, my dear. Just you go back to sleep.'

I realised nothing, only that my body and mind were consumed by this dreadful sickness, and I wanted to die. I remember waking up and it was dark again, except for a night light that seemed to bob up and down like a cork on a wave, and through it I saw a shape sitting by my bed and I thrust my hand out to it and fell asleep yet once again in the firm grip of my father's hands . . .

It was forty-eight hours later when I drank my first cup of tea, and, looking at my mother, asked wearily, 'How is he?'

'Holding his own.'

The reply brought me from the pillows and I whispered, 'He's that ill?'

'Well . . . well, the head'll mend as quick as those things are able to, but' – she turned her eyes from mine – 'he's got a bit of a chill, and no wonder. You were lucky, my girl, to get off so lightly, but with him, with the loss of blood and all that – well, he's got pneumonia.'

As I pushed the bedclothes back my mother's hands stayed me quickly. 'Where do you think you're going?'

'I'm getting up.'

'That you're not. Not today, or tomorrow either if I know it . . . And the doctor. You've been poisoned, lass, with that stuff.'

'But I'm all right now.'

'You will be until you stand on your legs. Doctor's orders, you stay put there the next couple of days at least.'

'Can I just look in and see him?'

'No, you can't. He doesn't want to see you or anybody else – not at present, anyway.'

'Who's looking after him?'

My mother was busily tucking the clothes round me, and her hands stopped and her face lengthened as she said primly, 'Who do you think? I may not have got any certificates, but don't forget I did five years in the hospital. There now, and nurse's orders.' She patted my cheek gently. 'You stay put . . .'

For the next two days I stayed put. The sickness had left me, but I had to admit to myself that I still felt ill. It was on the afternoon of the fourth day that my mother showed Patterson into my room, and awkwardly he took a seat by the bedside and smiled at me.

'How you feeling now, miss?'

'Oh, I'm all right, Patterson.'

He nodded his head at me. 'You're lucky, you know. You could have been much worse with one thing and another. By' – now his head moved from side to side slowly – 'I've never seen a woman as drunk as you were.' Patterson meant this in a jocular way, he was making light of the matter for my sake, but I couldn't take it in a light way. It seemed to me, at this moment, shocking that I had been paralytic drunk and that the dreadful feeling of illness was nothing more than a hangover, a giant hangover.

'But you know,' he went on now, 'it's just as well you were bottled. It would have been a good thing if Mr Logan had taken on a similar load, for he wouldn't have got pneumonia then. But if he hadn't kept that coat on things would've been worse. He wouldn't have lasted this long, I'm sure. Pity they didn't bottle him, too.' Then seemingly noticing my expression, his own became grave and he said, 'I'm not trying to make light of things, miss, not really. The stuff could have killed you, raw spirit like that, and then the exposure.'

As I looked at this man I thought to myself: I owe him my life, as does Logan Rossiter, and I put out my hand impulsively and touched his, saying, 'If it hadn't been for you . . .' I shuddered, then went on, 'How did you know?'

'Well, miss.' He cast his eyes downwards. 'It was like this. I came to the top of the cellar stairs and saw how things were going. Mr Logan had then been knocked out. You see, I had been over in me room for not more than ten minutes; it seemed impossible for all that to happen in so short a time, but it had. So . . . well, I made myself scarce. I knew Weaver, I knew that he wouldn't finish there. I also knew that it's only on the films that one fellow can beat four, especially if they're hurling bottles. So I used a bit of brain against their brawn, so to speak. I went back to my room and lit the lamp as if I was settled in there for the night. I knew one of them would come looking for me. So my idea was to tackle them just like that, one at a time, or even two, but not four.' He smiled shyly. 'But they got one over on me. It was simple. They just barricaded the door and I couldn't get out. Well, not for a long time, because, you see they also locked up Hollings and the old gentlemen. But they didn't bother with Bennett; they reckoned he was too old to do anything, and he'd never taken sides, had Bennett. He wasn't too old to come and get me out, but that was some time later, because he had to bide his time until the coast was clear, or doubtless they would have brained him. And he's too old to stand knocking about, is Bennett.'

'Where are they all now?' I found I couldn't name the minister, or even Weaver, without feeling sick again, and I'd had enough of feeling sick.

'Well, miss, you know the saying: As ye sow so

shall ye reap. Well, Weaver's idea was to finish Mr Logan off by simply leaving him in the drain and letting the cold do its work. His mad idea was that when he was found with you, miss, stinking of spirits as you were, the reason for your deaths wouldn't be far to seek. You'd been having a party, you were all drunk, there'd been a fight, and that was that. You see, it wasn't an unknown thing to happen at Tor-Fret, at least in the old days when Weaver was a boy at the turn of the century. And Weaver, miss, never grew up, not really. Weaver wasn't bad, he was just a bit mental. The one that was bad and still is, is Fallenbor.'

'Where is he now?' I asked.

'Weaver, miss? Well, at this minute he's in the mortuary in Alnwick. They must have all parted company, taking a number of bottles with them, and Weaver was so dead drunk that he fell asleep in the snow, just like he left you. They found him stiff in a thicket at yon side of the lake. He was making for a cave – there's lots of caves round there, you know, miss – in the outcrop of rocks hidden by the bracken, and he spent most of his days there, and nights too. But he never reached there that morning. As for Connor and Smithy, well, they are comfortably settled in jail at the moment.'

'In jail?' I was sitting up in bed bending towards him. 'And Mr Maurice?'

His eyes moved downwards. 'Mr Maurice has been in a bad way for the last few days, miss. Something like yourself, very sick. Also with him is his conscience.'

'What will they do to him?'

'Nothing. Oh, nothing, miss. It said in the papers he was the victim of that little band of thugs, too.'

I screwed up my eyes as I repeated, 'In the papers? Is it in the papers?'

'Oh yes, miss, it's been big headlines. It was big headlines the first day; but big headlines, like everything else, are soon forgotten. Other headlines take their place. You see, miss, Mr Logan isn't unknown in this part of the world, and he was married that day. Although he did it quickly, everybody knew he was getting married. It all seemed a funny business, and there's been talk.'

I nodded slowly. 'Miss Noreen . . . I mean Mrs . . .'

'As far as I can gather she's still in the hospital in Newcastle. It's all caused quite a bit of a scandal.'

My mind was working now, pushing me back. I was in the cellar once again hearing Logan Rossiter's words. 'My wife is in Newcastle having a miscarriage.' Then Maurice's voice, crying, 'Your wife? She's never been your wife.' I said now very quietly, 'About Mr Maurice and Miss Noreen being married . . . was there any truth in it?'

'Well, they're trying to find the minister, miss. There's bets on all sides. You see, there's certain laws about marriage. It's got to be in a registered place and if there are no banns there's got to be a special licence. I think there can be two kinds of special licence, but I'm not up on that subject.' He smiled wryly. 'I was married once. It was in church and that was binding enough – God knows,' he added, the smile twisting his mouth now. 'But if you want my opinion, that was all a bit of a game. Mr Maurice liked to think it was legal to have one over on Mr Logan. They've never hit it off, miss, never. You couldn't imagine them being born of the same mother, they're so different. Yet mind, Mr Maurice has his points. I don't dislike him, but he's not Mr Logan. Never could be, not for me.'

I felt sick again but with a different kind of sickness now. This sickness was not created by raw spirit but oozed from the depths of my heart. I hadn't been in any condition to think what it would mean if Maurice's declaration proved to be true, yet when Patterson disproved it in such a way I could not but believe him. It was as if I had been living in hope for days that something would happen to annul the marriage. Perhaps my subconscious had been at work, for now my disappointment rose to the surface of my mind like a tidal wave and swept away any secret hopes I had been harbouring. But Patterson was speaking again and I brought my wandering attention to him. 'But you know, miss,' he said, 'it's my private opinion that Mr Logan should never have married Miss Noreen. Mr Maurice was really the one for her. I could never understand it really. They were both after her years ago, but it seemed as if she preferred Mr Maurice. So Mr Logan gave her up without much of a battle, as if he wasn't greatly concerned like. And then recently she swings from Mr Maurice back to him . . . and there it was, what could a man do? For she's an attractive girl, is

Miss Noreen . . . Mrs Rossiter I should say.'

'Yes, she's very attractive, Patterson, very attractive.'

Perhaps it was the tone of my voice that brought him to his feet, for he said now, 'Look, I'm tiring you, I must go. But I'm glad to see you as fit as you are.' Then in an effort to cheer me up he bent towards me and, smiling, finished, 'By, you did give me a time that night. I had more trouble with you than with Mr Logan. The times you fell in the snow flat on your face. I can laugh at it now, but it wasn't funny then.'

'No,' I said, managing to smile at him, 'it wasn't funny then. Goodbye, Patterson, and thank you very much . . . very much.'

'That's all right, miss. I hope that tomorrow you'll be up.'

'Yes. Yes, I'll be up tomorrow. Goodbye, Patterson.'

'Goodbye, miss.'

I got up the next day, and with legs that wobbled and with a head still a bit swimmy I went across the landing towards my parents' room, and, knocking gently, I opened the door.

The man in the bed was not The Big Fellow, he was no-one that I knew. His head was swathed in bandages, his cheeks were hollow like those of an aged man, and his face was very red. His eyes were open and held me from the minute I entered until I stood by his side, and then he spoke to me. 'Kate,' he said, 'how are you?'

I could only swallow and stare at him and prevent myself from dropping on my knees and laying my head on the bed and giving vent in a spate of tears to the emotions that were choking me.

His breathing was coming in short laboured gasps, and he said now, 'Lot of trouble . . . to your people . . . lot of trouble.'

I shook my head and forced the words steadily through my lips. 'It's no trouble. No trouble whatsoever . . . Only get . . . well.' My voice cracked on the last word, and he nodded and reached for my hand.

At this point the door opened and my mother entered. She was evidently surprised to find me there, but she said quietly, 'Well now, who told you to get up? Away to your bed.'

I drew my fingers from Logan's clinging grasp and, turning, went silently out of the room. I waited on the little landing for her, and when she came out I said to her, 'I'm not going back to bed, I'm going to nurse him.'

She stood looking at me hard for a long moment, perhaps it was a matter of minutes, and whatever she saw in my face she did not comment on, she simply said, 'All right, have it your own way. Only remember this. He's very ill; the doctor says it'll be touch and go. We've got to be prepared for that. There's one thing in his favour: constitutionally he's strong. So we can only do our best and pray to God he pulls through. The crisis is some way off, but it will come.'

On this she turned and went down the stairs, and

I went into my room and got dressed. My body was cold again, but with fear. A person in his low state could easily release his hold on life if that life appeared too complicated to take up again. And God knew, his must appear to him more than complicated at this stage.

We were into December and Christmas near, but this fact did not matter to me. Our house during the next few weeks became more like a hospital ward, with Patterson as the running orderly, running between it and Tor-Fret. Every day he helped to lift and wash and change his master; sometimes it was me on the other side of the bed, sometimes my mother. Sometimes he kept a night watch with my father, sometimes with me. We all insisted that my mother must have her rest at night, for the strain was now telling on her, and although she would not admit it she was very tired.

The crisis came and it passed and it left just a shadow of The Big Fellow. But the shadow required more careful nursing than the man had done. As I had foreseen, Logan lost all desire for life. Sometimes in the middle of the night he would wake and, groping for my hand, would hold it and repeat my name, saying, 'Kate . . . Kate,' in a weary kind of way. I had been embarrassed by this the first time it happened because Patterson was sitting in the shadows, but no longer did it embarrass me. I didn't mind now who knew what I felt for this man, and I would grasp his hand and try to infuse my natural robust strength into him, willing him to get better, willing him to have the desire to live.

Then one day – it was the second of January – he sat up and smiled. I had been sitting by his bedside all night and had gone to my own bed about eight o'clock in the morning. In the afternoon, before going downstairs, I had quietly opened the bedroom door and there he was lying back on his pillows, more raised up now, and on the sight of me he pulled himself up a little further and he smiled. And his voice was different when he said, 'Hello, Kate.'

I was crying now and I did not try to hide my tears, but I stood near him and answered, 'Hello, Mr Logan.'

He took in a long thin breath before saying, 'No mister, Kate, no mister.'

'As you wish.'

'It's snowing again,' he said, looking up into my face.

'Yes, it's snowing again.' I nodded at him, then looked towards the window, and when I looked back at him we both smiled, we even laughed together – a weak laugh on his part but nevertheless a laugh. Snow would always be significant to us.

He said now, 'Sit by me, Kate.'

'I've been doing that for weeks,' I said.

'I know. I know. I'll never be able to repay you, or your people . . . your mother is a marvellous woman. They're both very fine people.'

'I think so.' In an endeavour now to make him

smile again I said significantly, 'And my mother's name is Kate.'

The effect was what I had played for, and he smiled enough to bring a fullness to his hollow cheeks. And then he said, 'Oh, be kind to me, Kate, although I don't deserve it.'

There was that phrase again, 'Be kind to me.' How meaningful it was and how strange the people who used it. People who you would never dream needed kindness. I was reminded in this moment of Noreen Badcliff, and inevitably then came the thought that, to all intents and purposes, this man was still married to her. But I sat on near him, talking to him, but not now touching his hand. Nor did he make any attempt to touch me. He was on the road to recovery, he did not need my strength now . . .

From this day the pattern of the house changed further. There were visitors. Logan's partner came twice within the next fortnight. On his second visit he brought another distinguished-looking man with him and they were a long time upstairs talking. But some time before this Patterson brought the uncles over. It was as if during the time since I had last seen them they had put on a great number of years. Perhaps it was only within the walls of Tor-Fret and their own environment they appeared younger, for when they came into the sitting-room of our small house they looked two old, two very old shrunken men. Their delight at seeing me was almost pathetic, and I was both moved and pleased by it.

It was my mother who took them upstairs, and

when they came down again, Mr Bernard, the grumpy, stiff, taciturn Mr Bernard, was crying. My mother gave them tea, and my father, being a really tactful man at heart, talked fishing, and by the time Patterson came in to take them home before the light failed, they looked a little like the Mr Bernard and the Mr Stanley that I remembered, yet not quite.

And Hollings came; he came a number of times. It was nice to see Hollings again. And on one of his visits he took me aside and handed me a letter, and to my surprise he said, 'It's from Mr Maurice. He would like an answer, madam.'

The letter was brief and to the point. 'Dear Kate,' it said. 'Can I ask you to come up and see me. You will be doing me one last favour if you will comply. Yours sincerely, Maurice Rossiter.'

I lifted my eyes from the letter and said to Hollings below my breath, 'He wants me to go up.'

'I know, madam. Will you come?'

I hesitated before saying, 'Yes. Yes, I suppose I had better. Tell him, I'll come . . . Tomorrow afternoon.'

'Very well, madam, thank you.' He said nothing more concerning this during his visit, nor did I.

Naturally I did not mention this request to Logan, but that night, when I took his drink up to him, he said to me, 'Sit down, Kate, just for a minute. You've been flitting about like a migrating bird these last few days. What is it? Are you troubled about something?'

I sat down, and then looking at him straight in

the face I shook my head, and said, 'No. No, I'm not troubled. Why should I be?'

'Yes, why should you be? Your life is uncomplicated. How could it be otherwise living in this house?' His voice was slow and weary-sounding again. And then quite suddenly, reaching for my hand, he bent towards me and asked, 'Can we talk, Kate? Not just pleasantries. And forget that I was ever ill. I'm ill no longer; I'll soon be up and about . . . Not that I want to get away, believe me. In spite of everything it's been like . . . well, like going into retreat. But now I want to talk to you . . . You understand?'

I shivered and looked away for a second before bringing my eyes back to him and saying, 'Yes. If you want to talk, talk.'

'Tell me' – he lay back on the pillows again but still kept hold of my hand – 'what did you feel like when that . . . that fellow let you down?' It was a surprising question. I thought he had wanted to talk about himself and Noreen Badcliff – I couldn't think of her as Noreen Rossiter – and of course he did, only he came to it in a round-about way.

I closed my eyes for a moment and thought back, and then answered him truthfully. 'Like death,' I said.

'So humiliated that you felt that you wanted to crawl into a hole and die?'

'Yes, something like that.'

'Did you hate him?'

'Yes, I loathed him for a time, and myself for being such a gullible fool.'

'It's good to know that one isn't alone with such feelings.' He thrust his body forward now and, releasing my hand, placed his palms flat on the counterpane, and with his head on his chest and his words rumbling and indistinct he said, 'I hate her so much that even now I feel I could kill her.' His body was shaking with the intensity of his emotion.

I shook my head. 'Don't feel like that, not so bitterly . . . at least not against her. She wasn't all to blame; Mr Maurice was to blame and . . . and you yourself.'

He did not lift his head but raised his eyes and looked at me from under his brows in a questioning way, and I answered the question with, 'You shouldn't have left her dangling between you for years. When Mr Maurice wouldn't marry her . . . you should have done something if . . . if you cared for her enough.'

He straightened up and lay back against the head of the bed and, looking towards the ceiling, said, 'Yes, you have something there, I know you have. In a reasonable frame of mind I can see it myself, but' – he brought his eyes down to me – 'apparently he thought he had married her. Yet he couldn't have been sure as to the legality of it, or I'm positive he would never have let me go through with it.'

'I think he would.' My voice was quiet as I thought of the devils that were at work within Maurice, and I repeated, 'I think he would, and you've got to face up to that, too.' Then I asked a question that had been niggling at my mind for days, weeks in fact. 'Have they proved that the service was legal?'

He was looking down at his hands now, examining his nails, and his tone was one I couldn't translate as he said, 'No, Kate, they found it was illegal. My marriage to her stands until . . . until it is annulled and . . . and I can do nothing, legally speaking. There is no question of adultery. The act . . . er . . . only becomes such when either of the parties is married.' He closed his eyes now. 'Our marriage can only be annulled if she refuses to consummate it.' Now his eyes came up slowly to meet mine, and I blinked once or twice but continued to look at him. At last I had to rise to my feet in case my hands went out to him for he had made no gesture towards me. Not outwardly anyway; I had only the look in his eyes to go by. I stood a little away from the bed now and said, 'Good night.'

'Good night, Kate,' he answered, but as I turned from him he stopped me and in a flat tone added, 'Just a minute. I think I'd better tell you. Tomorrow I'm getting up and as soon as I am able I'm going away. Although, mind' – he moved his head slowly – 'I'll hate to leave this house and your people, but I've stayed long enough. I'm going abroad for a time, Kate.'

'Abroad?' I had turned squarely to him now. 'You'll be away . . . long?'

'I'm not quite sure, Kate.' He screwed his eyes up tightly for a moment. 'I can't go back up there, not yet awhile. Nor can I face my friends and acquaint-

ances in the county. I suppose I'm not big enough –
inwardly, at any rate. These things die, I'm told, a
natural death. Well, as soon as I feel this one is quite
dead' – he pointed now to his chest – 'inside here,
too, I'll come back. You understand, Kate?'

I tried to keep all feeling from my voice as I said,
'Yes, yes, I understand.'

I turned quickly about and went out of the room
and across the landing, and as I sat on the side of
my bed, my head in my hands resting against the
rail, I told myself it was best he should get right
away. But, being a woman, I also told myself there
was a danger in it for me. Men did strange things,
even strong ones, big fellows, they did strange
things after going through an experience such as
Logan had. They jumped off on the rebound, and
in a foreign land there would be many ready to
catch them.

I went to bed, and there returned to me the feeling
of emptiness that I had lived with before the night
on the fell road when Logan Rossiter and I had
kissed.

9

The following afternoon I sat facing Maurice Rossiter in the very position I had taken up when I had first come for interview, but this was not the same Maurice Rossiter. The man opposite to me had changed in his way as much as his brother had. All the devils seemed to have died in him, or fled. There was no bite of sarcasm in his voice. There was no pain-inflicting glint in his eye. He went on speaking to me as he had been doing for the last quarter of an hour. He was saying now, 'You came in, Kate, at the beginning of the end. In fact I think you heralded it. Noreen told me of the day you took the top road and came down by the lake.'

I could still blush at the memory and I lowered my eyes from his. He went on, 'You became entangled with us, but, believe me, I never wished you any harm.'

'I can believe you, Mr Maurice.'

'I am leaving here tomorrow, Kate.'

'What!'

'You seem surprised. But what else is there for me to do? It would be quite impossible for Logan and me to live together in the future. Quite out of the question, you can see that.'

Yes, I could see that, but I hadn't been able to see a solution, for I couldn't imagine Maurice leaving this house. He went on, 'I'm going across the valley to Noreen's. Strange as you may think it, I consider her my wife, although officialdom says differently. If I hadn't been eaten up inside against fate and the blows it had dealt me, I would have done as she wished years ago and there would have been none of this. But there, life is very strange. The pattern is set at the beginning, and, do what you may, you are kept in the tracing lines. If it wasn't so, you wouldn't have come into our lives, Kate, and there wouldn't have been Logan for you.'

'Mr Maurice!' My tone was one of high indignation, mixed with amazement.

'Don't get on your dignity, Kate.' He smiled quietly at me. 'And this isn't one of my old devils speaking. I'm just stating what you know to be a fact.'

'But how . . . how did . . . ?'

'Don't worry, don't worry, Kate. No-one would have guessed. No-one had the least suspicion. None but my henchman who was lying in the bracken the night the man molested you. He was still lying there when Logan intervened and he saw what followed. Oh, please. Oh, please, Kate, don't hang your head like that. There's nothing to be ashamed of.'

'I'm not ashamed of it, Mr Maurice.'

'Then don't act as if you were, Kate. Remember,

Weaver, bad as he was – kept a still tongue about it. And you must give me my due, I didn't taunt you with it, did I? Nor him, not even on the night of the show-down.'

No, that was true enough. He had not mentioned it and he could have done. As Patterson said, Mr Maurice had his points.

'You know' – he was smiling kindly at me – 'if I had been in his place I would have gone ahead. For the fact that he had let himself go with you proved that it wasn't a surface feeling. Oh, I know my brother, Kate. He would rather crucify you than allow his feelings to divert him from the straight road. There couldn't be two people more opposite than Logan and I, that is why we could never pull together. But in my own defence I would say that people of my timbre are easier to live with. You will find his high principles trying at times, but you won't mind . . .'

'Please, Mr Maurice, please. There's no talk of anything like that.'

'All right, Kate, all right. But there will be. When everything is cleared up there will be, you mark my words . . . It's funny.' He smiled wryly. 'It only takes a matter of minutes to tie two people together, yet even in the most straightforward cases it takes weeks, even months, to untie them. You see, Noreen is answering the law by living openly with me. What more could they want? Apparently a signing of papers and an appearance at court. When? In their own good time. But eventually we'll be . . . as we were.'

I hoped so from the bottom of my heart; but to change the conversation I said, 'How is Miss Noreen?'

'She is very well, Kate. Oddly enough, she's better than I've seen her for years. In fact, I can say that she has grown up – if you know what I mean. I must tell you something.' He leant towards me. And now I glimpsed a little of the playful side of the old Mr Maurice as he said, 'She's learning to type.'

This brought a smile to my face, but I said, 'Why not? Anyone can type.'

'I hope so, Kate.'

'Is it the lodge you're going to?'

'Yes, it's the lodge. I'll find it different.' He glanced round about him, then looked towards the window. 'There's no long view. But still, I've had a long view all my life. I, too, must grow up and look at the world that's close about me. I'm a very selfish individual, Kate.'

I did not contradict him but said, 'I feel that you'll be happier there somehow, and you'll work better.'

'You mean that my work will improve?'

'I didn't say that.'

'All right, we'll let it pass. But now Kate . . . I want to tell you why I asked you up here. It's simply this. I want you, in your own way, to pass on to Logan what I could never say in a letter. I want you to pass on to him what I've told you: that I'm going and he can come back whenever he likes. I know he will never come back as long as I am under this roof. And, you see, the old uns depend on him. I depended on him, but now I must learn to stand on my one good leg. But the old uns are different – the uncles, and Hollings, and Bennett. They can't be thrust aside, they can't be left to rot, and only he can see to them.'

I did not speak. I realised that Maurice Rossiter was making sacrifices which would probably be the making of him. I said, 'I will tell him, Mr Maurice.'

'There's something else, and this is very difficult to talk about. I have always accused him of being tight-fisted. All my life since my father died I have fought with him over money, and now I hear through his partner that he has made me an allowance and almost trebled what he allows me now. I can't do anything about it. Will you, Kate . . . will you tell him . . . ?' His voice was thick now and trailed off.

'I'll tell him,' I said softly.

As I rose to leave he held out his hand and asked, 'Would you come and see us sometime, or is it too much to ask?'

'I would be only too pleased, Mr Maurice.'

'I'll leave it to you then, Kate. Goodbye.'

'Goodbye. Don't worry, everything will be all right.'

'I hope so, Kate, I hope so. Thank you. Thank you for coming. You'll see the uncles before you leave?'

'Yes, of course.'

'Goodbye, Kate.'

'Goodbye, Mr Maurice.'

*   *   *

When I reached home my mother was in the sitting-room. She turned her face to me and smiled, saying, 'Well, how did it go?'

'Very well,' I said. 'Very well.'

I looked towards my father, who was sitting, his head on one side, waiting for me to relate my visit, and I said, 'It's nearly the last episode, I'll give it to you later on.'

He nodded and said, 'Good enough, lass, good enough.'

My mother, motioning her head towards the ceiling, now remarked, 'He's up and in his clothes. By, it's taken it out of him, he's nothing but an outsize skeleton.'

When I went into the bedroom and saw Logan sitting at the window I had to endorse my mother's description. He was nothing but an outsize skeleton.

'How do you feel?' I asked.

'Wobbly, very wobbly. It's surprising. You think you can walk a mile when you're in bed. Dear, dear, I've never felt so weak in my life.'

I looked at his face, at the second scar, the one that reached now from the corner of his eye socket and went up over his brow and well towards the top of his scalp. The jagged line would pale a little more, I knew, but it would always be in evidence. The line running up from his lip to the corner of his nose, the result of Weaver's first attack on him, and then the line from his eye disappearing into his hair, gave the impression that someone had tried to slice off that side of his face. I wanted to touch his cheek and say, 'Oh, my dear.' But instead I sat down at the side of the small hearth and, bending forward, I picked up a piece of wood and put it on the fire. And as I straightened up I said, 'I've been up to the house.'

'Oh?' I knew his face was turned towards me.

'Mr Maurice sent for me.'

He asked no question but sat in silence, stiff silence, and so I went on talking. And in my own words I gave him Mr Maurice's message. I did not look at him during all the telling, but when I finished I turned towards him and found he was looking out of the window. He did not speak, and when I rose to my feet he made no effort to keep me in the room and I went out and down the stairs.

My parents were both in the kitchen, and I did not refer to anything that had transpired upstairs, nor yet could I begin the episode for my father, but I said, apropos of a question that had not risen in the house for the last few weeks, 'If Bill hasn't got anybody yet I'll start again on Monday. I'll manage on half-time during the winter. I don't want to go into the town again – not yet, anyway.'

'No, lass, of course not.' My mother glanced at my father, and he, coming to my side, said, 'Look, there's no need for you to take up at Bill's again if you don't feel like it; we can manage fine, there's nothing to stop us. We've done it afore.'

'Thanks, Father,' I said. 'But if Bill's post is still open I'll continue there.'

The post was still open and so I continued to work for Bill. And for quite a while I was a source of interest in the village. Bill said I was good for business, for people were always dropping in, having discovered they wanted paint or brushes or some such. When I was confronted with old newspapers and asked if this or that was true, what could I say? Was I looking forward to being called as a witness against Smithy and Connor? they asked. No, no, I wasn't. It was difficult to be evasive, in fact it was quite impossible. But I was most thankful for one thing. No-one was shy in using Logan Rossiter's name, which meant that they hadn't an inkling of my true feelings.

10

'By, I do miss him,' said my father. 'The house isn't the same. Can't get used to the quietness. He had some good crack. What he didn't know about fishing wasn't worth learnin'. Aye, he was a nice bloke.' He laid aside his book and looked towards my mother. She had a stocking in her hand again and for the first time for many weeks she was knitting, but she made no attempt to endorse his words, so he said to me, 'Do you suppose he's there now?'

'Yes,' I said, 'he'd get there about tea-time.'

'By, here one minute, Switzerland the next.' My father shook his head. 'It's unbelievable when you think about it, isn't it?'

'It would be,' said my mother caustically, 'if he had done it in a minute.'

'You're so sharp, lass, you'll be cutting yourself . . . you know what I mean, don't you? I wonder if he'll write?' finished my father now.

'He'll write,' said my mother. 'He said he would and he will.'

They talked like this for quite some time. It was a two-sided conversation and I wasn't drawn into it. They were my parents and they weren't blind. They knew how it was with me, but they pretended that they didn't, on the principle that if you don't acknowledge a thing exists it can't hurt you. They were terrified of me being hurt again; in fact they felt I was in the process of being hurt. Mr Logan Rossiter from Tor-Fret . . . and me? Well, things happened like that in books but not to their daughter. Not that she didn't deserve the best. Oh, yes, she was their daughter and the highest in the land wasn't good enough for her . . . in theory. But when it came down to actual practice, then their workaday souls were troubled. And mine was troubled, too.

Yesterday afternoon Logan had said goodbye. We were standing in this room alone and he had taken my hands in his and looking steadily at me he had said simply, 'I'll be back, Kate, I'll be back.' That was all.

What did it mean: 'I'll be back.' Of course he'd be back, but did it hold any special significance for me? Couldn't he have promised something, given me hope?

Last night, as I had lain thinking, my eyes dry and burning, I had clung to Maurice's explanation of his brother's character. He was so high principled he would crucify you, Maurice had said. Yet he could have said some word to me, some telling word, couldn't he? I asked myself. Just one word. Yet was he not, in his own eyes, still a married man? And in mine was he not still on a par with Arthur Boyle? No. Not any more. Not any more . . .

Then there was the business of the rebound. He might look like a living skeleton, his face might be scarred, but nevertheless this in no way detracted from his innate attractiveness. I spent the early hours of the night torturing myself with pictures of all the women he would meet. Slim girls dressed for winter sports. They appeared alluring creatures. Everybody appeared alluring except myself, for my body with its ample curves was not built for slacks, or tight jumpers.

My mother's voice broke in on my thoughts now, saying, 'I shouldn't be surprised at seeing him back in a week or so.'

This was meant to soothe me, and I thought to myself: I should. He wouldn't be back in a week or so. Nor was he.

The first letter I received from him began, 'My dear Kate.' It told me of the journey, of the comfortable château high up on the mountainside. And in the line before the end, he said, 'I miss you, Kate.' But this was qualified, as he went on, 'and your mother and father. I'll never be able to repay you all.'

'What does he say?' asked my father. The letter was such that I could hand it to him and say, 'Read for yourself.' He read it, then read it out aloud to my mother, who was working at the sink. The only comment she made was with her eyebrows – she raised them high.

It was shortly after this that Patterson came to the house again with a request that I should go up and see the old gentlemen. They were rather lonely. So once again I started going up the hill to Tor-Fret. My first visit was deeply moving, for Mr Stanley and Mr Bernard held my hands and hovered over me as if I were someone who had been lost to them, someone whom they feared they would never see again. Hollings and Bennett too, their greetings were such they warmed me and made me feel wanted, especially that of Hollings, for he treated me with deference that endeared him to me. One thing I noticed immediately: they seemed all so much older. The twins seemed to have aged even more since the visit to our house. The only one who appeared the same as when I had last seen him was Mr Stephen. This was probably due to the fact that he had not been present on that memorable night in the cellar.

So, as I said, I returned to Tor-Fret; weather permitting I visited them at least three times a week. A month passed, and during this time I had had three letters from Logan, nice letters, informative letters, letters that I could hand over to my mother and father, letters that left me cold inside, shivering at the bare prospect of the future.

Then one afternoon, as I got off the bus to go up the hill to the house, I saw two men in the bottom field. They were doing surveying of some sort, with long tapes and poles. Further up the road I met a short stubby man with a big head; he had his hands thrust deep in the pockets of his overcoat and was looking across the valley towards where the men were measuring. I said to him, 'What are they doing down there?' and he turned to me and answered,

'Eh? Oh, we're just seein' how many houses we could plant.'

'Houses you could plant?' My voice sounded awe-stricken. 'Who said you could build houses here?' I spoke now with a dignity, as if the land were mine.

'Well, that's what will happen when it's sold, an' it's going to be sold, isn't it? I've always had me ear to the ground an' that's put me where I am the day . . . Bradley's the name. An' what do they want to hang on to all this for, anyway, you tell me? What good is it to them, eh? And people living on top of each other like rabbits in the towns.'

As I looked at this man I knew he wasn't worrying about people living on top of each other like rabbits. His concern would be how cheaply he would get the ground, and how dearly he could sell it again to a builder. I turned from him abruptly and hurried up to the house, to be greeted immediately by the old men who were definitely in a state of nerves. And this included Hollings, and did not exactly exclude Patterson. I found them all in the kitchen. Mr Bradley had apparently paid a visit to the house and had startled them with his information.

It was Mr Stanley who turned to me as if I had the power to wipe out their fears, saying, 'It isn't true, is it, Kate? Logan wouldn't do this. He wouldn't sell the whole place, not without telling us?'

Before I could speak, Mr Bernard, his head bobbing like a golliwog, spluttered, 'Could, you know. Not entailed, no heirs, nothing. Own boss, own boss. Couldn't blame him.'

'But he wouldn't.' I looked around them. 'He wouldn't do anything behind your backs.'

'No.' It was Hollings now speaking. 'No, madam, I think as you say, he wouldn't do it behind our backs.'

'Well, something's moving.' Mr Stanley was speaking again. 'There's never smoke without fire . . . What would we do?' The two brothers now looked at each other, these two men who had been born in this house, and then Mr Bernard muttered, 'Stephen, poor Stephen.'

As I looked from one to the other of these old men, and at this moment even Patterson came under this heading, for he seemed to have jumped over the boundary of middle age, I felt like a mother responsible to a number of children, and as such I went out of my way to soothe them, and I said, 'I'll write to him now and post it on my way down.'

'Do, do. Do that, Kate. Yes, you're a better hand at it than any of us.' It was Mr Stanley speaking again, and the others nodded eager agreement. 'Yes, that's it. You write.'

I left them and went into the room I still called my room, and, sitting down, I wrote to Logan. I cannot remember word for word what I said, but as I wrote I know I became angry, for by now I too felt that there was something afoot. Men didn't come measuring the land for houses unless they knew that that land was available, and not just a strip at the bottom of the road, but this house also, the home that meant so much to so many because it sheltered lives that were running to the end of their courses.

It was on a Tuesday when I posted the letter. I reckoned he would receive it by the Thursday and perhaps I would get a reply by the Saturday. So Friday seemed an empty day, a day of waiting when nothing would happen.

On the Friday morning I went down to Bill Arnold's and did my usual work. It was a nice morning, very cold, but with the sun shining, and when I left Bill's I had a reluctance to return straight home. What I really wanted was to do something to make the time pass quickly until tomorrow and the post arriving. So I went into Rodney's shop and bought some rolls and a cake. The rolls were hot and I broke a bit off one and ate it. And Rodney, seeing me do this, laughed and split another one open and, thickening it with butter, handed it to me. And then he said, 'Would you like to come to a weddin', Kate?'

'Oh, Rodney, you are going to be married?'

'Aye, yes, I'm goin' to be married. The sooner the better I think now.'

'I'd love to come, Rodney. When is it?'

'Well, not till Easter.'

'I hope you'll be very happy, Rodney. You deserve to be.'

'Thanks, Kate. And now you must come out of your shell and follow me lead.'

'Yes, yes, I must, Rodney. I'll have to see about it.'

He saw me to the door of the shop, and I was still smiling when I turned from him. But I had not gone many steps before the smile slid from my face. Why should the news of Rodney's coming marriage make me feel so unhappy? I was glad for him, really glad, but I was sorry for myself for I felt lost and lonely, and I told myself once again as I had done over the last few weeks, that I was a fool. A fool for a second time.

When I came on to the level of the fell path I saw my mother at the door and she waved to me and I waved back. She was enjoying the sunshine. Her face was bright and she looked happier than I had seen her for a long time. In the little hall she helped me off with my coat, and then she nodded towards the sitting-room. It was a motion of her head which she used when she was indicating that my father was up to something. So it was with the expectation of seeing my father and what he was up to that I opened the sitting-room door, and then I stood still.

Logan was standing with his back to the fire and he was alone in the room. I closed the door behind me and leaned against it for a moment before I said, 'I didn't expect . . . When did you come? . . . Why?'

He was smiling broadly, his eyes hard on my face, and it was quite some seconds before he spoke. 'One thing at a time, Kate,' he said. Then, 'You didn't expect me, not after that stinker of a letter you sent me? Don't you think that was enough to catapult any man out of his complacency?' I could not answer, and he went on, 'I arrived in Newcastle this morning, but as to why I've really come back, well, it will take a little time to explain that.' He took a step nearer to me and held out his hand now, but I found that I couldn't move from the door. It was as if I was glued there. I ignored the outstretched hand and asked in a flat-sounding voice, 'Are you selling up then?'

'Well, what do you think?'

I did not know what to make of this reply. I could gauge little from his tone, yet it seemed to confirm what had been in my mind since I saw the men measuring the ground, and so I blurted out in a high indignant voice, 'You can't do it, you can't sell the place. If it was empty, yes, but not with all those old people there, and they depending on you. They'll rot in a nursing home. The uncles would die.'

'You're very concerned for them, Kate, aren't you?'

His hands were hanging stiffly by his sides now, and as I continued to look at him I found myself being again consumed by anger. I had never known such a force. It became so overpowering that the perspiration began to run down my arms. I found I must not look at him any longer and I turned my face away as I said, 'Yes, I'm concerned. Any ordinary person would be. I think it's terrible, scandalous. You talked about Mr Maurice.' He hadn't. 'I think this is worse than anything he ever did. I'm sure he'd never have . . .'

He held up his hand and cut in quietly, 'Say no more, Kate . . . until I tell you something . . . Your letter was the first indication I had that I was going to sell Tor-Fret or an inch of the land.'

I turned my face slowly towards him. My anger seeping away, I was left feeling drained, weak, and very foolish. My head drooped and I muttered, 'I'm sorry, but . . . but the men were there measuring, and they said . . .'

'That man Bradley would say anything. It was he who was after the land before. Whoever set the rumour about, it didn't originate from me or anything I might have said . . . You think I'm the kind of man to throw aside my responsibilities, Kate?'

'No. No, I didn't . . . I don't . . . I'm sorry. But it was seeing the men there, and them actually measuring. And they had been up to the uncles and everybody was upset . . . I'm sorry.'

Now I looked at him with eyes clear of anger and saw that here was The Big Fellow, or nearly so, he looked so much better. I said somewhat sheepishly now, 'How are you feeling?'

'I just don't know at the moment, Kate.' The corner of his mouth was lifted. 'I'll be able to tell you better in a little while. You see, I was coming home on Monday in any case. I had intended to stay away until . . . until my affairs were put in order . . .' I knew that he was not referring to his business because his partner was quite competent to carry on for the time being, but was referring to the proceedings which would annul his marriage. 'I wanted to play fair but the strain has been so great that I . . . I . . .' He spread his hands towards me. 'I just had to come and see you, tell you what I felt.' He stopped speaking and moved nearer to me until there was only the breadth of a hand between us. 'Have I got to tell you, Kate?'

Had he got to tell me? Use words when his eyes were pouring love into my body, sending my senses swirling, and filling the void of loneliness with trust and security and tenderness? Had he got to tell me?

I shook my head vigorously, I was gasping like a runner. I could not speak, not one word, and then we were enfolded again as on that night on the fell path. So close did he hold me, and so tightly did I press my arms about him that our bodies seemed to merge one into the other. When eventually my lips withdrew from his I dropped my head on to his shoulder, and with his mouth moving in my hair now he said, 'Oh, Kate, I've been lonely for the sight of you. At times I felt like a boy again, crying for my mother. Does this sound silly? It may do. But, Kate, I need you in so many ways, as wife and . . . and mistress . . . and mother. Does this frighten you? Tell me, Kate, does this frighten you?'

I lifted my face and looked into his eyes as I said, 'Nothing that you could demand of me could frighten me, Logan.'

'Not even being mistress of the House of Men?'

'Not even that. Nor of the tongues that will surely wag. Nothing will frighten me as long as the master of Tor-Fret stays by my side.'

'He'll stay by your side, Kate, never fear. He'll never want to leave your side, that will be the trouble. You don't know what you've taken on, my Kate. The Big Fellow of Tor-Fret is no angel, as indeed you know, and if I know anything about him

I should say he's the kind of fellow whose demands will wear you down. What have you got to say to that?'

'So be it,' I said. 'So be it.'

And my heart and every vein in my body echoed joyously: 'So be it . . . so be it.'

THE END

JUSTICE IS A WOMAN
by Catherine Cookson

The day Joe Remington brought his new bride to Fell Rise, he had already sensed she might not settle easily into the big house just outside the Tyneside town of Fellburn. For Joe this had always been his home, but for Elaine it was virtually another country whose manners and customs she was by no means eager to accept.

Making plain her disapproval of Joe's familiarity with the servants, demanding to see accounts Joe had always trusted to their care, questioning the donation of food to striking miners' families – all these objections and more soon rubbed Joe and the local people up the wrong way, a problem he could easily have done without, for this was 1926, the year of the General Strike, the effects of which would nowhere be felt more acutely than in this heartland of the North-East.

Then when Elaine became pregnant, she saw it as a disaster and only the willingness of her unmarried sister Betty to come and see her through her confinement made it bearable. But in the long run, would Betty's presence only serve to widen the rift between husband and wife, or would she help to bring about a reconciliation?

0 552 13622 0

THE MALTESE ANGEL
by Catherine Cookson

Ward Gibson knew what was expected of him by the village folk, and especially by the Mason family, whose daughter Daisy he had known all his life. But then, in a single week, his whole world had been turned upside down by a dancer, Stephanie McQueen, who seemed to float across the stage of the Empire Music Hall where she was appearing as The Maltese Angel. To his amazement, the attraction was mutual, and after a whirlwind courtship she agreed to marry him.

But a scorpion had already begun to emerge from beneath the stone of the local community, who considered that Ward had betrayed their expectations, and had led on and cruelly deserted Daisy. There followed a series of reprisals on his family, one of them serious enough to cause him to exact a terrible revenge; and these events would twist and turn the course of many lives through Ward's own and succeeding generations.

0 552 13684 0

A SELECTION OF OTHER CATHERINE COOKSON TITLES AVAILABLE FROM CORGI BOOKS

13576 3	THE BLACK CANDLE	£5.99
12473 7	THE BLACK VELVET GOWN	£5.99
14633 1	COLOUR BLIND	£5.99
12551 2	A DINNER OF HERBS	£6.99
14066 X	THE DWELLING PLACE	£5.99
14068 6	FEATHERS IN THE FIRE	£5.99
14089 9	THE FEN TIGER	£5.99
14069 4	FENWICK HOUSES	£5.99
14050 7	THE GAMBLING MAN	£4.99
13716 2	THE GARMENT	£5.99
13621 2	THE GILLYVORS	£5.99
10916 9	THE GIRL	£5.99
14071 6	THE GLASS VIRGIN	£5.99
13685 9	THE GOLDEN STRAW	£5.99
13300 0	THE HARROGATE SECRET	£5.99
14087 2	HERITAGE OF FOLLY	£5.99
13303 5	THE HOUSE OF WOMEN	£5.99
13622 0	JUSTICE IS A WOMAN	£5.99
14091 0	KATE HANNIGAN	£5.99
14092 9	KATIE MULHOLLAND	£5.99
14081 3	MAGGIE ROWAN	£5.99
13684 0	THE MALTESE ANGEL	£5.99
10321 7	MISS MARTHA MARY CRAWFORD	£5.99
12524 5	THE MOTH	£5.99
13302 7	MY BELOVED SON	£5.99
13088 5	THE PARSON'S DAUGHTER	£5.99
14073 2	PURE AS THE LILY	£5.99
13683 2	THE RAG NYMPH	£5.99
14602 X	THE ROUND TOWER	£5.99
13714 6	SLINKY JANE	£5.99
10541 4	THE SLOW AWAKENING	£5.99
10630 5	THE TIDE OF LIFE	£5.99
14038 4	THE TINKER'S GIRL	£5.99
12368 4	THE WHIP	£5.99
13577 1	THE WINGLESS BIRD	£5.99
13247 0	THE YEAR OF THE VIRGINS	£5.99